WHY SHE LEFT US

By

DAVID DENNIS

This book is dedicated to all those whom I have loved and lost, with the fervent hope that someday the Great Reunion will take place.

Cover design by Graphicz X Designs

(http://graphiczxdesigns.zenfolio.com)

CYCLE ONE:

MONICA'S MEMOIRS – March 26, 1986

BETSY'S DIARY – June 14, 1985

ELLEN'S MEMOIRS – December 23, 1985

BETSY'S DIARY – June 16, 1985

AUNT LUCILLE'S DIARY – December 23, 1985

BETSY'S DIARY – June 20, 1985

CARL'S DIARY – January 1, 1986

BETSY'S DIARY – June 21, 1985

CYCLE TWO:

MONICA'S MEMOIRS – April 4, 1986

BETSY'S DIARY – June 23, 1985

ELLEN'S MEMOIRS – December 24, 1985

BETSY'S DIARY – June 28, 1985

AUNT LUCILLE'S DIARY – December 24, 1985

BETSY'S DIARY – June 29, 1985

CARL'S DIARY – January 3, 1986

BETSY'S DIARY – June 30, 1985

CYCLE THREE:

MONICA'S MEMOIRS – April 8, 1986

BETSY'S DIARY – July 1, 1985

ELLEN'S MEMOIRS – December 25, 1985

BETSY'S DIARY – July 2, 1985

AUNT LUCILLE'S DIARY – December 25, 1985

BETSY'S DIARY – July 3, 1985

CARL'S DIARY – January 4, 1986

BETSY'S DIARY – July 4, 1985

CYCLE FOUR:

MONICA'S MEMOIRS – April 13, 1986

BETSY'S DIARY – July 5, 1985

ELLEN'S MEMOIRS – December 26. 1985

BETSY'S DIARY – July 6, 1985

AUNT LUCILLE'S DIARY – December 26, 1985

BETSY'S DIARY – July 7, 1985

CARL'S DIARY – January 5, 1986

BETSY'S DIARY – July 8, 1985

CYCLE FIVE:

MONICA'S MEMOIRS – April 16, 1986

BETSY'S DIARY – July 9, 1985

ELLEN'S MEMOIRS – December 31, 1985

BETSY'S DIARY – July 14, 1985

AUNT LUCILLE'S DIARY – December 31, 1985

BETSY'S DIARY – July 15, 1985

CARL'S DIARY – January 7, 1986

BETSY'S DIARY – July 30, 1985

CYCLE SIX:

MONICA'S MEMOIRS – May 25, 1986

BETSY'S DIARY – September 1, 1985

ELLEN'S MEMOIRS – January 1, 1986

BETSY'S DIARY – September 2, 1985

AUNT LUCILLE'S DIARY – January 1, 1986

BETSY'S DIARY – September 3, 1985

CARL'S DIARY – January 8, 1986

BETSY'S DIARY – September 4, 1985

EPILOGUE:

MONICA'S MEMOIRS – May 26, 1986 ("MEMORIAL DAY")

CYCLE ONE

MONICA'S MEMOIRS – March 26, 1986

I sit here in this gloom and gaze silently upon the ring on my finger, the ring that was supposed to be a token of complete bliss and happiness, the culmination of all of my hope and all of my joy. After all, they always said great things about me. They said that I was destined for happiness, that with so much going for me there was no reason to see anything but a bright and rapturous future for me. I can't remember the last time I looked at it, but it's there in black and white for everyone to see: my yearbook picture with the caption underneath it. "Most Likely to Succeed." Just another in a long series of cruel jokes that Life chose to play on me, I guess.

Funny. I can't even laugh anymore at my own sardonic attempts at humor. It's strange how all the emotion can leave you at certain times, and you wonder how it was that you had ever been capable of so much of it at one time in your life. Responses to external stimuli no longer come so spontaneously from me. Right now, if I were a shell on the beach, someone would pick me up and look inside to find it thoroughly empty and barren.

But it's better this way. Better to have no emotions at all than to be driven by passion, revenge, and hunger. Better to live out the rest of one's life as an empty shell rather than to be consumed by, worst of all, a surge of erupting, violent, unbridled passion.

It's shocking to even think about it. Just a few short months ago, I would have shed tears at the very thought of it, and only a few short months before that, I would have been literally unable to deal with it at all. I'll never forget the night they came in here, and I actually envisioned the moment when they would finally have me bound tight and my head would split open in sheer insanity and it would be all over.

It wasn't that way at all, though. I screamed and groaned that night, and a wall of black came down in front of my eyes. They held me down, yelling nonsensical entreaties into my ears, and I felt my body lurch with agony as a hand came over my mouth and silenced that awful wail that came from deep in my throat. Deeper than that, in fact. It was my very soul that screamed out in that horrible moment. That horrible moment during which I saw Hell itself opening up before me.

Why do I torture myself with dismal thoughts like this? It's springtime. My favorite time of the year. My birthday is just around the corner. I'll be nineteen years old. God, may that day never come!

It's a sacrilege, I know, for me to utter a word of prayer – to utter His name in this hell-hole. I stopped praying a long time ago so that He needn't be outraged by the sound of my pleas. Now I know how she felt that night last September when she took it upon herself to commit suicide, thus starting the ball rolling in the direction my life has now taken.

I must remain hidden. I vowed long ago that I would remain hidden from the sight of the Almighty and from the sight of all mankind. Perhaps, in curling myself up into a little ball, I won't be able to bring any more suffering to the outside world.

I'm glad, so infinitely glad, that hardly anyone comes to see me anymore. Once a month, on the same day of each month, that one visitor comes, and in the eyes of that one visitor, I see such pain and hellish torment that it tears the heart from out of my body just to witness it. Why does he come here? It's so senseless, so futile to look for peace and for a tranquility that is so far beyond our reach that it probably no longer exists.

Aunt Lucille hardly comes by anymore either, putting in a periodic appearance to show that she cares. The one person who really ought to care doesn't, and the other person who would have cared so much that she would have done everything within her power to exchange places with me – the other one who cared for me as a mother cares for her young – She is gone forever.

A tranquil, blue horizon is conjured up in my mind, belying the violence with which she took it upon herself to leave me. Would that I could have immediately followed her and spared myself this horror!

But I'm not fooling anyone. Just as my entry into this world was fraught with pain and terror, so shall my exit from this world be similarly characterized, only I anticipate that it will be a lot worse because, in the meantime, I have developed a soul. One that is black with self-disgust, but a soul nonetheless. I know that when my time comes, when that day that I am so looking forward to does arrive, it will only send my horrible black soul into an abyss, and I will never see her again. I will never see that angel again for all eternity.

I can hardly believe it, but I think a shudder passed over me at the thought of it. Mom would tell me not to be morbid, and I used to listen to her and accept everything she told me as gospel truth. She, along with Aunt Lucille, always had a preconceived notion of what I ought to turn out to be as an adult. No wonder my life is such a disaster. They should consign children to the care of adults who are specifically trained by experts on how to rear the young, whether or not an actual biological connection exists between them. That's only one of the faults of our society, that young, innocent, pure gifts from God fall into the hands of horrible, corrupt, and evil people. How the hell is one to survive? How the hell is one expected to endure such wholehearted stupidity?

In spite of all that, I made it to high school graduation. Top of the class. "Most Likely to Succeed" and all that other meaningless crap. And I met Carl. And we were married.

I thought for a moment that I just heard someone approaching. God, no! I don't want a visitor. I don't want anyone to see me looking like this. Hell, I don't even know what I look like, I'm so terrified, I won't even look in a mirror.

It's all over anyway. As soon as I finish writing, I'll find my cot, preferably in the dark so I won't even for the briefest of seconds imagine that I was somewhere else in a happier time. And then, if the saints are willing, shortly after my eyes close, I'll go to sleep.

They say that God is Love. Well, then, if He truly loves me, He'll take me in my sleep. Some saint should ask Him," Isn't her time up yet? Isn't it totally unnecessary for her to contaminate that pitiful planet a second longer?"

I think whoever it was who was walking in this direction has now gone. I think they're all tired of trying to get to first base with me. It's just as well. Even if their intentions are of the most noble and selfless kind, I don't want them to come here with their sympathy. It only reminds me of how low I've fallen, to have some stranger come in here and start spouting advice at me. They're only doing their job, I suppose, and Lord knows, I don't hate them for it. It's just that I wish they'd all get the message once and for all that I just want to be left alone. I never asked them for any favors. I never craved their attention, did I? Did I ask for treatment? Did I demand that they expend so much time and energy on my behalf? What makes them think that I actually have any desire at all to return to a state of what they call sanity? Why can't they understand that the offer they're making me doesn't tempt me in the least? They should just stop trying, it's such a pathetic waste of time!

That last doctor was really something. Kind of young, too. About thirty-five or so, I'd say. He looked shocked when I asked him if he was married. Only at first, of course. He'd been too thoroughly and efficiently trained to let on to me that he could actually be flustered, even momentarily, by anything at all. So, he simply put on a little smile and said," No. Why does that interest you?"

I gave him no reply, and I'll bet my silence was further proof in his mind that I was insane. But boy oh boy, I could have given him an earful if I thought it would do any good. I would have told him in no uncertain terms that, instead of wasting his time talking to me and trying to rehabilitate me, he should be out spending a quiet romantic afternoon with the woman he loved. Life is too precious for it to be wasted in idle pursuits and meaningless gestures. We should all do what we enjoy doing most. Even restrict and limit ourselves if we have to. Once you've found what makes you happy, you should stick to it and not feel guilty or let others talk you into doing other things that you know will be a waste of time for you.

I had my head together. Right. I was the level-headed one. That's what they always told me. Hadn't over one hundred students picked me as Most Likely to Succeed? I wasn't even that popular, but it was no secret that I was a straight-A student. On that basis, those poor misguided people sought to equate academic achievement with success in Life. Those poor misguided, half-blind people even saw fit to vote me and Carl in as Ideal Couple.

I looked pretty good in that yearbook photo. I had on my cream-colored sweater, not that it showed up in the black-and-white, with my tan slacks. My hair was long in that picture. For some reason, I'd forgotten to ask Betsy to shorten it for me. I was all set to have her do it, too, and then bang! Carl and I got called down to have our picture taken as Ideal Couple, and we both giggled like the naïve school-children we actually were at that point in time – giggled like a couple of little toddlers because we were getting out of Mr. Ballard's science class, even if it was just going to be for only ten minutes or so.

Carl had on his preppie brown shirt and those slacks that accentuated his cute rear-end, and I remember noting, as we stood in front of the camera while Jill Michaels was trying to make us laugh, how fiery those dark eyes of his looked. He seemed to have all the energy and fierceness of youth concentrated in those dark brown eyes, and I remember how I instinctively touched the side of his face with my hand, and my bottom lip quivered a little bit while I stood there next to him. Someone said Smile, and the flash went off just as we put our cheeks together, and I swear, even though it didn't come out on film, there had to have been just the smallest, daintiest teardrop coming down my right cheek-bone at that precise moment. I studied that photo as soon as I purchased my yearbook. I even took out a magnifying glass when I got home and tried to see if I could detect the vaguest semblance of a tear coming down that right cheek-bone. But I never could find it. Maybe it just wasn't there after all, just like a lot of other things I once believed existed, only to discover later on, with the most excruciating sadness, that I had been wrong.

If I could live the whole experience over again, I would tell Betsy about that silly teardrop fantasy of mine. It would have been just the sort of thing she would have supported me in, and I would have been happy, so blissfully happy, even in my ignorance of the actual truth.

Oh, God! Now I have a new anxiety to deal with, because now, more than ever, I want to go back in time and tell her the whole thing. I want to relive that moment when, stretched out on the top of my bedspread and holding the magnifying glass over that picture, I felt a sense of panic when I heard someone walk into the room.

"What are you doing?"

I can almost hear the gentle way she said it. In my mind, I can hear her voice. I really can! The voice of that angel.

"Just looking at my picture. The picture they took of us for the yearbook. Me and Carl."

Betsy came towards the bed, and I immediately shifted my position so that she could sit there alongside me. I believe I was trembling ever so slightly as she took the book from my hands and allowed me to lean in towards her and point out the photo to her.

"Oh, Monica," she murmured, as if in genuine awe. "You look beautiful. And Carl. So handsome."

We were both flooded with happiness, she for me, and I for the bright and unsullied future that I thought lay ahead of me. And to think that, only a few short months later, I would become seized with such agonizing doubts. I thought I had had them mastered. My God, isn't that why I'm here? If I had only been able to master those horrible doubts and suspicions, I never would have entered that room that night, and I never would have ended up killing –

Let's be calm. It's almost time to go to bed. The peace of sleep is about to enfold me, and I may just imagine myself, as sleep comes upon me, re-entering the womb as if I possessed the miraculous power to, not only go back in time, but to actually set Time itself going backwards for everyone else. Only then could this horror be erased. Only in blotting out my entire existence from the face of humanity can I obliterate the guilt and self-disgust of my life.

I'm trapped. I can't change it. I can't alter the course of my own life, let alone the course of Time itself. I just feel so totally helpless.

I feel as if chains weighing tons and tons of metal were enclosed about my ankles and wrists, and the wrath of Heaven itself were about to pour down upon me and choke me in my screams of filth. God Almighty, how could You have allowed a monster such as myself to escape from the womb? Suffocate me, I beg You! Kill me and have done with it. Then perhaps the roses of this coming springtime may bloom everywhere without the risk of becoming contaminated by the stench of my very being. And to think that You allow stinking filth like me to exist, and yet You take away the innocent ones.

I'm supposed to be so smart. So intelligent. So level-headed. I don't even know what I'm saying, what I'm thinking, or why I'm writing this. I can never get it to make sense. Never get it to somehow cleanse me, or purge me of my guilt. But I feel urged on by some mysterious compulsion, some occult desire or need to get it all on paper – some of it, anyway – before Satan takes my hand and causes me, in one final victory over my black soul, to take my own life in one immense, horrible outburst of self-inflicted violence.

And when I'm dead and buried, I know – I know that he will not be visiting my grave with the same regularity and devotion as he now visits the other one. I know this as surely as I know that I will never be with her again to receive the blessed magnanimity of her forgiveness.

BETSY'S DIARY – June 14, 1985

Dear Diary: Today really was quite wonderful. Monica came home from school with her yearbook, and I caught her looking at it in the privacy of her room. I use the word "caught" because she became so flustered when she heard me come into her room. She was looking at a picture of her and Carl Peters that had a caption under it saying "Ideal Couple."

Monica looks absolutely beautiful in the photo, not like a young girl in her teens, but like a grown woman of some maturity. She hasn't told me as much, not in so many words, that is, but I think she's in love with Carl. And quite honestly, I'm very happy for her. He seems very bright and very clean-cut. If I'm not mistaken, she showed me his yearbook picture on another page, and he was listed as Most Popular. Or was it Best Personality? I can't remember exactly which. All I know is she seemed sincerely proud as she showed it to me.

I only wish that Mom could show a little more interest. I'm sure that it would mean a lot to Monica if Mom expressed a desire to learn more about Carl, for example. The two have been dating for quite some time, so it would seem only natural that Mom should be interested in learning more about him. Instead, she behaves as though he doesn't even exist, and I honestly don't know how she can ignore the fact that Monica positively glows whenever she speaks his name. I suppose Mom is so used to my not dating very frequently that she doesn't seem able to acknowledge the possibility that my younger sister may very well have fallen in love with somebody already.

And to think that I could have had a date this weekend! There's a young man who's been coming to the library lately. Mrs. Evans told me this morning that he'd had his eye on me, and in my embarrassment, I merely laughed and moved away from her on the pretext of having some books to stack in the reference room. Then, later on this afternoon, the young man approached me, initiated some small talk with me, the particulars of which I cannot now recall, as I was so taken aback by his ease in speaking with me. Before I knew it, he inquired about my plans for the coming weekend. I know I handled the situation quite ineptly, and I was probably unnecessarily rude when I told him that I really didn't see that it was any of his business. I sincerely hope that his feelings weren't hurt, but I simply could not bring myself to assume the relative ease and self-assurance that he himself possessed while the two of us stood there conversing with each other. I hastily removed myself from his presence, and it wasn't until a few minutes later that it dawned on me that perhaps I was letting my scruples stand in the way of the possibility of my seizing upon some unexpected happiness and good fortune. Then I soberly reminded myself that I didn't even know the young man, and if I were to entertain the idea of getting seriously involved with a member of the opposite sex, I would have to be stirred initially by some sort of unfathomable passion. And so, this coming weekend will be like all the rest. I will immerse myself in my books and tend to my household duties, basking in the safe and comfortable shell that I have found for myself in this house.

Ellen seemed a bit moody today. Not that she's exactly been a joy to be around, even on her good days; but I'm sincerely troubled by a certain bitterness I've been able to detect in her manner recently. I suppose it's to be expected. Maybe it's my fault, though. Perhaps I'm not patient enough with her. I'll try. I promise to try and spend more time with her, try to be more understanding, and try to get her to forget about those things that tend to make her distraught.

My vacation starts in a few weeks, and I can hardly wait. Not that I'll be doing anything exciting, of course. But perhaps having a lot more free time for a little while will enable me to spend more time with Ellen. And then maybe I can drive out to the beach. Or read a blockbuster novel that will sweep me away with its excitement, beauty, and passion. We'll see.

P.S. I have a feeling that it's going to be a wonderful summer!

ELLEN'S MEMOIRS – December 23, 1985

At last I have a moment's peace, and I'm going to start doing something I've never done before. Write a book!

Well, not really a book. I guess you could say I'm just going to write down a few thoughts. God knows it's about the only thing I can do these days without someone else's assistance, that is.

O.K. Let me start out by saying I'm handicapped. Good. Maybe someone will take pity and publish my memoirs someday just because of that. You know, kind of like: "The poor girl's handicapped, so let's show how nice we are, and publish her stuff, even if it isn't even any good."

Well, I wasn't always this way. I've been this way only about six months. No, longer than that. Christmas is two days away. That makes this December. Real smart, aren't I? No, let's see. The accident took place in May. Memorial Day weekend, in fact.

Boy, it had been a great weekend or, as I used to say back in those days, a total blast! Lisa and I hitched up with these two gorgeous guys, and I do mean gorgeous! What was the red-headed guy's name? Marty, I think. Yeah, Marty. How could I ever forget that powerhouse stud? Yeah, I'd been with that stud like a thousand times already, and it was always totally awesome! Well, anyway, Marty got a hold of his father's station wagon, and Lisa and I went along with him and his friend Duke or something like that. We had beer, grass, coke, and a little bit of meth, and the four of us planned on partying, and I do mean partying! Well, the beaches were opening up that weekend, too, you know, so Lisa told her old lady some cock-and-bull story and I told Mom pretty much the same thing, and that was it. Real simple. The rest I don't care to go into. Let's just say Lisa wound up in intensive care, the guys wound up with minor scrapes and bruises, and Yours Truly wound up in this wheel-chair.

I don't want this account to be morbid. Mom always said not to be morbid, and she was right. She had the right idea about living, I'll say that for her. No sense in being morbid. I mean, if I wanted to be morbid right now, I could be really, really morbid to the extreme. So, let me go way back. Way back to the day I first met the great big love of my life, and let me tell it kind of like it was a real story. And I won't leave out any of the juicy parts either. Then maybe when I'm all done and have had a chance to put it all down on paper, I'll take out that knife I've had hidden under my pillow for the past two days so Aunt Lucille won't be able to find it. And then I'll stick it right into my stupid heart. And you know what it'll say on my gravestone? Nothing. That's right. Absolutely nothing. It'll be one of those charity funerals, you know? The kind where absolutely no one cares about the deceased, and nobody even gives a damn about what the deceased's name was either. That's the kind of funeral I'd get.

But this is no way to start a story. I know that, and I didn't even get anything higher than a C in English or anything else either, for that matter. So, let me start by telling you about the day I first laid eyes on the big love of my life, and hopefully, Aunt Lucille won't come bursting in here to tell me it's getting late and I need my rest. When that happens, fine, let it happen. But at least for the time being, I can breathe a little in peace, so let me begin.

It was April vacation. This past April, that is, just about a month and a half before my accident. Lisa and I had been to an indoor movie. Monday night, I think, because there wasn't anything better to do. Lisa still had the hots for this guy Jason, and I was still waiting for that redheaded guy Marty to ask me out on a real date for a change, after I'd already given him head something like a thousand times already. So, it was just me and Lisa sitting at good old Burger King, sipping on strawberry shakes and then taking out all our loose change to see if we could scrape enough cash together so we could buy us a couple of joints when who-in-the-world strides into the place with a couple of his buddies but the Man himself: Wayne Brown!

"Do you see what I see?" Lisa said to me with these really big eyes as she kind of curled in a little closer to her shake.

I turned around and saw him. I mean, I'd seen this guy plenty of times before. He was Monica's age. Maybe a year or two older because he wasn't in school that often and everybody said he must have stayed back a couple of years ago. But I'd seen him around, and I knew his rep and everything else, and I'd always thought to myself: What an ass on that dude! But I never thought to do anything about it or drop any hints or anything of the sort because here I was, a meek little freshman, and there he was, a big, tough senior who could take his pick of any girl he wanted.

I guess it was Fate. All girls like to think that everything that happens to them is Fate, so forgive me if I care to indulge in the same ridiculous delusion, O.K.? I mean, out of all the places in Burger King he could have sat, where do you think he and his pals chose to sit? Right next to me and Lisa, of course! Now that I look back on it, a lot of the other booths and tables were either occupied or messy, so it very well may have been the only table they could have picked at that particular time. But no, let's call it Fate just for the sake of pacifying a poor little crippled girl like me, O.K.?

Wayne Brown, sitting practically right next to me. This had to be the climax of my entire existence. In looking back on it, those two months I spent with Wayne were actually the greatest, most exciting, mind-blowing times I ever spent in my life. I call it two months, but it was really a lot shorter because, you see, by the end of that two-month period, I'd already acquired these wheels, and I'm sure it comes as no surprise to you that, after my Memorial Day weekend fiasco, good old Wayne would have nothing to do with me. He probably told himself there were other factors involved, but that's bullshit. If I weren't in this wheel-chair today, I know for a fact that none of that other garbage with Carl, Betsy, Monica, and my mother would have happened. In the short time Wayne and I were together, I loved that guy, and he loved me. If I hadn't become incapacitated from that accident, he'd be mine right now. We'd be in bed this very second, too, I'll bet, and he'd be craving me the same way he did back in April and the beginning of May.

Last April and May were like another time and another world to me. Forgive me if I grow sentimental for a moment, but I really did love that guy. He was the first guy I ever went all the way with, you know? And the last, too, in the sense that I haven't had any more "fun times" with a guy, except for those few hours my redheaded boyfriend Marty and I cavorted around in unbridled lust, shortly before the accident brought all of that to a big, crashing halt.

But I'd rather not dwell on any of that right now. Let me instead dwell on that first night. That night we met for the very first time at Burger King. Real romantic setting, huh? I'll bet you're thinking this is all kid stuff, right? Well, I may have been a kid back then in April, but you see, there's something about being confined to a wheel-chair for the rest of your life that kind of forces a person into aging quite rapidly. Why, sometimes I look in the mirror, and I can't believe I'm only sixteen. I actually have wrinkles around the corners of my mouth. Just like Mom, and I remember, even in my early childhood, how she used to complain about those stupid little wrinkles of hers. And my hair! Jeez, is it possible for girls to lose their hair from lack of sex?

It's Wayne's fault that all of this has happened to me. Yes! It's even his fault I'm in this chair. Because if he hadn't dumped me for that bitch Charlene, I wouldn't have hitched back up with Marty that weekend, and Lisa wouldn't have wound up in intensive care and then –

Well, she's better off than I am, anyway. At least, she's dead and doesn't have any more worries. I remember how my fool sister broke down in tears when we got the news that Lisa had died. "Betsy," I said to her," you didn't even know Lisa. Why the hell do you even care about what's happened to her?"

But the fool couldn't even answer me. She was so choked up, so distraught. I remember she even had to leave the dinner-table, and Mom shook her head and looked at me as if to say: Let her cry. She's a hopeless case, anyway.

But I'm getting way off the track, aren't I? I started out by saying that I would tell what happened as kind of a story, and instead, I find myself veering off in all different directions. I must be losing my grip, that's all. Have patience with a poor paraplegic, won't you?

As I was saying before, Wayne Brown parked his gorgeous buns right next to me and Lisa, and I swear, I thought I was going to have an orgasm right there in the middle of Burger King. I mean, I know that sounds stupid, but I remember saying something about the way I felt to Lisa. As luck would have it, she had her eye on one of the other two guys Wayne was with, so the two of us just sat there having multiple orgasms over these guys, you know? And then Lisa finally gets the guts to lean over in their direction and then starts asking them if they know where we can get our hands on some pot. She purposely sounded real naïve, as if she didn't know the first thing about drugs of any kind when, truth to tell, she probably could have written a book about them. I won't pin all of the blame for some of the scrapes I got myself into on her, but I do know that if I'd hung around with, say, Monica's crowd, for example, things would have been a little different. Much different, I should say. A hell of a lot more boring, of course. But then, I may not have met Wayne if I hadn't been chumming around with Lisa, and Lisa always had these great contacts with these really super-cool guys. If it hadn't been for Lisa, I wouldn't have known what to do about getting the pill, and believe me, the pill definitely came in handy, especially during those action-packed two months I spent with Wayne.

Barely had Lisa spoken to these guys than they all started laughing and guffawing like we were a couple of babes straight out of the woods or something. I say they all started laughing, but it was really just those other two guys, the two that ended up getting it on with Lisa that night. As for Wayne, he just sat there with his chin propped up against his fist, looking down at the table and not making a sound, almost as if laughing at something stupid like me and Lisa wasn't even worth the effort for him. And that's when I started losing my grip on my sanity, I guess you could say. The guy wasn't even reacting to our presence, and that bugged me to no end.

I don't know how long it took. I didn't have a stop-watch handy at the time, but Lisa and I eased closer and closer to their table. Pretty soon Lisa was sitting on this one guy's lap directly across from Wayne. Then the guy whose lap Lisa was sitting on said," Sure, I think we can accommodate you chicks," and he and the other guy chuckled. Probably some secret code between guys which translates as: "We'll be getting the booty tonight for sure. It's only a matter of time."

I know I don't have to say it, but I'll say it anyway: Wayne just sat there looking down at the table-top with his fist propped up against his clenched jaw. He wouldn't even establish eye contact with any one of us that whole time we sat there and shot the breeze. I don't even think that during our entire relationship we ever really looked each other squarely in the face. I tried looking at him. I mean, really looking at him very deeply a few times during the course of those two months, but it never seemed to work. I recall wondering on several occasions if he was guilty of some terrible crime or something, and perhaps that was why he could never look anyone in the eye.

I wonder now if he ever looked *her* in the eye. I know he did. The way she carried on about him, he must have. And if he looked her in the eye and let her stare back at him, did he then let her see the real Wayne Brown? Is that what destroyed her?

My mind is wandering again, and I feel that my fists are about to clench up again in anger and rage. I mean, I know it was virtually all over between us, but if I couldn't have him, then why should she? And to think of him actually making love to her! Making love to that cold damp fish. It turns my stomach just to think about it. He couldn't have had sex with her. It's impossible. If he were in this room, I'd kill him. Kill them both, in fact, if that were humanly possible.

I guess the cruelest blow of all is having to remain chained to this wheel-chair when there are literally thousands of more important things I should be doing right now. If I could, I'd put something in Aunt Lucille's coffee. Nothing too potent, of course. Just something to keep her on ice for a while so I could slip out of the house and go out and find him. I'd take that knife, too, the one I've got hidden away under my pillow, and go after him with it. And when I found him, I wouldn't care where he was or whether he was with anybody or not. I'd stab him with one swift, dynamic stroke. Stab him in the groin, too, so that, even if he survived, his life would be over and done with for all intents and purposes, the same way mine is.

I often wonder what might have happened if Lisa and I hadn't taken in that movie that distant Monday night last April. We never would have wound up at Burger King, and even if Wayne and his buddies had gone there, they simply would have found some other whores to bang. Maybe I still would have gone out on that Memorial Day weekend and messed up my legs even if Wayne had never entered my life, but at least I wouldn't have had to endure all the rest. The gross indignity of watching him working outdoors in our back yard, bronzed by the sun, looking for all the world like one of those Roman gods, with his blond curls shining in the sunlight. I'd watch him from my position in this goddamned wheel-chair, and I couldn't even walk over to him. Couldn't even feel his arms go around me, his lips coming over mine, his tongue engaged in my mouth with my tongue. That horrible car accident may have taken away all the feeling from the bottom half of my anatomy, but I still nourished that aching feeling in my heart for him.

But I swear, that guy had no feeling in his own heart! Not from the beginning, either. He was incapable of it. Despite what she said about him, yes! Despite the way she supported him and proclaimed that he was a changed person.

It was bullshit. None of that was supposed to happen, and it damn' well wouldn't have happened either if I hadn't been crippled. It was supposed to turn out all differently. I was a virgin that night at Burger King. A virgin who was ready for the man of her life to scoop her up and carry her off to the sacrificial altar. I was playing with dynamite at the time. I should have known that. I was only fifteen, but I still should have known better.

He scooped me up, all right. Carried me to the sacrificial altar, too, if that's what you want to call the back of his van. And the entire time, I imagined that it was something really wonderful and meaningful. Something that I would live to tell all my granddaughters about some day.

Well, it was wonderful, dammit! And I conducted myself in quite a mature fashion, if I do say so myself. Acted as though I was used to it. I don't really think I fooled him, though. I don't think he really cared whether I was a virgin or an experienced whore, even, come to think of it.

Come to think of it, I don't think he cared. Period!

Oops! Sounds like Aunt Lucille's back from doing her last-minute Christmas shopping. Last-minute until tomorrow, anyway. Wonder what she's bought me. A new pair of legs, I hope.

BETSY'S DIARY – June 16, 1985

Dear Diary: I've hardly spent any time at all with Monica over the past two days, she's been seeing so much of Carl Peters. I don't mind, of course. I want her to see just as much of him as she cares to. The two of them must certainly be in love. I can see it in her face, the way she positively glows when she picks up the telephone and realizes it's him on the line. She looks so happy, so fresh and young. It warms my heart to see her flushed with joy as she appears so constantly to be. It is definitely a miracle, a supreme miracle of love that she has found this wonderful young man and that they seem so compatible, so full of life and the desire to live it to the fullest.

It must be wonderful to be in love. I see how completely it has transformed my sister into a veritable fountain of pure, refreshing bliss. I certainly read enough about it in the novels I've devoured over the past few years. Although I have never experienced it myself, I feel as if vicariously I have come to savor just a little bit of its overpowering beauty. I fervently pray that one day, God willing, I will come to know what it is like, first-hand, to be in love and to be loved by a positively pure man of noble character.

Do such men exist in this day and age? Or am I simply deluding myself into thinking that, somehow or other, I could possibly recreate in my own humdrum existence something of the aura and mystique of unadulterated and unblemished pure romantic love that may or may not have existed in better times? I may be hopelessly naïve as far as worldly affairs are concerned, but I do know that if the right man were to invade my life with his dynamic fervor, I would instantly recognize my emotion as love, pure and simple. Whenever I take Ellen through the park or go off into the woods by myself, I seem to sense Nature itself, breathing as if it were a living organism, and whispering to me that there really is such a thing as Love. The Prime Mover. God. Whatever men may call it, it is there, and I know that my existence will never be complete until I have discovered it for myself and drunk in the essence of its being so that it has become a part of my very nature and my very soul.

I am twenty-one years old and have not known what love is. By other people's standards, that fact alone might classify me as, to say the least, eccentric. But I am still young, and I feel that I should console myself with that thought and, also, the thought that I have never deemed it necessary to settle for anything that I could ever regard as less than first-rate. May I someday slip into my grave a virgin rather than give my heart and love to a man who could not understand the true meaning of this divine phenomenon which we call Love. And so, as I retire to my warm, chaste bed this evening, I will enter a serene sleep, knowing that the best is yet to come. The best years of my life lie ahead. With God's blessing, I will not disappoint Him but will yield to every circumstance He feels compelled to send my way. I know that He will not fail me.

P.S. It's after midnight, and Mom's not home from her date with that man from the office. Mr. Sellars, I think his name is. I do hope she knows what she's doing, but most of all, that she is safe, happy, and healthy.

AUNT LUCILLE'S DIARY – December 23, 1985

I came home tonight a little earlier than I expected and caught Ellen doing something underhanded. She tried to pretend that everything was fine, but I know she's up to something crazy. I know these past few months haven't been easy for her, but God knows they haven't been easy for me either. It's Christmas in two days, and I feel like the world's biggest hypocrite in making even the slightest attempt to acknowledge the holiday season in any way, shape, or form. It's not easy for me, especially having turned forty this past year, to find myself saddled with a handicapped girl with questionable morals. I know, I keep reminding myself that it's not her fault. The accident was unfortunate. Not only for her, but for that poor girlfriend of hers who passed away. And it seems as though things, after that, just went from bad to worse.

I can't deal with this. Not at my age. It was always easy for Jean. She had a way with men, and I suppose Ellen inherited that sensuality from her. But me? After Arnie left me for that tramp, I gave up on men, and that was – let's see, next February makes it twelve years ago. Not once in those twelve years have I ever even had the slightest desire to go out on a date with a man, and I haven't regretted it thus far. Maybe if those poor nieces of mine had stayed clear of them as I have, none of this would have happened.

Well, I've tried to see my way through this holiday season as best I could. But I made a big boo-boo this afternoon. I actually went up to Norfolk with the ludicrous thought in my head that seeing Monica would help me cope with my emotions. But it was the most shocking thing. They wouldn't even let me see her. One of the attendants explained that she had been heavily sedated and that they feared that she might actually attempt to "do herself some harm" (as he put it).

I don't know whether to cry or give way to my bitter rage at this point in time. I know that I should hate that girl, but I can't. She had her reasons for what she did. Stupid ones perhaps, but undoubtedly they must have made sense to her at the time.

How morbid! My own niece in that horror chamber. I hate to say it, but things aren't getting any better. Just when I thought they couldn't get any worse than they already were –

It was unnerving, to say the least, and it's becoming more and more difficult to parry Kathy and Melanie's questions when I see them at lunchtime and they ask me," How's the girl doing?" and I have to say," Which one?" and then the conversation just dies away in horrible discomfort. I'm trying to be fair about this, and I feel that it's my duty to carry on as best I can, but this constant strain is getting to be too much for me. Why, I wouldn't be at all surprised if I were to lose all my friends over this!

Oh, God, and then I made the miserable mistake of going to the cemetery. After becoming catapulted into a state of depression up in Norfolk, I should have known better. But for some unfathomable reason, I thought I might be able to purge myself of these morbid feelings by going in there and allowing some of its peace to filter through me. Weather-wise, it was such a brutally cold afternoon, I never expected to run into *him*. But there he was, dressed in mourning – at least, it appeared that way to me. He tried to conceal himself behind a tree so that I wouldn't see him, but I'd already seen him from a distance, so I knew it had to be him. I mean, who else besides him would be there all alone in that bitter cold, ready to carry on as though the funeral had taken place just yesterday? Oh, yes, I'm sure Monica would pay her respects, if she weren't already in her own figurative grave right now. I mean, not even that other dreadful young man visits the grave as often as Carl does, and if there were any justice in this world, it ought to be him, not Carl, who should be haunted by guilt.

I knew he was trouble the minute I laid eyes on him. For one thing, he was an animal. I could tell from the way he moved and the way he perspired when he worked outside with his shirt peeled off in the hot sun. And those ridiculous head-bands, and those bandannas he always wore. I thought that sort of thing went out with the Indians!

Enough of him. I'd prefer to think he never entered our lives. It was bad enough I had to deal with Carl Peters, I pretended I didn't see him hiding behind that tree, but it was a complete waste of time. I felt so tense, just knowing that he was lurking such a short distance away, that I couldn't concentrate my thoughts on what my original purpose had been in going there. So, I came away quickly, feeling sicker and sicker by the moment, and I swore I'd never go back there again. After all, I'm doing my part just in taking care of my invalid niece. I don't need to feel guilty, do I, even if I never set foot again in that cemetery for the rest of my life.

Instead, I'll say my prayers daily. I'll try to act happy and cheerful, especially around Ellen, and I'll continue to lead this lonely life of mine as best I can. I have nothing to reproach myself with. Absolutely nothing.

That's it for today.

Postscript: While Ellen was bathing herself in the tub this morning, I went through some of her things and found a knife hidden away under her pillow. I know I ought to have confronted her with my discovery. Maybe if I just ignore the whole thing, nothing will come of it. She couldn't actually figure on using it on herself, could she? Omigod! Could she possibly figure on using it on --?

I'll get rid of it, first thing tomorrow morning.

That's it for today. For sure.

BETSY'S DIARY – June 20, 1985

Dear Diary: I'm so excited, my thoughts are rushing through my mind with such speed that I can hardly control myself. I've never been this excited in my entire life. It took a good two hours for me to bring myself to sit down and begin writing this, and I daresay it will take a lot longer than that for me to actually absorb the significance of all this. I do know one thing: This has definitely been the most thrilling day in my entire life up to this point.

It all started when the telephone rang, and I discovered that it was Monica and that she sounded so excited. Almost in a frenzy, as I recall. She asked me to meet her and Carl at Donovan's Restaurant and not to breathe a word about where I was going to either Mom or Ellen. Luckily, Mom had already gone off with Rick Sellars from the office and Aunt Lucille had been called in to sit with Ellen for the evening. Dear Aunt Lucille was a bit huffy with me when I returned after eleven, and honestly I don't know how I managed to get her out of the house without blurting out what had happened. I'm sure she's wondering what it was that could have made me so positively ecstatic when I walked through the door, but she'll find out soon enough. I just thought I should break the news to Mom first.

When I arrived at Donovan's Restaurant, Monica and Carl waved me over to their table and invited me to sit down. They had already had dinner and offered me a dessert, which I refused, of course, since I was so anxious to find out what the mystery was all about as Monica had neglected to let on any clue at all on the telephone a short while earlier.

They were a bit tentative at first. Understandably so, of course. But I sensed what it was they were going to tell me even before they managed to get the words out of their mouths. They were going to elope, and they wanted me to stand up for them as a witness.

At first, I was simply nonplussed. All I could think of was that Mom would surely stage a scene as soon as she got wind of it and that she'd be perfectly impossible to live with for the next few weeks. I also felt a slight twinge of inferiority over my not having managed to find a husband before my younger sister was able to do so. Then I began to see how selfish it would be for me to think only of what the consequences would be for me when it was Monica's happiness that should take precedence over all else.

At the same time, I've always felt that, since Monica deserves the very best of everything in every possible area of her life, she should be given the opportunity of experiencing a huge, elaborate wedding and reception, expenses being no object, and that I should be afforded the sheer joy of being able to watch my younger sister walk down the aisle looking pure and radiant in a white wedding-gown. Monica never said it herself, that she would prefer a lavish wedding when her time came to marry, so perhaps my own idea of what would be best for her is not identical to her own. Just seeing the look of positive rapture that was on her face as she informed me of their plan to elope convinced me that she was doing the right thing, that in running off with him tonight and tying the knot in secret was simply another manifestation of her youth, drive, and spontaneity, and why should such impulsive joy be denied her? I only wish that my own bland existence could be characterized by some such sudden impulse of sheer and glorious romantic passion.

They had procured the marriage license, had taken the blood tests, and arranged to be wedded by a justice-of-the-peace over in Glendale. Carl had told his parents that he'd be spending the weekend up in New Hampshire with some friends, so he didn't foresee any problem in having to explain his absence from home for a few days to his parents. The only bad taste that was left in my mouth came when Monica begged me to explain to Mom when I got back home that she knew she was doing the right thing. Carl had enough money saved up for an apartment. They had even made arrangements to move into one, not too far from here, in fact, as soon as they got back from their little honeymoon. She hoped, and so did I naturally, that by the time they got back, Mom would have recovered from the initial shock of learning that Monica and her sweetheart had run off secretly to get married.

When Mom gets back from her date with Rick Sellars, whether it be later on tonight or early in the morning, I will tell her. It will be difficult for me, but Mom has been acting so strangely lately that there's no way I can accurately predict how she will react to this whole business. If she takes it upon herself to fly into an insane fury, I'll brace myself, wait it out, and then later on when she's relatively calm, I'll ask her to be as understanding as she possibly can. For Monica's sake, anyway. Then again, she may surprise everyone and respond indifferently to the news that Monica and Carl were married in secret. Ever since Ellen's accident, Mom's moods have been highly erratic. These all-night escapades with Rick Sellars and the like may indeed be her way of getting it all out, although it still doesn't explain all her former indiscretions with certain men whom

I'd rather not bring back into my memory. Even before she married Pop, Aunt Lucille asserts that Mom was quite the playgirl, and even went so far on one particularly grisly occasion to suggest that my own parentage was not above suspicion. But Aunt Lucille is so much the opposite of her sister that Monica, Ellen, and I have always been inclined to take everything she tells us with the customary grain of salt.

Why can't life be just a little bit more predictable? I mean, I'm happy for Monica, all right. More than just happy, in the ordinary sense of the word. I just wish things didn't always have to be so frantic. At times, my days go by in boring mediocrity. Then all of a sudden there's a spurt of strange and unusual activity, and through all of it, although I never play a leading role, I feel as though I were being bombarded with cruel attacks coming from over a thousand different directions simultaneously. Perhaps the problem is that I'm too sensitive for my own good. When Pop died all those years ago, I'm told I became seriously ill for over a month. That same feeling of weakness and helplessness assailed me not too long ago, too, when we heard about poor Lisa Dobbs passing away. I mean, I realize that death is a fact of life and that sooner or later we all have to deal with it in some fashion. Hopefully by the time it is necessary for me to experience the death of a dear loved one in my adulthood, I will have a firmer grip on my emotions. I certainly hope so, because I feel that if I were to lose my dear sister Monica into the fierce hands of Death, I would be devastated. I don't know if I'd ever be able to function again as a human being if I were to lose her.

But I refuse to dwell upon such morbid issues. Just let me thank God that I was able to perform a part, be it ever so small, in helping to bring about Monica's happiness for her this evening. I will never forget that moment, that absolutely sacred moment when they were officially pronounced husband and wife. I felt as though a spirit of supreme calm passed through my soul. Then, when the two of them drew apart after their embrace and I caught a glimpse of the elation on my dear sister's face, I simply quivered. A feeling of indescribable bliss took hold of me, and I stood there and cried in a helpless state for several minutes. And to think that, in the midst of her supreme happiness, Monica came over to me at that moment and embraced me.

I find it so amusing to recall the look Carl gave me when he saw her embrace me. He wasn't smiling. He wasn't frowning either. He just seemed to be in awe of me. It wasn't until he realized that I was looking back at him that he smiled. Why? I don't know. I can see why Monica was attracted to him from the first because he certainly is a handsome, clean-cut young man. The fire of those eyes! The two of them have so much fire and brilliance of personality between them. They are, after all, made for each other. The Maplewoods High School yearbook staff certainly knew what they were doing when they nominated those two for consideration by their classmates as Ideal Couple. I am sure that the years ahead for them will be ideal in every sense of the word. Nothing in my life thus far could be more certain.

P.S. What makes this marriage so perfect and beautiful, in my eyes, is the fact that they're both virgins. Monica assures me of this, and I have never had any reason to doubt anything she's ever told me in her entire life.

CARL'S DIARY – January 1, 1986

Dear Diary: This is my first entry in the first diary I ever owned. I never thought I'd ever find myself writing in one, but when I spied it in that little novelty shop last week and thought about the kinds of things I could write in it, the idea kind of appealed to me, so I bought it and now, the start of a new year, seems like an appropriate time to begin using it.

Let's see. How do I begin? Where do I begin? Do I begin with something poetic? Maybe I ought to start with a preface or an introduction. A dedication would be nice. Nobody will ever get to read it except me, anyway, so why hold back?

On second thought, dedications are queer. I'm a man. I should start with something assertive, something macho, something aggressive that will really make a statement.

"This – my first, only, and last diary – is dedicated to My Angel, just as my every thought and breath is dedicated to her."

Not manly enough? Too effeminate perhaps? Well, why not? How can a dedication be defined in masculine or feminine terms, anyway? All that matters is it's the truth. My life *is* dedicated to her. My life, my soul, my heart, my every thought, my every breath. It's true, and that's all that matters.

I visited the grave this afternoon. It was cloudy, cold, and drizzly. The air was damp, and my clothes stunk with sweat and filth and the smoke from the last joint I'd had. I wanted to take them off and fling them to the ground, and embrace the tombstone with my cold, naked body. I wanted her to sense that I was willing to go to any lengths and any depths to prove my love to her so that she would recognize that I am the one who loved and loves her still. She couldn't comprehend that when she was alive, so I must prove to her now that she's dead how strong my love for her really is. Who the hell goes to see her every day besides me? Not even that dowdy middle-aged spinster aunt of hers loves her enough to see her as often as I do. It's just as well, anyway. She gives me the creeps. The last time she looked at me, she made me feel as though everything was all my fault, the bitch! God damn her! God damn all of them! Not even my own stinking wife had the nerve to look me straight in the eye when we stood at the coffin shortly before it was going to be lowered into the earth.

No. I promised myself I would remain calm and not succumb to any vulgar language. But then again, who's going to read this, anyway? I couldn't afford to have anyone get a hold of this book and start leafing through it. Why? Because I intend to put my soul into this book, and no one would ever understand it. No one appreciates the worth of a soul like mine. They've all got their stupid arrogant pride, their holier-than-thou, tight-assed attitudes. They'd never understand that a man like me needs something loftier and far more ennobling than the kinds of crap they wallow in. And if I never have to see any of those people again for the rest of my life, then I'll be much better off. The problem is: Just how do I get through the rest of this life?

I know how, of course, although nobody would ever understand why I do the things I do. I went to that party last week and experienced the most excellent high of my life. I seemed to acquire new spiritual dimensions that night, and then I came home to the real world and almost puked as soon as I walked in the door. Luckily, my parents were asleep, and I was able to clean up the puke without them finding out about it the next day. I've got to get out of this house, though. It's so confining, so limiting. If I expect to get away with the kinds of crap I've been pulling lately, I'd better find somewhere else to live. Maybe that freaky Samuel will take me in. He'd appreciate the bread, I know that. But even he can be a real downer at times, spouting all that religious crap at everyone all the time. What makes him think he even has any idea of the true meaning of existence when the strongest stuff he's ever gotten off on was cheap grass? Still and all, it might not be a bad idea to move in with him. At least, he may have some connections, and it's getting to the point these days where nothing satisfies me anymore.

I haven't had my mind on sex for a while, and that's a good thing. Masturbation's a downer, that's for sure, and I'm lucky if I can ever stay focused on an erotic thought long enough to get the pony out of the stable, you know? That last girl I tried to have sex with was a real downer, too. Stupid really. I'm kneeling with my head in the toilet, puking my guts out, and she's wondering why I can't get a hard-on. The whole night was a disaster, totally depressing with a capital D, and God knows I don't need any more depression in my life. If only I can hold out a little longer. I think I've got a little over a thousand in the bank. I'll be fine in a month or so, get myself a little job or something, just enough to sustain my lifestyle, of course.

Christ, I don't even want to think about tomorrow, let alone the months ahead. I'm calm now. I'm doing fine. Those two joints I smoked earlier this evening have settled me down. Just as long as I don't let anything get to me. Just so long as I can escape each day for just a few hours. That's all I need, and then I'll be all right. Just as long as I don't have to think about the future. After all, things were pretty rough there for a while, but now I've got a good, firm grip on myself, and I can handle whatever comes my way. I don't have to think about those people anymore. Those other people. I don't even have to worry about Wayne anymore. I think I'll be able to handle him all right the next time I see him. I won't let him try anything fancy on me the next time. I've got to show him I'm a man, a superior being, and that I'm not afraid of the kind of trash he represents. Then the stupid bum will lay off me, you wait and see.

Who am I trying to kid? Christ, I'm scared. I'm scared of him, and I'm scared of tomorrow, and I'm scared of just plain living. If I can't get my hands on some really strong shit, I'll crack up, and I can't afford to do that. I can't afford to veg' out. Then nobody will take me seriously the next time I try convincing them of my superiority and my amazing self-assurance. I never used to have trouble convincing them before, did I?

Christ, in high school I had them all eating out of my hands. There wasn't a slime-ball in that whole damned class that wouldn't have felt privileged just for getting the opportunity of kissing my crotch. They all voted me Most Popular and Best Personality, right? And it was a clean sweep, too. I mean, the competition for Most Popular was practically nil. What with my fantastic looks and everything, I had it made. And Best Personality was a cinch, too. All I had to do was lend a few bucks to a few influential people, let Kenny borrow my car for a few weekends, hand out a few pills to some of the riff-raff, and once again, with my incredible good looks going for me as well, there was simply no way I wasn't going to win. The only votes I didn't get was those losers, stupid Wayne and his twice-as-stupid buddies. Christ, I don't think they even had the intelligence to cast a ballot in the first place. All I know is, when those yearbooks hit the stands and those jealous dicks saw my face peering out at them on practically every other page, I knew I was king. I reigned supreme. Even the teachers were totally in love with my ass.

That's why Wayne hated me. If he'd so much as laid a hand on me, I would've reported him and had him expelled, and he knew it. Maybe he didn't care much about getting his diploma, but he knew I had power in that school, and he didn't dare touch me back then. All he could do was ignore me, pretend I didn't even exist. His way of ignoring the fact, I'll bet, that I was better than him. A better scholar, a better person, a better man. Superior with a capital S. That's why he kept his big mouth shut. He tried to pretend he wasn't fazed by all the glamor I was constantly surrounded by from one day to the next, but I know he must have hated me. Why else would he have pulled that stupid crap on me last summer?

I could kill him when I even so much as think of how inferior he was to me, and so much grief came into my life because of the sheer stupidity of those other people. Everybody actually began starting to say," He's good. He's kind. He's wonderful." And I wanted to puke in all their faces.

I'll never forget that day last summer. It must have been in August because Wayne was already in the marines, and I was feeling really depressed one day and then deliriously happy the next. I sat at the dinner-table eating something boring, and Monica started in on me with how maybe we were all wrong about him and maybe they knew what they were doing and maybe we shouldn't interfere, and I felt like saying to her," Maybe you should just shut the hell up."

How he fooled them all will remain one of the supreme mysteries of my life. Just an inferior intellect. An inferior being in every way imaginable, and he fooled everybody! Everybody except me, so I guess it makes sense insofar as my keen mind was the only one capable of deciphering his true worth as a human being. I recognized him from the beginning back in ninth grade when he and his old man moved into this town and he got enrolled in one of my classes. Gym class, it must have been. Yeah, I remember saying to my good buddy Kenny," Since when do they allow retards into this class?" Then, when we were all taking our showers after gym class, I turned to Kenny and said," Big prick, tiny brain." And then Kenny and I killed ourselves laughing over the exceptionally brilliant observation I'd just made, until Wayne took his eyes off the floor to look up at us briefly, and the two of us clammed up.

I don't know why me and Kenny were so scared of him. I mean, at the time, Wayne was new in school, and he hadn't managed to befriend any of those losers he eventually started to chum around with. But it didn't take long for him to acquire a few morons for friends, and even some of the sluts on the cheerleading squad started taking an interest in him, the ones with subhuman intelligence, that is. For a while there, I thought Monica was going to say something about him being cute or some such brainlessly female statement, but she never verbalized such thoughts. Not to me, anyway. All I know is I should have had him killed back then in ninth grade. Had I known he was going to royally mess up my life, I would have paid somebody off to have him beaten, castrated, flagellated, and then killed. It would have been worth the money to hire the Mob to do it, too. If only I had thought about it. If I had only known back then what I know now, all my troubles would be over completely. I could be happy now with the woman I love. I wouldn't have to drive myself into a drug-induced state periodically in order to cope with the horror of daily living. I wouldn't have to drive out to that cemetery and torture myself with this incredible grief, this grief that is so strong and so overpowering that I can't even put it into words. I wouldn't have to live with the constant fear that some kind of violence is going to come upon me when I least expect it. When is it going to end? When?

What's today? January First? I ought to be hearing from good old Wayne any day now. It's been nearly a month since our last confrontation. A month since that horrible night I actually thought he'd killed me. How I ever got myself off the ground and crawled home in one piece is totally beyond me.

But it doesn't make sense. When he walked up to me that night, the first thing he said to me was," You know what today is." That's how he was able to catch me off my guard. I couldn't for the life of me figure out what he was talking about. I stammered, started asking him all sorts of questions. The moron actually caught me off-balance. Then what was it he said next? I can't remember. Something like," It's the fourth," and I thought to myself: Sure. It's the fourth. It's the fourth time he's done this to me.

But that's not it at all! Christ! As I sit here writing this, it's starting to make sense. The first time he beat the hell out of me was about a month after the funeral. Well, he didn't exactly beat the hell out of me. One punch. That's all it was. But he caught me off my guard, and I was out cold for an awful long time from that one punch of his. That had to have been in October. Early October. The second time, how'd it happen? I forget. It's a strain to get this all straightened out in my mind. I'm getting mixed up now, and I can't think.

The second time it happened, I was just going over to my car after getting out of work. It had to have been early November then because I quit my job a couple of weeks before Thanksgiving. Early November. Right. I was going over to my car, and I heard him say my name. I turned around, not having recognized his voice at first, and when I saw him standing a couple of feet opposite me, he said something soft to me. I don't think it registered in my mind at the time, I was so shocked, seeing him again after he'd knocked me out that other time. I mean, I know I should have been more alert. I should have dived for the car door and made a run for it. But he caught me at an off moment, you see, and I heard him say something like," It's that time again," before he raised his fists. I don't know what I should have done at that moment, but he took me totally by surprise, appearing in that parking lot so unexpectedly like he did. What did I do when he put up his fists? Christ, writing about it like this makes it seem like it happened only yesterday, and yet, I can't remember.

Yes! He put up his fists and waited, almost as if he expected me to engage in some sort of boxing match with him, or something! But I wasn't going for any of that stuff. I know I should have made a dive for the inside of my car, but I figured he might grab me and pull me out of the car before I had a chance to get the engine started, so I called out for help. A couple of lowlifes I worked with were in the vicinity, but nobody stepped in to help – not even while I stood there and let him punch me several times in the face.

That makes twice, right? Then the third time was early last month. But Christ! That's when he said," It's the fourth." Is the moron so fundamentally stupid that he can't even count to three without running into serious difficulties? What did he mean," It's the fourth?"

It's getting late, and my mind is sore with the strain of dealing with this. I'll sleep late tomorrow, possibly till noon. Then I'll drive out to the cemetery and see that angel of mine. I love her so much, it's killing me. Then I'll drop in on Kenny, and hopefully he won't be in the middle of some massive sex session like the last time I dropped in on him unexpectedly. But Kenny's cool, with a capital C, so I'm sure everything will still be O.K. between the two of us. Later on, I suppose I'll drive out to Samuel's pad and see if he'd be willing to take me in. Even if he says no, I'm sure I'll be able to talk him into it sooner or later. All I have to do is catch him when he's totally spaced out and, with my superlative charm and personality, I'll have him handing over the keys to his pad in a flash. He's putty in my hands, only he's too limited in intelligence to realize it.

And now I'm going to put down my pen and rest. Maybe I'll have something vitally interesting to write in this diary tomorrow night. Or maybe, if luck is on my side, I'll be able to report with acute pleasure that Wayne Brown Junior has been the victim of some horrible freak accident and may no longer be counted among the living.

Or better still, I won't be alive myself to write another entry in this dumb diary. I'll be with my angel. I'll be in the company of the most perfect human being who ever graced the planet Earth with her sublime presence. And then, when we are finally together, we will consummate our love in a union on a far more spiritually elevated plane of existence than the one here, where a physical union with her was denied to me.

BETSY'S DIARY – June 21, 1985

Dear Diary: At the end of this long day, I feel rather as if I were being pulled in several different directions. This is not to say that I have lost sight of my true aim, only that in order to keep all the factions appeased, I feel compelled to make certain compromises in my ways of thinking along the way.

The first thing I did when I woke up this morning and went downstairs to have breakfast was to leave a brief note for Mom explaining what had happened last night, just on the off-chance that she was curious to know why Monica wasn't home this morning. I also urged her to call me at work in case there was anything she wanted to discuss with me. Apparently she had spent the entire night with Rick Sellars, and although I had never regarded that liaison with anything approaching approbation, I feel that, in this particular instance, her timing was very opportune insofar as a night of physical pleasure has always had a positive effect on Mom's usually unpredictable disposition.

I had been prepared to deal with Ellen later on, but as luck would have it, she accosted me just as I was about to leave the house. I mentioned to her that I felt it to be rather early for her to be so wide awake. I was also tempted to allude to her rather hostile manner, but ever since the accident that has deprived her of the use of her legs, I have tried to refrain from making any such comments.

Needless to say, Ellen's reaction to the news of Monica's elopement was caustic and abrasive. She referred to the two of them in such degrading terms that I honestly felt quite sorry for her in the sense that her condition has made her literally incapable of sharing in the joys of others, even the joys of her own sister. It is difficult for me to fully understand why she should be so brutally insensitive, but then again, I have been fortunate in the fact that my physical well-being has remained unimpaired all these years. It is unfair of me to judge her too harshly, and I feel that, whereas Monica's happiness is fundamentally my primary concern and has been for many years, I must not forget that it is perhaps my youngest sister who needs my time, patience, and understanding more than anyone else.

What I didn't expect, and what I really wasn't prepared for, was for Mom to appear in person during my lunch break and begin to upbraid me, as if I were the one who had actually suggested to the two of them that they should elope. It was quite embarrassing for me to sit quietly while she abused me in every conceivable fashion with two of the other librarians sitting within hearing distance of the whole scene. I'm afraid that my lack of composure didn't help matters any either, especially when I found myself incapable of continuing the conversation and finally broke down in tears. It wasn't until after Mom stormed out of the room, leaving me sobbing in my chair and trying to gather myself together to assume at least a semblance of self-dignity, that I began to feel the hurt even more. If Mom had always been demonstrative in her love towards the three of us, her anger could have been justified to some extent. All of this could have made more sense. The fact remains that she is becoming more and more difficult to deal with as the days go by, and I often wonder which of the two is more serious: Ellen's physical deterioration or Mom's emotional instability.

I can't help feeling that there might have been more I could have done. If I had done something quite wonderful in the past few years, something wonderful that would have made Mom proud of me, perhaps she would have treated all three of us with a bit more understanding and compassion. I know that, although I've never brought any shame upon the household, she is disappointed in me and feels that I could be making more of my life. As the weeks and months pass and I remain a single, unattached female with absolutely no romantic prospects, she must view me as a mortifying failure. It's obvious I haven't made her happy. I haven't fulfilled my function as her eldest daughter. I haven't married and given her grandchildren. I haven't performed a single, solitary act that would endear me to her. I simply exist from day to the next without affecting anyone's life in any significant way, and for that, I am truly sorry. For that, I am ashamed of myself, and I acknowledge my guilt and all of my shortcomings as a human being.

It may be possible for me to justify my existence by caring for Ellen a little bit more. By encouraging Mom in her relationship with Rick Sellars. By saying nice things to everyone and making our home a little brighter on a regular daily basis. I will try. I promise myself right now that I will try to be a better person, so that they could love me just a little bit and feel that it is, after all, worth it just a little bit to have me around.

This would all be so much easier for me if Monica were here. But even when she returns from her honeymoon, she will be moving into an apartment, and I won't be able to see her that much anymore. I must release her in order to let her grow so that she may fulfill her potential as Carl's young, beautiful, and loving wife. If she needs me, if she wishes to confide in me or seek my advice, I will try to satisfy her as best I can. Maybe in simply being here for her in case she needs to consult me on some problem, or in case Ellen needs someone to act as the object of her bitterness, or in case Mom must have somebody to rail at – maybe thus I will be fulfilling their needs in some way and, in this, I may justify my being alive.

Let me rest now and try to find a little peace. I fervently pray that they all remain happy. All of them. And if they are not happy now, may they find their happiness very, very soon.

P.S. I am consoled by the sudden realization that, by this hour of my writing, Monica has now discovered the joys of physical love with the man of her dreams.

CYCLE TWO

MONICA'S MEMOIRS – April 4, 1986

I'm calm now. I heard somebody say as they walked out of my circle of Hell that I could be left alone for the remainder of the night. Shortly, the strong sedative should begin to have its full effect, and I will be able to slip into a milky-white bath of nothingness. How I wish that it could be an eternity of oblivion! It's what my soul longs for more than anything else. The peace of the grave should be as sweet as the nothingness I crave.

I envy her that peace. I envy her the serenity of an existence that is alien to the ghastly horrors that I face in my daily living. I envy her the power to blot out the accusing cries of a relentless conscience – those cries of my own implacable conscience as my guilt continues to corrode my soul just as thoroughly and irrevocably as it has already corroded my sanity. The disease that eats away at me, at every fiber of my being, is one that cannot be treated, so why don't they all just desist? Why don't they release me from this eternity? This eternal waiting for the moment when my lungs will take in their final breath of self-disgust. Why don't they inundate my arms and legs with an accumulation of intoxicating drugs and needles that will render me a complete nonentity with neither a mind, heart, or soul?

At least an entire month will elapse before my solitary visitor returns. It was his appearance today which, they say, triggered my present traumas. They may even forbid his visit next month on the grounds that my already tenuous mental stability might be endangered. Should that happen and I am then deprived of the one experience in my present life which even remotely succeeds in cleansing me of some of my unbearable anguish, then I may rest assured that the real End is near.

It is spring. A time of flowering. A time of renewal. A time of hope when all those things and creatures that took on a semblance of death are given a chance to redeem themselves. A chance to justify themselves through sheer beauty alone.

I saw the buds on the trees this afternoon. Actually saw them and wondered with amazement at their reappearance. I took fresh air into my body and expelled it slowly, trembling at the very realization that I was still alive. I heard a bird twitter overhead, and I remembered that bird that used to live in our house, and I was too empty of all feeling to weep at the remembrance of all the tears that had been shed in our home when that bird suddenly caught a draft and expired at the bottom of its little cage.

I was only ten, and Betsy was a teenager already. And Mom got rid of the bird before we came home from school.

"Where's the bird?"

Betsy ran into the living room where Mom and I were sitting, apparently having noticed that it was no longer in its cage in the corner of the kitchen.

"It died," Mom said," so I wrapped it up in the garbage and threw it out."

We were never allowed to own another pet after that. Mom claimed that she had no intentions of going through the same ordeal again when our next pet died. I couldn't understand it then, but I now know that if we had gotten another bird or, even worse, a dog or a cat, Betsy would never have been able to endure its eventual death.

"Where's the bird?"

Why does the sound of her voice continue to haunt me? It's not the thought or the image of the bird being wrapped in the garbage that pains me, nor the picture I have in my mind of an empty cage standing in the corner of a silent kitchen that was once alive with the sounds of bright music. It is the tremor of her voice, quivering with the dread that must have already seized her imagination as soon as she had discovered that the cage was empty. She had begged Mom to let us have a bird. It had been a routine scene of begging every so often until Mom told her to go ahead and get the "dumb bird" if she had enough money to pay for it on her own. And Betsy proceeded to save up all her pennies so that she would not only be able to purchase the animal at the pet store, but be able to buy the cage and all the food necessary to keep the bird in good health. She went to the library every day after school and read books on the proper care and management of birds and other household pets; and months afterwards, when the bird had already become a part of our environment and Mom insisted that it had been a waste of money, referring to it as a "common pest and germ-carrier" – Betsy still fed it daily and took it to the vet on a regular basis. And in the middle of the night, she would get out of bed to check on the bird. In the middle of a dark and chilly night, she would tiptoe downstairs and take the bird-cage cover off, open the tiny door, and stroke the tender little trembling body of the bird. And the bird loved her and trusted her completely.

"Where's the bird?"

The drug is beginning to take effect as I can feel my eyelids droop, and yet, part of the calm that I feel coming over me stems from this escape into a happier time. The escape that my mind so desperately needs if it is to hang on to a mere vestige of sanity and rational thought, even if it should be only by the most gossamer thread imaginable.

The sounds of springtime that I heard this afternoon continue to tingle my sluggish thoughts, mocking me even in their comparative feebleness. I can almost feel my lips smiling as my mind, teasing me with delusional thoughts, leads me back to those carefree days of my childhood. The days we spent in the park, smelling the flowers and laughing in the sunlight. Those sultry afternoons at the beach, too. Especially that day when all three of us were suddenly taken with fright because we somehow lost track of where Mom was, and then we ended up finding her talking to that stranger in the convertible. I was only about eleven, and yet, Betsy saw fit to lead me behind some parked cars so that I wouldn't see Mom and the stranger.

I remember how I knelt down while Betsy's arm enclosed my shoulder. And Ellen tried to look up and get a better view of what was going on.

"Tell me if she gets in the car with him," I pleaded with her.

I was so terrified at the thought, you see, that Mom would get into the convertible and ride off with the stranger, and then the three of us would be orphans. But Betsy pulled me in a little closer and assured me that Mom loved us and that she would never abandon us. How ironic it was that, only a second after Betsy had managed to calm my fears, Ellen then took it upon herself to shriek," She's getting into the car with that man!"

No! I cried No in a loud, piercing voice so that Mom would hear me and stop herself from committing that terrible sin.

I can still hear the sound of her laughter as I saw the man pull her in against him and enclose her in his arms. We stayed still, the three of us, for less than a minute, and then Betsy took us, one in each hand, scampering back onto the sand. I thought at the time that Mom hadn't seen the three of us scampering away, but then I remember how she screamed at Betsy all the way home about how the whole day was ruined and how it was all her fault, too.

My God, that was eight years ago, and it seems as though it happened only days before the cataclysm that engulfed our lives. How could we have spent so much time together and not been able to judge one another's characters, not been able to distinguish between the lies and the truth, fact and fiction, honesty and deceit? If it had only been us three girls and Mom, it might have been simpler. Even Aunt Lucille's feelings were easy enough to decipher.

But we had no way of dealing with Carl and Wayne. We had no way of knowing that, by adding the two of them into the mix, our emotions would become so tangled that it seemed as though none of us could even see straight anymore. I envy Aunt Lucille her position on the outside of all of it and, most of all perhaps, her ability to recognize that, strategically, such a position was the safest one to be in from the start. However, even from her vantage point of seeming neutrality, she was never able to see the truth. To this day, I don't believe she knows the truth.

At the funeral, she wept with all the others, and she even held Carl's hand when he put his out to her. But what was so strange about that? At that time, not even *I* knew what the actual truth was. Even then, I was blind. Even at that point in time when they were on the verge of lowering the coffin into the ground, I was unable to discover a good enough reason to grieve as I stood there, tense and uneasy and in mental agony, knowing that Carl was gazing forcefully in my direction with those horribly fierce dark eyes of his.

I didn't even know the truth when we left the cemetery in the hearse and began our slow and tortuous journey back home. Nor did I know the truth when the hearse started to leave the gates of the cemetery and I saw – We all saw Wayne's van coming at us, then tearing past us at the very last instant so as to shoot towards the grave we had just left. I didn't hear his scream on that occasion. No. Not on that occasion did I hear it. I was spared that agony for the time being. It wasn't until that other night. That other night when the two of us screamed together, and my mind has not stopped screaming since.

One month from today, he will come back. And if the air is pleasant, if the birds are singing that day, if I have been calm and they heed the pleading in my eyes, they will let the two of us walk the grounds as we did this afternoon. And together, we will listen to the sounds of the air, the voices of nature, the whispers of the trees. And I will hold his golden curls against my breast, and together we will strain all of our senses so that we can hear that sound we both so long to hear: the pulsation of her pure and innocent soul.

BETSY'S DIARY – June 23, 1985

Dear Diary: At this point in time, I feel deliriously happy. At least, I keep telling myself that I should feel this way as I seek to suppress the doubts that would desperately plague me if I were to allow them to do so.

The day started out as usual for a quiet, summery Sunday morning. I woke up, and the air seemed filled with a sense of nature reclining with bated breath. I felt stirred to get the day started as soon as possible even though I had no idea of what the course of the day's happenings would have in store for me.

Mom had spent the night with Rick Sellars. I think. At any rate, she was still fast asleep when I awoke at nine, and as I was to learn later on in the day, she hadn't taken a shower until three this afternoon. She seemed erratic in both mood and behavior, so I purposely stayed out of her way. After church, I decided that taking Ellen down to the beach seemed like the best way of avoiding any possible confrontations at home. Since the weather was so splendid, it ended up being an altogether refreshing idea. My vacation will begin at the end of the coming week, and I look forward to spending a lot of time at the beach, either by myself or in Ellen's company. If I remain home all day long, I won't be permitted a moment of privacy since I know that Mom will seize upon my leisure as an excuse to demand that I cart Ellen around the entire state if she and Ellen should deem it necessary. If that is what they wish, it certainly won't interfere with my plans, because I don't have any anyway, outside of being given an opportunity to catch up on my reading and possibly warming myself in the sun's rays.

I know that I will miss Monica, having so much time on my hands to notice her absence, but at least I can fortify myself with the thought that her own time must henceforth be spent with the man she loves. Her husband. I find it somewhat jarring to discover that I must now refer to Carl Peters as her husband. He seems so young. They both appear to be so tender and vulnerable, albeit flushed with the emotion of their newly found love. When they called me this afternoon and asked me to see them at their apartment, as if seeking my approval for all that they've accomplished in the very short time they have been married, I felt so abundantly happy, not only on their behalf, but also because it was my company that they sought. I will forever be in Monica's debt for the way she has accepted me as her dearest friend and confidante through all of this. Her desire to see me and share with me the delirium of her happiness makes me feel that my life is not such a total waste after all, that even if I should live the rest of my days in total solitude, I will have served some sort of purpose in that I was able to be here when Monica needed me. Would that I could always fill some need in her heart, some craving of her spirit, for the rest of our lives.

Oh, I know that, from here on in, the person who shall reign supreme in her heart and mind is Carl, and I will gladly subordinate myself and find the beautiful peace and fulfillment in the knowledge that, although I am not the queen of her heart, I at least inhabit some special chamber of her soul. It is perfectly awe-inspiring for me to realize this truth, and I may now re-assure myself with the consoling thought that my life is worthwhile, if only for this.

The whole time I spent with her this afternoon, I felt that I was perhaps even more consumed with delights and enthusiasm than she and Carl were, and I so desperately wished for just the tiniest of moments for us to be left alone together, just Monica and I, so I could look into her eyes and into her heart with my own and discover the secret of her joy. And just as luck would have it, Carl stepped out for a few minutes to pick up some odds and ends at the store, and I remember how I took my sister's hands in mine, brought her over to the kitchen table to sit opposite me, and gazed at her intently as I asked her how the honeymoon had gone.

Dear Monica! How disappointed I felt when she averted her eyes upon hearing the question and simply said," Fine." Had I been in her position, having just returned from a passion-filled elopement and honeymoon in New Hampshire, I would have been overcome with such total ebullience that no human being would have been able to prevent me from shouting out my rapture in no uncertain terms. And yet Monica simply swerved her eyes away from my probing look and said," Fine."

I know that I shouldn't have laughed at her modest simplicity. I now realize that I must have embarrassed her with my rash inquisitiveness because she instantly pulled her hands away from me, rose from her seat, walked over to the kitchen window, and asked my opinion on the color of some draperies she proposed to buy for the apartment. I suppose she must think me a meddlesome idiot, but I rose, too, and approached her. I took her in my arms and laughed and cried at the same time and told her, as I clutched her two hands within my own once again,

"Monica, you can tell me anything you want. You know that. And you may also withhold anything you wish, also. I'll understand."

And then the tears of what I hope were joy started to flow from my sister's eyelids, and I smiled warmly into her slightly averted face, neither of us speaking for the next few moments. When Carl returned, she ran over to him for an embrace – or, at least, that's what I expected her to do. Instead, however, she ran into their bedroom, closing the door behind her, and Carl and I were alone together.

He has the most piercing dark eyes I have ever seen. And he's so incredibly handsome in a very boyish, clean-cut sort of way. No wonder Monica is driven by such uncontrollable passion these days. No wonder she trembled as I held her hands clasped within my own. She was a virgin before all of this happened, and now she is a woman who has suddenly found herself in the throes of limitless and boundless ecstasy. Carl, too, must surely be in the grips of the same dynamic fervor as my sister, because I have never seen a young man with such an impetuous stare in all my life. The way he looked at me when the two of us were alone together, the way his lips curled into a smile, the way his slender body held itself coiled in front of me –

I quickly left the apartment, knowing that as soon as I was gone, he would want to enter their bedroom and, once again, unite his body with hers and his heart with hers and his very soul with hers in the kind of breathlessly beautiful union I can only conceive of in a very insignificant way. How fortunate for those two that they have found each other, and that that vibrant young man has opened the portals of pure and immense loving devotion for my dear sister who, of all creatures I know, is most worthy of receiving such a precious gift.

When I entered this room early this afternoon and sat down with my book, I barely finished reading one chapter, my mind was so filled with thoughts of my younger sister and the enormous happiness that is now unfolding before her. I was hardly aware of the book on my lap, sitting there practically unread all evening long. Nor was I aware of the sounds of the television set downstairs where Ellen and Aunt Lucille were whiling away the time watching the Sunday night movie. And I was not aware, either, of my mother's not being here for the fifth night in a row.

Why does she leave us here every night? Doesn't Aunt Lucille mind constantly being called upon to share with me in our roles as Ellen's attendant and companion when Mom is certainly capable of exerting herself in some capacity or another, at least once in a blue moon?

I must chide myself for being selfish. I vowed only a few short nights ago that I would spend more time with Ellen and be more patient with Mom and more tolerant of Aunt Lucille's idiosyncrasies. I certainly have no pressing need to go out every evening and socialize, so my time might as well be spent here in this house with Ellen. Lord knows, the poor girl must find it a grievous trial to simply live out the rest of her life from one day to the next. My complaints and my worries are nothing compared to the endless torment my baby sister must feel as she sees her very youth passing her by in the confines of that wheelchair. If only her moods were more peaceful, I wouldn't continue to find it a trial, myself, to spend long hours alone with her. If my own character were stronger, my own personality more accepting of other people's woes, I would be able to withstand the situation a lot more easily.

So, from now on, I will make that effort. If I should spend the rest of my life as Ellen's nursemaid, I shall never raise my voice in complaint, even should the poor, desperate girl decide to slice me to ribbons with her vicious tongue over and over again as she has begun to do more frequently within the past couple of weeks.

I really feel exhausted now, and I will retire for the night. May God bless Monica and her husband. May He keep watch over my baby sister and ease the anguish of her mind and soul. And may He fortify me with the wisdom and generosity of spirit that will enable me to endure what I must for the long years ahead of me.

P.S. Mom mentioned this afternoon that she's going to hire somebody to paint the house and do the gardening this summer. I don't think she can really afford to pay somebody to do it, as she has been attending so many social gatherings these past few months and buying a lot of new clothes and the like. I must remember to put aside a good portion of my pay-check this week and offer it to Mom to help pay for the new workman. And if it's not enough, I'll take that money out of the bank. The money I was planning to use to throw Monica and Carl a big wedding-party sometime next month. We'll see. Everything should work itself out just fine. If worse comes to worst, I'll do all of the odd jobs myself.

ELLEN'S MEMOIRS – December 24, 1985

Today wasn't a total disaster as I would have expected. I mean, I did have a few laughs watching Aunt Lucille decorate the tree, using all that frizzie garland she's had for eighty-five years or so and still thinking it's "divine." And all the while she was putting up the tree, she kept saying that it was just what we needed to brighten up the place after the disastrous year we all had. Then she looked at me with that pathetic face of hers and said," I'm sorry, dear. I didn't mean to remind you of all that." I swear, the woman has gotten to be feeble-minded. She didn't mean to remind me of all that, huh? Well, all I need to do is look down at my legs if I want to be reminded of all that, right? She keeps telling me it's Christmas, a time of peace and good will towards men and all that other mumbo-jumbo sad people like her take heart in believing in. And then she wonders why I'm always in such a sour mood. I swear, if she pops in here tomorrow morning and wishes me a Merry Christmas in that sickening sweet voice of hers, I'll take that knife out from under my pillow and –

That's right. I almost forgot. She took away the knife early this morning while I was in the other room bathing. Didn't even mention having found it either. What did she suppose I'd think when I'd discovered it was missing? She's trying to play it cool, acting as if nothing out of the ordinary has taken place. And in the meantime, I'm supposed to go on thinking that this Christmas is going to be just like any other. What a joke! To think that this Christmas will be just like any other when our entire family has been torn to shreds just as completely as my two legs were in that accident last Memorial Day weekend. Who the hell are we going to celebrate Christmas with this year, anyway? Aunt Lucille planning on having her dumb friends Kathy and Melanie over here to cheer me up with a rousing rendition of "Silent Night" or something? First thing those two old crows will do is look down at my legs and then look up guiltily into my face and say," How are you doing, you poor thing?" I ought to look them right back in the face and say," Great, guys! I wish every Christmas were like this, me stuck in a wheel-chair, the rest of the family blown away to smithereens, and the great love of my life spending his nights playing with himself."

I don't know. Maybe Monica is the luckiest one of us all. At least, she gets to hide up there in Norfolk and doesn't have to put up with all of Aunt Lucille's "charity" day after day like I have to do. And even if Aunt Lucille were to go up there every single day and pay her a visit, at least Monica can get around under her own power. It isn't as if she's missing out on all the thrills in life like I am: the simple thrill of swinging your legs out of bed every morning to stuff your feet into a warm pair of slippers. The simple thrill of walking over to the refrigerator when you get a sudden craving for a snack or a cold drink. Or better yet, the simple thrill of having a man like Wayne lusting after you like no man ever did before.

Yes! It was a simple thrill, simply because it happened so many times. It was getting to be like when smokers light up one cigarette after another and never even taste them.

But what am I saying? It was much more than that. My redheaded stud-man Marty was always up for the b.j. any old time of the day or night. Now *that* was nothing but a routine, for the two of us, you'd might as well say. But it was Wayne who sent me into orbit as I felt as if I were being shot through space in the midst of all the acrobatics we engaged in. Even that first night when he put it to me in the back of his van while those other two guys had their way with Lisa in the next car over – even that first night, I felt we really clicked. Sexually, that is. As a conversationalist, the guy was strictly zero. Personality-wise, the same thing. And after we'd finished doing the deed, it would be a really rare event if the two of us exchanged a couple of words till the moment we parted for the night.

I can't believe he's forgotten about me. Not even now. He's kidding himself if he actually thinks that what she said about him was true. Once a louse, always a louse. At least, that's what Lisa always used to say whenever she got misty-eyed and nostalgic over her former boyfriends. If I know Wayne –

The problem is, I don't know him. Maybe I never really did know him. Why, he was the love of my life, and still is, of course. But I couldn't possibly have known him. Not really. I couldn't have really known him and then been unable to predict those fancy moves of his that he used on all of us. No one would have been able to convince me, not even after my accident, that he would be responsible for the way things currently stand in my family. I mean, who was he? What was he? A gorgeous hunk, and that was it. All the rest is pure bullshit.

That's the one point Aunt Lucille and I see eye to eye on. She never trusted him for a second. I remember that day last summer when Wayne had that little accident in our back yard and he was in the hospital for a little while. It made me sick to think that he was getting sympathy, and Aunt Lucille waited until Mom and Betsy were both out of the house before sitting me down, in a manner of speaking, of course, and telling me not to give it a second thought. "All men are bastards," she said to me. Well, maybe not in so many words, but I caught the gist of what she was trying to tell me. "In a way, you're lucky," she said. "Now you've got an excuse for not having to deal with men anymore, whereas people are always prying into the reasons why a basically healthy woman like me never bothers with them. Ever since my Arnie went off with that tramp, I've written them all out of my life. You'd be smart if you took my advice, Ellen. Forget about them because they're all pricks. Every single one of them."

As stupid and brainless as she normally is, I do believe right now that there was some sense to that. After all, the only men who ever had anything to do with our family were losers, each in his own way, and Wayne had to be the supreme loser of them all. I have yet to get even with that sucker, but when I do, he's going to remember it. I'll make him rue the day he ever laid eyes on me. That's for damned sure.

What a way to express it: "the day he ever laid eyes on me." We never even established eye contact, the two of us. Not once. And it bothered the hell out of me. What was he trying to hide? It was obvious to everyone that he was trouble. It was obvious, that is, to anyone who had a shred of intelligence. Then why were some of them fooled?

I'll never forget the day of the funeral when we were riding out of the cemetery in that hearse, and Aunt Lucille was making a fuss, scolding Mom for her lack of decorum during the ceremony; and then, to my utter amazement, there he was! Screeching past us in his van! The nerve of that bastard. I wanted to fall into my very own grave myself when I saw him in his van screeching past us like a maniac. Aunt Lucille immediately started raving, saying that the cops ought to be called in, and Carl looked up suddenly. I don't think he'd seen what the rest of us had seen. When he heard what Aunt Lucille was saying, he yelled at the driver to stop the hearse. What a fool! "Shut up," Mom said, and I couldn't tell if she was saying it to Carl or Aunt Lucille. And wouldn't you know, the two fools actually clammed up, and we made it the rest of the way home in silence.

Mom, trooper that she was, walked in the front door when we got home, and the first thing she said when we all piled into the living room was," What an ordeal. Thank God it's over. I hope I didn't miss any important calls while I was out."

Then the screaming started. All that fuss, and what did it accomplish? Nothing had changed. For two days, everything remained the same. Mom went back to work immediately, just like nothing had happened, and Aunt Lucille came to stay with me. And during those two days, I waited to hear from him. I hadn't seen him in weeks. None of us had, except for that brief glimpse we got of him racing past us outside of the cemetery.

I was asleep when he finally did come. I missed seeing him enter the house. Didn't hear a sound while he apparently made his way up the stairs. I missed everything that happened that night, prior to the gunshot.

I woke up with a start, but I was still too groggy to take it all in. And nobody would tell me anything! They kept me in the dark. Kept me in suspense like I didn't even count. Like it didn't even concern me that a gun had gone off in my own house.

Amid all that commotion, all I remember is one thing: Wayne's eyes boring into mine for the very first time in that one horrible moment when the cops were hauling him out of the house, and he spat at me!

That's right. He spat at me. Spat at a poor crippled girl. The man I loved. The love of my entire life chose that awful moment to look at me. To look me in the eye for the very first time and spit at me. Months earlier, he had had all those opportunities to look me squarely in the eye and tell me he loved me, and he never bothered. Never bothered despite all the times I told him how much I loved *him*. No! The bastard couldn't look me in the eye – not then! He had to wait until that night, two days after the funeral when he had no right being in our house, even! He had to wait until that night to finally establish eye contact with me, so he could spit at me like I was a goddamned pig or something.

It was all *her* doing! It had to have been. She must have poisoned his mind against me. That's always the way with those inhibited-virgin types. People feel sorry for them all the time because they act so timid and so vulnerable; and yet, they're the ones who go around knifing people in the back. She was jealous of me. That had to have been it. He told her about all the times we'd made love in the back of his van, and it turned her stomach, so she slung accusations at my otherwise noble character and got him to hate me. That had to have been the way.

They were always jealous of me, both Monica and Betsy. I was the prettiest one, and they knew it. Mom knew it, too. That's why, when I was a mere toddler, she'd always put ribbons in my hair and show me off to all her boyfriends. At least, that's what Betsy told me. And whenever we were out somewhere or in the park or whatever, people would pass by and tell Mom," What a pretty girl." I know it was me they were talking about. I could tell by the way they said it. I was the baby of the family. The cutest, you know? It's just too bad for my two sisters things turned out the way they did.

Too bad for me, too, of course, but I suppose that even though my sisters were kind of screwy, they deserved better than what they got.

What am I doing talking about those two? When I began writing my story last night, I intended to write solely about the one big love of my life. But just like in real life, those two keep interfering, and I can't stay on track. I want to write about the great times, not the pathetic ones. I want to write about the great passion the two of us aroused in each other, and how he made a woman of me virtually in one night. We never spoke, we never exchanged words, glances, or looks, it's true. But when our two bodies were entwined, we didn't need any of those unimportant frills.

Carl Peters was an O.K.-looking guy, I'll admit. "Pretty Boy" was what Wayne called him once on one of those rare occasions when he actually spoke, and it was to one of his buddies, not me, right? I guess Carl must have poked Monica a few times once they were married. Not before, that's for sure. They both had to have been virgins. But afterwards, something must have gone on in their bedroom every night. I'll even give Monica credit for a certain amount of good looks, too, so I guess it's possible she might have turned the guy on once or twice. But I swear, she had that untouched look about her, even after they were married. I don't suppose she even had the nerve to tell Betsy what actually went on between her and her husband, and I'll bet that, whatever it was, it was nothing compared to the kind of hi-jinks Wayne and I were up to every time we got within two feet of each other.

And Betsy? I don't care what anyone says. I don't care. I know what I know. I refuse to listen to what they said. Everybody said something different, anyway. How could anyone be intelligent enough to separate the truth from the lies? And I don't want to dwell on it either. I know that it will only end up infuriating the crap out of me if I allow myself to think –

I was the one he loved. No one can tell me anything different. He loved me from the moment he bedded me down on the night the two of us met at Burger King, and he's loved me ever since. And I know that he'll come back to me. Charlene had her abortion, so there's nothing to keep him tied to her either. He'll come back to me, and I'll glide gracefully across the space that separates us, and meet his embrace. And the two of us will have sex, too, right here in this room, or wherever we want to do it. And I'll then be cured of every ill that now consumes my mind and my body.

Tell me, Wayne. Tell me that it's me you love. Not her. You were crazy when you said it was her you loved. You were on drugs or something. It must have been drugs. Or the exertion of basic training. You were never stupid enough to say you loved Charlene, were you? Then why say it about *her?* Why can't you just come back to me now? You can have me any time you want, but you can never have her. I am here. Here in this cold, dark room. You can be my Christmas present this year. You can make me want to live again. You once made me so happy – so happy that I wanted to live forever. Live forever and love you for the rest of my life. I thought that I could do that, and that nothing could stop that from happening.

And now I have nothing to live for.

Tomorrow is Christmas Day. I won't get out of bed, I don't think. I think I'll tell Aunt Lucille I have the flu. Maybe she'll stay away from me and leave me in peace. Then I can lie here all by myself and dream about the great big love of my life. That! That will be my Christmas present: Being able to lie here alone in my bed and imagine that he was here with me, looking into my eyes and, this time, not wanting to spit at me like he did that other time. Is that possible? Is it at all possible that he could ever look at me again without spitting?

BETSY'S DIARY – June 28, 1985

Dear Diary: I should be happy today, but I'm not. Today marks the beginning of the two-week vacation I've been looking forward to for such a dreadfully long time, and yet, I'm feeling hurt and disappointed right now. Why do all of my good intentions end up being misinterpreted and treated with scorn? This whole past week I have been making a determined effort to make everyone happy. I have really tried to keep peace in this family. In my own small and insignificant way, I have tried. I guess that, no matter how hard I try and no matter how much effort I put into keeping all of these warring factions appeased, my efforts do indeed remain very small and insignificant. If this is the best I can do when I try my hardest, then I must surely be one of the most pathetic and worthless individuals on the face of this planet.

It has been difficult for me all week to adjust to Monica's absence from this home. Although she has phoned me every night and assures me that everything is going well, I do miss seeing her bright and sparkling smile every evening at the dinner-table. Now that it is just Mom, Ellen, and I who are seated at dinner every night, there's very little reason for me to think that we'll be able to get through the meal without some sarcastic remark being passed, usually at my expense; or is that just my imagination? And today I displayed such stupidity in believing that I would be able to make Mom happy by offering her my entire pay-check to pay for the painting and gardening that she has hired somebody to do around the house this coming week.

I'll never forget the searing look she gave me when I handed her the money and explained that I hoped that this small contribution might lessen the financial burden for her, and she snatched up the money and said,

"Really, Betsy! If you'd wanted to be helpful, you should have volunteered to do all the work yourself. You'll just be hanging around here for the next two weeks doing absolutely nothing all day long. The least you could have done was to offer to do the work yourself."

I tried to exonerate myself. Tried my best to suggest to her that I never dreamed she expected me to make that offer in the first place, seeing as I've never impressed anyone as being very handy around the house when it came to outdoor chores. I thought that she would have felt that doing the dishes and all the other indoor chores I usually do, plus taking care of Ellen from day to day, would have left insufficient time for me to take care of everything that needed to be done outside. Then when I finally offered my services to her, telling her that she could still keep the money if she needed it – after I'd swallowed my pride to such an extent that I felt like crying, Mom then accused me of being inconsiderate. A charge of such a nature coming from anyone else would have been bearable, but it hurts me so much to hear my own mother express such a low opinion of me in so severe a tone of voice. And to think that I've been trying so hard to make her proud of me, or at least, ward off censure of this kind by simply being agreeable around the house at all times. Even my strongest efforts to maintain harmony in this house go for nothing. She must truly hate me, and if I am to live the rest of my life failing in my efforts to win her love, then perhaps life isn't worth living.

I know I shouldn't entertain such unhealthy thoughts. Deep down, somewhere inside of her, she must have a speck of love, a speck of compassion for me. I know that I was the first-born and that the pregnancy was the last thing she had wanted at the time. She's expressed her views on that issue a countless number of times over the past twenty years. But what does she expect me to do to erase the injustice of having been conceived at a time that was inconvenient for her, at a time that didn't strike her as being agreeable?

Pop had done the honorable thing, and nobody suspected anything when I was born "prematurely" so as to keep everything aboveboard in the eyes of whatever society they hoped to impress twenty or so years ago. It is sinful of me to even think it, but sometimes I wonder if she now regrets not having had me aborted. Then she and Pop never would have had to get married, and her life wouldn't have been "hell", as she has succinctly summed up her entire married life with Pop on various occasions. I wonder if, had Pop not passed away within a year after Ellen's birth, they might have eventually wound up in divorce court, and if there had been any kind of scandal, would she have referred to my birth as one of the causes of all her grief?

How do I justify my existence when I'm not even sure myself just why it is that I had to be brought into the world? And now that I'm here, a living and breathing testament to the love that she and Pop must have had for each other once upon a time – Now that I'm here, what is expected of me? What must I do to prove that I can live from one day to the next without causing her so much shame and disappointment?

I will go out there tomorrow morning and do some work in the gardens. Perhaps when Mom sees that I mean to carry out my offer to save her some expense, she'll call the worker she hired and tell him to forget about coming here. Then she can keep the money I gave her and go out and buy some nice party dresses. And then maybe the unexpected will take place, and she will come to me one day and say Thank You for the money for the party dresses. Or Thank You for waiting hand and foot on Ellen during your vacation. Or Thank You for not doing anything to annoy me or make me angry. Or Thank You for not being such a waste of a human being. If I were to hear a Thank You from her, it would be like a divine blessing. It would be as if a choir of angels had called down from Heaven to bless me, and then I could live out the rest of my days with a sense of peace and self-fulfillment in the knowledge that I was appreciated.

Oh, Monica, when will I see you again? Why couldn't we for just one day pretend that we were little girls, all three of us, running along the beach and playing in the sunlight? Those were the days of my innocence, the days before I became so serious, sobered by the realization that I wasn't going to experience love in the same way as other people. The days before I began to feel that I was viewed as an ugly blemish upon this family's honor. The days before I came to understand that my value as a human being was negligible. If only the three of us could go back for just one day and lift up our hearts in the sort of carefree, unbridled joy that *used* to seize our hearts on a daily basis.

I am exhausted now, and I'm sure that, when I finally do fall asleep, I will sleep soundly. As exhausted as I am right now, I will get up early tomorrow and, weather permitting, spend the entire day fixing up the house. Maybe when the day is nearly over, I'll be able to do a little reading up here in my room. Maybe, just maybe, because tomorrow is Saturday, Monica and Carl will stop by, and I can see the flush of joy on my sister's face as she relates to me the exquisite bliss that is now a part of her soul. Just maybe.

P.S. I almost forgot about that other young man who stopped in at the library this afternoon. This was not the same one who'd seemed interested in asking me out a while back. This individual came right out and said," Let's go to the movies together tomorrow night." The other girls teased me for not accepting his invitation, but it's only natural, seeing as the young man was quite personable and attractive. Little do they all know, but I've got standards I intend to remain faithful to. If I am to accept a young man's offer to spend the evening with him at the movies or anywhere else, I must first of all feel certain that he's been prompted to ask me out, not by a physical desire alone. I have not dated anyone on a regular basis since I graduated high school, and I don't care how many years I'd have to wait until the right man finally comes along. When he does, I will recognize him. I will know, I am sure, after only being with him for a couple of minutes, too. Because that's all it will take for my soul to sense that inexplicable, yet beautiful longing to become united with his in a common bond of love.

AUNT LUCILLE'S DIARY – December 24, 1985

I'm so tired, I could drop into bed and not come up from it for the next thirty years or so, but first I have to get my head cleared out, and the best way to do that would be to get some of my prominent thoughts here on paper.

It was a hectic day, to say the least. I did some last-minute Christmas shopping. Every year I promise myself that I'll get all my holiday shopping out of the way before the beginning of December, and every year I find myself standing in line and fighting over merchandise in overcrowded stores and shopping malls. There's an excuse for my having put everything off till the last minute this year. After all, it was such a tremendously dismal year, from all angles, that I never even wanted to face the holidays in the first place. It was only at the last minute that I decided I'd better do something around here to acknowledge the season, if only to hold onto my sanity for just a little while longer. Years past, I used to sit gazing wistfully into the fireplace every Christmas Eve and ponder the idea of finding a man to spend the holidays with. I used to think having a man around the house, especially at Christmastime, would be just the ticket. Then I remembered how cruelly my Arnie treated me twelve years ago, and I chucked the idea of ever wishing there were some kind of romantic involvement in my life. My life has had enough complications this last year. I certainly don't need a man to come along, fill me with all kinds of silly romantic notions, and then have him choose an ideal time like Christmas to dump me for some tramp just like my Arnie did all those years ago. You'd think my nieces could have been smart and listened to my advice instead of entertaining all kinds of crazy romantic ideas about men and relationships. But then again, with Jean setting them such a poor example, sleeping around with any new man that happened to be handy at the time, I guess it was only a matter of time before the girls would start getting sexually involved with one man or another.

I suspected, very strongly in fact, last spring that Ellen was having sexual relations with some of her boyfriends. I warned Jean about giving her so much freedom and independence, but that crazy young sister of mine was so occupied in conducting her own love life that I don't think she took me seriously. Not seriously enough, I'm afraid, because maybe if she hadn't let Ellen go out all the time and stay out till after midnight so often, Ellen would still be walking today. I warned Jean so many times, too. I told her that, to let a sixteen-year-old girl with Ellen's good looks to go off for the weekend without being informed of an exact itinerary was foolhardy to the extreme. And look what happened! There had to have been young men involved. Ellen was so pretty. She reminded me so much of Jean when Jean was in her teens, and *she* never had any problems attracting members of the opposite sex. That's a fact.

And then the way Monica up and eloped with that Peters boy. I still can't understand how Jean could have failed to foresee that that was going to happen. Monica may not have been promiscuous, though. I'll say that for her. She was a bit like Betsy, not as withdrawn as her older sister perhaps, but she took her schoolwork seriously and didn't stay out till all hours of the night the way Ellen did. I don't think she did a lot of serious dating either. Not until she took up with Carl Peters. I don't know why they had to rush into marriage the way they did. She obviously wasn't pregnant. All I am able to surmise, in looking back on it now, is that she must have swallowed some cockamamie story Carl Peters must have given her. The kind of story that got me into Arnie's bed that one time. At any rate, I was just beginning to feel happy for Monica. That is, she honestly appeared to be in love with the boy, and he certainly did have that innocent, boyish look about him. Then, before you knew it, there was all that talk and all that friction, and then the whole thing just blew up in everyone's faces.

And to look at the other girl, you never would have expected it of her. She was so quiet and gentle compared to everyone else. Almost as though she didn't fit in, but belonged to another age and another sphere of existence. As sad and lonely as my own existence happens to be, I don't think I would ever want to see, for myself, what it must have been like for that girl last summer.

God, it's depressing! Whenever I think of what happened last summer and, worst of all, the way it all ended, I feel so totally helpless. I hated them all then. Hated them for months. Hated them to such an extent that, when the request was made that Ellen live here with me from now on, I almost told them all to go to hell.

My anger and indignation, however, have abated in the intervening months. Now, instead of becoming infuriated over what happened, I grow increasingly sad and practically sick to my stomach with the pathetic futility of it all. I want to hold that girl in my arms and never let go of her, and now it's too late. It's too late for me to ever tell her how much I loved her. I loved her from the moment she was born, and I never brought her face up against my own and held her as tightly as I ought to have done.

There are only two people, apparently, who know the whole truth about what happened last summer, and I can't get to either one of them. I don't even think Jean knew either. She couldn't have known what actually had gone on.

I remember the day of the funeral. Quite vividly, of course. Jean was in rare form, and the responsibility of mourning seemed to be mine and Monica's husband's only. And even I didn't quite know why I was crying at the time. I was so ashamed and stunned over what had happened. But the thing that unnerved me the most was when Jean returned home, stepped into the house, and made that ludicrous statement about feeling relieved that the ordeal was over and she could renew her usual lifestyle once again. Only two years younger than me, and she was behaving like a callous, unfeeling adolescent. I couldn't help myself. I just started screaming at her, and then she started screaming back at me. There we were, the two of us, having a screaming match just like the one we had had a few days earlier over Rick Sellars, and it was only a short time after the conclusion of the funeral service. I suppose we would have just stood there screaming at each other for hours, only Monica staged that awful scene to distract us. Not on purpose, of course. But it was then, when I saw her writhing on the couch as if she were not in her right mind, that I suspected she was going to have a permanent breakdown. I recall how the idea popped into my head at that very moment, and now I feel guilty about thinking it then, because at that point in time, she hadn't yet committed the grievous crime that she is now paying for. And will be paying for for the rest of her life.

I ought to hate that girl for what she did two nights after the funeral, and I did hate her immediately afterwards and, indeed, for a good long time after that. But it's not her I blame. Yes, it was primarily her fault. She's the one who pulled the trigger. But it was *him!* He's the one I hold responsible – just as he was responsible for what happened on the Fourth. I knew it from the first moment I saw him that he was bad news. I even told Jean as much, and she simply laughed and said,

"He may look like he's bad news, but he's got the most gorgeous ass I've ever seen on a man."

Right then and there, I should have walked out of that house, packed a bag for Florida, and flown way the hell out of this state so that none of this would have affected me the way it now does. The girls may be forgiven at least partially on the basis of the fact that they were young and relatively inexperienced in dealing with members of the opposite sex, but my sister should have known. She should have known better than to bring that young man onto her own property. And now she's paid for it, too. They all have.

I shouldn't be feeling so bitter right now. Tomorrow's Christmas, and I must be cheerful, if only to keep Ellen's spirits buoyed up to the extent that she'll refrain from being obnoxious and disagreeable during this holiday season. Kathy and Melanie told me they may stop by and have a bit of turkey sometime in the afternoon. I asked Ellen if there were anybody else she might want to see on Christmas Day, but she mumbled something so softly and with such painful sadness that I couldn't make out what she had said. It's too bad that girlfriend of hers had to pass away last spring. She might have been able to cheer Ellen up if she were around right now. It's too bad.

So, it looks as though it's going to be a pretty dull affair. No matter how you slice it, this is going to be the worst holiday of my entire life. Thank God I was able to take that knife out from under Ellen's pillow. That's one less thing for me to obsess over. And if she ever brings it up and asks me what happened to it, I'll just pretend ignorance. I've fooled men all these years by pretending I don't know what they want from me, right? It ought to be a piece of cake to fool that poor niece of mine, then.

That's it for today. At last.

BETSY'S DIARY – June 29, 1985

Dear Diary: Today was a very strange day indeed. While I usually consider myself a fairly good judge of character, the events of the day had me floundering in a whirlpool of confusion. Even now, I am not quite sure what to make of things, and it is the first full day of my vacation, too.

Well, at least I meant well this morning when I got up out of bed, took a shower, and then put on some old clothes to go outside and do some gardening. It was selfish of me, I know, but I was hoping that Mom would see me on my knees in the dirt and that she would run out to tell me that I needn't fuss about it. But apparently Mom didn't get back from her date with Rick Sellars last night until very late, so she wasn't up and around when I first got outdoors. Neither was Ellen, for that matter, and as far as I was concerned, it was just as well because I didn't quite have it figured out how I would be able to do the gardening and tend to Ellen's considerable needs and demands at the same time.

It couldn't have been much after nine o'clock when I was digging up some weeds in the garden right underneath the kitchen window. Before I knew it, a van pulled into the driveway, and a young man came out back dragging a ladder over his shoulder and holding a bucket of paint and some rags in his free hand. He looked quite a bit younger than I expected someone Mom would hire would be, but there was no mistaking the fact that this was the very person Mom had spoken to about doing the work around the house because he immediately put the ladder up against the side of the house and then went back towards his van to get some brushes and other paraphernalia. And he did all of this without even casting a single glance in my direction or saying a word to me as if in explanation of who he was and what he was doing here.

I confess that I was very nervous in his presence. I have always found it difficult when a man is near, especially one my own age whose interest in me might possibly end up being more than just platonic or impersonal. At the library, when some of the teen-aged boys and some of the younger men come in and ask me for assistance, I sense that they have sought me out from the other girls in order to pursue some ulterior motive. Oh, I know that I'm not beautiful like so many of the other girls these days, and that I lack the type of sex appeal that seems to come so easily to so many of them. I may be extremely naïve, but I do know that I have occasionally been looked upon by certain strangers at the library with more than just a passing interest.

The young man who came to paint the house this morning was different, at least in the respect that he appeared completely disinterested in making any kind of contact with me whatsoever, even though we were situated only a few yards away from each other. I wanted to say hello, simply to be civil, but I was not able to catch his eye. It wasn't until at least an hour later when I heard someone ringing the front doorbell that I stood up and said," Excuse me for a moment," in a polite tone of voice. He was only a few steps up the ladder, so he very easily could have nodded his head or mumbled something to indicate that he had heard me, but he simply continued his work without making a sound or revealing the slightest indication that he'd taken any notice of me at all.

It ended up being Aunt Lucille at the front door, so I stayed inside for a little while and chatted with her. Then I heard Ellen calling from her room, and it took about an hour to get her bathed and freshened up for the day. Since the weather was perfectly gorgeous, I asked her if she wanted to sit out on the patio and watch me do the gardening, and she agreed somewhat moodily. By the time I wheeled her into the kitchen, Aunt Lucille had evidently discovered that there was someone in the back yard painting the house.

She asked me very sharply who the young man was, and I told her that I supposed he was the person Mom had hired to take care of the painting and gardening. I don't really know why, but Aunt Lucille began to click her tongue in severe disapproval, and then she said something that I found very strange, or at least I considered it to be so at the time she said it: "Jean should get rid of him. He looks dangerous."

I was speechless for a moment, but then I calmly explained to her that I'd been working out there with him for about an hour and that he hadn't bothered me in the least. By this time, Ellen had wheeled herself over to the back door and was looking outside through the screen. It was so peculiar what happened next. Shocking, really. I just got through explaining to Aunt Lucille that there was no reason to feel threatened by the young man's presence when Ellen suddenly backed her wheel-chair away from the door and screamed that she didn't want to go out there.

"Take me away from here!" she cried. "I need to get out of here, and as far away from this house as possible!"

The words in themselves were frantic enough, but the absolutely terror-stricken voice she used in saying them was positively chilling. For a moment, I was completely dumb-struck, and Aunt Lucille didn't help any by telling Ellen to shut up and stop acting like a child.

So, I remained calm and told Ellen that I would gladly take her to the beach this afternoon if she thought that would please her but that I really would prefer to do a little gardening first. I felt that I was speaking in a reasonable enough manner, but Ellen grew even more vehement and stated her demand that I take her out of the house immediately. And she kept stressing the fact that she wanted to be taken as far away from the house as possible, too. That's what alarmed me more than anything. I'm afraid that her testiness has become almost unbearable lately. I feared that, as time went by and she began to feel more acutely the limitations of leading a handicapped existence, this very thing would happen. Once again, I tried to remain calm and assured her that I would bring her to the beach just as soon as I packed a little luncheon for the two of us and slipped out of the old soiled clothes I had on. She was still very distressed, but I suppose she was able to exercise enough rational thought to understand that a few minutes of preparation were required before we could start on our way, and she gradually calmed down.

When I came back downstairs a few minutes later, she was seated before the open front door, looking outdoors with such a forlorn expression on her pretty little face. Perhaps I was being foolish again. Perhaps my timing was off, but I felt such a rush of compassion for my poor baby sister that I impulsively reached down and hugged her.

Ellen thrust me away from her, and her next words cut me very deeply as she said to me,

"Get away from me, you bitch."

I didn't say a word. I felt like saying to her that if she wanted to adopt such a hostile attitude towards me, then maybe it would be better for us not to spend the day together. But I didn't. I know that many times I have been accused of not having enough back-bone and that too often I allow people to verbally abuse me without fighting back. But there was no way, this time, that I was going to answer her tartly, or even entertain the expectation that an apology would be forthcoming. I know that, next to her, I am infinitely fortunate in that I have the full and complete use of my legs, and if my life happens to be limited in much the same way hers is, it is of my own choosing. I should be more accepting of her emotional instability. She has been under such a strain lately that I'm sure she couldn't have meant to snap at me that way, so I tried not to take it personally.

The beauty of this summer day did much to restore her spirits, just as it did mine, and we spent several pleasant hours at the beach, even though we barely exchanged two words the whole time we were there. I read my novel, and Ellen just sat there in her wheel-chair, looking out at the ocean with that sad, forlorn look on her face.

As soon as we got back home, she went straight to her room and turned on the radio. The van was still parked in the driveway, and I could hear Mom talking outside in the back yard although Aunt Lucille sat in the kitchen reading a magazine and looking rather disgruntled, I thought. I took a quick peek out the kitchen window and saw Mom standing in the sunlight, her face turned upwards while she shielded her eyes with her hand held against her forehead as she spoke. She was dressed in a swim-suit, so I imagine she had been sunning herself all afternoon in the back yard while the workman was painting the house. The whole time she stood there talking to him, I tried to discern an answering reply of some sort, but I heard nothing. I had already started getting dinner ready when Mom came inside, her skin moist from the suntan oil she usually applies quite generously to every exposed area of her body whenever she goes out back to sun-bathe, and I must admit, she looked extremely fit and trim in her swim-suit. She definitely has a very sensuous and earthy kind of physical beauty that many men must find undeniably attractive.

Aunt Lucille abruptly asked her why she'd been speaking at such length with the young man outside, adding that she couldn't imagine what the two of them could possibly have in common, and Mom replied that the young man's father was an old friend of hers. Wayne Brown Senior. And that they had actually dated shortly before she and Pop had gotten married. She also stated that she'd been unaware of the connection last week when she'd initially run into Wayne Brown Junior at an auto garage where the young man worked as a mechanic. She said she had struck up a conversation with him, found out that he was in the market for making some extra money, and she told him she had a few odd jobs for him to do around our house. Aunt Lucille then responded by saying quite pointedly that that still didn't explain why Mom had seen fit to spend the whole afternoon out there sunning herself in such close quarters with a virtual stranger like that. Mom simply laughed off the insinuation that she had been improper, saying that she was just trying to be friendly. She told Aunt Lucille to "loosen up" for a change.

I pretended not to be interested in their conversation, but I know that they realized I heard every word they said. In fact, with the back door wide open and the kitchen window partially open as well, it's altogether likely that Wayne Brown heard their conversation, too, especially when Mom raised her voice suddenly and said to her sister,

"I know you think he looks like a punk, Lucille, but that doesn't take anything away from the fact that he's got the most gorgeous ass I've ever seen on a man."

I was so embarrassed at that point that I quickly left the room and entered the parlor, hoping they wouldn't find my sudden departure cause for concern. It's not simply the language my mother occasionally uses that disconcerts me; it's her blatant way of flaunting her sexual outlook in front of Aunt Lucille that disturbs me more than anything else. I'm sure my aunt wanted to put her in her place. I believe I heard her say something to Mom, just as I was leaving the kitchen, to the effect that his good-looking rear-end didn't justify any of it and that he definitely looked like bad news as far as she was concerned. But as soon as I found myself in the parlor, I put my hands over my ears because I didn't want to hear the rest of their conversation. Sometimes I wonder why Aunt Lucille even bothers to come here to visit so often. She rarely sees eye to eye with Mom on anything. She thinks we baby Ellen too much. She is also of the opinion that Monica shouldn't have been allowed to elope with Carl, not suspecting that there really wasn't much any of us could have done to prevent it from happening. And she usually criticizes me for being too introverted and lacking in initiative.

Well, I knew sooner or later I would have to walk back into the kitchen to tend to the cooking, and I was a little relieved when I heard the van pull out of the driveway a few minutes later. I recall wondering how long it would take to get all the work done outside that needed to get done. I hate myself for thinking it, but I wish that young man wouldn't come back here. Ever again.

As it turned out, dinner was tolerable. Ellen kept quiet the entire time, and Aunt Lucille let Mom talk incessantly about the party she was going to tonight with Rick Sellars. I was relieved that the tension had cleared, and it was good to see Mom looking so cheerful and so excited when she described to Aunt Lucille all the new clothes she had bought at the mall within the past few weeks. I was just getting ready to wash the dishes when the phone rang.

I was so delighted to hear Monica's exuberant voice. She has called me every night this week, and I've found that her daily telephone calls are the highlights of my current existence in this house. First, she asked if Mom were going out for the evening. Then she wanted to know if Aunt Lucille intended to sit with Ellen for the evening, too, and it was then that I gathered that she wanted to speak to me alone. I assured her that I would love to speak to her privately if that was what she wanted, but at the time I said it, I wondered what we were to do with Carl. Almost as if she were reading my thoughts, Monica informed me that Carl had planned to go out with Kenny and some of his other friends from school, so she would be alone for some time.

The long and short of it is I was able to slip out of the house for a few hours after I'd tidied up the kitchen. Mom had already left, too, so I didn't have to worry about getting tangled up in any messy explanations as to why I, of all people, was bustling out of the house on a Saturday evening. When I arrived at Monica's apartment, she embraced me as soon as I walked in the door. Briefly. But I felt a very strange urgency in her mood, so I tried to steer the conversation in such a direction that would bring us closer to what it was that she seemed so desperately to want to confide in me.

She said that she and Carl were happy. Very happy. She said that he was very patient with her and that he never raised his voice at her – all of which observations I considered to be rather bizarre. Then she turned her face away from me as tears started coming into her eyes, and said to me,

"Something's missing, Betsy. A vital ingredient to our marriage – to any marriage – is missing."

Perhaps I was so confused and bewildered as to what I should say and as to just how far I should pry into the matter, that I let just a little bit too much time go by without saying anything, and then Monica turned to me with a forced smile and took both my hands in her own.

"It's nothing, I'm sure," she said to me, although in a way it seemed as though she were really saying it to herself. "It'll work itself out. It just needs a little time, that's all." And she squeezed my hands and kissed me briefly on the cheek, and I knew that she would be all right. I find it rather odd that she should have asked me to go over there for a private talk and then, just as she seemed to get close to whatever it was that was bothering her, she seemed anxious to simply shrug it off as if it were nothing.

Well, my sister is a strong girl. And a level-headed one, too. I am sure that if she encounters any difficulties or has any questions about things having to do with married life, she can always consult her own husband on such matters.

With that re-assuring thought, I will put my pen down and go to bed. The weather forecast is for another bright and sunny day tomorrow. Just as luck would have it, though, rain is predicted for Monday, the first full-fledged day of my two-week vacation. I won't be troubled by that fact, however. I can always stay indoors and watch television with Ellen. Or read a book.

P.S. Monica couldn't really be hiding anything terribly important from me, could she? And if she is, can mere scholastic aptitude and intelligence rectify the problem? I must be sure to keep from prying, but I promise myself now that I will be there for her whenever she feels called upon to seek me out.

CARL'S DIARY – January 3, 1986

Dear Diary: Here it is. My belated entry in the diary in which I have vowed to pour out my feelings and somehow or other purge myself both of the great grief that possesses me and the great love and adoration that consumes me daily. I didn't write anything here in my diary last night because my mind wasn't exactly working right. I'd seen Samuel and a few other guys at Samuel's pad. One guy – I think his name was Vince – was there, and he was cool with a capital C. He turned me on to some of the most excellent hash I've ever had. Then we popped a few pills, and I was on the most wicked high. I had a hell of a time explaining to my old lady the next day (today) why I didn't come home last night, and she ran true to form, telling me I'm irresponsible and asking me point-blank when I was going to get a job. I told her I was working on it, but I don't think she swallowed it. I think she's been discussing my unruly behavior with the old man. Any day now, they ought to be kicking me out into the street, and I don't really give a damn, anyway.

Well, they can just go to hell, for all I care. My old man and his fat paunch, smoking that foul pipe of his all the time and thinking he's some kind of sophisticated intellectual because he listens to Mozart on the radio in his car on his way to work every morning. When I look at him and see what an uptight ass-hole he really is, I'm amazed at how good-looking and put-together I am. And my old lady, putting up with all of his shallow pomposity all these years. She has got to be the one woman who could singlehandedly set the women's rights movement back thirty-five centuries or so. And to think that I'm the offspring of such sad and pathetic human beings. I must have been adopted, that's all. That's the only explanation I can come up with for why they're so vastly inferior, and I'm such a brilliant marvel. I'll bet my old man never got voted Best Personality or Most Popular when he was in high school. I'll bet he never even had half the friends I've got either – friends who would stick by me through thick and thin no matter how rough the going got. I've outdone my old man in practically every facet of my life, and I'll bet he's jealous of me. And with my sterling good looks, he probably wonders if my mother cheated on him twenty years ago so as to produce a child of such obvious superiority to the usual Peters stock.

Enough of that. The sooner I get out of this house, the better. And I've got to keep the ball rolling with Vince. That guy really had some excellent shit to offer, and he's cool, too, with a capital C. Connecting up with him will ultimately prove to be one of my most brilliant inspirations. I can feel it in my bones. Yeah, I know I've made a few blunders in my life. My life wouldn't be so incredibly messed up right now if I hadn't. But it wasn't my fault, of course. I mean, how can an unquestionable genius accomplish anything noteworthy in life when the supreme morons of the world keep getting in his way?

Speaking of supreme morons, I'll bet I'll be hearing from good old Wayne Brown any day now. It's about time he started knocking at my door, so to speak. Well, I'll be ready for him this time. I even told Vince about him. Vince is over six feet tall. I've never seen him fight, naturally, but I'll bet he could beat Wayne, no problem. So, I told him about the three times Wayne sucker-punched me, and Vince says the next time Wayne bothers me to let him (Vince) know and it'll be curtains for Wayne Brown Junior. Finally!

If only I'd known last summer what I know now. If only I'd had that sucker wiped out when I had the chance. The problem was, most of the guys Wayne hung around with were pretty tough, so if it ever came down to a rumble or something like that, things might've gotten a little sticky. But I'm sure with me being Most Popular and all that, I could have got Kenny and quite a few of the other guys together, and we would have beat his ass, but good.

Man, I go nuts, just thinking about all those stupid chicks at our school who went for that moron. Even Tiffany Mason had the hots for him for a while, and she was supposed to have a certain amount of class, too. I remember how – I think we were juniors at the time – word got around school that Wayne had knocked her up. And a couple of Tiffany's friends said he'd banged them a few times as well, and they were afraid they might've gotten pregnant just because Tiffany was. As if that wasn't bad enough, I told Tiffany that somebody ought to put him in the hospital and that that would straighten him out, and then the stupid bitch goes and tells Wayne!

Christ, I'd never bunked school before that – never in my life – but I think I missed about two weeks of classes. I wasn't about to enter that building and run the risk of having Wayne jump me from behind and attack me when I was off my guard. I was too smart for that. Even after I went back to school, thinking things had calmed down, some slut goes and tells Wayne I'm back, and that whole day I'm sweating bricks. I had to give Kenny ten bucks just to stick by me between classes just in case that moron decided to try anything. Man, I had so many friends in that school, I'm sure he was just too scared to come out in the open and challenge me like a man. The best he could come up with was when we were playing basketball in gym class later that week, and he bumped into me two or three times and knocked me down. Thornton caught on after the third time and told him to hit the showers. Needless to say, I changed back into my street clothes real quick that day, and practically ran all the way over to my next class.

But all of that was nothing compared to the way he screwed up my life after graduation. Christ, when I ever found out he was doing work outside my in-laws' house, I nearly blitzed out. I'll never forget that Sunday afternoon when Monica and I popped over the house for Sunday brunch. My stupid-bitch mother-in-law asks us to step on over and meet a good friend of hers, the three of us walk over, and lo and behold, good old Wayne is standing there painting the side of the house. He had his shirt off, of course. Guys like him, just because they've got some muscle on them, figure the whole world's got to see what they look like with their shirts off. They know that's just about all they've got going for them, that's why. He was sweating like a filthy pig, too, and wearing that stupid bandanna around his neck and an even stupider-looking headband across his forehead. I don't even think the dumb moron recognized me when he glanced in our direction as Monica's mother introduced us to him. He was probably too spaced out on cheap drugs to recognize me. Or maybe, when he saw it was me, he got scared and pretended not to know me. I swore right then and there I wouldn't go back to that house ever again. Or at least, as long as I figured he might still be working there.

Then, before you knew it, things started getting out of hand. I was relieved when we found out he'd enlisted with the marines and was going south for boot camp. Man, I was sailing on Cloud Nine when I heard that one. It meant I had free and easy access to my angel, too. Add to that the news that he'd recently gotten that flooze Charlene knocked up, and I knew I wouldn't have any problems getting what I wanted.

Christ, it should have been so easy. But I was foiled every step of the way, man. That whole time Wayne was in basic training, I swayed between periods of the most intense rapture and other periods of the most incredible gloom and anxiety. I don't think I masturbated once the entire month of August. I was so damned tense and nervous about everything. I was unable to achieve an erection, no matter how hard I tried. At one point, I figured maybe the drugs were responsible for that, and I actually went two days without smoking – but the pressure was too much for me. A guy can only take so much, you see, even a guy like me who's usually so together and on top of every situation.

Then that night came in early September when I thought I was actually going to pull it off. I had her alone with me. All the right music. All the proper lighting. The atmosphere was ideal for the most romantic adventure of my entire life. And when I held her in my arms, I even thought I was going to get hard.

Christ, I don't even want to think about the rest of it. It'll literally kill me if I start reliving that agonizing night all over again. The night of my undoing. Christ, I never thought I'd be able to look at myself in the mirror ever again after that horrible night, and then –

Jesus, the worst thing possible happened after that, and I had nobody. Absolutely nobody. Not even my own bitch of a wife could look me in the eye during the entire time we spent standing near the coffin. I was totally and immensely alone. I experienced the most awful depression of my life. I might have been able to manage a little better if I'd only been able to get my hands on some strong stuff that day. But when I dropped in on Kenny early that morning to see if he had anything potent on hand, I interrupted one of his massive sex sessions he happened to be having with a couple of slutty ex-cheerleaders from school, and he wasn't in the mood to carry on the drug trade with me at that particular moment in time.

When Wayne showed up at the cemetery, screeching straight past the funeral car we were in, I didn't notice him at first. I was so depressed. I think I was sobbing, bent over with my hands over my face, sitting in back next to Monica. I remember the stupid spinster aunt saying something, and then I looked up to see that moron in his van speeding past us in the opposite direction. Christ! He was supposed to be in South Carolina. He wasn't supposed to be here in town, ready to screw up my life even more than he'd already done. How the hell had he found out? How the hell had he managed to weasel his way out of boot camp and wind up at the cemetery?

First, we got to my in-laws' house, and the two old bags started screaming at each other almost the instant we walked through the door. And as if that wasn't bad enough, my stupid wife started having these crazy spasms on the couch, putting her hands over her face and groaning the word No over and over again. It took good old Aunt Lucille an awful long time to get her calmed down, and I'm standing there, getting worked up with tension and waiting for Monica to get a grip on herself so the two of us could head back to our apartment. And all the time my wife is having convulsions over on the couch, I'm saying to myself: What the hell am I going to do if Wayne comes over here? He'll beat the living daylights out of me, for sure.

Well, luckily, I managed to get Monica out of there and the two of us back to our apartment before Idiot Wayne ever showed up, and once we got home, I put it right to her: Were you the one who told Wayne about what happened?

I thought I was being pretty damned patient and low-key about the whole thing, but my stupid wife wasn't having any of it. I remember how she sat at the kitchen-table, looking like a seventy-year-old woman with her hair uncombed, no make-up on, and circles under her eyes that were so dark, they made her look as though she was the one who'd just passed away, and not that precious angel of mine. She sat there as I stood over her and demanded that she tell me if she'd been the one who'd told Wayne about what happened. My wife just sat there, not saying a word. My wife, I tell you. Wasn't she supposed to answer me? I mean, isn't a woman supposed to do what her husband tells her to?

When I backhanded her across the mouth, I felt a tremendous sense of release. Of pleasure, even. At that moment, she must have known, once and for all, that I was a man. She must have realized she wasn't dealing with any candy-ass just then, but with a real, honest-to-goodness, powerful man. And a man who wasn't about to tolerate any of her stupid crap, either.

She never did answer my question, though, the bitch! Instead, she ran into the bedroom and slammed the door shut. But at least I'd shown her a thing or two. At least I'd resolved all the doubts she'd ever had about my being a man, and I showed her the exact kind of man she was dealing with, too. Plus, I figured I got my answer anyway. If she hadn't told Wayne, I'm sure she would have been so scared of me and the power I had over her, she would have proclaimed her innocence, hoping I'd lay off her. She had to have been guilty then. Simply by not answering my question, she was telling me that it had been her, after all. What a bitch!

That whole night she kept the bedroom door locked, but I didn't hear any crying coming from behind the closed door. She probably thought that locking me out of my own bedroom would really drive me wild, but I was glad I didn't have to sleep with her that night. It would have been a total disaster, and we both knew it, so it was just as well she bolted the door shut. So, I just went into the bathroom and tried to masturbate for a while. I thought of my angel and how beautiful she had been during our last evening together. And I tried picturing in my mind how gorgeous her pink breasts had appeared during that all too brief moment when I'd managed to get them exposed. And I tried to imagine what it might have felt like to get closer to them and kiss them and caress them, and I tried with all my might to bring myself to a point where I would know, once and for all, that I could have performed sex with her if I'd had the chance.

But Christ! I was having a lousy, pitiful day. Plus, I was scared Wayne might turn up at the apartment and try to beat the crap out of me. I was too tense and scared, so I gave up trying to masturbate and decided to leave the apartment for a few hours. It was perhaps one of my most uninspired thoughts, too, because as it turned out, I was apprehensive about running into Wayne somewhere out on the streets. Every single van that was out on the streets seemed to resemble his. And then when I ran that stop sign and nearly got rammed by that station wagon, I realized I was screwing things up royally.

That's when I decided to visit the grave. And yes, I realized she had only been put to rest that very day, but I knew instantly that it was the only place on this earth, the only place on this whole God-forsaken planet, where I could find peace and repose for my agonizing spirit.

Like I said, I drove into the cemetery, parked the car, got out, and knelt at her grave. The stars were out, I remember, and the air was a bit sultry for that time of year. But I remained oblivious to all of that as I remained kneeling there, weeping softly for what seemed like hours and hours, until I finally got back into my car, sat behind the wheel without turning on the engine, and fell asleep.

The last thing I remember thinking, just before sleep descended upon me, was that it didn't matter if she never really loved me the way I needed her to love me. Nothing mattered anymore, because despite all of that and despite what had happened and what didn't happen, I would continue to love *her* for the remainder of my miserable life here on this rotten and disgusting planet.

BETSY'S DIARY – June 30, 1985

Dear Diary: I woke up this morning, feeling refreshed. I even put on a summery outfit to go to church in and was feeling just about as wonderful and positive about everything as I possibly could when I heard a noise just outside my window. When I approached the window to look out, I noticed that a ladder had been placed just below where I was standing, and I drew back immediately lest the young painter should climb the ladder suddenly and find me looking out at him. Although I was fully dressed at the time, I felt a distinct shiver run up and down my spine as I entertained the thought that, had he decided to begin painting outside my bedroom window about a half an hour sooner, he might have caught more than just a glimpse of me getting dressed. As peculiar as it may seem, I have never allowed any man to see me in an unclothed state, and the thought of having a stranger peer at me at such a moment I found to be quite unnerving.

At any rate, I felt a bit relieved with the realization that I would soon be leaving the house, and I even suggested to Ellen when I got downstairs that maybe I'd take her out for the better part of the day if she were feeling up to it. I was totally surprised when she not only agreed but also expressed the desire to accompany me to church. I can't even calculate the number of years that have passed since that girl has attended Mass. Naturally, I agreed wholeheartedly with her suggestion and proceeded to pack another luncheon for the two of us when she further persuaded me to do so, thereby eliminating a return trip home after church to change up and prepare for a second outing.

As happy as I was to see Ellen's enthusiasm this morning, I was still a trifle concerned that our leaving the house all day long would necessitate Mom's being alone in the house with the workman in the vicinity all those hours. Aunt Lucille had told us yesterday that she was going to spend the day today with some of her girlfriends, thus leaving Mom all alone to fend for herself, so to speak, all day long. I was going to rouse Mom from her sleep and ask her if she wanted to come along with me and Ellen, but then Ellen told me Mom hadn't gotten home until five o'clock this morning, so I felt it would be better to leave her alone and let her sleep as late as she wished.

It felt good to have Ellen in church with me, and so many people seemed pleased to see her, although a few of them were a little less than tactful in alluding to her present physical condition. However, Ellen seemed to be so grateful to be out of the house that I don't believe she revealed any visible signs of distress or annoyance. And then she didn't even seem to mind when I introduced her to some of the youngsters from the Bible-study class I taught a few months ago. Some of them seemed uncomfortable at the sight of Ellen in her wheel-chair, but I don't think any of them were openly rude or insensitive. I did so try to instill compassion in the souls of my pupils the whole time I was teaching them. Perhaps, that and a little common courtesy played a part in the excellent manner in which they conducted themselves this morning.

It was after four o'clock when Ellen and I returned home from the park, and I was overjoyed when, upon returning, I discovered that

Monica and Carl had dropped by for a visit. When I wheeled Ellen on out into the back yard, all three of them were there, smiling and talking around the patio table while the painter appeared to be just finishing up his work for the day. I glanced up at the side of the house and saw, much to my perplexity, that he had hardly done any work at all since yesterday; and yet, he had been here this morning, outside my bedroom window, as early as nine o'clock. All I could figure was that Mom must have gotten out of bed earlier than Ellen and I expected and that she had probably gone outside and engaged the young man in continual conversation all day.

No sooner had I begun to chat with Monica and Carl than Mom noticed that the painter was about to leave, and quite unnecessarily, I thought, she got up from the table and asked him to walk over to where we were sitting. Ellen immediately demanded that I take her back inside the house, and I was ready to obey when Mom told Ellen not to be foolish and then proceeded to introduce both of us to Wayne Brown.

For my part, I was very embarrassed. First of all, I felt that the young man was being pushed into an introduction that he had no desire to participate in, seeing as he had efficiently avoided my glance yesterday morning while we had worked outside together for at least an hour. Secondly, I found my suspicions about his own embarrassment confirmed when, upon being introduced to me, he found it impossible to even raise his eyes from the ground. He barely muttered Hello even though I put as much friendly warmth into my own greeting as I possibly could under the circumstances. And third of all, I could sense that Ellen was growing positively appalled by the whole scene, and before Mom could introduce the two of them to each other, calling Ellen "the prettiest girl a mother could want," my poor baby sister screamed at the top of her lungs that she wanted to go inside. I noticed that even Monica and Carl winced upon witnessing the thoroughly hysterical nature of her behavior.

Perhaps I did the wrong thing in hastily wheeling Ellen into the house. I know for a fact that Mom must have considered it rude of me to scamper off, barely a moment after the introduction had been performed; but my first instinct was to spare Ellen the acute embarrassment she must have felt upon having that young man look upon her in her disabled state. As far as Wayne Brown was concerned, I doubt very much that he cared. In fact, I don't believe, not even at this very moment, that I would recognize his voice if I were to ever hear it again, his Hello to me had been so muffled as to be virtually inaudible. By the time I returned to the patio after leaving Ellen in the parlor in front of a blaring television, he was already inside his van and getting the engine started.

I do know that Carl seemed quite vocal in his condemnation of Mom's employing the likes of "a bum like Wayne Brown" to do the work outside our house, and he even went so far as to state that Mom had better watch out that all the silverware didn't disappear from the kitchen while Wayne was in the vicinity. I did think Carl was exaggerating more than just a little. That is, as far as I could see, no harm had come to anyone in the two days Wayne Brown has been working here; and I'm sure, while Ellen and I were at church and Mom was still in bed, he could have entered the house and pilfered anything he pleased if such were his intentions. When I told Carl exactly what I thought, he turned upon me with those blazing dark eyes of his and informed me in no uncertain terms that Wayne Brown probably had a criminal record, for all he knew, that he had been nothing but trouble the whole time they had been in school together, and, finally, that I was too trusting and naïve. This last observation, I must admit, was spoken with great tenderness compared to the heated manner in which he had attacked Wayne Brown's character a few moments earlier. In fact, his criticism of me was spoken in such a way that one would almost construe the words as a compliment of the highest order. Then my sister Monica, practical-minded as ever, commented that Carl was right about

Wayne Brown being something of a shady character while they were in high school but that he seemed to be doing a pretty nice job painting the house, so who were we to complain? And then Mom, in perfect candor, added,

"What it comes down to is he's got one hell of a great-looking ass on him, so let's leave it at that."

I recall casting my eyes downward when she said that, and I believe Monica, too, must have felt a little uncomfortable. But it was Carl who reacted the most strongly by getting to his feet very abruptly and storming into the house without saying a word to any of us. Monica hesitated a few moments, smiled apologetically in my direction, and then followed her husband into the house soon after; and that left me and Mom sitting at the patio table, uncomfortable in our silence together.

I love Mom just about as much as I can, given the fact that she has always made me feel as though there's nothing I can do to convince her of my worth as her daughter or even as a human being either. I know – she's told me often enough in the past – that it had been a very sad day for her twenty-two years ago when she had discovered that she was pregnant. And despite all of this, I love her immensely and pray to God on a daily basis that I can do something wonderful in her eyes so that someday she will put her arms around me for just a few seconds. That's something she hasn't done to me in – I was going to say "in years" but the truth of the matter is that I have no recollection of that ever having happened.

"What's wrong with Ellen?" she asked me a few moments after the two of us found ourselves alone together at the patio table. I suppose she said it just to get some semblance of a conversation going between us, and I was grateful to her for making the effort. But then I committed the serious blunder of telling her that I didn't know what was wrong with Ellen, and she immediately accused me of being stupid and insensitive. "You spent the entire day with her, and you say you can't figure out what's wrong with her. My God, Betsy! Aren't you good at doing anything around here?"

She went into the house as soon as she finished her attack, and I sat quietly for barely thirty seconds before I began to feel tears well up in my eyelids. Even now, I can still hear the abrasive sound of her voice as she raised it in scorn against me out there on the patio, and when she walked into the house and left me alone, I felt as though I really were supremely and infinitely alone.

It was with great difficulty that I was able to pull myself out of the chair and go inside to make dinner for the five of us, but when dinner was finally ready and even though Monica was there and I had been missing her so much, I couldn't eat a morsel of food and found myself, instead, excusing myself from the table and retiring to my room.

And it is here that I have remained for the entire evening. I read for a little while, but for the most part, I lay on my bed and looked up at the ceiling, dry-eyed, as I pondered the meaning of my sad and unproductive life. If only there were somebody who cared. Somebody who cared enough to put his or her arms around me for just a few seconds and give me a hug. I don't need to hear," I love you." I have given up hoping that such ecstasy could ever be a part of my life. I just want a little bit of warmth from another human being, even if it's just for a few seconds. Those brief few seconds would fortify me with enough strength to last me the next twenty or thirty years. Monica has found her happiness. Why not me, since my happiness would not demand too much from any single human being? Why not me, so that I could feel as though my every breath weren't such a total waste of energy? When can I begin to feel useful? When can I begin to feel loved?

I am tired now. Even though tomorrow marks the first full day of my vacation, I feel as though everyone would be quite satisfied if I never even woke up at all in the morning. Everyone would be quite content if I should die in my sleep.

P.S. I had to get up and write this down: I want to erase such selfish and sinful thoughts from my mind. Who am I to demand happiness? I should be grateful for what I have and "count my blessings" (as they say). May I be forgiven, then, for being so selfish and unappreciative of all that I have been blessed with. May the good Lord forgive me. Amen.

CYCLE THREE

MONICA'S MEMOIRS – April 8, 1986

They played soft music for me today. They said that even plants reacted favorably to the strains of soft, consonant music, and I let them play it for me, and I sat quietly and still and pretended that I had discovered the kind of peace that they so desperately wanted to force upon me. I don't know how much longer I can keep them fooled, but I know that, if I expect to kill myself someday soon, I must first delude them into thinking I am improving. They can call in the most astute, their most accomplished doctors and analysts to examine me, and I will feign calmness. They can bring in experts and specialists from all corners of the globe, and none of them will ever be able to find a way of really bringing about a cure for the poison that consumes me daily. The poison that has invaded my entire body for so long now that its effects are completely irreversible, and these well-being physicians and therapists are powerless to deal with it effectively.

Only one who has been infected with such a disease as I have can fully understand the feeling. I have faced the gaping jaws of Hell so many times these last few months, and yet those pathetic "doctors" fail to realize that their mere earthly training can do nothing to combat the power of Hell. And it is from Hell itself that I draw my stamina, my ability to fool them all, so that my eventual suicide will be all the more easy to accomplish.

What will Aunt Lucille say when they bring the news to her that her poor, demented niece has killed herself? Will the horror of it all be severe enough, after what she and the rest of us experienced last summer, to drive her to despair? Or will she be able to accept it with perfect composure as the inevitable upshot of this whole stream of events? She will then have one last funeral to attend, and this one she will be able to attend without crying bitter tears.

What will my beloved husband say when they deliver the news to him that the aching embarrassment of his life has finally been erased from this planet? Will he then see fit to cast aside all of his delusions of self-inflicted grief and start living the life of a normal, shameless human being?

I hardly think so. That self-imposed mantle of grief that encloses him is as endless and impenetrable as the pain of self-guilt that eats away at my soul. Just as I failed him in our marriage, I will fail him, too, in my death; and there will be no need for him to mourn the death of a defective human being – and out-and-out murderess.

I no longer shudder with quite the same violence as I used to when I recognize the fact that I am nothing but a common criminal. In this respect, at least, the doctors have succeeded in alleviating the symptoms of my so-called illness. Yes. I can call myself a murderess now without feeling the need to tear my eyes out from their sockets as I did when they first brought me here and had to dope me up for weeks at a time in order to avert the danger of my destroying myself as fully and completely as I had destroyed *her*.

They call people like me "unnatural," I believe. People like me who take lethal weapons and use them against the very people they are supposed to love. Would that I could have spared myself this overwhelming shame and disgust and turned the gun in towards myself, just as Wayne tried to do to *himself,* just before the door opened and, without even seeing her appear, I fired the shot that put an end to her miserable life – the life that she led, utterly devoid of mercy and compassion for the people *she* was supposed to have loved.

And Wayne, stupid and weak and seized with a sudden crazy desire to be rational, tried to shield me, even though he should have known, after what the two of us had just discovered, that I meant to kill them both. To kill them both and make them pay for what they had done!

How he suffered that night! When he turned the gun in on himself, I should have let him pull the trigger. Perhaps I could have spared him the cruel ordeal that he was to face – the cruel horror that he now faces every single day of his life. I know how he feels. I know exactly how he feels because I, too, bear that pain constantly, and it's killing me. It hurts so much sometimes that I open my mouth to cry out with the sheer pain of it all, and no sound comes out. No sound at all escapes my lips as I lie in bed and feel my soul being wrenched and wrung and twisted about inside my chest.

But I suffered even more before I pulled the trigger. Even before I took the gun out of the closet downstairs, knowing full well what I had to do with it. And I began to suffer even more before I learned the truth of what happened last summer. Even before Wayne and I held each other in our arms and screamed -- simultaneously – the scream of unlimited pain.

No. My insanity began two days earlier than that. When we returned home from the funeral, that's when I started to become unhinged – when my body fell onto the living room couch as if of its own accord and I began to groan. It all appears very vividly in my mind right now: Mom and Aunt Lucille bickering about Mom's lack of decorum during and after the funeral, Carl insisting that he and I get back to the apartment before "that lunatic" came and started a fight with him, Ellen sulking off in her corner with the only tears in her eyes those of self-pity. And my mind, as if quite on its own, curled itself inside out as the realization hit me that I would never see her again.

I could not deal with the tremendous loss, more tremendous than any other pain I had ever had to endure, and I just flung myself onto the couch and groaned; and I tossed my body from side to side over and over again with the horror of it all, and I had no idea what I was saying or what I was doing while I thrashed about in sheer agony. I was no less insane then than I am now, at this very moment, because even then my mind could not cope with the enormity of her absence.

Oh, God in Heaven! You call yourself a God of Love, and You took her away from me! You took her away from me before I had a chance to grovel at her feet and beg for her forgiveness. Before I could clutch her whole body against me and tell her that I loved her. Oh, God in Heaven, how could You do that to me? How could You be so heartless, so cruel, so relentless in Your desire to make me suffer?

There it is: the misery of my life in a nutshell. The moment I was born, the moment I first took in oxygen – That should have been my final moment on this earth. How can the rest of my horrible existence now be erased? I curse this God of Love! I curse Him daily because He is so weak and stupid that He allows these atrocities to exist. Oh, God, why did You allow all of this to happen? Why can't You show a tiny bit of mercy towards me at this time and stamp me out completely?

There is nothing for me to do now except wait. I must simply wait for the end to come. There is nothing I can do to bring her back.

Nothing I can do to erase what happened last summer. Nothing. And I curse God for depriving me of the ability to alter the course of last summer's events. I curse the God Whom people revere as Love for making me so blind that I could not see the truth on my own. Not until it was too late. And then my powerful rage took over and forced me to commit the ultimate sin any child can ever commit against a parent. And even when the bullet went plunging into her heart, I wasn't satisfied because I was unable to accomplish a double-murder with the firing of that one shot. In any case, my soul should have gone straight to Hell right then and there. End of story.

"Describe how you felt when you pulled the trigger," one of them proposed not too long ago.

"Happy," I said without any hesitation.

"And yet, now you're having trouble dealing with the overwhelming guilt of having killed her," he said with that little knowing smile.

"Yes," I replied, again without any hesitation.

And that's the way it goes every time with little variation. Oh, they know what they're doing. They're wasting the taxpayers' good money is what they're doing, attempting to discover what makes a despicable murderess like Monica Peters tick. They hope that someday they will be able to proclaim that I am cured, so they can pat themselves on the back. They hope that they'll be able to send me back out into the real world someday and praise themselves for their expertise in rehabilitating a dangerous psychopath like Monica Peters. Maybe I should let them get their way. That's what I should do. I should allow them to bring me out of my room and lead me to the gates outside. I will let them take me up to the gates. I will let them shake my hand and kiss me on both cheeks. I will stand at the gates and gaze at them while they gaze back at me with pride and self-satisfaction, proclaiming," Go forth, young lady. You are now cured of all infirmity." And then I will stand at the gates, smile at their own smiling faces, and plunge a dagger straight into my heart.

Then everyone will be happy. Even those who betrayed me and whom I then saw fit to betray in return. And the nightmare of this earthly existence will follow me into the grave where the talons of Hell will pin me to a scorching plate of fire where I will roast and writhe in agony forever and ever.

Just where will the Almighty God of Love be, while *that* is happening?

BETSY'S DIARY – July 1, 1985

Dear Diary: The rains came today, but I didn't mind. In fact, I was thankful for it. I stood outside the front door for a few moments this morning and let the rain sprinkle my face and hair, and it felt good to be alive and to stand there and witness the gentle splatter of refreshment upon our front lawn. The rain also was most welcome because there were a few things I needed to do indoors, one of them being my having to take Ellen in for her doctor's appointment this morning.

I got up and dressed at a leisurely pace, then came downstairs and found Ellen waiting for me, fully dressed, in the living room. Her face looked a bit flushed, and she seemed uptight for some inexplicable reason. Scarcely wishing to engage in some sort of quarrel, I tried to be pleasant and reminded her of her doctor's appointment. Then I suggested that the two of us could run some errands together and possibly take in an afternoon show. I must admit Ellen seemed very agreeable to my every suggestion. Then when she told me that Mom wasn't feeling up to par and had called in sick early this morning, I felt more anxious than ever to get going.

Mom in a good mood has been difficult to deal with; I was in no frame of mind to cope with her while she was ailing, although I realize in saying this that once again I am revealing my own weakness of character and total selfishness.

At any rate, Ellen's visit with her doctor went well. I would have spoken to the man privately for a few minutes and discussed her present moodiness with him, but the opportunity did not present itself. I suppose her wildly variable behavior of late is to be expected. All in all, I'd have to say she has adjusted to her present situation remarkably well, and I am certain that, if I had met with a similar misfortune, I never would have been able to withstand the torment of my own physical affliction quite as well as she has.

As soon as we were free, I drove the two of us to the bank and made a rather sizeable withdrawal. Since I had given Mom the entirety of my last week's pay-check, I figured I'd might as well splurge a little bit on myself, it being my vacation and all, so I next drove the two of us to the mall. Ellen and I had been there once before – since her accident, that is – so I felt confident that being seen by so many strange people all at once would not trouble her.

The mall wasn't very crowded, luckily, and whenever I spotted a group of teen-agers a short distance away, I carefully steered Ellen in a different direction just in case they might have been former acquaintances of hers in front of whom she might have felt extremely uncomfortable. I know that a few times on the beach some of the people from her school have noticed her, and she became a bit flustered the first few times it happened. Still and all, I was very careful, and just to keep her in a good mood, I catered to her every whim and desire all day long. At the jewelry store, I saw that she was eyeing a pair of relatively inexpensive earrings, so I bought them for her, not trying to make a big deal out of it. It was well worth the meager expense, too, to see her face light up when she opened the bag and discovered I'd bought them for her a few

113

moments after we'd left the store. Her smile of delight overjoyed me so much, in fact, that later on I decided to surprise her with a pair of sun-glasses and some perfume. I don't believe she actually said Thank You, but the smile that creased the corners of her lips as I presented these little knick-knacks to her was all the thanks I could have asked for.

Perhaps it was foolish of me to spend so much money, but I saw a set of wine-glasses in one department store that I thought Monica and Carl might be able to use in their apartment, so I bought that, too, hoping I could maybe take a run out there later this evening and see how my sister has been getting along. And so as to make sure Mom didn't feel left out, I bought her what I thought to be a beautiful pair of dress shoes, and I saved the receipt just in case they weren't the right size or they weren't quite to her liking. Then, on the spur of the moment, I got her some more suntan oil as I was sure she would be running out of it fairly soon, the way she seemed to be doing an awful lot of sun-bathing lately.

It's strange, I know, but in one of the stores, I spotted some bandannas, and I recalled that Wayne Brown had been wearing one around his neck yesterday afternoon while he was painting the house and that there had been smudges of paint on it. Without really thinking about it, I picked out two of the more colorful ones I could find and bought them, too. Maybe I'll never get the chance to give them to him because I really would feel rather odd giving gifts to a virtual stranger, but they were really so inexpensive, it doesn't matter.

After making a couple more stops so as to buy some cologne for Carl and some perfume for Aunt Lucille, I stepped into the bookstore and saw a set of historical novels I'd been dying to get my hands on for quite some time, but when I reached inside my purse to count out the remainder of my cash, I figured I'd better not make the purchase after all. Ellen and I still hadn't had lunch, and I'd promised her an

114

afternoon show. I could go to the bank tomorrow maybe and take out enough money to buy the books later on in the week.

The movie was great. I'd purposely picked a comedy so as to avoid giving Ellen an excuse to become moody or depressed, and I was relieved to hear her laugh occasionally at some of the goings-on in the film. After the movie, I had just enough cash on hand to get her an ice cream cone, and as it was getting late, I suggested that she eat it in the car while we drove home.

It was still raining, and as far as I knew, had been doing so all day long, so I was more than a trifle mystified when I saw Wayne Brown's van pulling out of our driveway just as Ellen and I were coming down our street. For one ludicrous moment, I started to wave as his van went past us, and then Ellen yelled at me to cut it out, so I put my hand back on the steering wheel, admitting to myself that it didn't make any sense for me to wave hi at him. Ellen was right.

Once inside the house, I went upstairs with the shopping bags, heard the shower running in the bathroom, and entered my room. I was in a wonderfully happy mood, and I wanted more than anything else to surprise Mom with the shoes I'd bought her. Personally, I thought they were quite lovely and would complement a few of her outfits quite nicely.

It must have been bad timing on my part, however, because when I finally got up the courage to enter Mom's room where she was changing up after her shower, I made the mistake of mentioning that I'd seen Wayne Brown pulling out of the driveway when we neared the house, and I asked her," Isn't it strange that he should have come here to paint the house in the rain?"

"I've been sick in bed all day," Mom told me, shooting one of her angry and impatient stares at me. "For the life of me, Betsy, I don't know what you're insinuating by all of this."

When I told her that I hadn't meant to insinuate anything at all, she quickly told me not to bother her with any of my "nonsense" and to leave her alone, as she still wasn't feeling well. I started out of the room, feeling embarrassed over having upset her, when I remembered the box of shoes I was carrying. The thought crossed my mind that I should pretend to forget what had just happened and go ahead with some sort of presentation of the little gift I had brought her. But my knees were shaking so much and I was so afraid of saying the wrong thing, that I quickly reminded myself that she wasn't feeling well and had asked to be left alone. So, I simply left the box on the top of her dresser and went downstairs to get dinner ready.

About two hours later, I was on my way to Monica's apartment. Aunt Lucille had stepped in to keep Ellen company for the evening, and Mom was apparently staying in bed, so I didn't think anyone would miss me not being around.

When I arrived at the apartment, it was Carl who opened the door for me. I apologized for dropping in unexpectedly, but he was very pleased, he said, and actually looked delighted to see me. Monica was in the bathroom, he told me, but he invited me to sit down with him for a few minutes, and I then gave him the cologne I'd bought for him earlier in the day.

It was only a bottle of relatively inexpensive cologne, but Carl seemed so delighted, you might have thought I'd just handed him a check for ten thousand dollars. I can recall his exact words as he gazed across at me with those brilliant dark eyes of his: "That was really very sweet of you, Betsy. You're really a very wonderful person, you know that?"

I quote his words in my diary here tonight because I felt so warm inside upon hearing them. Not even Aunt Lucille had seemed quite as pleased with the perfume I gave her back at the house, and Aunt

Lucille does tend to gush with emotion at times. I was so tremendously moved, though, and embarrassed, too, that I'm sure I blushed, and I looked down uncomfortably at my hands in my lap.

In the next moment, Monica came in from out of the bathroom. For one very strange second, I imagined that she had been crying only a few moments earlier, but I was still so overcome from Carl's compliment that I didn't think much of it. I got up from the couch and handed her the wine-glasses without any further hesitation.

Monica smiled and thanked me warmly, but her mind seemed to be elsewhere. She scarcely looked me straight in the eye the whole time I was there. Carl, on the other hand, seemed unable to take those piercing dark eyes of his off me for a second. In fact, he was the one who pressed me to stay longer when I later mentioned that I ought to be going.

Monica walked me over to the door, leaving Carl to stand in the kitchen doorway, and just before I was ready to walk out, she clutched my hands suddenly, looked deeply into my eyes, and said, "Call me," in barely above a whisper. I know I must have seemed callous, but I kind of laughed a little, kissed her on the cheek, waved good-bye to Carl, and drove home feeling totally carefree and even a little bit smug with the thought that perhaps I had made a few people happy today.

It wasn't until I got home and came up here to my room that I began to have misgivings about the course of today's events. I fully understand that nothing truly earth-shattering took place today, but at the same time I feel a little shaken when I think of the uneasy look Monica gave me when we said good-bye to each other a little while ago. I love her dearly and am, in fact, envious of her good fortune in being married to such a charming young man as Carl. And yet, I sense that there is something not quite right about their marriage. Although I can't put my finger on it, it's there. Monica intimated as

117

much the other night when I saw her alone in her apartment, then she had quickly pushed her worries aside with the assurance that things would work themselves out, if given a little bit of time.

Well, they've been married only a very short while, and they're both so very young. Monica was right. Things will work themselves out. Things couldn't possibly go wrong for them for very long, could they?

P.S. Tomorrow is supposed to be a beautiful, sunny day, so I suppose Wayne Brown will be back to finish painting the house. Why does that thought disturb me?

ELLEN'S MEMOIRS – December 25, 1985

It's all over now, and I can breathe a little more freely. All that
Christmas nonsense is over, and the house is back to its normal,
boring self. I never thought I'd actually be looking forward to things
to be the way they are now, but it certainly is a relief not to have to
pretend that I was enjoying so much Christmas cheer with Aunt
Lucille and her idiotic friends. Oh, the Christmas tree will still be lit
up for a few more days, and pretty soon Aunt Lucille will be getting
herself all worked up for the coming New Year. But at least we can
put all this Christmas crap to rest for a while.

I got some pretty nice clothes, though. Aunt Lucille really went all
out this year. It makes sense, I guess, seeing as I'm just about the
only person in the family she's got left to buy Christmas presents
for. The only problem is I don't see why she had to buy me such
fancy clothes. I'll never have any place to wear them to. I'd might as
well wheel myself around this house in the nude, nobody ever comes
around here to pay me a visit, even. Lisa was the only real friend I
ever had, and after she dropped dead, there was nobody. Mom got
me a tutor to finish off the school year. Then when the next school
year was about to begin, the whole world caved in on my family, so
it was pointless for either me or Aunt Lucille to think about my

schooling. Aunt Lucille hired that one guy last October to come in and get me started on my studies, but I made such an awful scene, the guy took off and never came back. Besides, he looked like a total nerd, anyway. Now, if she'd decided to bring someone in here who was gorgeous to look at, it might have been different. The guy may have even succeeded in taking my mind off the big love of my life, but it would have taken quite a hunk to get me to forget *him*.

I remember the time early last summer when Betsy brought me to the mall to do some shopping. She was so careful we didn't run into any of the kids from school, it was pathetic. All the while she kept dodging from store to another, I was hoping she'd cut it out so maybe I could catch a glimpse of some hunk from school. But no such luck, of course. At one point, I'm pretty sure I saw my redheaded stud-man Marty coming out of one of the stores, but when I noticed he had his arm around that stuck-up ex-cheerleader Lori Adams, I turned away, feeling sick to my stomach at the very thought of him being with a girl like that, when he could have had me, right?

But naturally I couldn't get Wayne out of my head, and I still can't stop thinking about him, especially when he used to come around our house back then and strut his magnificent stuff all around our back yard. What a fool I was for trying to avoid him the first few times he came over to paint the house. I was so embarrassed about the way I looked that I didn't think I could bear the sight of him looking at me with nothing but pity in his eyes. How stupid of me! The guy never even looked at me, with or without pity, all those times we got together last spring. But finally, one day, I did get up enough courage to go out there on my own and see him, and not a moment too soon, either.

It was a beautiful summer day, and the two of us were alone, what with Mom being at work and Betsy off doing some stupid errand of some sort. I'll admit I felt timid at first, but once I made up my mind as to what I was going to do, there was no stopping me. I wheeled myself out onto the patio and saw him just as he was coming down the ladder, wiping the sweat off his forehead with the back of his forearm. He looked magnificent, sweating like a powerful animal and with one of those colorful bandannas he always wore around his beautiful neck. I knew he wouldn't make the first move – he never did, really – so I said Hi in a clear voice, just so he couldn't pretend he didn't notice me, and I wheeled myself a little closer to where he was standing.

"Fancy meeting you here," I said to him, or something equally gauche. I knew I didn't need to say anything brilliant to him, since the only brilliant things we had ever done together were in bed.

He didn't say a word, of course. Didn't really look at me either. He just calmly stood there and pulled a cigarette out from behind his ear, put it between his lips, and stuck a hand in his pants pocket, probably so he could take out a match or a lighter. And as he did that, he kind of arched his torso upwards a bit so that he reminded me of one of those statues of those Roman gods I used to see pictures of in my ancient history textbooks. I'll never forget how incredible he looked just then, as I imagined that he was standing there waiting for me in the sunlight.

We were all alone, just the two of us, and the back yard hedges afforded us all the privacy we needed. I knew he wasn't going to say anything to me just as surely as I knew he wasn't going to look directly into my face, so without any further hesitation, I wheeled myself right up to him, reached over, and unzipped the front of his denim jeans.

I'm beginning to feel feverish, just sitting here and recalling the hunger I had been feeling just before I saw him that morning and the fact that I was about to satisfy the deep craving I had always had and will always have in the future for that tremendous body of his. It had been over a month since I'd had any sexual contact with him. Hell, I hadn't had any sexual contact with anybody at all since the accident – not even good old Marty who was always up for what I was about to do to Wayne.

But in that moment of pure Heaven, the fury of Hell broke loose upon me because that bastard suddenly pulled away from me and zipped his pants back up, tight. I looked up at him with all the fury of Hell breaking loose in my own eyes, no doubt, and called him an ass-hole. And wouldn't you know it, he simply put his stupid unlit cigarette back behind his ear, turned around, and started back up the ladder as if the only reason he'd come down in the first place was because he expected to have a leisurely smoke for himself.

I stayed right where I was. What else could I do? And I watched him calmly walk away from me as though it wasn't even worth his time to have me get nice and friendly with him again, like he had so many other important things to do. Like get it on with my mother!

I knew it! I knew he'd been to bed with her! I wasn't as stupid as Betsy when, just the day before, we got back from the mall and saw his van pull out of the driveway. In the rain, no less. Nobody paints the outside of a house in the rain, right? With me and Betsy gone all day long, he had to have been up in Mom's room. She'd called in sick that morning. She'd had it all planned. She knew I had that doctor's appointment, too. Sure, she must have had it all planned. Call in sick, then call Wayne and invite him over for fun and games. They had it all worked out. And even if Betsy and I had returned early, it would have taken several minutes for Betsy to help me out of the car. The two of them would have had plenty of time to discover we were back. Wayne could have rolled out of bed, put his clothes back on, and his bandanna, too (couldn't go too far without *that,* could he?). Then he could have come downstairs with some lame explanation or, more likely, simply ignored the two of us if we'd entered the house and accosted him before he had a chance to escape in his van. None of that did happen, of course, because that dude always had luck on his side. Later that night, Mom came downstairs and complained that she hadn't had such a complete rest by staying home from work after all, and I wanted to say to her, "Sure, Mom, I can understand that. When a thirty-eight-year-old woman takes a young stallion like Wayne to bed with her, she can expect anything *but* rest." But I didn't say a word because a part of me didn't want to believe that it had really happened. I didn't want to have to picture my own mother going to bed with the man I loved. The man who belonged to me, and nobody else. Who the hell did she think she was, anyway? Why couldn't she stick to guys her own age, right? She couldn't have been too good, that's all I can say, because after that, they never got it on together. But then again, that wasn't entirely of my mother's own choosing.

But I'm getting off the track here. When I wheeled myself out onto the patio that morning, I was only thinking about how he would rush over to me when he saw me, scoop me up from out of my wheel-chair, and take me with him for a wild and exciting journey into Fantasyland. That was the stupid delusion I was entertaining when I went out there, and I honestly thought something like that would happen, too, especially when I got so close to him and made my little "pass" at him. So, what was his problem? Why did he have to draw back? Why did he have to recoil from me like that, as if I was poison or something? And then to just turn away, climb back up that ladder, and resume his painting just as if nothing at all had just taken place. That was the prime insult!

So, I drew back, too, and watched silently as he assumed a position on one of the top rungs of the ladder. I watched quietly, burning in my anger, as he calmly dipped his brush into the paint bucket and then lifted his arm to slap paint against the side of the house. I looked up at that magnificent specimen of manhood, and thought: He thinks I'm not even worth his time. He's pretending I don't even exist. As if he could just turn his back on me and I'd disappear, go back in the house, and entertain myself with a stupid magazine or something. Well, I'll show him a thing or two, the prick. I'll show him that I'm still a force to be reckoned with. I'll make him take notice of me, all right. He thinks he's all that, right now. Well, I'll knock the props right out from under him!

I know I shouldn't have done what I did; but then again, he shouldn't have pulled away from me and acted like I wasn't even fit to touch him. In all my fury, I just wheeled myself straight into that ladder he was perched on top of, and then I watched him drop.

I think he cried out for a moment, just before he started to fall and was thinking he could somehow retain his balance in mid-air or something. I know he didn't scream. He had to show how macho he was, no doubt, by not screaming, but I know how good it felt to see him hit the ground.

I still remember the sound his shoulder made as it hit the ground and the way he kind of curled up. Just like when you step on a spider and, after you pull your foot away to see if you got it, you see that it's all squished up and dead. That's exactly what happened to Wayne when his shoulder hit the ground. He curled up and was perfectly quiet, and I honestly thought I'd killed him. He was the love of my life, and I was happy I'd killed him because he'd just rejected me and acted like I wasn't even good enough to touch him. Because I was a cripple, he'd made up his mind he was going to pretend I didn't exist anymore. He was going to pretend nothing had ever gone on between the two of us, and somehow or another, that was going to justify his ignoring me from that day forward.

Well, in that one moment when my chair hit that ladder and that bastard found himself struggling to keep his balance just before the whole damned ladder folded up under him – In that one glorious moment just before he dropped, he must have taken notice of me. He must have known, right then and there, that I was a force to be reckoned with. And if he'd ended up crippled for life because of having fallen that distance to the ground, it would have been the most delicious twist of Fate!

But no! I didn't want him to die. I didn't want him to be crippled either. I wanted him to live, to go on living and looking so handsome. I didn't want anything really serious to happen to him.

I wheeled myself closer to where he was lying there, curled up and motionless as if he were dead, and my arms were trembling like crazy and if I'd had two good legs, I'm sure they would've been trembling, too. I leaned forward in my chair and called his name, praying as I'd never prayed before that he wasn't dead, that he would speak to me, say my name or something. To hear him tell me that he had forgiven me would have been such a divine miracle that it might have even inspired me to start walking again.

But no! No! He was too much of a macho prick to do anything of the sort. I leaned in towards him and called his name, and he just lay there and waited a few moments, just long enough for me to work myself up into a frenzied state of hysteria. Then he straightened himself up, clutching his shoulder with his other hand, and laughed.

I turned and wheeled myself back into the house in a complete rage. He was hurt. He had to have been! Nobody falls from the top of a ladder and hits the ground, shoulder-first, without sustaining injury. Not even a macho freak like him! Well, he wasn't kidding anybody. He was hurt, all right, and it was all because of me, too. And from that point on, he knew that I could hurt him any old time I wanted to. And I did hurt him. I hurt him real bad, too. I was soon to learn the secret to hurting him, and I spared him no pain whatsoever. That's why he spat at me the night the cops came to take him away. He'd seen the truth, and he realized just how badly I had hurt him, and so the big baby had to show what a complete ass he could be by spitting at me. Me, a poor, helpless cripple! I knocked him off a ladder, and he laughed at me; but when I hurt him later on that summer, hurting him so badly that he actually found the guts to look me in the eye, all he could do was spit at me!

Now that that's all behind me and things have changed so much, I can't bear the grief of not being able to see him. Couldn't he have dropped by this afternoon and wished me a merry Christmas? God! Would that have been so hard for him to do? What's he got to live for now, anyway? What have any of us got to live for? It needn't have been any big deal, right? Couldn't he have just dropped by for a few minutes, possibly carrying a little gift or some little trinket or something, a little peace offering in the form of a bottle of perfume maybe, and handed it to me and wished me well? Then I could tell myself that I could go to my grave without having only the remembrance of his spitting at me as the last sign of recognition he ever gave me. I could convince myself that he still loved me despite everything that happened, despite his having loved *her,* despite his having loved her to the point that he seemingly became a different person and swore he would never love anyone else ever again.

It's impossible to imagine that he could have changed so completely. I tell myself that he must have somebody in his life right now to replace her, somebody just to keep his interest in life sustained. But I know that's not true. I know, way deep down inside of me, that he doesn't have anybody, either. He's in mourning. Continual mourning. How can that man, who never seemed capable of any sincere and deep emotion, be suddenly consumed by so much grief? How can he continually mourn her death as he does and be oblivious of everything else that life has to offer him? How can these things be?

I'll go to sleep now, and I'll pretend that none of this matters. I'll pretend that this Christmas was just like all the others in the past. All the others when the three of us would spring out of our beds in the morning and run downstairs to see all those fantastic presents under the tree. How Monica's face would shine when she'd open her gifts and find that Santa had given her all those dolls and new dresses! And how Betsy would glow with a kind of restrained joy when she'd unwrap her solitary little gift and discover some stupid book inside or a picture of a puppy or a bird or some such nonsense, and she'd think it was the treasure of the Amazons or something. And how my own eyes would light up with desire at the sight of all those wonderful toys and make-up and ribbons and perfume and earrings they'd shower me with every Christmas. Every Christmas I'd make out like a bandit. I was the prettiest one, you know? The little cutie-pie of the family, and Mom knew it, too. Everybody knew it. And whenever I was decked out in all my Christmas or Easter finery, Mom and Aunt Lucille would have their cameras clicking so excitedly, they'd run out of film before they even had a chance to take any pictures of Monica or Betsy.

Yes. Just let me sleep and dream of the Christmases of the past. The days when I was the queen of our house, and every other girl my age wished she had my looks and charm and personality. Let me dream about all that glory I once had, because right now that's all it is is a dream. Just a stupid dream.

BETSY'S DIARY – July 2, 1985

Dear Diary: What a strange day this has been! I've been having such weird dreams the past few nights, I can just imagine the kinds of dreams I'll be experiencing tonight after the bizarre events that took place today.

The day did start out in a commonplace manner, however. I woke up with sunshine falling across my face to remind me that I was still at the beginning of my vacation and that I could go about whatever business I cared to attend to in a leisurely enough manner. I remembered that I had run out of money yesterday, so I set about the business of getting showered and dressed with the idea of taking a run out to the bank to make another withdrawal. Things would be a lot easier if I had a credit card, of course, but Mom said I would be too careless with it and probably lose it somewhere without even realizing it was missing. Well, anyway, I thought I'd ask Ellen to come with me, too, and just play it by ear. Once again I reminded myself that the sun was out, good and strong, which meant that some work would need to be done outside, and Wayne Brown would be around to do it, too. The idea of hanging around and wondering if I should go outside and assist him in some manner didn't really appeal to me, so I was more anxious than ever to go out on a few errands and maybe spend some time at the park or beach, with or without Ellen.

I was surprised when I got downstairs to find that Ellen had no intentions of going out today. When I pointed out to her that the workman had just pulled into the driveway as he had, in fact, done so a few minutes before I came downstairs, Ellen replied that that didn't make any difference to her because she was planning on staying in the house all day, anyway, and watching some television. I didn't argue with her, naturally, but told her that I'd probably be out for the better part of the day and that there were some cold cuts in the refrigerator if she got hungry later on.

Everything went well during the morning hours. I took out some money from my account, browsed in a couple of bookstores and found a few interesting novels. I would have stayed out a little longer, but my car was making some strange noises, so I thought I'd better head on home. Mom had mentioned that Wayne Brown was an auto mechanic, so I wondered if he might be willing to take a look under the hood and see if he could spot the trouble. I'd pay him for his time, of course.

When I got home, everything appeared normal at first. That is, I found Ellen sitting in front of the T.V. with a rather set expression on her face. I asked her if everything was all right, and she snapped at me for distracting her from the show she was watching, so I went into the kitchen and got out a soda. It suddenly occurred to me that since it was very warm outside, Wayne Brown might possibly be quite thirsty, so I took out a beer from the pack Mom had stashed away in the back, behind some bottles of soda, and walked on out into the sunlight.

Wayne Brown was there, all right, but he was leaning against the side of the house, holding his right side as if he were hurt. I noticed, too, that the ladder was lying on the ground with a spilled bucket of paint not too far away from it. Without even thinking about what I was doing, I put down the beer and soda and rushed over to him. I asked him, quite stupidly, I would imagine, what had happened. He didn't answer me, nor look at me either, for that matter, but the expression he had on his face told me that he must have been in considerable pain although he didn't make a sound to indicate that the pain might have been that severe.

I next did a very silly thing by trying to take him and lead him over to a patio chair, for he winced in pain as soon as I touched him, and it was then that it dawned on me that, if he had indeed fallen from the ladder, there was no way of me knowing exactly from what height he had fallen. He may very well have broken a few ribs or fractured his arm or his shoulder. Without any further hesitation, I informed him that I was going to drive him to the emergency room immediately. He shook his head a few times, looked down at the ground, and said he was O.K.; but I knew I wouldn't be able to live with myself for the rest of the day if I allowed him to kid me into thinking he was perfectly all right. It took some doing, but I finally escorted him around the side of the house and over to my parked car. He got inside on his own, but the whole time we drove to the hospital, he kept clutching his side, and I glanced occasionally in his direction and saw his pain written quite plainly on his face.

Sure enough, after he had been examined in the emergency room and X-rays were taken, he was found to have fractured his right shoulder and was advised to spend the night there as some pretty strong pain-killers had been prescribed for him. It was truly heart-breaking for me to see him looking so miserable and so desolate. Like a normally strong-looking animal that's dying of pain with its foot caught in a merciless trap. I stayed with him all afternoon, actually feeling it to be my duty to do so since the accident had taken place on our property and I hadn't even been around to help him when it first occurred. For a moment, I wondered why Ellen hadn't gone out there to see what was wrong. But then I remembered that the television had been on quite loud, so it is altogether possible that she didn't hear a thing when the poor young man fell off the ladder outside.

At one point in the afternoon, I told him I would call his father to tell him what had happened and that he'd be spending the night in the hospital, and Wayne simply shook his head and wouldn't answer me when I asked him why he didn't want me to call his father. I felt so awkward, sitting there next to his bed, not really knowing what to say to him and not really knowing what I could do for him, but simply knowing that I couldn't leave him there all by himself in that condition. He was still perspiring, even while he lay there in his hospital bed, and I wanted so desperately to reach over and pull some of his curly blond hair away from his forehead as I would have done to Monica or Ellen if either of them had been in this position. But I was afraid that he would misconstrue the gesture or, worse than that, push my hand away and tell me to leave him alone.

No, I shouldn't think that. Throughout all of it, he never showed any kind of hostility or impatience. He was in pain and, no doubt, concerned about his future well-being, but he didn't seem to resent my staying there by his side all afternoon. Neither did he appear to resent my feeble attempts to converse with him on some casual pretext to sort of break the ice between us. No, he didn't seem to resent me in any way. He just looked so sad and so lonely. And bashful, too. In all the time that we spent with each other today, I don't believe he ever once looked me fully in the face. Not even when I touched his hand lightly to get his attention to tell him I would be missed around the house if I didn't get going pretty soon. I thought I caught a flicker of a smile pass over his face when I told him I'd come back later to see how he was doing, but I don't recall that it was anything more than a mere wisp of sound when I left the room and fancied that he had just said Good-bye to me.

When I returned home, I discovered that Mom had just gotten in from work. I was about to tell both her and Ellen about the accident, but I couldn't even begin to relate my story because Mom immediately railed at me for leaving Ellen alone for so many hours. I wanted to remind her that, ordinarily, when I was at work, Ellen was left alone for quite a few more hours than she had been today and also that I was always willing to stay with her, except that something else had come up today – but Mom wouldn't hear any of it. She was also infuriated over the fact that nothing had been prepared for dinner and, seeing as I was on vacation, the least I could have done was to see to it that dinner was taken care of. When she said that, I realized that it was true. I was on vacation, just as she said, and there was no reason for me to be so irresponsible. So, I went into the kitchen and put a few things together for us to eat. It wasn't until the three of us were eating dinner that Mom asked if either of us had seen the painter today.

"His van is parked in our driveway," she said, "but he doesn't seem to be around, does he?"

Ellen put her head down and pretended not to have heard what was being said, so it was left to me to explain to Mom that Wayne Brown had, indeed, been here to do some painting but that he had fallen off the ladder and needed to be taken to the hospital. "If you want," I suggested to her," I'll do the rest of the painting myself if it turns out he won't be able to finish the job because of his injury."

"There's no rush," I was surprised to hear Mom say. "And besides, I'm sure Wayne would do a much better job than you ever could."

There was no denying the truth of that statement, so I decided not to take issue with it. I was a little alarmed, though, that neither she nor Ellen seemed the least bit concerned over the young man's current state of health, so I didn't even bother to tell them, later on, where I was going. I had promised Wayne that I'd stop by in the evening to see how he was doing, and I aimed to keep my promise. For all I knew, he had forgotten about the promise I made him, but just on the off-chance that he'd be lying there all night alone, I thought it would be best to stop in and say Hello, even if it was only for a few minutes.

As it turned out, there were three young men standing around his bed when I stepped into his room. I thought it extremely peculiar that they all stopped talking as soon as they saw me enter the room and even more peculiar when one of them whistled a little under his breath when I reached for Wayne's hand to give it a friendly squeeze. I hadn't meant to interrupt anything, but Wayne's visitors left the two of us alone within perhaps two or three minutes of my arrival. I did feel more relaxed after they'd gone, and that in itself was odd, too, because Wayne and I had been introduced to each other only two days prior to his accident. Nonetheless, I found it extremely difficult, all over again, to establish eye contact with him, let alone get a stimulating conversation going between the two of us. I guess I stayed there with him a good fifteen minutes without saying anything that I can now recall, and when my nervousness began to show, I reached into my purse and pulled out the present I had wrapped for him before I left the house this evening.

Wayne took the little package I gave him and simply frowned down at it a few moments as if he really didn't know what to make of it. I began to feel tense and anxious all over again, wondering if I had really gone a bit too far this time, but I knew I had done the right thing when he unwrapped the package and pulled out the two bandannas I had bought for him just yesterday at the mall.

A smile, just a trace of a smile creased the corners of his lips as he held the bandannas out in front of him and looked them over. Then he chuckled a little and tried to sit up, but the pain in his shoulder prevented him from shifting his weight about as he had intended to do, causing him to lose his smile for a few seconds. Then he turned his face in my direction, and I immediately lost all my nerve and dropped my eyes to the floor, so I don't know for sure whether he actually looked directly into my face or not; and now that it's too late to find out, I wish to God with all my might that I could recapture that moment and find the strength to keep looking at him when he decided to turn his face in my direction. The next thing I knew, after I lifted my eyes from the floor, he was looking down at the bandannas that were clasped in his hands, and he wasn't exactly smiling anymore.

Without quite knowing what to say to him, I arose and mentioned that I hoped he'd be feeling better very soon, not that we were all that anxious to see the house get finished painted, but just that it would be good to see him up and around again. I know I sounded like a klutz, but I was very nervous and flustered. I'm afraid I'm not in the habit of spending any great lengths of time with young men, especially young men who seem to travel in different circles than I do. Then it suddenly occurred to me that I'd spent practically the whole day in this young man's company and now I had topped things off by embarrassing the two of us with my sheer inability to conduct myself with the slightest degree of self-confidence and self-assurance.

I tried to leave his room quickly, after having just made a fool of myself, but then I was arrested by the sound of his voice as he called my name from where he lay in his hospital bed.

"Betsy," he said to me in a very clear voice. "Thanks."

If I weren't so stupid and so naïve as they all say I am, I would have driven home as clear-headed as I would have been had I just returned home from doing some routine grocery shopping. But I felt so muddled and confused, I even forgot that Monica had urged me last night to give her a call and I had meant to do that right after dinner. It wasn't until I walked in the front door that I remembered Monica's request, as I directed my steps to the phone in the kitchen and dialed her number.

It wasn't Monica, but Carl who answered. He sounded very pleased to hear that it was me, and asked me several questions relating to how I was passing the time now that I was on vacation. I didn't tell him anything really specific, since I was very anxious to speak to Monica, and in a minute or so, I was able to tell him that I wished to speak to my sister.

"Monica can't come to the phone right now," he told me, his voice suddenly sounding very serious.

I was being foolish. I know that now. But at the time, I saw reason to become alarmed after hearing him say that, so I asked him if anything was wrong. Then Carl laughed briefly and said,

"Nothing that a little rest and relaxation won't cure. You know how it is with newlyweds. Monica is resting right now. She just kind of conked out around eight o'clock or so."

I think I said something extremely brilliant at that point. Like "oh," for example. Then I urged him to have her call me as soon as she got a chance, and hung up.

Well, that return call hasn't come, and it is now pretty close to midnight. I suppose Carl was right when he seemed to imply that I perhaps didn't quite realize how newlyweds carried on with each other when they were alone. Still, I do recall the urgent note in my sister's voice when she asked me to call her, and I know that she wouldn't have stared at me the way she did for those few moments – not unless there was something pretty serious on her mind that she wanted to discuss with me. I will make it a point to call her tomorrow. Perhaps in the morning, and we can meet for lunch or something. And I'll have to make arrangements to pick Wayne up from the hospital. His van is still parked in our driveway, and I'm sure he'll be needing it to get around in as soon as he gets out.

Now that it is time for me to retire for the night, I feel as though a long day has now ended and that, for once, it wasn't a total waste. At least I was able to help a person in distress – and to even make him smile, even though it was only for a few moments and even though I never had a chance to see what color his eyes were.

P.S. These words came so easily to me tonight. I almost felt inspired as I wrote these last pages of my diary. There must be some profound reason for why I feel so fresh and spontaneous all of a sudden, although I would be very hard put to explain, even to myself, why this should be so.

AUNT LUCILLE'S DIARY – December 25, 1985

Well, the day is nearly over now, and an incredible sadness has descended upon this house. I always grow nostalgic and sentimental around Christmastime, but today I didn't fare too well at all. In the past, at least, all I would do is mope around and wonder what it would be like if Arnie or some other man could share the holidays with me; but this time I forced myself to put up such a cheerful front in front of Ellen and my friends that, by the time I was left alone to tidy up the place, I just sank onto the couch and cracked.

Why is it that we force ourselves to be cheerful and carefree when it's just a phony sham? Who do we really expect to fool? I know I certainly didn't fool Ellen. She's too sharp to think that, after everything that's happened to us this past year, I could possibly carry on during this holiday season as if nothing out of the ordinary had taken place. And I'm sure that the girls from the office knew that my insides were churning during their entire visit here this afternoon and into the evening hours. It was really nice of them to come and share a little Christmas cheer with Ellen and me, but I could tell that they felt uncomfortable. Oh, they'd seen Ellen before in her wheel-chair, but I don't think they've ever seen her looking so haggard and withdrawn.

They should have been here this morning when Ellen opened up her presents. I honestly thought for a second there that she was going to laugh and smile with delight over all the wonderful clothes I had bought for her, and I actually said to myself in a stupid moment of insanity: Nothing has changed. She's still a little girl, brimming over with innocent enthusiasm as she opens her presents on Christmas morning.

But what about the other two girls? There will be no more Christmas mornings for them, will there? Oh, I remember quite vividly how in the past Jean would have me drop by early, and I'd have my camera ready to roll while the girls, sleepy-eyed but seized with a tremulous excitement, would enter the parlor and gaze upon their gifts with positive rapture. Ellen was always so cute the way she used to gather all her gifts together in one big bunch and then open them up one by one, smiling up at the camera in pride as she held up each item close to her dimpled, radiant face. I'd spend so much time with the camera focused on her, half the time I'd forget about Monica who'd be off to one side, gingerly unwrapping each gift as if afraid to spoil the wrapping paper. She'd smile, too, but with a little more reserve than her younger sister, and I'd take a few pictures of her, too, although she was never quite as photogenic as Ellen. And then there'd be Betsy off in her own corner with perhaps one or two small gifts, and when I'd bring the camera over in her direction, she'd laugh softly and cover her face with her hands or with some wrapping paper and say," No, Auntie, no. Don't take my picture. Take more pictures of Ellen and Monica. They're so pretty."

I don't want to dwell on those moments any longer. Those moments were just too precious and too sublime for words. They weren't even my own children, but I would pretend, on each holiday when I took their pictures, that I was married and that these were my three little girls. I loved them as if they were my very own flesh and blood, and that's why I considered it such a tragedy when I watched them all get washed down a drain of filth so rapidly that I couldn't even raise a finger to prevent them from being destroyed, each in her own way. Oh, if only we could all go back to those days of innocence and joy! If only those days could have continued forever and ever and ever!

I should drive up to Norfolk tomorrow. If only for my own peace of mind, I should visit my poor niece and tell her, once and for all, that I don't hate her. I should reach over and embrace her. Finally. That's something I haven't done in so long, partly through indecisiveness and partly through fear. I know she's not in her right mind, and I'm afraid she may scream or go completely hysterical if I touch her. It frightens me to even think of what she might possibly do if I say or do anything to excite her. And to think that, just the other day, when I drove up there to see her, they wouldn't even let me in. Oh, God! Is it all over for her now? Already? She's only eighteen years old, and her life is already ruined beyond repair. I'm afraid that if I drive up there to see her tomorrow, they may tell me that she's done away with herself, and I couldn't go through that – not again! That would make the third funeral I'd have to go to in less than six months.

If the first one I attended last September was awful, the second one was a virtual horror show, if only because I was practically all by myself all the way through it. All by myself and consumed with hate and numbed by shock, all at the same time. Not even Carl Peters had the decency to attend. After Monica was put away, he just kind of disappeared as though he had finally renounced all ties with our family; and my only contact with him these past months has been on those rare occasions when I visit the cemetery. It's all well and good that he chose to disappear, I suppose. He and that other one, too. Why did they have to stick around, anyway? They'd already done all the damage they possibly could in the short time they were a part of our lives. It's just as well I was practically all alone during that second funeral. If I had seen any one of them – Carl, Monica, or Wayne – I would have done something so violent, they next would have had to put *me* away!

So now it's just me and Ellen, and when the two of us pass away, there'll be no one. I can't imagine Monica ever being released, going out and finding another husband, and having children. Of course, if Ellen would only give herself half a chance, she might meet up with some nice boy with a good background who would be able to love her, despite her physical handicap.

But that's as far-fetched as to expect that Arnie will come crawling back to me on his hands and knees, begging for my forgiveness. God, how could we women be so stupid and trusting? How could we allow ourselves to be deluded so easily into thinking that, by taking a man into our beds, we would find happiness and companionship and everlasting devotion? Such things are a mere fabrication of playwrights and storytellers and movie-makers. The truth of the matter is there are no guarantees for happiness or even comfort and security. None whatsoever. In a space of a few short months, my entire family was practically wiped out. If there'd been any real guarantees, we'd all be together right now, celebrating Christmas in a mood of festivity and joy, instead of going to bed each night, alone, and waiting for the world to end.

On that note, I think I'll go to bed. Maybe I'll have another crying jag before I finally fall asleep. If I do, maybe I'll feel better in the morning and I'll be able to put on a happy face for Ellen without feeling like too much of an incredible hypocrite.

That's it for today.

BETSY'S DIARY – July 3, 1985

Dear Diary: Weeks ago, as I sat back and tried to visualize what my vacation would be like, I never expected that such strange events would characterize it. I just thought that I would be spending my days reading and taking Ellen shopping or out for some air. I never imagined that Monica would be married, for one thing, or that I would begin to feel such strange emotions over a person I didn't really know much about at all.

Let me start at the beginning, then, and perhaps as I write this, I'll be able to make some sense out of it. The day began with my getting out of bed and almost wishing that I could hear the sounds of Wayne Brown stirring outdoors. Then it hit me suddenly that he was in the hospital with a shoulder injury, and despite myself, I found that I was filled with an eerie sort of anxiety as I hastened to shower and get dressed for the day. I also remembered that I ought to call Monica, and so, as soon as I got downstairs, I called her at work and made an appointment to meet her at noon so we could have lunch together and possibly have an opportunity to talk, hopefully about whatever it was that seemed to have been on her mind when she practically begged me to call her the other night.

I was all set to go out the door with the intentions of stopping at the hospital for a wee bit before lunch when it suddenly occurred to me that, if he had been released already, he might have hitched a ride with a friend by this time and might even be on his way here to pick

141

up his van. So, I went back to the phone and called the hospital. It's a good thing I did, too, because the shock might've been even worse if I'd entered his room without first finding out what had been going on all morning. Apparently one of the doctors attending him was of the opinion, I was told, that an operation was necessary to reset the bone in Wayne's shoulder, and at the time I made my call this morning, he was just coming out of surgery. For some strange reason, I found myself trembling when I heard the news, and all I could think of was the way I had found him yesterday afternoon, leaning against the side of our house and pretending he wasn't in as much pain as he evidently was. I hung up the phone and started out the door, relieved that Ellen was sitting in front of the T.V. and taking no notice of what I was doing, so at least I was spared the necessity of having to explain to her what had happened and where I was going.

Minutes later, I found myself on the threshold of his hospital room, and my heart sank to the pit of my stomach when I saw him there with his eyes closed and the I.V. unit hooked up to his arm and those horrible bandages wrapped around his shoulder and his upper body. He looked so helpless and vulnerable just then that my legs immediately carried me to his bedside and I leaned over him and did what I had been so tempted to do to him yesterday when he had lain there, conscious, and perspiring heavily. I stroked his forehead and pulled a few of his blond curls away from the sides of his face and gazed down upon his motionless form in complete pity. I'd never expected to see him like this, not when, just yesterday, he appeared to be in steadily improving spirits.

An intern came in and asked, quite unnecessarily, if I was Wayne's girlfriend or wife, and I was so startled by the question, my voice just kind of got stuck in my throat for a few seconds before I finally managed to tell the man that I was just a friend. Then I asked him if Wayne's father had been kept up to date on his son's condition, and the intern replied that no one had as yet been able to get a hold of Wayne Brown Senior. Before I knew what I was doing, I told the intern that everything would be all right and that I would be staying with him so he wouldn't have to come out of the anesthesia all by himself. The man smiled politely and left a short time later, and I felt nervous and foolish. It seemed so similar to that time a little over a month ago when we heard that Ellen had been in that horrible car accident, and I'd rushed Mom, Monica, and Aunt Lucille over to this same hospital, and the four of us were so distraught, particularly Monica and Aunt Lucille, and I kept telling them that Ellen would be all right, just to keep everyone calm and in control. Then, when the severity of Ellen's condition became known to us, I sank to the nearest chair and broke down completely, not even listening with my full attention to the rest of what the doctor had to say to us and not even hearing Mom when she then took it upon herself to scream down at me, saying that I was so stupid for having told them all that Ellen was going to be all right.

Well, I certainly knew that Wayne's condition was nowhere near as serious as Ellen's had been, but I've always had a hard time dealing with death and sickness and the like. I couldn't help crying a little bit when I noticed that Wayne was lying there for so long without even moving, and the time kept ticking away, and he seemed to be making no visible signs of coming to. And for one desperate, insane moment I said to myself: What if he's dead? Was if he's never going to regain consciousness? Ever?

The tears welled up in my eyes all over again, and I rose from my chair to lean over him as I had done when I'd first entered the room. And I took out one of the bandannas I had given him last night where he'd left it on the little dresser next to his bed, and I gently wiped his brow with it while, with my other hand, I stroked his blond curls further and further away from his damp forehead.

It was then that his body began to quiver slightly, and I imagined that I could detect a certain amount of movement under his closed eyelids. I drew my hands away from him but kept leaning over him and looking down into the face of that poor, helpless young man, and minutes passed without my noticing it. I didn't care what time it was either, because I knew that I just had to be there for him when he opened his eyes and became aware that he was still a vital, living part of the real world.

When his eyes did open, it seemed that he really couldn't focus them on me right away. I believe that he had been at least semi-conscious for some time before he actually opened his eyes, because his lips had parted several times and he had seemed to be trying to get some sound out. Finally, he appeared to get his eyes and his mind adjusted to my presence; and without thinking, I reached down and touched the side of his face.

"Betsy?" he said in a small voice, full of awe, surprise, and sheer wonder.

"Yes, Wayne, it's me."

That's all I said to him as I leaned over him and kept my hand held gently against the side of his face. He let out some breath, and with the exhalation of that air, his body seemed to discover a certain amount of new-found peace, so I was surprised when his eyes swerved away from my face instead of remaining trained upon me as I would have expected. He didn't say anything after I spoke, but he closed his eyes again, his face slightly averted from mine, and before I knew it, I found his left hand being raised towards me. I didn't even give it a second thought, but reached out with my other hand and enclosed his in mine.

Even though his grasp was considerably stronger than I thought it would be under the present circumstances, a sort of peace suddenly began to engulf me while we remained close to each other for the next fifteen minutes or so with our hands clasped together. I felt such contentment in the knowledge that I was there for him just then. He had been detached from reality for a few hours, and when the moment came for him to be reborn, as it were, my face had been staring down into his and my hand had been ready to take his, and he was them able to re-close his eyes, let out some air, and perhaps re-discover some of the peace he might possibly not have been able to feel in a very long time.

I don't know why I've been spending so much time in writing about this. In retrospect, I no doubt will feel that my emotions had been unnecessarily stirred by a perfect stranger's temporary helplessness. But my life has felt so empty and devoid of purpose that even this small a gesture on my part on this young man's behalf has seemed to restore hope within me, hope that my life may actually be worth something and that my mother may yet live to see a speck of a reason for not regretting that I had ever been brought forth from her womb.

Well, the time went by, a nurse came in for a few minutes, and I sat back in my seat and waited for Wayne's gradual recovery from surgery; and it wasn't until twenty minutes after twelve that I remembered about my luncheon date with Monica.

Wayne still seemed to be drifting in and out of consciousness, so I waited until I was able to find a lucid moment before I told him that I'd be gone for a little while because there was an appointment I wanted to keep. Then I made the mistake of asking him if he wanted me to come back later to see how he was doing. I call it a mistake because, in a ridiculous surge of emotion, I was expecting to hear from him an ardent confession that he was counting on my return. Instead, however, he kept his eyes lowered and made a little awkward movement with his lips which I interpreted as signifying that he really didn't care that much after all. I smiled nonetheless, to no avail of course because he wasn't even looking at me at the time, and found myself walking out of his room without really having said good-bye to him.

Luckily, I had my luncheon date with Monica to transfer my thoughts to, and I soon found her at the restaurant, not looking angry over possibly having been stood up, but looking rather tense and moody with a tall ice cream soda sitting in front of her. She smiled weakly when I took a seat opposite her, and I apologized for being late. I'm afraid I rattled on a bit too long about how the painter had hurt his shoulder and so on and so on. Monica didn't seem to be the least bit interested in what I was saying, and I don't think she would have appeared any more intent, anyway, had Wayne been one of her best friends. She just seemed so pre-occupied, giving me half-hearted smiles every so often and mumbling an occasional Yes or Really. Finally, I just had to stop my idle prattle and ask her, point-blank, what was bothering her.

"Nothing," she said with another feeble smile. "I just have doubts about certain things, that's all."

I couldn't derive much information from that remark, and I was trying to be tactful, too, in that I didn't want her to think I was being nosy, so I kept quiet for the next few minutes. A waitress came over, and we gave our orders. Then Monica sipped some more of her ice cream soda in perfect silence, and I started to grow a bit teary-eyed at the sight of my beautiful sister looking so tense and out of sorts at a time in her life when she ought to have looked simply delirious with happiness.

Then, almost with complete abruptness, she stopped sipping her drink, looked at me, and asked me a very strange question.

"Betsy?" she said to me, rather tentative-sounding. "Do you think that – if you were a man, you would consider me – attractive?"

I'm forever doing the wrong thing, I know, and of all times for me to act stupid and insensitive, I actually ended up laughing a little at the question she'd just asked me in such a serious manner. Then when I saw that my light-heartedness was inappropriate, I reached across the table to touch her hand and told her that, of course, she was attractive, and that there never had been any doubt in anyone's mind about that either.

"Oh, I know I'm not ugly – or horrid to look at – or anything like that," she stammered, dropping her eyes back down to the table. "I was just wondering if you thought – I was wondering if I was – considered – attractive enough in a man's eyes. That is, from a man's point of view, do you suppose I might be considered – desirable? Or even – sexy?"

"Yes, Monica," I told her in complete and utter sincerity as I applied pressure to her hand which I held in my own. "You are a beautiful young woman, Monica. Beautiful in every way. And I can't understand why you should be having these doubts. You don't mean to tell me, do you, that Carl doesn't find you as completely irresistible as the rest of us do?"

And I laughed once again because of the intense pain I saw gradually creeping into my sister's face while I had been speaking to her. I laughed because I thought, by laughing, I could make her pain go away. I thought I could help her even more than I had ever hoped to help Wayne just a short time earlier. I wanted somehow to be able to bring back the bloom of red roses that had always been in her cheeks all these years. And I hadn't been lying either about her being beautiful. And I'm just so proud of the fact that such a beautiful human being is my very own sister. I would gladly lay down my life for her if, by doing so, I could prevent any sadness whatsoever from ever entering her soul or depriving her of her zest for life.

My failure to bring her round I ascribe to my own ineptitude. I shouldn't have laughed when I did, even though I had meant well. I know it now because she suddenly shrugged her shoulders, sipped some more soda, and told me to forget everything she had just said. It was too late, at that point, for me to pursue the matter any further, so we finished our lunch in a rather subdued manner and, just before we parted company, I reminded her that she could feel free to phone me anytime she felt the inner need to do so.

As I drove my car out of the parking lot, I glanced into my rear-view mirror and thought I caught a glimpse of her getting into her own car with her face streaked with tears, but I had just put on my sunglasses, so I may very well have been mistaken about that.

I drove straight back to the hospital, really kind of anxious to see just how much Wayne had recovered in the brief space of time I had been away from him, and when I stepped over his threshold, I received a bit of a jolt upon coming face to face with a tall, slim brunette who was standing over his bed and who looked up the instant I entered the room.

"Who are you?" she asked me in a kind of snappy tone of voice. Or maybe it just seemed that way because she lost no time at all in addressing me as soon as our eyes met.

I did manage to give her a little smile, and then I walked forward, reaching out my hand, and introduced myself. She told me her name was Charlene and touched hands with me briefly. Then she immediately turned her attention to Wayne and started telling him different things about different people who were unknown to me. At one point, she referred to a certain individual as a "whore" and then to another person as a "bitch" and, although I was making no conscious attempt to follow the thread of what she was telling him, I felt that I had obviously walked into his room at the wrong time. Not only that, but Wayne himself didn't seem to exhibit any particular desire to acknowledge my presence in any specific way, but kept his face averted both from me and from Charlene. Once in a while, he'd grunt or make an appropriate negative or affirmative response to what she was telling him, but he didn't seem to be in tune with what was going on. Had the two of us been there alone, I might have stayed longer than I did, but I was beginning to feel extremely out of place, so I excused myself rather meekly, told Wayne I hoped he'd be better in a short while, and left.

I didn't go back there tonight, either, although a call to the hospital about an hour ago furnished me with the information that he was sleeping soundly. And I didn't go to Monica and Carl's apartment because I felt that, at this stage of the game, it was probably up to Monica to get the ball rolling if she really expected to benefit in any way from confiding in me.

All told, it was rather a mixed-up day. Tomorrow, then, I will take it slowly. I'll read a book or watch T.V. with Ellen or tidy up my room or cook something really special for dinner tomorrow night. One thing is definite: I will not go to the hospital. I think perhaps Wayne Brown doesn't really care to see me, and I don't want to be in a place where it's obvious I'm not wanted. And besides, he has his friends, so it's not as if I'm abandoning him to complete solitude or anything of the sort. So, I think I can go to bed now with a relatively free conscience, and I expect to sleep soundly. It's been a long day.

P.S. That girl Charlene who was visiting him this afternoon must be his girlfriend. I find that rather saddening, as she didn't strike me as the type of person who would be capable of giving him a pure and impassioned love that would be boundless, the kind of love that that poor young man must surely deserve. I pray for him right now. And I don't simply pray for his health. I pray for his soul. I pray that it may find peace and fulfillment and the kind of love and joy that we are all entitled to if we sincerely try to do His will. Amen.

CARL'S DIARY – January 4, 1986

Dear Diary: Wayne Brown is dead meat!

Now I finally know what he meant that other time when he said it was the Fourth. Sure. The Fourth of the month! How could I have been so stupid all this time? As if the Fourth of September wasn't the worst day of my life because it marked the last day my angel ever drew breath on this planet. Oh, God! To think I could have been so stupid! And I used to get straight A's on all my report cards, too. I was prime material for college and everything, and then I went and screwed up my life and married Monica, a girl I never really loved. At the time, sure, I thought I was doing the right thing. I thought, if I married her and bedded her down, I'd find out once and for all if –

"It's the Fourth!" he said to me. Sure. The moron had enough intelligence to read the date on the calendar, and he had some stupid pig-headed idea in that underdeveloped brain of his that he'd pay me a visit on the Fourth of every month and beat my head in. Well, now I'm prepared, and it won't ever happen again because I'll see him dead before the end of the week, man. Nobody messes with me the way he's been doing and gets away with it. Nobody.

And I was just telling myself yesterday that it was getting to be that time. I was just saying to myself just the other day that it'd been nearly a month since we last tangled; and yet, I was so stupid, I didn't even figure it all out until the last minute. Until it was too late.

All day long I'd been doing some pretty heavy partying. I was too spacey to realize I was in danger. I didn't get up this morning till noontime, and as soon as I was dressed. I drove on out to the cemetery and went to visit my angel. Mine and nobody else's. The only woman who ever made me feel like a man, she was so beautiful and so perfect, with her silky blonde hair and those brilliant blue eyes with a hint of tragedy in them. I stayed there at her grave, humble and quiet, for several minutes. Everything was so calm and peaceful out there this afternoon. I was barely conscious of the snow that was beginning to pile up on my shoulders as I knelt in front of her tombstone and tried to focus in on the past for a little while. I wasn't even aware of the wind when it kicked up and blew my hair around. Someday, I'm sure of it, I'll hear her voice. I'll hear the voice of her spotless soul as she tells me that I'm the man she loves. Me, and nobody else. Only me.

I picked myself up and went back to the car and met Vince and Kenny at the mall. We went driving around in my car and smoked a few blunts. I told Vince a little bit about my angel, and he said, "Man, she sounds like a mighty special chick, all right. When am I gonna meet her?" Then Big-Mouth Kenny goes and tells him," She's been dead since last September," and then Vince looks at me with real concern and says," Man, you've got it bad, you know that?"

I don't know what made him think he could sum me up like that – as if he were some kind of mental giant with an I.Q. that topped mine, even. I didn't say anything at the time because I was kind of mellowed out, and like I said before, I viewed Vince as a vital link to some pretty strong dope, so I didn't want to antagonize the guy, even though he was carrying on like a complete dick. Where do these limp brains get off, anyway, thinking they can judge me and the way I feel according to conventional standards? If even one of them were capable of the powerful emotions I feel, then maybe they'd be entitled to offer some criticism. But none of them happens to have an inkling of the kind of boundless and noble passion that is a part of me from day to day and literally moment to moment.

Then those two got the brilliant idea of heading on back to the mall on some kind of beaver hunt, and Kenny actually had the nerve to suggest to me that maybe if I got myself laid, it'd help take my mind off my problems. "What problems?" I said to him, and he just clammed up. I'd obviously put him in his place and made him realize he was contending with a genius here, and not some stupid moron. Despite my better judgment, I did go back with them to the mall and hung out with them. What helped me get through the better part of the day was the coke Vince sold me, and when I started to feel myself winding down later on, I bought a couple of pills off him and got back on track.

Later we drove to McDonald's, the three of us in my car once again, and Kenny starts complaining about how he needs to get laid real fast, and then Vince goes and says he never has a problem finding girls that want to go to bed with him.

"I was with this chick once," he was saying to us at one point, "who was so nuts about me, she even started following me around like a little puppy-dog till I told her she needed to see a shrink real fast, and that was the end of it."

I wanted to tell him that I knew exactly what it was like to be stalked – except in my case, it was a different kind of stalking, of course – so, I kept my mouth shut while Kenny picked up on what Vince had been saying, only in Kenny's case, you'd think he was the prime stud of the century – at least, according to him. How some guys wind up with such over-inflated opinions of themselves is something I'll never even begin to understand.

A short while later, a couple of the high school girls Kenny and I used to know showed up. I thought they were going to walk right past us, but then stupid-balls Kenny goes and waves at them to get their attention, and they decide to come over and start talking with us. One of them – Sherry Day – looks me over, and out of the blue, she says to me," Boy, you look like shit." I wanted to tell her I felt like shit, too, but I didn't like her attitude, so what I did was basically ignore her as much as I could. But it was embarrassing to have to sit there and listen to her go on and on about how she used to think I was so cute and now she couldn't understand how I could've gone downhill so fast.

"It's the drugs," Soft-in-the-Head Kenny tells her.

"Oh, yes," Sherry's side-kick joins in in a prissy voice. "I've read that extended usage of marijuana and other hallucinogens can actually accelerate the aging process of one's skin, and can even have a debilitating effect upon one's metabolism." Or something like that.

I was getting ready to say," Up your metabolism, you scuzz," when suddenly I saw, out of the corner of my eye, that Wayne's van had pulled into the parking lot.

I didn't feel too nervous, you see, because there were two other guys with me, not to mention Sherry and her pal, and I figured even a prime moron like Wayne Brown wouldn't dare start anything with me, being outnumbered the way he was. And then, when I noticed he shut his engine off and turned his headlights off and still didn't get out of his van, I realized I was getting nerved up over absolutely nothing. McDonald's was pretty crowded, and so was the parking lot. I didn't think he'd been able to spot my car so easily along with all those others, unless he'd been following me around all day, or something. But then I wondered why he wasn't getting out of his van and coming inside to get something to eat. Instead, he seemed to be just sitting there behind the wheel, not making any move to get out of the van.

In the meantime, those other four were have a jolly old time talking about nothing in particular. I could tell Kenny was getting his rocks off, though, because Sherry was batting her stupid eyelashes at him and leaning way over him with her disgusting boobs nearly pouring out of her blouse. Even Vince seemed to be eating up all the attention those two chicks were giving us, and I just sat there munching on fries and wondering, with the passing of each individual second, when Wayne was going to start up his engine, roll out of the parking lot, and get his stinking butt as far away from me as possible. If he'd looked in and seen me sitting there with Kenny and Vince, he would have figured it would be supremely stupid of him to entertain the notion of confronting me with the same crap he'd used on me those other three times.

But no such luck. He just sat there without making his move, looking so cool about everything, and I'm sitting there with Kenny and the others, perspiring like never before and wishing I could just melt into thin air on the spot. Then Kenny gets up, saying he's going up to the counter for another burger, but when he gets up there, I can see him motioning for me to get up and join him up there at the counter. I took one quick look out the window to make sure Wayne wasn't making any moves, then joined Kenny and asked him what was up.

"Gimme the keys to your car, man," Kenny says to me. "I'm gonna fuck Sherry."

Here I am, sweating bricks wondering whether I'm going to live to see the dawning of a new day, and all Kenny's got on his depraved mind is that equally depraved sex life of his.

"I can't do it, buddy," I said to him. "Not right now."

"Don't be a bone-head all your life," Kenny then said to me. "Just gimme the keys before you catch a smack."

Well, I had too much on my mind to stand there and argue, so before I knew what I was doing, I handed him the car keys, then shuffled back over to our table with Kenny, and we sat down again and started shooting the breeze like before. Around five minutes later, Kenny and Sherry got up and started moving towards the exit, five minutes after that the scuzz moves off to another table to sit all by herself, and that leaves me and Vince alone, with that dangerous psychopath still sitting out there in his van and I'm about to start hemorrhaging at any second.

Sure enough, Vince gets this sudden urge to smoke a joint, suggesting the two of us go outside around back and do it while we're waiting for Kenny to get back with my car. I needed the buzz really bad, but I wasn't about to take any chances going out there and having Wayne creep up on me from behind and try doing something fancy to my head. No, what it boiled down to was this: I had to tell Vince about Wayne being outside in his van, probably waiting there with the intention of starting a beef with us. I said "us" just in case Vince jumped to the conclusion that I was scared on my own account and not his. After all, I've got my pride, you see.

Then we got up, and Vince kind of hitched his trousers higher up around his waist and said," No problem, man. If he wants a beef, he'll get one. C'mon." And I felt a great deal of relief when he said that and started striding towards the exit. Like I wrote in my diary last night, Vince is at least six feet tall and looks to be pretty tough, so I figured that, if worse came to worst, I could let Vince handle Wayne for me, and I wouldn't have to worry about getting my pretty face bruised like he did to me the last time he attacked me without warning.

And that's pretty much the way it all started out, too. The two of us walked outside, Vince right out there a little ahead of me, acting real nonchalant, and sure enough, Wayne spots us right away and steps out of his van to intercept us.

Vince didn't back down from him for a second, man, but goes right up to him and says if Wayne's got a problem, then he (Vince) is exactly the man who'll straighten it out for him. Wayne must have thought he was acting pretty slick just then, however, because he walked right on past Vince, even going so far as to bump his shoulder against him when he did that.

Vince called him a bastard and swung at the back of his head. I don't know, man. I don't know if Wayne had radar attached to the back of his head, or what, but he swung around, before Vince had a chance to hit him, and knocked him in the jaw.

As soon as I saw Vince hit the dirt, I started running for my car. Then, in a frenzy, I remembered that Kenny had borrowed it and wasn't back yet from his massive sex-session with Sherry Day. But it didn't matter. I kept running, anyway, but before I actually knew what was happening, Wayne was right behind me, and he grabbed me by the elbow and then threw me against the side of McDonald's. When I cried out for help, he took me by the throat and pinned me against the wall with his other fist cocked.

I'll never forget it, man. I'll never forget the way he looked me in the eye and snarled at me all kinds of bullshit. Everything he said was a lie. Everything he accused me of, while he held me pinned against the wall, was an outright lie! I never meant anyone any harm, least of all *her!* I choked out at him that it wasn't my fault. How was I to know she was going to slash her wrists in a hot tub of water? None of it was my fault. None of it!

I wanted to tell him all this. To tell him I loved her and never meant her any harm, but he had me by the throat, so I could barely get a word out to defend myself. He just stood there with his fist cocked and accused me of all sorts of bullshit. I felt like puking all over him. He was so full of it! – And me? All I'm full of is this immense love that I have for her, but I had to stand there, pinned to the wall, and listen to him fling accusations in my face.

Then it started.

First, he started punching my face. Then he started in on my stomach. Then my ribs. Then my face again.

When he left me, I don't know why, but I could hear that he was sobbing. The fool!

I stumbled over to the back of McDonald's and began vomiting. Christ, I must have stayed there for at least a half hour. Each time I'd hurl and think I was all through, then I'd start feeling sick all over again and start hurling some more.

Finally, I'm kneeling on the ground in my own puke, and Kenny and Vince both come up to me. Kenny's looking down at me, too, with this kind of half-grin on his face, and Vince is holding his hand to his jaw, looking dazed as all hell.

"He's dead meat!" I screamed up at them. "I want to see him dead! You hear me? I want him dead inside of the next week!"

"He's dead meat, all right," I heard Vince say. "Nobody knocks me down like that and gets away with it."

I told them Wayne's address. I also told them where he works, too, and Vince assures me he'll be dead meat within a week or so – or maybe two or three weeks, he wasn't too sure when he'd get around to doing it. But it would get done, for sure!

And that was that.

So, now I know what I have to do. I have to concentrate all my energies on seeing Wayne's ass fried within the next week. Within the next week, I intend to see him laid out on a slab in the morgue. So, my angel will just have to forgive me if I spend a little less time with her for a few days. But I know for sure, man, that my primary objective in life right now is to make sure that that bastard gets what he deserves. And inside of a week, too!

Or maybe, with any luck, by the end of the month.

Or before the spring thaw, at any rate.

BETSY'S DIARY – July 4, 1985

Dear Diary: As I write these lines tonight, I can hear the fireworks still sounding in the distance. It is a warm summer evening, and we have all the windows open. The night is simply glorious this time of year, and pretty soon I'll be hearing the crickets chirping outside when the fireworks cease completely and I know that a wonderful peace will envelop me when that happens.

The day went extremely well. We had a little cookout late this afternoon out on the patio. While I was quite busy running around trying to keep everyone's appetite satisfied and making sure I didn't burn the hamburgers or hot dogs that were on the grill, I still managed to have a wonderful time. My good humor was heightened, of course, by the fact that Monica and Carl were able to join us. Although I didn't get much of a chance to speak with Monica, either in private or in front of all of the others, it was so good to see her. She seemed rather spirited, in fact, possibly more of a chatterbox today than she's ever been. Why, she practically dominated every conversation, keeping all topics on a very impersonal level, but still looking as bright-eyed as ever. It was such a joy to have everyone here. Not only did Aunt Lucille come by with two of her friends from work, but Mom also had invited Rick Sellars. This was the first time I had ever met him, and I must say he seemed nice enough. From a physical point of view, he struck me as being very different from Pop. Whereas Pop was tall and slim with dark brown hair, Rick is about medium height but rather on the husky side, with wavy, light brown hair and a full mustache. Mom was certainly in her element today, clinging to him quite a bit, and I suspect, when Aunt Lucille and her friends arrived, Mom became even more affectionate with Rick Sellars, almost as if she wished to prove something to Aunt Lucille as to her obvious ease in attracting men. I'm sure Aunt Lucille sensed this, especially since she hasn't had a man in her life in about ten years. I feel sorry for her, in a way. Although she doesn't have the figure Mom has and doesn't dress quite as stylishly as she might, she's really such a sweet and loving person. I'm sure any man would be proud to be seen with her. In fact, I mentioned it to my aunt casually enough, I thought, that she had so many years ahead of her, I was sure she would meet someone as nice and good-looking as Rick Sellars someday soon. Aunt Lucille didn't exactly snap at me when I said that, but I could tell she regarded my opinion with a certain degree of contempt, so I quickly dropped the subject.

Carl was very helpful. For one thing, he gave me a hand with the grill when it occasionally appeared that I had my hands full. He even offered to do some of the cooking himself, but I told him not to be so silly. After all, he may be one of the family now, but he's still entitled to be treated as a guest in our home. Even after we'd all had our fill of food, he came over and gave me a hand with the clean-up. There were a few moments when I felt a bit nervous, like a couple of times when I thought he was staring at me for no particular reason that I could fathom.

Monica looked gorgeous, though. She had her dark brown hair pulled back, and the cute outfit she had on really showed her trim figure to good advantage. She actually looks a little older than her eighteen years, but I mean the remark in only the most flattering sense. It's hard to believe that, only a few short years ago, she seemed like a helpless, naïve young girl who became very alarmed over having started her first period. I remember how I had to hold her in my arms and kind of rock her back and forth as I re-assured her that nothing was wrong with her, just as though she were my own daughter. Naturally, we have lost that physical closeness over the intervening years, and in a way, I miss it. But I know that my being able to see her looking so fully mature and womanly is more than adequate compensation for the need I have recently felt to pretty much let go of the reins, so to speak, a little bit more than I would have liked.

It's hard to believe, but Ellen, too, looked rather cheerful. She has always been exceptionally pretty, and I know that, before the accident, she had several boyfriends. Lord knows there were times when she didn't get home till well after midnight, and I'd be waiting downstairs for her, nervous as a cat about to give birth to a litter of kittens. I knew that Ellen would resent my concern for her safety, just as she often did when she'd come waltzing in way past her curfew. But I was willing to put up with her verbal abuse and her disrespectful attitude because I was always afraid that there might be an accident. I know how terrible it was for her and for all of us last Memorial Day weekend when she didn't come home at all, and we received a call in the middle of the night that she'd been involved in a car crash. Well, we hadn't expected her to come home that night anyway because Mom had let her have the whole weekend with Lisa and some other friends of hers. Then, when I finally had a chance to see my baby sister in the hospital soon afterwards, she glared up at me from her hospital bed and accused me of *wishing* the accident on her. She claimed that my constant fretting over the possibility of her being injured in a car accident had put the jinx on her or something, and that it was all my fault. Of course, I realize now that I could hardly be held accountable for what had happened to her, but at the time, I recall having been consumed by guilt. And I blamed myself for several days afterwards for, in some mysterious way, being responsible for the whole awful tragedy.

But enough of that. And enough of the cookout. I have to relate, now, what happened earlier in the day which accounts for the light-headed mood I was in later.

I had awakened, feeling a bit tense because today was a holiday, and that meant Mom would be around all day long to pressure me into doing all sorts of impossible things with my time. I was also a bit on edge because last night I vowed that, after seeing Wayne and Charlene together and feeling all sorts of discomfort as a consequence, I would not go back to the hospital today to see how he was coming along. I was on edge because I knew that, despite my promise, emotional weakness and insecurity were liable to get the better of me and I might wind up breaking the promise I had made to myself and then hate myself afterwards.

Well, as it turned out, I was doing some cleaning in the kitchen, trying to be very quiet, too, since Mom was still asleep and I didn't want to disturb her. Suddenly the kitchen phone rang, and I answered it. Our conversation was so brief and free of superfluous comments that I believe I can now relate it verbatim:

"Hi," I heard a low, masculine voice say. "Betsy?"

"Yes?" I said, not really having recognized his voice but hoping with everything I had inside of me that it was him.

"Hi," he said once again, without raising his voice the least little bit. "How's it going?"

"Fine. And you? How are you doing?"

"I'm O.K."

There was a pause. A long pause, in fact, and I felt my knees shaking as I asked myself: Where do we go from here?

Then he said," What are you doing right now?" I told him that I was simply doing a little housework, and again there was silence. Not the kind of silence that spoke volumes, as they say, because we obviously weren't discussing any key issues at the moment. Then, when it appeared that he wasn't going to say anything, I steadied myself with an effort and took the plunge.

"Would you like to have some company?"

There was another pause, but not a very long one by any means, before he said Yes, and I do believe that I shot out the door within two or three minutes. That is, I did run upstairs to get my hand-bag and car keys and so forth. Then, like a fool, I brushed my hair in the mirror, even though I'd just finished brushing it less an hour ago just after I'd taken my shower. I didn't have any make-up on and, no doubt, looked quite wretched, but I really wasn't thinking rationally at the time. Now that I look back on it, I was so silly and immature. I'm twenty-one years old, consider myself to be fairly level-headed, and yet, I had obviously lost my bearings for a few moments. And to think, I even left the house without leaving a word with either Mom or Ellen as to where I was going or for how long I expected to be out. The truth of the matter is I don't think I really knew what I would have said, even if I had left a note.

At any rate, I was seized with a sudden desire to do something extravagant on his behalf. Just my luck, it was a holiday today, and all the shops nearby were closed, but I did manage to find that the general store a few blocks away was open, so I went inside and picked up a few auto-mechanic type magazines, not being the least bit familiar with the type of literature I was looking over when I decided to bring them to the counter and pay for them. Then I recalled having seen a pack of Kool cigarettes on the table next to his bed, so I purchased a couple of packs of those. For all I knew, I was behaving like an incredible scatter-brain, but I just don't think I could have functioned for the rest of the day if I were to walk into his room, empty-handed.

It was all quite worth it, I believe. When he saw me walk into his empty room, I do think he wanted to smile even though it wouldn't be fair of me to say that he actually did do just that. I felt nervous upon entering, and didn't know exactly how I should greet him, so I simply said Hi, and he said Hi back to me. Then, at a complete loss for words, I opened the bag I was holding and pulled out the two packs of cigarettes. "Betsy," he said in some surprise when he saw what I was holding. I smiled and said something stupid about not being sure if they were the right brand, although I knew fully well that it was of no consequence. Then I gave him the magazines and, again, stammered out something to the effect that I didn't know if he'd be interested in them or perhaps had already seen those particular issues. All he did was say "Betsy" again, but he never looked at me. To tell the truth, I was kind of mystified over his inability to look up at me and smile, which is something I suppose I would have done, had I been in his position.

But I felt, at the same time, that I ought to take his rather odd manner in stride, because the fact of the matter was that he *had* taken it upon himself to call me and, in a way, expressed a desire to see me. That, in itself, was probably the most demonstrative gesture I could expect from him, so I tried not to let it upset me when he continually failed to establish eye contact with me or even permit himself to smile openly in my presence.

As soon as he had the magazines in his hands, he rapidly flipped through the first one, then put it aside and opened up the other one. I stood quietly and watched him for a few minutes, then decided that I might feel a little less tensed-up if I sat down, so I did. About halfway through the second magazine, he lighted upon an article that appeared to spark his interest. He looked at the page, frowned, and then leaned his head back against his pillows and appeared to be in some discomfort. He closed his eyes, and I thought maybe he was experiencing some physical pain in his shoulder, so I asked him if anything was wrong. He didn't answer me for the longest time. Then, with his eyes still closed, he folded up the magazine and just let it lie there on his lap. I continued to sit quietly. At one point I thought he might've drifted into sleep without my being aware of it at first. Then when I got up from my chair and went to take the magazine from his lap, he reached out slowly and took my wrist, and then he opened his eyes and appeared to be looking down at my hand.

"I'll read you the article, Wayne," I said to him, instinctively understanding the source of his discomfort.

He then let go of my wrist and opened up the magazine to the page he had been trying to read. I pulled my chair closer to the side of his bed and read the article out loud to him while he lay there quietly and listened. I read page after page, not even comprehending what I was reading, but he never told me to stop, so I continued for quite a long stretch of time until I finished first one, then another, and finally a third article.

"I really do enjoy reading," I told him at the end of the third article," but my eyes are getting a little tired. And maybe you'd rather just rest and have me leave you alone."

He didn't answer me, so I closed up the magazine and rose from my seat to put it on the dresser next to his bed. And it was as I stood close to his side that I felt his hand reaching for my arm once again, and with his eyes half-closed, he touched my hand, and I quite instinctively took his hand in mine and squeezed it firmly. With my other hand, I reached over and stroked his forehead which was damp with perspiration, pulling some of his curls away from the glistening

165

skin and smiling down at him as a mother would smile down upon a sleeping child.

"You are beautiful, Betsy," he said to me in a very low voice, and we remained perfectly still after he said that. The tears struggled to come out of my eyelids, but I fought them back because I saw no reason to shed them. I only saw a reason to keep still, perfectly still, and to drink in the beauty of that moment.

It wasn't until sometime later that I released his hand, and I gently loosened the soiled bandanna that was still around his neck from the other day and replaced it with one of the new ones I had given him yesterday. I took extreme care to knot it perfectly and then to adjust it around his neck so that it nestled at his throat, slightly off-center.

He is a handsome man. His hair is curly. And golden, just like the sun and like newly harvested wheat. The complexion of his face is golden, too, without a single mark or blemish. And he has full lips and a dimpled chin that is marked by strength and determination. And yet, for all the strength that he seems to project, what I find all the more appealing in him is his aura of child-like simplicity. Although he has not allowed me to look into his eyes just yet, I pray that someday soon he will grant me that awesome privilege because I sense, almost intuitively, that I will see in those eyes of his a reflection of myself – or rather, I should say, a reflection of how I would most ardently wish to appear in his sight.

I didn't stay too much longer after I finished adjusting the brand-new bandanna around his neck. I had been standing there looking down upon his motionless form for so long that I didn't even realize, when his hand had begun to relax in mine, that he was falling asleep. So, I quietly turned, picked up my hand-bag, and started for the doorway; but when I walked across the threshold, I turned to look back at him for a moment.

He had his head turned away from me so that he faced out towards the window, and he was lying completely still, bathed in the sunlight that flooded the room via the window opposite him, and his hair looked completely yellow on his scalp. He looked as though he were basking in the comfort of some special, almost otherworldly serenity.

When I went back to the hospital to visit him later on in the day, I never made it into the room, and I doubt that he was even aware that I was standing just outside his threshold. I was afraid to enter because there was a man standing opposite him, dressed in rather grimy-looking work clothes, and he was glaring down at Wayne and pointing his index finger at him in a rather menacing fashion. He was of medium height but quite ruggedly built, like Wayne, and had the same curly blond hair. I couldn't see his eyes, but I heard his voice as he pointed his index finger at Wayne and said," If that broad is pregnant, then it's your problem, not mine. You just remember that."

I backed away the instant I saw that the man was making as if to leave the room. I was afraid of the anger that was in his voice and of the way he'd been thrusting his finger in Wayne's direction in such a forceful and threatening manner. I held myself against the wall next to the doorway to his room, so nervous that my ears suddenly seemed to have become blocked up. Then a moment later, the man came storming out of the room, and I was able to catch a glimpse of his face.

The fierceness that was in his blue eyes frightened me. He was Wayne's father. He looked just like Wayne. And he had the most horrible expression in his eyes. It was intense. Just too, too intense.

I was so scared that I left after only a brief moment of indecision. If this man's eyes could convey such intensity, then with what fierce and impetuous a look would Wayne greet me if I were to walk in just then and experience the shock of having him suddenly raise his own eyes to my face? For the very first time!

No. I decided right then and there. If Wayne were to bring his eyes to meet mine, I would want them to be filled with tenderness, not anger. And if his look were destined to be intense, then let it be intensely passionate. That, I could endure. Anything else, I was afraid to confront.

When I returned home, I gradually applied myself to the business of getting the grill heated and all the food straightened out, and then all the good memories of my earlier visit with Wayne started to come back to me, and I found myself in a buoyant mood. Like I said before, the cookout was a great success, and I'm so happy that I didn't say or do anything stupid to annoy Mom and cause her to criticize me in front of the others. She was with Rick Sellars, and I expect that she was primarily concerned with creating a good impression for him in front of the family.

Now it is time for me to sleep. Already the sounds of the fireworks have subsided considerably, and something of the peace of this beautiful and heavenly summer night is beginning to seep alluringly into my system. I thank God for the bewitching beauty of my surroundings, for the beauty of the heavens, and the beauty of the earth and sea. And I thank God for having given me my first breath, so that I may now live and partake of the richness of being alive here on this earth.

P.S. Why did he say that I was beautiful? I know I'm not. Far from it, I would say. Ellen is beautiful, and Monica is, too. They're the ones he should be calling beautiful, not me.

P.P.S. Nevertheless, I *felt* beautiful when he said it.

CYCLE FOUR

MONICA'S MEMOIRS – April 13, 1986

It is cold and damp and dismal in here tonight. It's supposed to be
warmer this time of year; and yet, nothing seems to be going
according to nature's plan. Nature is supposed to be so powerful a
phenomenon, and although the calendar may have us all believing
that springtime is upon us, there are no guarantees that a warm day
in March will necessarily herald even warmer days in April. There
are no guarantees at all that such things should happen with any kind
of logic. Nature has a tendency to deceive us at various and
unexpected times, as if God Himself wishes to remind us all that He
can do just as He pleases. He can bring a raging snowstorm into the
area in the middle of July, if He so wishes, and there's not a damned
thing any of us can do about it either. He can send this planet
hurtling towards the sun, and we must all deal with it somehow and
go scrambling towards the North Pole in some foolish, pig-headed
attempt to simply delay our inevitable incineration. And – again –
there's nothing we can do about it. He can cause monsters like me to
come out of the womb to contaminate the environment, and then He

takes away those who are pure and without the stain of sin. And there's nothing we can do about that, either. Nothing anybody can do about it.

If I could have had my way, I never would have turned my back on her. Hell, if I could have had my way, I never would have allowed myself to spring forth from my mother's womb. But I didn't know any better, of course. Nature forced me to spring into existence, to take in my first independent breaths of life, and to grow stronger and more independent and self-sufficient with the passage of each year. And the priests told us that we were lucky to be alive, that life itself was a precious gift, and we should thank the Lord for having given us the opportunity to live and get to know Him and experience His loving kindness. Aunt Lucille used to take the three of us to church on cold, damp Sunday mornings – mornings when I, for one, would have preferred to remain huddled in the warmth of my bed sheets – and she'd tell us that it was our duty to attend Mass. That we owed it to our Savior in gratitude for all the wonderful gifts that had been bestowed upon us. And I swallowed it all. I listened to her, too, when she told me I had a responsibility to live my life to the fullest and not complain if the going got rough. I would be making her, Mom, and even God and all the priests in the parish happy by being a good girl and getting good grades in school and then marrying a fine, upstanding, morally upright young man and populating the earth with children. And there was nothing I could do about it.

Well, I did do something about it, didn't I? I attended Mass, just as I was expected to, and I achieved high honors upon high school graduation. Oh, yes, I was a good girl, wasn't I? They even voted me Most Likely to Succeed. And there was no finer, more morally upstanding boy in the whole graduating class than Carl Peters, and he told me he loved me. And even Betsy told me that we made such a handsome couple. Yes. I was considered moderately good-looking.

I even held onto my virginity despite the efforts of a few aggressive adolescents in my tenth, eleventh, and twelfth grade classes. And when Carl kissed me in front of the justice-of-the-peace, with Betsy watching, flushed with excitement and filled with teary-eyed happiness – at the moment when Carl held me in his arms and implanted his first tender husbandly kiss upon my lips, I said to myself: "They were right. This is it. I have done what they all wanted me to do. I have been a good girl and a devout Christian, and now I am going to go forth and populate the earth."

I remember, too, how I trembled in his embrace, and continued to tremble during the long drive up to our little love-nest in New Hampshire. And I thought to myself: "This is it. I am an independent woman now. And the man of all men is going to make love to me with all the fervor and passion that all young men crave to call their own."

I remained a virgin that night. And the next night, too. And I am a virgin to this day. And the significance of that fact ceases to stun, puzzle, or even grieve me. It is simply an accepted fact. Where does it say in the Books that such a state should necessarily be condemned? And even if my still being a virgin at this point in my life is actually deemed unnatural by anybody of any consequence, isn't it nothing compared to the other atrocities I have been guilty of?

Oh, God! The atrocity of all atrocities is that I'm still alive! I'm sick. I know that. It's sick for a person to want to die, isn't it? For thoughts of suicide and self-inflicted harm to be stronger and more obsessive than one's natural instincts for self-preservation. But I have stopped believing what Aunt Lucille told me all those years ago. I have ceased to put any credence whatsoever in the delusions all those priests fed my brain with. And those know-nothing classmates of mine, in their complete ignorance, entertained the far-fetched notion that I was most likely to succeed, basing their judgment on their belief that I had good grades, good looks, and what they thought to be a good personality, too. So, they stupidly appointed themselves as the all-knowing clairvoyants of Maplewoods High School, deluding themselves into thinking that there would be any guarantee at all that their predictions could come true, simply because the scant evidence at their disposal seemed, to them, to be so all-convincing. What are they all saying now? How can they look one another in the face, after what has become of me, and admit that they made such a gross and obscene error in judgment? Well, they were partially correct, you might say. It would genuinely appear that I *was* most likely to succeed – to succeed in screwing up my whole life as well as those of a few other people!

It's Sunday, and I long to go back to the days when the three of us would run through the park on a Sunday afternoon while Mom and Aunt Lucille sat around and talked about men, Mom talking about her romantic exploits and Aunt Lucille warning her about all the pitfalls that spread themselves out before women like Mom who regarded men as mere playthings, instead of the treacherous demons she herself knew them to be. Or if it were raining out, they'd take us to the mall where Aunt Lucille would win Ellen over with gifts of all sorts and maybe a doll or two for me and a book for Betsy, which was all she wanted anyway, and Mom would drift off, terrifying me with the thought that she had taken advantage of an opportunity to escape from our family for good and seek her true happiness with some good-looking stranger. Then she wouldn't have to be burdened with the three of us ever again for the rest of her life.

Even then, I knew that her principal interest in life lay in the pursuit of sensual pleasure and nothing else. She was always attractive. Alluring, even, in those tight slacks and low-cut blouses she donned on nearly every occasion. She amazed me with her sheer stamina in being able to draw men towards her, as though she wasn't even aware of it half the time but took it for granted the same way we all take breathing for granted, for example. And I'll admit I was a little jealous of her. And I knew, after I married Carl and discovered that I had absolutely no sex appeal, that I wasn't even in her league.

But what does it matter after all? The reasons why I married Carl were far different from the impulses which prompted her to seek out her sex partners. I call them "sex partners" because that was exactly what they were, and I'll grant her the fact that she never pretended, not even in front of me or Aunt Lucille, that they were anything else. I knew, the minute I met Rick Sellars and saw the way she was all over him out on our patio last Fourth of July, that the bond they shared was based purely on the supercharged sexual attraction they felt for each other. Yes, I even saw how aroused he became when, perched on top of his knee, Mom leaned back to put her arm around his shoulders and push her breasts against his chest. And I thought to myself: How much power she must have over him, that she can cause him to become sexually aroused with such little effort on her part; and at the same time, I'm so inept that even my most earnest and energetic attempts at romancing my own husband in our wedding bed could produce no such reaction from him. And I couldn't believe that our lack of success in the bedroom could possibly be connected with some sort of failing or impotence on his part, not after he threw in my face the allegation that he had been enjoying sex with multiple partners for over five years and that all these nubile wonders of nature had never failed to arouse him. Naturally, it was all my fault. How could it possibly be his?

Seeing my own inadequacies as compared to my mother's prodigious talents blatantly flaunted before me, I drowned myself that afternoon in stupid chatter and idle banter. I even tried to walk provocatively about the patio, thinking that I could somehow assume an air of such self-assured confidence in my own womanhood that Carl might sit up and take notice and, on that very evening, make long and passionate love to me in our bed, hot with the remembrance of how stimulating it had been for him to watch me in front of all those other people all afternoon. The only thing I succeeded in doing, however, was inciting his anger. When we returned to the apartment, he instantly accused me of acting like a tramp in front of the entire family. "Who did you think you were turning on with that grand performance of yours?" he furiously demanded, and when I said," Nobody," I perhaps gazed back at him a little too intensely, and that's when he backhanded me.

I had never been struck before this. I had never known violence, first-hand, but my beloved husband had to be the one who introduced me to feelings of pain that I had only heard about and imagined about, though I never thought such sensations would ever become a part of my own life. Not even Mom, what with all her erratic behavior during my upbringing, had ever raised her hand against me. If she inflicted pain upon me, it was through neglect rather than out-and-out physical violence. No, she never struck me with her hands or fists, and violence of this kind was alien to my existence. It happened to other people, other families. Not me. But the man I loved, the man with the fiery dark eyes – the man my blind classmates took to be the one with the best personality – he had to be the one who struck me in the face with the back of his hand and, in so doing, inducted me into the world of violence and the disintegration of all that I had always regarded as sane and logical. And in that moment when the back of his hand flew across my cheek, I cried out for the first time in my life in a voice that was not my own. The sound that came from my throat just then was the most awful and unnatural sound I thought I was ever capable of producing. Little did I realize, at that all so distant point in time, that I would henceforth produce even more horrible and unnatural sounds and perform even more horrible and unnatural acts. As soon as I became an inhabitant of the world of violence, I adapted to my surroundings with surprising ease; and in doing this, I closed up my heart. I ceased to view the outside world with the same awe-struck sense of joy and wonderment that I was accustomed to. As my heart became acquainted with perversity, I could no longer understand the things I had always accepted as real and true and good. I could no longer respond to the purity of a moonlit night in the forest, and my heart no longer responded to the glow of innocence and warmth that constantly radiated from her saintly being.

I will never see her again. I won't even allow myself to be admitted to her presence, even if the powers of Heaven were to compel me to stand before her. I have lost her forever, and my mind cannot cope with it at all. My mind cannot even begin to grasp the horrifying immensity of her absence.

When I lay on the couch after the funeral and flung my head all the way back and groaned so horribly that even Aunt Lucille lost control and let her tears spill down upon me while she sought to free me from the iron grip that insanity already had upon my being – In that moment, I came to understand the utter finality represented by my never being able to see her again. And I could not deal with it. Not then. Not now. Not ever.

Whatever happens to me, however my life ends, even should the saints themselves dictate all else to the contrary, I will never be able to face her. I will never find solace in the purity of her smile. I will never bask in the sunlight afforded by her radiant soul. And I will never feel the gentle touch of her hand upon my brow, and in this, I can never experience my salvation.

My heart knows nothing but emptiness now, and my eyes crave sleep, forgetfulness, and oblivion. The violence is now over. I won't scream anymore. Neither my mind nor my vocal cords will allow it to happen ever again. I will simply resign myself to the emptiness of her absence, and the peace of the grave will be all that I will ever have the strength to long for, from now on. Oh, how tired I am! How exhausted I am from accomplishing nothing and amounting to even less than nothing. After all, isn't that what it all signifies? Nothing?

Peace. Sterile and elusive peace. Descend upon me and help me to forget that, just as love, joy, and sanity are no longer possible for me, it may very well be that peace, too, will ultimately be denied me as well.

BETSY'S DIARY – July 5, 1985

Dear Diary: I will retire to my bed soon, and I ardently pray that tonight's dreams will not be as frightening as the ones I had last night, although the events of the day and the mood they have created in me would lead me to expect even more disturbing dreams.

Last night I dreamt about Wayne's father. It's silly, I know, that I should have allowed myself to become so unsettled by the presence and appearance of a man who is a perfect stranger to me, who never even came face to face with me, let alone spoke to me – a man who appeared in my vision for only a few brief seconds, but a man whose awesome countenance and intense voice poured forth upon his son in such wrath that I can practically still hear it ringing in my ears. And that look! The look of those boiling blue eyes nearly scorched the walls on either side of him as he stormed down the hospital corridor after sending his bolts of lightning down upon his son just a few moments earlier. That look haunted me all last night, and I found that his fearsome presence invaded my subconscious to such an extent that he figured prominently in every dream I had all night long, rendering a certain frightening reality to each of them by virtue of his fiery gaze. When I awoke, I felt relieved that reality would soon dominate my thoughts and that there would be no need for him to appear to me today in physical form if I allowed myself to stay out of his path.

It was so early when I awoke that I was afraid to move about the house or take a shower for fear of awakening the others, so I stayed in bed and read for an hour or two. It wasn't until after I heard Mom stirring about and was finally convinced that she had gone to work that I roused myself into the routine actions of getting ready, physically, for the day. When I arrived downstairs, I found that Ellen was already up, too, sitting in the kitchen and munching on some toast. I made conversation with her by alluding to the wonderful cookout we'd had yesterday, hoping to draw out some compliment from her as to how lovely Monica looked and how splendidly everything in general had turned out. Her only observation, however, was that in her opinion Mom should get rid of Rick Sellars because he was too good for her. I laughed at her flippancy and started to say something to the effect that I thought the two of them were amazingly compatible, when Ellen made a very peculiar face and then appeared to be totally disinterested in the whole subject itself, so I dropped it and fixed myself something to eat. Within twenty minutes or so, Ellen and I ended up playing cards at the kitchen table. The weather was beautiful, and I wasn't sure what I wanted to do for the rest of the day. In fact, before I even was able to make a decision of any kind, the front doorbell rang, and then Aunt Lucille popped in, explaining that she had the day and the rest of the weekend off from work and had come by to see what we girls had planned. In her poor distress, my baby sister responded by saying that she had been planning on running in a marathon, and that started heated words between the two of them, prompting my immediate departure from the room.

It was still so early in the day, and already I felt the need to escape into the sedate and secure contours of the world my books had always allowed me to slip into. I felt like rushing up the stairs and devouring those books, hour after hour, in my bedroom and later finding, with a huge sense of relief, that it was once again time to retire for the night.

But I was living in the here and now, of course, and time wasn't going to go speeding by me just because I wanted it to. And so, it turned out that I gradually made my way back downstairs. By then, Ellen and Aunt Lucille had calmed down, and the three of us were sitting in the living room watching television, when I thought I caught a peek of a car pulling up in front of the house and then stopping. I rose from my seat and looked through the curtains of the front picture window, then instantly regretted that I had done so.

There were a man and a woman in the front seat of the car that had just stopped in front of our house, although the engine was still running. The woman was behind the wheel as the man leaned over and kissed her, and their embrace, at least on the part of the woman, seemed almost excessively passionate. She was a slim brunette – the one I had met briefly at the hospital – and her name was Charlene, and the man in the passenger seat beside her was blond-haired with a colorful red and blue bandanna around his neck.

I drew back and started to retrace my steps back to the couch. I guess I'd drawn away from the curtains a little too awkwardly because Aunt Lucille instantly asked me what was wrong and what was going on out there. I sat down and told her as quietly and unemotionally as I could that the painter was outside, and Aunt Lucille got up from her chair and hurried over to where I had been standing.

"What's he doing out there? I thought you people said he was laid up in the hospital with some kind of shoulder injury."

As it appeared that some response was expected from me, I hastily cleared my throat to answer her when the doorbell suddenly rang, and Aunt Lucille herself stepped over to open the front door.

Wayne stood on the other side of the screen door and mumbled something to Aunt Lucille, something I couldn't hear, partly because he didn't have his head raised to face her on an even level. His eyes, no doubt, were downcast, and he stood with one foot supporting more of his weight than the other, a stance that apparently led Aunt Lucille to take him for a punk because she quickly put her hands on her hips and spoke sharply to him.

"Well, when do you think that will be? It's taking forever to get this house painted. And I'll tell you another thing: I warned Jean from the outset that she would be making a big mistake, hiring you to do the work instead of a professional – somebody who knew what he was doing instead of spending his time falling off ladders and driving around the streets with promiscuous young women."

It was as though a knife were cutting right through me!

I wanted to leap from the couch and put my hand in front of her mouth to stop those atrocities from escaping her lips. I wanted to push her away from the threshold of the front door and hold my hands out to Wayne and tell him to go home and rest and come back when his shoulder was feeling better and that I would help him paint the house. I would get down on my hands and knees and do all the gardening myself. I just didn't want him to get hurt, and I didn't want him to have to stand there and suffer the abuse of a woman who was judging him harshly because she couldn't see past his bandanna, or past his stance, or even past his gender, for that matter!

But I sat quietly in my seat. And I fought the urge to clap my hands over my ears because I needed to hear him defend himself. I needed to hear what words he would choose to clear himself of any fault or wrongdoing. Most of all, I didn't want him to adopt the same hostile tone Aunt Lucille had chosen to use on him. No, that would be disrespectful and would only serve to re-enforce the negative feelings she already bore him. No. If only I could hear him gently tell her that he would try to come back and finish the work as soon as possible, and then she would calm down and agree that such an arrangement on his part would be prudent; and then perhaps she would even go so far as to apologize to him for having been uncivil. If only a little rational thought could be applied to the situation. Then I could be spared – and Wayne, too, could be spared. We could all be spared.

But no such gratifying conclusion was to result. Aunt Lucille's refusal to adopt a moderate tone of voice set him off, and before she could get out another word, I saw a flame rise in Wayne's cheeks, and he said to her, without either raising his eyes or the tone of his voice,

"If you don't want me around here, I'll load my gear into the van and clear out of here – for good."

Then he turned his back on us all and walked out of view, and I leaned back and sighed, feeling myself about to uncoil, only to be seized with a new and more intense dread as it then came upon me that, if Wayne intended to be true to the words he'd just spoken, then that could mean only one thing, and I had no way of dealing with it just then.

And neither can I deal with it at this very moment. I cannot understand what has happened to me in the short space of time that I have known him. I am afraid to give it a name, a tag, or a label, because the truth frightens me so much – the thought that I may have actually fallen in love with him terrifies me to the point that I almost wish to fall on my knees and pray that God might erase the events of this past week, erase them completely rather than compel me to acquaint myself with thoughts and feelings that I am so ill-equipped to deal with.

I could not possibly have fallen in love with him. I don't know what love is, have certainly never experienced it first-hand, and have even been told by my own mother that I wouldn't be able to handle it even if, through some freakish twist of fate, the opportunity to experience it should ever present itself to me.

I behaved like a fool all day long. I know it now, although I am certainly unable to discern an alternate path, even at this time, to the one that my actions took all day long.

As soon as Wayne left the front of the house, Aunt Lucille slammed the door shut and told both Ellen and me that she had been right all along, that Mom never should have allowed the likes of him to set foot upon our property, and that it was a good thing we'd never see him again, as she surely hoped Mom would agree that such an outcome must be considered best for all concerned. I glanced at Ellen while Aunt Lucille voiced her opinion on the matter, and it shocked me to see that my baby sister was actually smiling, as if gloating, along with Aunt Lucille, over a combined feeling of victory after having ousted an alien substance, as it were, from their immaculate environment.

It was just too much for me to bear, but I remained perfectly silent through all of it. I heard Charlene's car engine still purring outside, and a part of me wanted desperately to run out there and see if Wayne was with her, talking with her, kissing her, embracing her. And another part of me wanted to run out the back door instead and take him by the arm, should I find him in the act of getting all of his equipment back inside his van. I would take him by the arm and get him to listen to me. Get him to look me in the eye. Finally! Yes! Look me in the eye and listen to me as I told him that I didn't want him to leave. I wanted him to stay and finish painting the house. I wanted to be able to wake up tomorrow morning, to actually be awakened by the muffled sound of his ladder being propped up just outside my bedroom window. I wanted to be able to raise myself from my bed, walk over to the window, open it wide, and lean out to see the top of his golden head coming nearer and nearer, and for him to lift his face towards me, smiling and getting closer and closer, until our two faces would be so close that I wouldn't be able to do anything or think of anything except the expression of melting tenderness that would be in his eyes when I leaned down and took his face in my hands and planted my first welcoming kiss of love upon his lips.

There were so many things I wanted to do, so many things I wanted to tell him so that he wouldn't leave our house this morning, never to return. But I stayed on the couch and watched them gloat, and I put my hand over my face for a moment, very quietly and unobtrusively so that neither one of them would notice my distress, but then Ellen crisply demanded," What's the matter with you?" making the question sound more like an accusation than anything else, and in responding that there was nothing wrong with me at all, I betrayed too false an air of nonchalance, I guess, because Aunt Lucille walked over to me just then, actually took both my hands in her own, and said to me in a soft voice,

"Betsy, you don't know what it's like out there. Take it from me. I'm a mature woman. Some men will do anything to ingratiate themselves into a woman's bed, you know. My Arnie took advantage of me once, and then he ended up running out on me for that tramp from Elder Falls. Betsy," she added, laughing a little to mask her obvious pain," I loved that man. I trusted him. I would have married him if he had had the decency to ask me to, after I let him into my bed."

I turned my head away from her at that point because she then began to speak of Wayne, calling him "that bum" and implying that

183

if she hadn't sent him off packing, one day we would have discovered all our valuables missing from the house or all the windows broken or some other act of outright violence and vandalism. I remained silent with my head turned away, but I let her hold my hands, and it felt wonderful to think that she could still talk to me in gentle tones after having just unleashed her disgust upon Wayne.

In a few moments, we heard the slamming of his van doors being closed in the driveway, and Aunt Lucille let go of my hands and got up to walk over to the window. I stayed where I was seated and looked down at my hands. I noticed immediately that they were trembling, and I was afraid that Ellen would notice this and say something abusive, so I got up, too, and went into the kitchen.

Once alone, I leaned my back against the refrigerator and held my arms against my stomach. I didn't cry, nor did I close my eyes in pain, but my eyes, as if of their own accord – as if steered by the hand of God Himself – my eyes found their way over to the corner of the kitchen where Chippy used to sing on bright, sunny summer afternoons in her little cage when I was barely a teen-ager. She had been such a beautiful little bird, so dainty the way she would hop from one perch to another. Though Mom wouldn't let me take her out of her cage, I used to sneak downstairs in the middle of the night and take the cover off her tranquil little dwelling. And I would reach inside the cage, and Chippy would leap down from her perch to sit on my extended finger. And then I would slowly and carefully extract her from her little chamber and stroke her feathers. I was afraid that the slightest stirring in the air would disturb her, or that the least little pressure of my finger upon her body would ruffle the supreme fragility of her tender and innocent existence. So, I was careful, very careful, when I would raise her towards my face and, ever so slowly and delicately, bring her against my cheek, close my eyes, and dream that I had died and gone to Heaven with my little bird close to my loving touch.

I remembered all of this as I stood with my back against the refrigerator, listening to the van pull out of the driveway. I recalled how one day I came home from school, ran into the kitchen to see Chippy, and could not understand how it could be that the cage still stood in the corner of the room but with no Chippy inside. I remembered this incident quite vividly as the sound of the engine of Wayne's van gradually receded into the distance as he disappeared from our home. And I ran out that day, so many years ago, and Mom told me where the bird was because my mind, you see, could not conceive of her absence. My mind refused to accept the fact that my little Chippy was gone and that I'd never see her again and stroke her soft feathers and hold her precious little form against my cheek. The only little thing I had ever loved with all my heart, and she was gone.

I steadied myself against the refrigerator, now sure that Wayne's van was gone, and set about fixing lunch for the three of us. Ellen and Aunt Lucille were talking in the living room. I could hear the sounds of their excited chatter above the sound of the television set, and I said to myself: "Nothing has changed. Everything is the same as it's always been, and will always be this way, too."

We had lunch and played cards in the afternoon. Mom came home just when I was beginning to think I couldn't stand it any longer and wanted to be alone up in my room. I would write in my diary at four o'clock in the afternoon instead of the late evening hours as I usually did, because I planned on going to bed as soon as I finished writing in my diary no matter what time it happened to be. But Mom was home, and I had to get something together for us to eat. That meant I had to stay in the kitchen and listen to Aunt Lucille explain to her that she had "fired" the painter, and Mom didn't even act flustered about it, simply saying that "Betsy will have to finish the job, then,"

185

before leaving the kitchen to go upstairs to prepare herself for another big night out with Rick Sellars.

I came upstairs to my room shortly after finishing the dinner dishes in the sink. I had been debating all day long about calling Monica. I didn't quite know what I would tell her or even how I would go about broaching the subject of how I felt. But then I reminded myself that Monica had always been understanding and compassionate and that, even though she was younger than me, she might still be able to give me some advice on how I should handle my feelings.

Thus resolved, I called her apartment, and when Monica answered, I instantly detected a certain degree of uncertainty in her voice. I asked her how she was, and after some hesitation, she said she wasn't feeling well and that she hadn't even been to work all day on account of an extremely severe head-ache. I suggested that she might be cheered up by having some company, but she explained that she really didn't feel quite up to it. So, I calmly agreed that rest, peace, and quiet were probably more essential to a speedy recovery, and hung up the phone, only to sit quietly in the kitchen for a few moments after that.

Tomorrow is Saturday, I said to myself, and I have nothing to do.

Feeling thoroughly empty and spent, I raised myself from the chair I had collapsed into, took one last look at the telephone which was silent, of course, and came upstairs to my room.

It is only eight o'clock. I have no need to get up early tomorrow morning. But I want to go to bed and dream of absolutely nothing. I have no need to get up early, so I can sleep as late as I care to. Actually, I have no need to ever get up at all.

No, I must paint the house and do the gardening, as Mom requested. I must steep myself in work, keep every cell of my body engaged in some sort of activity if I am to ignore the emptiness within me. I must do as Mom asked and busy myself about the house all day tomorrow and all day the next day. I will do what they all want me to do. I will work and hopefully will forget this entire week that has just passed, and the final nothingness that has been its end result.

So. This is how it all ends. How stupid of me to have imagined a different outcome. This only proves my sheer inability to understand life and my perfect naivete in believing that I could have possibly meant anything – anything at all – to that young man who fell off a ladder and was lying helpless in a hospital bed for a couple of days.

This is how it ends, then. He's gone, and he'll never come back. It was nothing for him, I'm sure, to spend a couple of days in the hospital, undergoing minor surgery, and having a plain, naïve girl like me attend to him. He's used to having women constantly around him, I'm sure. He couldn't possibly have taken me seriously these past few days. He probably thought nothing of having Aunt Lucille send him on his way. He probably spent the rest of the day today with Charlene. That's probably why he didn't call me. I shouldn't have expected a phone call from him, anyway. He called once, yes. It's true. He called once because he was feeling a little down. A little lonely, I guess. He just wanted some company while he was in the hospital, that's all. Then when I came and stayed with him all those hours, he didn't give it another thought. I just helped fill up some empty time in the day for him, and that was it. He's gone now, and I'm sure he hasn't given another thought to that dull, unexciting woman who sat by his hospital bed yesterday morning and read to him out of an auto mechanic's magazine. This has all meant nothing to him, and I'm sure that he's forgotten all about me.

I was so stupid. I can see it now. Stupidly building up all of these trivial events in my mind as if they were of the most extraordinary consequence. I must get a grip on myself then and convince myself

187

of the folly of entertaining further thoughts on what may have happened if Aunt Lucille hadn't confronted him at our front door and sent him on his way. Why dwell on the if's of a situation? He's gone, and he'll never come back, and that's it.

Now, it would be such a vast and complete pleasure for me to simply lie down in bed tonight and sleep peacefully for a few hours. My mind and heart and body would relish such a state, and I would be eternally grateful to the good Lord for bestowing such tender kindness upon me during this time of such emotional distress in my life. Amen.

P.S. I must also remember Monica, Ellen, Mom, and Aunt Lucille in my prayers. Perhaps focusing on the needs of these loved ones of mine will help me to forget about all else. Because that's what I want to do more than anything else: Forget.

ELLEN'S MEMOIRS – December 26, 1985

Today Aunt Lucille took me to the mall, saying it would do me some good to get out of doors for a change. Out of doors! It was freezing out there today. The wind had really kicked up, too, and by the time we got from the car to the mall entrance, parking in the handicapped spot, of course, my hair was so messed up, I swear people started staring at me more because of that than on account of the spectacle I presented to them being wheeled around by a forty-year-old old maid who looked as though she ought to be wheeled around in a wheel-chair herself. Well, I can't complain. She did buy me a bottle of my favorite perfume, and even though I'll never get a chance to put any of it on for any special occasions, I can get a rush once in a while by just opening the bottle and sniffing it. The smell alone can transport me to those wonderful times I had last spring driving all the guys wild. Mostly Wayne, of course, although my redheaded stud-man Marty was always up for the occasion, to put it bluntly. Naturally, with my luscious lips, I never failed to drive that guy wild with excitement, even before we got down to business, which was practically every day there for a while – sometimes even two or three times a day, now that I think of it.

I always had a good build, too. I remember being one of the first girls in my class who had to wear a bra. Even Mom said it. Even when I was only eleven years old, I knew I'd end up having all the necessary ingredients to turn guys into wild animals the instant they saw me. That's why Marty always came back for more, over and over again, because he knew I'd always come through for him and make sure he walked away, totally satisfied and knowing that he could avail himself of my services any time he wanted.

But the first time I ever actually went all the way was with Wayne, and I always knew that first time would be a snap. There was even a time when Lisa and I took a couple of guys down her cellar, and we thought we were going to get laid for sure, only her stupid parents came home unexpectedly and the two wimps we had with us lost their nerve because they were afraid we were all going to get caught.

Well, I wasted too much time, that's all I can say. As soon as I entered junior high, even, I should have been having sex, because by the time Wayne came along, I was definitely over-ripe. I showed him a good time, too. I know it. And when I came home that night and it was already after two o'clock, Betsy was in the living room waiting for me as I was hours past my regular curfew. I couldn't help feeling somewhat embarrassed. I was sure the excitement of what had just happened to me was written plainly all over my face. But what was there to feel embarrassed about? I simply chose to take advantage of what Nature had given me by way of out-and-out sex appeal. And I'm sure – just as sure as I am that I'm sitting here right now, totally incapacitated – that my sisters would have done the same if things had been different.

Oh, Monica was certainly pretty. I'll give her that much. And she didn't have her head so much in the clouds as she always had her nose in her schoolbooks. She went with a few decent guys, and even Carl wasn't half-bad when it came to your basic good looks. But I wonder just how much of a woman she was when the lights were out, you know? Or how much of a man Carl was, for that matter. I do know I found it pretty hard to swallow when all that talk started up about what Carl was supposedly up to. And what he was even suspected for having done, too. There certainly was enough crap being thrown around here for a while, and it's a good thing Wayne never found out about it, or there would've been hell to pay. He would've kicked Carl's ass all over the streets of this sad town. But maybe he did find out about it, and maybe that's why Monica did what she did.

Oh, man, it's too confusing. I can't sort it all out, and I don't much care either. That was their problem, not mine. If only they hadn't all cared so much about everybody else's feelings. I had feelings, too, of course, but at least I was smart enough to face reality. For instance, I knew Wayne was still seeing Charlene on the side the whole time he was dating me – or seeing me on the side the whole time he was dating Charlene. It's hard to tell exactly what the hell was going on in that brain of his.

I was glad I'd put him in the hospital. I actually put him out of commission for a few days. And oh, it was so touching the way Betsy reacted when Aunt Lucille gave him his walking papers. She didn't say a word or try to stop Aunt Lucille, but I could tell she was hurt. She always knew how to get to Aunt Lucille, so after Wayne left, she put on that pathetic pout of hers and Aunt Lucille went over and told her Wayne was no good, and then Betsy ran into the kitchen. Probably cried her stupid eyes out, for all I know. It was laughable. Really stupid! I mean, here was a girl who knew nothing about sex, who knew nothing about anything, really, and she put on a little pout because she thought Aunt Lucille was treating him unfairly. I could see right through that dumb sister of mine. She was trying to play on our sympathies, all right, but it didn't work. Aunt Lucille didn't follow her into the kitchen, and neither did I, naturally. She probably thought we'd all go running to her to comfort her. She was probably furious, too, when her little display of distress didn't have its desired effect upon us.

I remember years ago when she came home from school and found out her stupid bird had died. Man, oh, man. You might've thought the whole earth had caved in, the way she carried on. But she didn't succeed in gaining any sympathy from me or Mom, that's for sure. I know for a fact that Mom was about as sick of that smelly little thing as I was. She didn't have to tell me how she felt. I could tell. It was almost as though she and I had a special connection – one that she never really had with either Betsy or Monica. She always seemed to have a soft spot for me, anyway. I was the prettiest, wasn't I? The cutest. And the sexiest. That goes without saying. And I think, in her own way, Mom saw herself reflected in me, and that accounted for that special bond we seemed to have between us.

She always had a good sex life, I'll say that for her. She could be a bitch at times. Even looked like one whenever she got ticked off, but all in all, she was pretty good-looking. For her age, anyway. I'll bet when she was seventeen, eighteen, or nineteen, she was a knockout, and she must've been sexually active at that age, too. In her day, maybe they didn't get into it as much as they do nowadays; but if they did, I'm sure Mom must have been one of the most active of the lot because, even in her thirties, she was pretty energetic. I can't even remember the names of most of the guys she went out with, there were so many of them, even when I was practically an infant and Pop hadn't been dead more than a couple of years.

I do remember Rick Sellars. Now, there was one pretty decent hunk. A bit beefy, maybe, but so what. I'd take beef over skin-and-bones any day. Well, it was too bad, wasn't it, that things didn't last too long between him and Mom. I kind of liked Rick, and I think he liked me, too. I think maybe if I'd put my moves on him, he would have let me. It's too late now to think about it, but I'll bet he would've been more of a man than Wayne and not turned away from me like I was poison the way Wayne did out in back of the house last summer.

I've said it before, and I'll say it again: I'm glad I put him in the hospital. He deserved what I gave him, and he must have known it, too. Maybe that's why he didn't let on to anybody that it hadn't really been an accident.

I remember how scared I was that he'd tell Betsy or let on to Charlene or anybody else, for that matter, that it had been me who had been responsible for putting him out of commission the way I did. I thought for sure he'd blurt it out. But no! He didn't have to, did he? He was already getting so much sympathy, he didn't have to resort to any such tactics. So, he kept it to himself and probably pretended that it had never happened the way it did, just like he pretended I didn't exist after I had that car accident last spring. I envy that man, let me tell you. I envy him the power to blot out everything from his mind that he wants blotted out, so that he can continue to live his life just as coolly and calmly as he cares to. All last summer, he acted like Joe Cool as he calmly and systematically screwed up everybody's lives, and it didn't bother him for a minute. Not until the damage had already been done, and then he decided to play the part of Joe Hero! Telling the cops it had been him who'd pulled the trigger. He was actually going to take the rap himself.

Jeez, that man was sure full of surprises. A changed man, I think they all called him. Well, somebody should have put his lights out. When he was in boot camp, some tough marine sergeant should have straightened him out and put him in his place. But no! He had to survive, didn't he? He had to survive and come back and play the

193

part of Joe Hero. But where the hell did that get him, huh? She was already dead, so what the hell did it matter? Huh?

I'm killing myself laughing right now because I know he's in pain at this very moment. He's in the most intense pain imaginable because he knows she's dead and there's nothing he can do about it. And if he hadn't been Joe Macho and enlisted with the marines, none of that other crap would have started up, and she wouldn't be dead right now – wouldn't have slit her wrists and dropped out of his life like a dead mosquito. He's got to be in the most intense pain of his life right now, and I'm happy for him. I'm ecstatic, because being Joe Cool and Joe Macho and Joe Hero didn't help him one bit. Right now, he's nothing but Joe Shit! Ha! Ha! Ha!

There's no denying it. I'm thrilled at the thought that he's still suffering right now, but I'm sick at heart because I'm suffering, too. Nothing has been resolved by any of this. Nothing good or beneficial to a single person has come out of it. If this were a movie or a play or a television program, it would get lousy ratings because it would have no happy ending to it. No ending at all, really. Just a continuation of misery for all concerned year after year after year.

That's why I'm planning on ending it all soon. Oh, I won't slit my wrists or do anything that sick. I'll take the sure and direct approach. A swift stabbing. A fall from a fifty-story building. Something that will be quick and violent and that will take my breath out of my body before I even have a chance to realize what I've done. No way am I going to stick around and wait for things to change. I know damned well that this misery is just going to continue forever. No way am I going to become a walking zombie like Wayne or a messed-up druggie like Carl or a schizoid murderess like Monica or even a dried-up old spinster like Aunt Lucille. There's just no sense to it. Life should be lived to the fullest, just like I was living it last spring. My redheaded stud-man Marty had the right idea: just keep getting head and doing the things that make you feel good and then walk away and come back later on and get serviced all over again, and the hell with any other person involved. The way the rest of us are living right now? There's no sense to it. No sense to it at all.

That's what I wanted to tell Aunt Lucille today at the mall when she poked around, looking for Christmas decorations and cards and wrapping paper at half-price. I wanted to tell her not to bother getting these things because I, for one, didn't plan on being around when the next Christmas rolled along. And neither should she. She has no real life to speak of. She's always miserable, the two things being related, no doubt. If she herself were confined to a wheel-chair like I am, it wouldn't even alter her lifestyle. What have the two of us got going for us? Between the two of us, we should put our heads together and come up with an ideal solution to all of our problems. A joint suicide pact. That would be fine. Truly inspirational, I think. And then, if Aunt Lucille and I actually had the guts to go through with it, we'd have the last laugh on the funeral parlor director because there'd be nobody left to pay for the funeral, let alone attend a service of any kind, so why even bother having one?

Oh, it's getting late, and my eyes are starting to close on me. Five more days, and it'll be New Year's Eve. Maybe Aunt Lucille and I can do the same thing Lisa and I did last New Year's Eve: Smoke a few joints and then go out and try and get laid. Who knows? Maybe one of us could get lucky.

And you know something? I think the smart money would be on Aunt Lucille.

BETSY'S DIARY – July 6, 1985

Dear Diary: It is a beautiful, clear night, and the stars are all out. Yes, I can even hear the wonderful sound of the crickets chirping outside my window. The air is still, without the slightest whiff of a breeze to stir the slender folds of my curtains. It is a glorious summer night once again, a night of such beauty that even the angels in Heaven must consider it worthy of praise.

And I am here alone in my room. Alone with my thoughts and seeking to find the strength to draw myself towards my window so that I can take in the serenity of the night and, in so doing, quench the longing of my soul. I would have thought there would be an emptiness inside of me similar to the one I always felt whenever I suffered a loss; but instead I am surprised to find that a strange but perceptible yearning has filled the void I would have otherwise expected, and I now know that I have fallen in love with him.

No, there is no logical or reasonable explanation for this feeling to have suddenly possessed me. Other, more worldly young women would scoff at such a notion that my heart could be seized with this incredible longing, but it's there, this undeniably strong yearning that cannot be suppressed or ignored. I always believed that when the time came for me to fall in love, I would instantly recognize my loved one with the eyes of my very soul – recognize him as the man to whom I would desire to entrust my heart and my spirit. Well, my soul failed to come to this awareness quite as swiftly as I would have anticipated, although unconsciously I may have fallen in love with him a lot sooner than I am now consciously able to determine.

And there is no reason for it either. It's unfathomable, inexplicable that this love should have come over me as it has; and just as I expected, I am unable to deal with it and have now begun to wonder if I should seek to cast it off as an undesirable invasion of the safety and serenity that have always clothed my existence up until now. I know nothing of such matters. I am completely naïve and inexperienced as to the ways a woman adopts in her efforts to please the man she loves. This feeling I have within me may very well never even have the chance to blossom forth, as I am sure my sheer ineptitude and awkwardness will doom it to failure.

Oh, dear Lord, what am I to do? I have spent this entire day thinking about him, fantasizing what it will be like when he returns – *if* he returns! But nothing material has resulted from any of this. I am alone in this house right now, just as I was alone all day long, although a number of familiar faces were around me from time to time. I am still alone, and I long for the unexpected, knowing that I am doomed in so wishing something to happen that will, no doubt, never happen at all.

He will not come back. This longing inside of me will never be appeased. It will simply remain there, stagnant and distressing and unsettling – yet, at the same time, so sweet and uplifting that it frightens me. When I woke early this morning and realized that I had actually fallen in love with him, I had such an extreme desire to do some good on this earth. I sprang out of bed, threw on some rags, and went outside to do the gardening that Wayne was to have done. I would have painted the whole house, too, except that he had taken everything with him in his van when he left our house yesterday, and I didn't have enough money to go to the hardware store. And since it was Saturday, I couldn't gain access to the money I have in my account. So, I just went out there on my hands and knees and did all the gardening that needed to be done. I even relished doing it, too, because I kept saying to myself: If Wayne does come back and finds that I've done all of the gardening for him, maybe he'll smile at me. God, he might even look right at me. Then I would see the color of his eyes and the glow of his emotions and the piercing and blinding light of his soul. Maybe he'll come back here unexpectedly and find me here on my hands and knees. And maybe he'll then put his strong, pure hands under my elbows and lift me up from the ground and tell me that I have found favor in his sight. In his sight, yes, because he'll be looking directly into my eyes as he tells me this. And then I'll laugh and tell him that I'm doing all of this for him and that, in doing it for him, it affords me the greatest possible joy. And then it'll be his turn to laugh, and he'll suggest that we do the rest of the gardening together, and the two of us will sink to our hands and knees and dip our hands into the dirt. Together.

Later on, I fancied, I would step into the garden against the side of the house while Wayne wasn't looking. In that garden grow the most gentle and delicate white roses I have ever seen. There is one in particular that is scarcely more than a bud, but it is pure and unblemished and, as yet, untouched by human hands. That is the rose I would pluck, while he wasn't looking, and it is that rose that I would offer him, quietly and gently, without having to say a single word to him because my soul, not my lips, would be speaking to him as I extended the pure, white rose and watched him take it from me and place it between the curls of his blond hair. And it would stay there for the next few days so that I could always see it there and be reminded of the beautiful intimacy of that moment.

We both would be silent, too, if by chance we were to find a fresh, clear fountain of distilled water in an imaginary park very far from here – a park that exists only in one's dreams. We would dip our hands into the fountain and cleanse them of all of the soil from the garden. Then, still without saying a word, I would dip my whole body into that holy fountain so that all my past sins would be wiped away; and in that one instant, I could stand before him in total purity, I myself a pure, white rose freshly plucked, and I would extend my heart to him and watch silently as he took it and pressed it against his own, and our two hearts would be joined forever.

I would like to kiss the earth at this time; and if it were humanly possible, I would kiss the sun. There is so much that is beautiful, so much that is heart-stopping in its gorgeous simplicity, so much that I want to share with this man. If God would only let me have the opportunity to do this! If only I could see him again! Just once! I want to open so many doors for him. I want him to be able to see the light of Heaven, to breathe its untainted scent into his lungs, and to hear the divine music that is now in my soul – the music that is known only to angels. I want to give him my hands so that he can press them between his own, my face so that he can hold it against his chest, my heart so that he can consecrate it with his love, and my soul so that he can unite it with his own. These are the fantasies and dreams that form the substance of my longing – a longing which my rational mind tells me can never be pacified. Not in the real world we are all forced to inhabit.

The longing is there, then, and I must deal with it all by myself. There is no one out there whom I can tell, no one who can advise me, no one who can fully understand what has happened to me. No one except the Divine Redeemer Himself. Only He knows what shall happen to me. Only He knows what will be the fruit of this seed of yearning which has been planted within me.

The other day he held my hand and told me I was beautiful.

Why then hasn't he made an effort to call me? Last night I told myself that it was over, and I know that allowing myself to entertain these delirious fantasies will only make my despair that much more tremendous when the awful reality of this whole situation sets in. But I must know where I stand. I must know whether he has thought of me since the last time we were in each other's company. If only I had some way of knowing what he's been doing the last couple of days, whom he's been with, what he's been thinking about, what his next move will be and whether or not that next move of his will bring my dreams closer to fruition.

What will become of me now? Will this love which now consumes me end up constituting the one final love of my life? Is this to be the extent of the love I am destined to experience? Is my happiness to be held in check like this forever? Is this, indeed, to be the peak of my romantic involvement with a man, simply the desire on my part that we may see each other again?

If it is meant to be, if God wills it, if He should find favor in such a union, He will lead him back to me – within a few days? Hopefully? But if Wayne does not come back to me, will it then become necessary for me to harden my heart against thoughts of a romantic nature, at least as far as Wayne is concerned?

I can only leave it in God's hands. I don't know what else to do. I don't know. I simply don't know.

I will now lay down my pen and pray for the sleep that may somehow enlighten me as to what my next course of action should be – if any. At the very least, the sleep which will eventually come upon me will, I hope, ease the longing that I cannot ignore, even though it can only be temporary and without any guarantee that the pangs will not begin anew in the morning.

P.S. Even if I should never see him again, I must be thankful for those moments of bliss that I spent in his presence, moments which now, in retrospect, seem so much sweeter and far more poignant than they initially felt. Yes, I must be grateful because, come what may, I now feel that I have finally had a taste – albeit a very tentative one – of what it's like to be in love.

AUNT LUCILLE'S DIARY – December 26, 1985

I decided to go to bed early tonight since I'll be getting up rather early tomorrow morning. Back to work for one last day before the weekend sets in. I'd just as soon work right through the weekend. While other people look forward to the weekends so they can carouse and celebrate and simply kick up their heels in excitement because all the pressures of their jobs have been lifted for a spell, my life is so dull and monotonous that the weekends merely consist of short periods of emptiness. If only I could find a way of feeling as the others do. If only I could motivate myself to kick up my heels the way other people do. I'm forty years old, and instead of feeling like a woman, I feel like a burnt-out shell. And Jean, while in her late thirties, was still a cauldron of seething sexuality.

I wasn't jealous of her. I didn't feel any bitterness towards her because I was so busy regarding her as a stupid, shallow woman who was hastening her own destruction. And now I wonder if perhaps I'd been way off the mark in judging her so. I don't think she ever went to bed feeling weary of life as I do, and that in itself would be a good enough reason for her having decided to live life in the relentless pursuit of sensual pleasure. After all, that wasn't what ultimately destroyed her. When Rick Sellars dumped her, she was bitter and outraged by it all, but it would have been only a matter of time before she set about reconstructing her outlook and applying herself to the task of finding a new man so that a newer, even more torrid relationship would result. Perhaps it was in her perseverance and her resiliency that I found cause to envy her, if I did indeed envy her at all. I mean, how could she spend months, actively engaged in sex with a single man, suddenly find herself cut off from him, and then carry on as if she'd simply finished breakfast and, a few hours later, would hunger for her next meal?

When my Arnie abandoned me for that tramp twelve years ago, the hurt I experienced was so tremendous and demoralizing to my ego as a woman, that I could not envision a quick recovery; and it's true that I have not recovered, even to this day. And yet, if it had been Jean, she would have bounced back in no time at all and started a relationship with another Arnie – another man who would take her to bed with him under the ludicrous pretext that theirs was a true and meaningful relationship. Maybe it was just my infernal bad luck that Arnie caught me at a time when I seriously believed that such a thing as true love existed, and I blindly took his words of undying love to heart. I was young and flushed with the passion and excitement of being in love. Or maybe I was just in love with the mere idea of being in love. I should have seen him for what he was. I should have opened my eyes to the way he carried on one New Year's Eve, gorging himself on spiked punch and then making a pass at Fran Woodstone. I should have realized, right then and there, that his idea of true and steadfast love differed greatly from my own, and I should have dumped him on the spot. Or, better still, for the sake of my own peace of mind, I should have compromised my ideals and accepted him purely on sexual terms the way Jean would have done, had she been in my position.

I wonder now about Ellen. She always had that "way" about her, the same as Jean. I'm sure she was no longer a virgin by the time of her accident. She always flaunted that sexy body of hers around the house. I even warned Jean several times that she had the look of a girl who was free and easy with her so-called charms, and Jean simply smiled, nodding her head, and said," She does have a mighty fine figure, doesn't she?" as if that, in itself, should cover all the bases. I won't be so cruel as to state that Ellen had that horrible, crippling accident coming to her, but I tremble inside as I confess that I was a little relieved when the doctors told us of the extent of her injuries. Yes, I was actually relieved because I knew that, if nothing serious came of her condition and she were then to renew her current mode of behavior – well, all I can say is she would have wound up pregnant and brought shame and degradation to the whole family.

The same thing happened when Jean got pregnant with her first-born. She and Norman hurried up and got married, but the shame was still there. For me, anyway, and our parents who were still alive back then. I remember the night Jean came home and told me, in our bedroom that we shared as young girls, that she thought she'd gotten pregnant. "You stupid fool!" I hissed at her. "You mean, you've been having sex with all these guys you've been going out with?" I was still a virgin, you see, and the idea that my younger sister could have been so "advanced" definitely appalled me. And it disgusted me, too. I then promised myself that I, at least, would be very careful, and I held onto my virginity well into my twenties. In fact, there was only that one man before Arnie, but we didn't go quite all the way, so that doesn't really count.

Why am I thinking about sex so much all of a sudden? I thought I was past all that. I thought I had a much firmer grip on my thoughts and emotions. I can live without a man, can't I? Maybe when I'm well into my sixties and the threat of being used purely for sex no longer bothers me, I will settle for the companionship of a gentle, kind-hearted, elderly gentleman who will provide me with a certain amount of financial stability in my declining years. At least, I would probably be able to sleep at night without worrying about waking up the next morning and finding out my man had decided to abandon me for some tramp.

I don't know why I even bother thinking so far ahead into the future. I have no way of knowing that I'll even make it to the end of '85, never mind the close of the century and beyond. That point was driven home today when I took Ellen along with me to go shopping. There I was, looking at the excellent bargains all the stores were offering on unsold Christmas ornaments, decorations, and so forth, and I began stocking up for next Christmas. I glanced at Ellen from time to time and saw the bitter expression on her face, and I was about to scold her for looking so grumpy, when it suddenly occurred to me that, if a mirror had been held up to my own countenance, the same expression of hopelessness and disgust would be registered there as well. I don't want to think about next Christmas because I know already that it will be as depressing as the one we've just finished celebrating, and I use the term loosely. Let other people recognize the holidays with some semblance of festivity and joy, not me. Why, I spent this whole Christmas thinking about the ones I lost. Instead of sitting at the kitchen table and eating turkey, instead of listening to Christmas carols on the radio, instead of decorating the house with splendid Christmas ornaments, Ellen and I should have driven out to the cemetery and paid our respects and then come home and tried to forget everything that happened this past year to our family. That family – Jean and her three girls – was my life. They were the family I knew I would never have, and now that precious assemblage of human beings has been torn apart. My darling little girls, as I had known them all through the years, have ceased to exist. There is a strange and horrible bitterness dwelling in the soul of one of them, and an even more terrifying and self-destructive urge governing the other one's mind and spirit. And the third of my three lovely little girls?

She never should have been born. I know that sounds like a terrible thing to say, think, or write down here in this diary, but I tried. I tried so desperately to understand her, to shield her, to talk some sense into her, to impart some of my wisdom to her, to advise her in every way possible, so that I could somehow prepare her for the storm of life that I knew would soon engulf her. My God, how I loved her, and yet, I don't believe I ever actually told her so – not in so many words, that is. And now I love her even more, and cannot cope with the very idea of never being able to see her again.

Oh, God! I will never see her again, and that thought is the most horrifying one I will ever have to live with. And it's partly my fault that she's gone. I should have found a way to save her. I should have fortified her somehow. I should have taken her, by force if necessary – taken her out of that house when I began to see the walls of her life collapse on all sides of her. I should have flung myself over her as one would protect a tiny, fragile flower that is vulnerable to the furious elements of nature. I should have been there that night to console her when she made her decision and wound up slicing –

I should have been there, that's all there is to it. But I didn't even live in that house, so I wasn't fully aware of what was happening. But I should have seen, or sensed something. If I had only been able to stop her. If I had only been able to impart a single word of hope into her bosom, all of this insanity could have been avoided. And our family would have been here, intact, to celebrate the holidays this year. Then there would have been a reason to don our Christmas attire, a reason to rejoice with the rest of the country over the birth of a Savior. There would have been a reason for me to get up tomorrow morning, because without her, there isn't a reason for living.

I should have known. I always considered myself an intelligent, perceptive person. I thought I would have made an infinitely superior mother to those children than Jean ever was. And for all my intelligence, and for all my superiority as a maternally guiding force, I was unable to put a stop to the act of violence that robbed us all of so much of the purity and selflessness that had been bestowed upon us, without our even realizing it or appreciating how enriched our lives had been because of all that.

And now we're all paying for it.

Tomorrow, after work, I will go up to Norfolk. I must. I must speak with Monica and find out why she did what she did. Once and for all, I've got to find some peace of mind – or try to, anyway.

That's all for now.

BETSY'S DIARY – July 7, 1985

Dear Diary: When I laid down my pen last night, I sincerely hoped that, by the time I lifted it again for this evening's entry, the most incredible miracle of love would have swept into my life and I would be consumed with joy and a radiant hope for the future. But it is nearly eleven-thirty, and my hopes are crushed. I see now that the path my life will inevitably take will be one of sterility, emptiness, and emotional isolation. It is as if I were being told right now by the powers above that Mom indeed is justified in regarding me as a disappointment, a nonentity, one who is unworthy of love, affection, and ultimately, anyone's concern.

My feelings of great inadequacy were re-enforced this afternoon when I drove Ellen to the beach with me. We sat together for hours, she in her wheel-chair and I on my beach chair, and I watched young people on all sides of us – most of them young and in the throes of the love-force. There actually were also many middle-aged and elderly couples walking along the beach, smiling confidently and undoubtedly breathing in the fresh air with a sense of gratitude for the opportunity to live yet one more day in the company of the person they loved. Even those people I saw, who appeared to be alone or simply in the company of a group of friends, all seemed as happy and self-assured as can be. As the glorious sun beat down upon them, so too did God's love, instilling them with a desire to live, love, and be happy.

It is selfish, I know, for me to dwell upon my own pitiful state when I realize that Ellen, too, must feel as I do: that life has played a cruel and shameful joke on us, and that we have been shortchanged. Of course, I cannot speak entirely for Ellen, but I myself feel so cheated – as if I've been robbed of the opportunity of experiencing a loving relationship that might have gone a long way towards restoring my confidence, a loving relationship that might have helped me to forget just how worthless and disappointing I am to my mother. How can a woman my age, unloved and unwanted, justify her existence? In years to come, some of the crass remarks Mom makes about Aunt Lucille's professed spinsterhood will probably also be leveled at me. With Wayne having obviously disappeared from my life, what hope do I have that I will ever be able to love again?

It's true then. I'm pretty worthless then, aren't I? If there had been anything positive one could see in me, if there were any attractiveness about me, physical or otherwise, then he would have come back. He would have been lured by some quality I possessed, lured back into my life because he feared he might lose whatever it was he felt I had to offer him. But his absence has only strengthened my belief that I am desirable to no one, either as a friend or a companion, let alone a lover. It's as if God Himself sought to drive home this point to me by allowing me to savor, all too briefly, what it would be like to be in love and to be loved in return by that person, and then to draw the cup of spiritual rejuvenation away from my lips before I became swept away by too much happiness. It is as though I were to finally crawl out of an abyss, and just as the light of pure and radiant love were about to unfold itself before my vision, I was forced to lose my footing, to fall back down into the pit of loneliness and darkness that I always inhabited, even sicker with pain now because I'd had that glimpse of a beauty that would forever be withheld from me.

Later in the day, after Ellen and I came back to an empty house as Mom and Aunt Lucille appeared to have vanished, I left Ellen downstairs in front of a blaring television, and I came upstairs to my room here, not even knowing why my steps had taken me here. It was still bright and sunny outside. I still had plenty of time before it would be necessary for me to fix dinner. I felt no inclination to pick up a book or even to write a premature passage or two here in my diary. But I came upstairs anyway, telling myself that I would weep bitter tears of self-pity as soon as the door was closed behind me.

But I did not cry. I simply sat at the edge of my bed in perfect stillness while the sounds of life could be heard floating up to me through my open window from the world outside. I sat quietly and listened to these bustling sounds of life, both human and un-human; but my own heart was silent. It was as if the longing to love and be loved had mysteriously disappeared, and all that remained within me was a drowsy acceptance. An acceptance that the moments of joy were gone forever, and that I should conduct myself in a very quiet and meek manner from now on. I would do all of Mom's bidding, and Ellen's too. And if one day Monica should be looking for a shoulder to cry on, I would supply her with one. But aside from these humble services I might be called upon to provide, there would be nothing else for me in life. Then, later on, in my old age, I would be looked upon as an annoyance to whoever might survive the long years ahead. I'd be Aunt Betsy the old maid, or the older sister who never did anything with her life, or the spinster niece who never really fit in, or worst of all, the oldest of the three daughters, the one who never should have been born.

Since Wayne has not returned, I can now see quite clearly the path my life should take. I will not struggle against a destiny that has already been mapped out for me. No. I will accept it and, perhaps, derive some small but painful joy from the remembrance of the extremely brief period of time I spent, thinking I was in love.

Mom and Rick Sellars had dinner with us this evening. It wasn't a feast, by any means. I just slapped a few sandwiches together, but everyone seemed to have a fairly good time. Mom was in her element, fussing over Rick and even literally spoon-feeding him when the ice cream was brought out, much to Aunt Lucille's silent disapproval. Even Ellen seemed to be in reasonably good spirits, her face showing a bit of color from spending time in the sun. Shortly after dinner, Monica came by with Carl. There seemed to be a strain between them, and I fancied that the skin under my sister's left eye was slightly discolored. I recalled how my recent telephone conversation with her had furnished me with the information that she hadn't been feeling well.

This evening, though, I made a fool of myself in front of her. I know she must think me an incredible idiot after I drew her into the kitchen with me while the others sat under a starlit night sky out on the patio. I drew her indoors with me, held her hands in front of me, pressed them with all my strength, and parted my lips to speak.

"Help me!" was what I wanted to cry out to her, but my vocal cords failed me. "I am so miserable, Monica. I want to die right now because I'm insane with love. Yes, Monica, it's true. I love him to the point of insanity, and now I've lost him, and I need you to help me to find a way to survive this as painlessly as possible."

But if I'd succeeded in actually saying all of that to her, she might either have not believed a word of it, or have taken me for a fool. And so, I kept my lips closed tight and dropped into the nearest chair, turning my face away from her in total embarrassment.

She asked me what was wrong, and I kept silent. What right did I have to bring her into my own sphere of suffering, when she was so recently wedded to the man of her dreams? How could I have even expressed myself in such a way that she would have understood what I was trying to say to her, without her thinking me totally irrational and over-wrought? No, I had to release her hands, drop into that chair, turn away from her, and plug in the ensuing silence by telling her that I was just feeling a little dizzy and that it was stupid and thoughtless of me to have troubled her over it.

But I know that she wasn't buying it, not for one split second. So, she just stood there, looking down at me, and it was just as she placed her hand upon my shoulder that Carl stepped in quite suddenly. I was so afraid he might sense that I was in distress, that I quickly rose from my chair and forced a smile upon seeing him standing before me.

"Anything wrong here?" he asked. "Has Monica been boring you with the intimate details of our sordid sex life?"

Then he laughed, throwing his head back so that the amusement in his dark eyes was thrown at the ceiling instead of in my direction. And I laughed, too, actually finding the inner strength necessary for me to simulate merriment at a time when my insides were pulling themselves in several different directions, all at the same time.

I don't know what we said after that, I was straining so hard to put up a front of carefree conviviality. I do know that it started drizzling outside, and Mom and the others came indoors. That's when I retreated to my room, and it is here that I've remained. My book has lain on top of my dresser, untouched, these past two hours that I have been up here. I have no desire to read a single sentence. That book is the most outrageous piece of fiction I have ever read, a story in which a woman gets her sweetheart despite the valiant efforts of her many and several adversaries. All the novels I have been reading lately are of the same stamp. The authors apparently adhere to the strict and steadfast rule that all women will ultimately find their true fulfillment in the arms of the man of their dreams and, most ridiculous of all, that this fulfillment is certain to be realized for every woman. It's all fiction. All fantasy. Not meant to be taken seriously.

Well, maybe I, too, will find some sort of fulfillment, some degree of happiness someday, but I am now beginning to feel that the happiness that awaits me is not that of this planet. No. Here on this earth I am not meant to be happy.

Enough of this disgusting self-pity that is getting me absolutely nowhere. I must retire now so that tomorrow morning I can get up bright and early and drive out to the hardware store to pick up some paint and other accessories. I have to paint the rest of the house tomorrow, and it will do me good to occupy my time in such a manner. Tomorrow is Monday. A work day, of course, and I must apply myself to the work that is at hand. And while I stand out there in the hot sun, applying paint to the outside of our house, I will try not to prick up my ears at the slightest sound of a car engine or a motor. I will try not to listen for his phantom van to pull up inside the driveway. I won't allow my mind to slip into that other world where two people can be united in love and where supreme happiness is realized in the arms of one's beloved. I will be dabbing paint against the side of a house. That is all.

P.S. A week from tomorrow I will be going back to work. My vacation will finally be over. I look forward to that and to the end of this delusion that has caused me nothing but pain and grief. I must triumph over the misconception that my life can ever be any different from the way it's always been. I must triumph over it once and for all, because if I don't, I dread to think what might happen to me. Or what I might do to myself.

CARL'S DIARY – January 5, 1986

Dear Diary: It's three o'clock in the morning, and I can't seem to wind down. I've been walking and driving around all day like some kind of zombie, and I've accomplished absolutely nothing. Last night I promised myself I'd see Wayne Brown dead inside of a week, and it wasn't until a very short while ago that I actually got the wheels turning in that direction. I know what I want. I want that bastard dead. That's clear as all hell to me. And I can't do it all by myself. Christ, I'd be a fool to try it all by myself. That sucker is out of his skull; plus, with his luck, he'd be the one who'd come through it all without a scratch on him. But I can't let that happen, so that's why I need just a little bit of assistance here. A little help from one or two of the many friends I have, all those friends of mine who are constantly putting their necks out for me.

What a day! I don't know how much longer I can keep this up without the old man kicking me out of the house. It's a good thing I managed to keep a low enough profile early in the day, but wouldn't you know, my old lady had to go and pick today as the day she'd barge in here and start straightening out my room.

I'd just finished smoking a joint, too, and she pops in here without knocking. Christ, I didn't even hear her coming up the stairs, I was so engrossed in trying to figure out how I was going to get even with that sucker for the beating he gave me last night. She comes into the room without warning, as if she owned the place (which she does, but that's beside the point), and sees me lying in bed with my face all swollen and bruised. Right away she starts in on me, accusing me of hanging around with punks and criminals, and laying all kinds of heavy crap on me like what a disappointment I've turned out to be and this never would have happened if I hadn't gotten married to that psychopath and ruined my chances of getting into college. As soon as she started up with her go-out-and-get-a-job crap, I stood up and told her to just chill out, I knew what I was doing with my life, so she says to me," I'm going to tell you father." The next thing you know, the old man is up here, yelling at me, calling me a disgrace and a lowlife and demanding to know when I'm going to stop hanging around with scum.

That's when I told him to go to hell. I put on my coat, grabbed my car keys, and split. Why can't those morons just mind their own business? Let me live my life the way I feel like living it. What's it to them if I get my face messed up, anyway? My whole *life* is messed up! Do they think I care about a few cuts and bruises when my whole aching heart is splitting in two, every second of the day? Don't they realize I don't care what happens to me anymore? They're such morons, they could never understand how I feel and the challenges I face every stinking day of my life. How could their small, inferior minds even begin to comprehend the repercussions of what happened back in September when she took her life and jolted everyone else's life out of whack? How could I ever make them realize that nothing matters anymore – not my education, my health, or even my sanity? When are they going to get it through their miniature mentalities that I just don't give a shit about anything anymore?

Nevertheless, I knew I had to see Wayne dead and buried inside of a week's time, man, and as soon as I bolted out the front door and got in my car, I shot right on over to Kenny's house.

The guy was getting laid again, do you believe it, only this time it's not Sherry Day but some other cheap slut who used to be in our senior class last year. His parents were gone for the day, and he'd invited that class-A slut ex-cheerleader Rebecca Lanigan over for one of his massive one-on-one orgies, as he liked to call them. So, he comes to the door half-naked, would you believe it, and pulls a face when he sees me standing there. Then he makes me sit around his living room for an hour while he bangs that ex-cheerleader piece of trash upstairs in his bedroom, the two of them making such a racket with all their groans and screams, you might think they were bent on destroying the house and taking it all down, with me in it, too. Finally, the two of them come downstairs with these obnoxious grins on their faces like they're King and Queen Tut or something, and Kenny makes me wait another ten minutes while he stands at the door, kissing her and feeling her up, like it's the last chance he'll ever get to see her again. Finally, she gets booking, and Kenny walks over to sit next to me, gets a cigarette lit, and doesn't even offer me one, the bum!

"That was great, man," he says, like I really need to hear this. "Even better than Sherry was last night in the back seat of your car, Bozo."

I don't have a clue why he felt the need to call me Bozo just then, but I was so bummed-out by all the crap I already had on my mind that I didn't bother raising any objections to the way he was treating me. Instead, I just sat there and listened to how he and the ex-cheerleader slut-faced tramp had gotten it on for something like the last three hours straight, and how she was already panting with excitement, looking forward to the next perverted adventure she hoped to share with him.

I remember how I used to get off, listening to his stories practically hundreds of times in the past. Yeah, Kenny was real cool. Cool with a capital C, you know? And hey! I could have had as many babes as he did if I'd put my mind to it, but half the girls he laid were easy to begin with, and I had my standards, you see. Still, I recall how I was a junior in high school, and Kenny and I got hooked up with these two cuties who just happened to come over and start talking to us on the beach. It started out as your basic getting-to-know-you chit-chat. Next thing you know, Kenny drags his chick behind one of the sand dunes, and the one I'm with starts dropping little hints here and there about how she'd love to have a little excitement in her life, just like her friend. Then, she even starts putting her hands in places they don't belong, and all of that. She's really getting hot for me, you see, and I do mean hot with a capital H! So, I remember how I came up with the brilliant idea of me and her sneaking up to the sand dune and spying on those other two, and she agrees. Next thing you know, we're peering over the top of the sand dune, and I'm kneeling there and watching Kenny nailing his chick just like they were a pair of German shepherds or something, would you believe it? At first, I was horrified, then disgusted, but little by little, I actually found myself getting aroused as they kept going at it for over fifteen minutes, not even caring that the two of us were watching them.

I'm sure. I'm absolutely positive that I would have had sex with the girl I was with, right then and there, but there was no room behind that sand dune and the beach itself wasn't exactly deserted, so I didn't make my move when I probably should have. I realize it now. I passed up the proverbial golden opportunity. And I even had one other opportunity that same day, and I went and blew that one, too.

Kenny and I and the two babes hopped into my car, and we went out for a bite to eat. Kenny even let me drive my own car because he wanted to stay in the back seat with his chick, you see. We eventually ended up sitting around at one of those drive-in places where you can eat your food outside, right in your own car, and I'm gouging down my burgers, and so is the girl next to me, but Kenny and his slut-faced chick are all over each other in the back seat, letting their food get cold. Then the next thing you know, Kenny tells me to drive out to Pelican's Landing, and everyone seems to be in agreement, so I go right along with it because I figure there's no telling what will happen once we all arrive at Pelican's Landing which is probably *the* spot to go to when you're in the mood to have some "fun." So, we drive out there, and Kenny takes Miss Slut-Face out on the rocks, way out so hardly anyone can see them, and I start crawling along the ledge to see if maybe I can get a better view without the two of them suspecting they're being watched. Sure enough, there they are, and Kenny's putting it to her all over again, only this time they're doing it on a flat rock. I just got so turned on when I saw this, and I immediately said to myself," I'm ready now. Where's my chick?" Then the next thing you know, the chick I'm with moves right on past me and goes over and joins the other two, and inside of the next thirty seconds or so, Kenny's got this nauseating ménage a trois going on, right there on that flat rock in the middle of Pelican's Landing!

I wasn't angry, though. I wasn't upset because I knew I'd get my chance someday. Someday I'd make love to the most beautiful woman in the world, and it would be heaven. Pure heaven.

Well, I never got that chance, although I came mighty close. If only I hadn't been so aggressive with her. If only I hadn't frightened her off the way I did with my overpowering sexuality. That had to have been why she resisted me. There can be no other explanation. After all, wasn't I voted Best Personality and Most Popular? I mean, I had everything going for me. Couldn't she see that? Not only that, but couldn't she see I was sincere? My God, I loved her from the very first moment I saw her. Even before that, you might say. When Monica would describe her to me, tell me about all the wonderful things she'd done and how she couldn't imagine what it would be like if she had to live without her because she was such a special person – When I heard all about these fine and upstanding qualities she possessed, I told myself that there was no way such a beautiful person could really exist. She'd have to be a dog or something, I said to myself.

But she was beautiful. I've never in all my life seen a girl so beautiful. Her hair was blonde, wavy, and infinitely soft and velvety-looking. Her eyes were like two stars of the deepest and most impenetrable blue. Her nose was just the cutest thing, with an almost impertinent uplift at the nostrils. Her mouth was small, her lips soft, but when she smiled, her face became illuminated with the kind of radiant joy and rapture that is given only to those who have been blessed from above. Her whole face had such mobility and character that you could just sit there and gaze upon her perfection for hours and hours without in the least becoming bored or disinterested.

Christ, what eloquence spews forth from my mind when I even so much as remind myself of her innocence and her purity. The earth never knew such beauty, and I! I held her in my arms that night. I held her in my arms and caught a glimpse of her exquisite flesh; and had the night continued as I had planned, there would have occurred the union of two absolutely perfect human beings.

So, I sat in Kenny's room earlier today and listened to him describe his filthy goings-on with Rebecca Lanigan, and it all sounded so disgusting. It was almost subhuman, you might say. Kenny might think he had a real hot time of it this afternoon, but what did he know? He'd never held my angel in his arms like I did. All he did was bang a stupid ex-cheerleader slut. Big deal! I pity him, man. I actually pity the poor moron because his small and insignificant mind can only understand unbridled raw sex with an energetic and insatiable slut-o-rama. How sad!

So, I'm ticked off. I've got every right to be with him. That dildo who calls himself my friend. I mean, I sat there and listened to how he nailed the Lanigan ex-cheerleader tramp and had her screaming in wild ecstasy, and the whole time he's telling me this, he's smoking his cigarette, acting like he's so cool, and throwing in these sad little remarks like," Too bad you can't get what I get on a daily basis," and even "Too bad you're such a loser." Then, as soon as I mentioned Wayne Brown and how he and Vince had promised they'd help me get even with him for what he'd done to me and Vince last night, Kenny got this annoyed look on his face. Then he stands up and stomps around the room for a few seconds.

"Listen, that's your problem, not mine," he finally says to me. "You can just leave me out of it."

"Kenny," I said to him, standing up and grabbing his forearm, really gently because I don't want to get Kenny mad at me. "You're my buddy, right? Don't let me down. You promised."

"Look, man," he says to me, and he actually shakes my hand off his arm. Then he slams me back down onto the couch real hard, but I don't think he meant anything by it because of him and me being such good friends, and all that. "I don't know what makes you think I got anything to do with this. As you recall, I was out getting laid when you were getting your face smashed in."

"But Kenny, you've got to help me. You just have to!"

"Don't go telling me what to do," he tells me, and he's got this real fierce look on his face when he continues," You've got problems, man, you know that? I think you're getting a little soft in the head, if you know what I mean."

It goes up my butt just thinking about the way that dildo-pal of mine spoke to me this afternoon, especially that bit about me being soft in the head, when my I.Q. has his beat by a couple of hundred miles. Worst of all, the two of us have been buddies all these years, you know? Why, I've known Kenny since grammar school. We've been buddies for ages. When I got my new car during my junior year, Kenny stuck to me like glue. We were inseparable. We'd cruise around practically every night of the week, me and Kenny. I can't even begin to count the number of times I let Kenny borrow my car, so he could go out and get laid. Half the time, he'd leave me waiting at the mall or at Burger King or somewhere, waiting for him to get back with my car, and all the stores would be closed and all the lights out by the time he got back. Once I even had to walk home because he never came back that whole night. But I put up with it all just for the sake of our friendship. Kenny's always been loyal to me, you know? Loyal with a capital L.

But this time I was getting pretty sore. I mean, I figured I wasn't the only one in town who hated Wayne's guts. Wayne had never been one of Kenny's favorite people either. Why was he copping an attitude with me all of a sudden?

Finally, I told Kenny that this was no way for good friends like us to be acting. I figured if I didn't at least try to appeal to his basically generous character, he might throw me out of his house with brute force or something, so I gave it a try. Next thing you know, Kenny stands off to the side, puts his hand to his chin, and appears to be heavy in concentration.

"Tell you what, man," he says to me. "I think I can get somebody to wipe out good old Wayne Brown for good. Only it's gonna cost you a few bills."

"You don't think the three of us – you, me, and Vince – could do it all by ourselves?"

"Hey, man, I could do it all by myself if I wanted to," Kenny tells me, and he inflates his chest a little bit, like suddenly he's Joe Tough-guy or something. "But I don't feel like getting my hands dirty, if you know what I mean. On the other hand, I've got some connections, you see, and according to what I hear, Wayne welched on a drug deal he had going with some pals of mine something like a year ago, and they'd jump at the chance to settle the score with that prick once and for all. But just to play it on the safe side, I think we'd better offer them some cash."

The long and the short of it is this: Kenny's agreed to get these dudes he knows to bump off Wayne inside of the next week, give or take six or seven days. All I've got to do is come up with a measly grand, and the deed is as good as done. Kenny told me I could bring him the cash tomorrow night at Samuel's pad, and Wayne will be dead meat inside of a week or so.

I left Kenny's place feeling relieved. In fact, I was on such a tremendous high that I drove straight out to the cemetery and spent some time communing with my darling angel. I apologized to her about being busy the next few days. I told her I was going to have Wayne killed, partly because he was an inferior human being, partly because she had been deluded by him, but mostly because if I didn't kill him, he'd probably end up killing me first.

I thought about that. It's been four times that he's confronted me, and when I least expected it, too. Four times that he's attacked me when I wasn't looking, and the beatings he's given me have gotten progressively worse each time. Last night I experienced hell on earth, puking my guts out all over the place behind McDonald's and not being able to function at all for the rest of the night. At one point I actually thought I'd wet my pants. I didn't know exactly when that could've happened, although it was probably an ongoing thing that started as soon as I saw Wayne's van pull up outside McDonald's and I realized I was on the brink of catching the beating of my life.

But all of my worries will be over very, very soon. I felt so high when I left the cemetery. I mean, this was a natural high. The thought of seeing Wayne Brown's ugly body stretched out on a slab in the morgue was far more mind-blowing than the strongest hallucinogen known to man, in my book. I was really feeling completely spaced-out. I didn't care about anything else for the rest of the day.

Later on, I wound up at Samuel's pad. There was quite a crowd there, so I had a chance to mingle with some really cool dudes. Even Vince showed up, but it's weird. He acted as though he didn't even recognize me. I walked over to him and said," Wayne Brown's gonna be dead meat inside of a week," and all Vince said was, "That's casual," and then he turned away from me and started talking with some girl with long brown hair and a strange-looking tattoo of a serpent on the side of her neck. I could tell he was going to make his move on her at any moment, though, because that's just the way Vince is. He's so cool and put-together, it's a marvel. I wish I were like him. The way he stood up to Wayne last night, like he was really gonna fight him. That took guts, and I'll bet Vince could whoop him if they ever crossed paths again. Maybe I won't give Kenny that thousand dollars to give to his friends. Maybe tomorrow I'll be able to catch Vince in a more receptive mood, and then I can suggest to him that he call Wayne on and duke it out with him and not stop beating Wayne's head in until he bleeds to death, or something equally fatal. That's what I should do. Like I said before, Vince is at least six-two, and he is very tough. I wouldn't mess with him, I know that, and I happen to be pretty tough myself.

Christ, my mind's getting soft, just like Vince told me. Or was it Kenny? Jeez, if I don't get my act together pretty soon, I'll crack. I just know it.

I don't know what I should do. Maybe I should just go to the bank tomorrow and withdraw the grand and give it to Kenny. I don't think

Kenny would have the guts to try and rip me off. Basically he's a loyal friend. Loyal with a capital L. I can trust him with the money, I'm sure of it. Then, by the end of the week, I'll be able to see Wayne Brown in the morgue. On a slab, too!

One way or the other, whether I get Kenny to have his boys do it or whether I convince Vince he should take him on with his bare fists – one way or the other, it'll get done. I'm sure of it. And then I can concentrate on other matters, like how beautiful it will be in Heaven when my angel and I are re-united for all eternity. I'm sure that that's the way it's going to be in the end. I'm as sure of that, in fact, as I am that Wayne Brown will be dead on a slab in the morgue inside of the next week. Give or take a few days.

BETSY'S DIARY – July 8, 1985

Dear Diary: It has happened! Finally! The most significant and rapturously beautiful day of my life has finally occurred, and each time I take in breath, I have to simply sit still in sheer amazement. I never dreamed life could be so beautiful, that the mere act of breathing and realizing that one is alive and experiencing all this beauty could be so exhilarating, so intoxicating. Just last night at this time I lay quietly in bed and wondered if perhaps I wasn't the most ill-fated and unimportant being ever created; and now, twenty-four hours later, I feel as though I am the most blessed and fortunate woman who ever walked the face of the earth.

This whole day I simply traveled from one peak of ecstasy to another. But I mustn't carry on in this mode, as exciting as it may be. Let me simply start out by relating that, at about ten o'clock this morning after I had seen to Ellen's modest needs and left her sitting in her room listening to some records, I went outside to my car, bank book in hand, ready to rush off to the bank so as to withdraw the money that would be needed to purchase the paint and other necessary supplies, intending to complete the painting of our house within the next couple of days. I was terribly depressed, as I had already resigned myself to what I was convinced would be my fate as a terribly lonely and forlorn human being.

It was one of those occurrences that was just meant to be, I guess, because if I'd been two or three minutes earlier in going out to my car to run my errands, I would have missed him, and the wonderful array of events which transpired during the course of this altogether perfect day. At any rate, as I was about to put the key in the ignition to start the car, a red convertible pulled up in front of the house and stopped. I had never seen the car before in my life, but I'd recognized its driver.

He was wearing a blue head-band which held his thick, curly blond hair tightly about the crown of his head in some places, allowing his curls to protrude more wildly than ever in other places. He was also wearing dark sun-glasses as well as one of the bandannas I'd given him, plus a loose-fitting blue shirt and denim jeans. Not the most romantic attire for a "knight in shining armor" – but as far as I was concerned, he could have arrived in tattered rags and I still would have welcomed his presence with an uplifted heart.

He immediately spotted me, waved me to the convertible he was then standing beside, and held the door on the passenger side open for me, inviting me to hop in. I was a bit reluctant, but he assured me that everything was O.K. The car belonged to a friend of his who'd requested him to do some work on it at the garage, with the understanding that Wayne was free to take it on the road to put it through its paces. Still rather shy and reluctant to get on in, I carefully explained to him that I had a few errands to run, and he instantly promised me that he'd take me back home as soon as I said the word. In the face of his candor, not to mention the tenderness of his smile, I quietly assented and got in.

I had never ridden in a convertible with the top down until this morning, and I must confess that, at first, I was amazed at the way my hair started blowing all over my face, especially when we accelerated once we were on the highway. However, I soon began to relish the idea of feeling so free and independent as we drove towards the beach. It soon began to dawn upon me that the feeling of having the wind sweep one's hair about and allowing the bright and marvelous sunlight to pour down upon one's shoulders in all its abundant glory was totally exciting; and from now on, it won't feel the same driving around in my own car.

Needless to say, these feelings of exuberance and intoxication with the pure fresh air may not have overwhelmed me quite so much had I not already been overwhelmed and intoxicated by the belief that my prayers were finally being answered with this beautiful young man being sent back into my life. Feelings of gloom and despair, in a micro-second, had been transformed into feelings of intense joy as soon as I'd seen him re-appear, and in fact, there was also a slight tremor of disbelief as I wondered whether this were actually happening in real life.

Once we arrived at the beach, Wayne got out, walked around the front of the car, and took me by the hand as soon as he saw me opening the door on my side. He didn't say a word but led me down to the rocks where an unusually violent surf was sending sprays of light and golden sunlit foam into the air. He kept my hand in his, gazing at the spectacle that Nature was entertaining us with, and said to me," Isn't this something? I've never seen anything like it. Have you?" And I squeezed his hand a little more firmly as if to emphasize the common bond I felt with him just then. "No, Wayne," I said to him. "I honestly can't believe any of this."

"This is my favorite spot in the whole world, Betsy," he continued, amazing me with this sudden desire to actually speak to me in more than just a few phrases and half-sentences. "I just love it here – But today it seems even more wonderful to be here than it usually does."

Then he turned in towards me and took my other hand in his free one. He was still wearing his dark glasses, and inside, I cursed him for denying me the privilege – the right, in fact – of being able to see the melting tenderness that I knew, in my heart, he held in his eyes just then. And he pulled me a little closer to him and kissed me.

As I sit here in the solitude of my room and look back upon that moment of sublime fulfillment, I feel that I could write fifty pages, right here and now, describing the veritable flood of feelings that surged up within me at that all too precious and poignant moment in my life. But I will refrain from dwelling for too long upon that utterly tender moment. At the time, I viewed it as the height of joy my dull and drab existence had ever known. I had been kissed by a few other young men in the past, of course, but it wasn't anything like this. I realize, too, that Wayne had the advantage of the roaring surf behind him, a background of symphonic dimensions, one might almost be tempted to say, but that wasn't it at all. It was just so simply incredible that a man who looked so solid and strong could make a kiss so tender and perfect last so long without any loss of passion or feeling from the moment of its beginning when our lips first touched, through the long and ardent middle when the passion in my heart mounted to such tremendous heights that I felt I had taken on a new, more flowering identity – and finally, to the last few moments during which our ardor abated. Sweetly and gradually our kiss ended, and with such utter perfection and ease that one would have thought we had, in that brief space of time, shared the same identical heart, the same identical mind, and the same identical soul.

And once again, the best was still in the offing, because once our lips drew apart and I expected his embrace to unfold with the delicacy of a gradually wilting rhododendron, he instead drew me closer and entwined his two strong arms about me. With my face pressed against his shoulder, he leaned his lips to my ear and whispered the words of honeyed sweetness that I had been yearning to hear from the start: "Oh, Betsy, I've missed you so much."

I wanted to tell him the story of my life over the past couple of days, only I knew it would distress the two of us to give life to such negativity. I wanted to hold him tighter and express my despair over not having been able to see him over the past two days. I wanted to describe to him how desperately my heart had been tugged from within me when I saw him disappear the other day after Aunt Lucille had abruptly dismissed him. I wanted to tell him so much of how I felt. I actually wanted to tell him, too, that I loved him, that I had even fallen in love with him before this embrace we had just shared, but I could not find the words. The thoughts were there in my brain, waiting for my vocal cords to pull sharply at the reins to set them into vivid motion. But it was just as well that I didn't speak, because shortly after telling me that he had missed me, Wayne held me close to his chest and told me that he had been desperate, himself, all weekend. A gate seemed to have opened inside of him, allowing the rush of impetuous words which then erupted from his lips.

"I couldn't think of a way," he said into my ear. "I couldn't figure out how I could come back and see you again and not risk having some harm come to either one of us. Your aunt fired me, and she made it sound so final. I spent the whole weekend, thinking about how I could come back and see you. The whole weekend without you, and I couldn't think of the right way of going about it, so you wouldn't misunderstand and think I came back just to get my job back. Betsy, I can't lose you. That's all there is to it. You are the best thing that's ever happened to me in my whole life, and I can't afford to lose you. I can't live without you – because if I had to do that, that would mean I'd have no hope of ever feeling alive again --"

That's when I interrupted him, pulling myself away so that I could face him; and once again, I found myself staring up into a pair of sun-glasses, and I felt so robbed, so cheated. We had come so far, and there was still this barrier. This nonsensical, foolish, meaningless obstacle that stood in the way of my ability to absorb his inner being. I actually became furious for a moment at the belief that he could actually willingly deprive me of the complete and unbridled joy of looking into his eyes.

But I stemmed my fury and smiled up at him. I wanted to tell him that each moment we stood together like this was like a precious jewel to me, to be treasured for all eternity and loved and coddled in my heart forever. But such language was beyond my power to verbalize because, when I smiled and began saying a couple of words to him, he suddenly creased his brow, put his hand under my chin, and tilted my face up towards his with such gentle seriousness that I abruptly cut myself short and gazed wonderingly into his face.

"Your smile goes right through me," he said to me, with his brows still creased as if he were actually experiencing some sort of inner torment. "You are the most beautiful woman, and you have the most beautiful smile in the world."

"Wayne," I murmured, allowing my smile to fade away as it became the object of his intense scrutiny. "Don't say that. I'm not –"

"You're not what?" he cut in, as if stung. "Not beautiful? How can you say that, Betsy? How can a girl with such luscious, golden blonde hair say a thing like that? A girl with the most perfect little nose, I just want to kiss it and tease it gently with my lips. A girl with a smile that could light up an overcast sky in the middle of December, and eyes that make me want to cry, they're so beautiful."

No, I said to myself. He's blind. That's what it is. That's why he won't let me see his eyes. He's been blinded by some strange force. Not blinded, perhaps, but with his vision altered in such a way that he sees the world through eyes that no other human being has ever been given. Eyes that distort reality and transform darkness into light and ugliness into beauty.

His words scorched me, they were so searing in their intensity. I could barely breathe when he clutched me suddenly after telling me about my nose, my smile – and when he spoke of my eyes, I heard a sob enter his voice, and I clutched him in return so that the two of us remained in another long, silent, and wordless embrace. Or perhaps it was simply a continuation of the one that had begun with our first kiss. I didn't know for sure at the time it was happening, and even now, I cannot determine just how many times we kissed all morning and all afternoon, how many times we embraced, held hands, stared into each other's eyes –

Yes! Shortly after our embrace, we stood opposite each other, hands held loosely, almost flirtatiously, his head inclined slightly towards the ocean, for we had stopped speaking for a few moments. When I saw that his face was no longer directly opposite mine, I let go of his left hand, disengaging my own right one, and quietly reached up and, then, took his sun-glasses away from his face.

"Let me see them, Wayne," I said to him, calmly and simply when he swerved his face towards me in some dismay, immediately lowering his lids over his eyes as he did so. "Let me see your eyes, Wayne. I want to know. Once and for all. I want to be able to look inside of you and know who the man is that I've fallen in love with."

As soon as I realized what I had just said – making a complete confession of my love to him – I suddenly wished to retract the statement. It was only a moment or two later, however, that the complete ease and casualness with which I had made the avowal could only re-enforce the rightness of our love; and seeing that there was nothing we couldn't face together from this point onwards, I believe that he, too, saw the folly of resisting any longer the force which compelled him to reveal to me the depths that lay mysteriously within him.

When he saw the inevitability of what lay ahead and understood that we belonged to each other, he released my other hand, lowered his whole head a moment or two, and then raised his face back into the harsh, glaring sunlight, his eyes wide open and seeking to fasten their gaze upon the intangible line of vision that my own eyes created in the direction of his face.

I saw them, his mysterious dark blue eyes, at the same instant a wave crashed violently against the rocks, and a gushing sensation welled up inside of me, sending involuntary shivers up and down my spine as I gazed directly into the dark blue vastness of his soul and caught a glimpse of the incredible and heartrending sadness that he housed within himself. It was the same vast and limitless sorrow that I have seen in my own dark blue eyes at various times of self-absorption in the mirror of my bedroom, only Wayne's eyes were much darker with pain, much more tortured with melancholy of the most aching kind, with pools of shame and self-disgust swimming within their centers. I quickly, in my ignorance, reached a hand out to touch the side of his face – a well-meaning impulse stemming from the huge amount of compassion that I felt for him at that instant – and he just as quickly lowered his eyes from my gaze once again and said clearly but in a mournful monotone,

"I've done things, Betsy. I've done things in my life that I'm ashamed of. I've been – a lousy person. I've tried to mind my business all these years, but trouble has a way of finding me. I've used people. I've fought people, ripped them off – broken practically every rule in the book. My father hates me. I hate him. It's always the same. Nobody understand why I do some of the things I do. I just keep on doing them, mainly because I don't and can't see the point of any of this. It's the only way I know how to live. And I've somehow managed to survive."

He then swung away from me and, for a moment, seemed on the point of stalking back up to the convertible which was sitting at the top of a hill a short distance away. But he stopped, just a few paces from me, and continued to look down at his feet. His arms were wrapped tightly around his own torso, and the glow of the radiant sky hung all around him like a halo of forgiveness as he continued to speak.

"I'm stupid. I can't read. I can't do anything right when it comes to stuff like that. I can only do certain things, so I do them constantly because they're the only things I *can* do. I know it sounds weird, but I'm an expert at ripping people off – using them – like the way I use certain women, you know? My old man keeps drilling into my head that between cars, drugs, and women, I won't make it past age twenty-five. And he's right, too. It's no wonder he hates me. I'm just a piece of shit."

Then he swung back in towards me, stepped a little closer, and absent-mindedly kicked a loose stone out of his path.

"And while I'm living the life of a worthless bum," he continued, still hugging himself and still keeping his eyes cast down to the rocky earth underneath his feet," wishing I could just drive my van off a cliff somewhere and end it all once and for all – Just when I'm telling myself that life just isn't worth living, the most incredible person appears and gives me a reason to live -- and maybe even a reason to smile. Someday."

And he looked up at me. And he let his eyes bore into mine for at least two full minutes while I stood opposite him, my hair swirling about my face with the intermittent gusts of wind and my eyes fighting to hold in check the immense flood that was about to unleash itself down my cheeks. I stood quietly myself, drinking in the pleading desperation that his dark blue eyes conveyed to mine, and I wanted to give him something precious that belonged to me, offering it to him as a token of my undying trust and devotion. Would that I could have performed some sacrificial act for him just then, an act that would have succeeded in cleansing his soul of every evil he believed himself to be infected with. I cursed myself for my own human limitations and prayed that God Himself would somehow see fit to intervene on this young man's behalf. That He could cover him with a mantle of forgiveness and divine grace that would bring peace and utter contentment to his dark and tormented psyche; and then, when the mantle was lifted, he would rise up a pure and untainted individual with his primary aim being the desire to love fully and to be loved just as fully.

Instead, we stood silently for those two minutes, transfixed by the utter inability each of us displayed in managing to cleanse one another of our own hurts and shortcomings as human beings. How could I tell him that I, too, felt worthless and unworthy? That I, too, could find no way at all of justifying my existence to the outside world? I know, of course, that Wayne's sins – past sins, at any rate – have been of a generally more harmful nature than my own. In those two minutes of silence during which I drank in the dark and foreboding gloom in his eyes as if wanting to absorb it myself and, in doing so, alleviate the severity of his own torment – in that short space of time, an unknown spirit of hope seemed to stir our two hearts. Simultaneously.

And suddenly we were in each other's arms again, assuring each other that neither of us would leave, or walk away from the other in a way that would create emptiness in our souls. No, I wasn't as eloquent in my speech as I seem to be in relating this right now, but I do know that Wayne held me tightly for a considerable length of time and he did tell me repeatedly that he didn't want to lose me, and I assured him, just as repeatedly and with just as much sincerity, that I had no intentions of walking out of his life. None whatsoever.

A short time later it was I, not Wayne, who broke the spell by suggesting that we should release the past and let its gloom fall away from us like a discarded garment, and Wayne agreed, taking my hand and leading me back up to the car. We drove around a bit and found, without any trouble at all, a stretch of beach where the surf wasn't quite as brutal as it had been down by the rocks, and the surroundings were moderately peaceful. The sun was bright, and the temperature seemed to have risen quite a bit since earlier in the morning. Our conversation assumed a more relaxed tone, and in almost a carefree manner, Wayne suggested a swim. Carried away with the spontaneous appeal of his proposal, I actually disrobed all the way down to my undergarments without even giving it a second thought, while Wayne was already heading towards the ocean wearing swim trunks he'd had on underneath his jeans. He did glance back to make sure that I was following him, and when I came closer, he reached back to take my hand so that the two of us soon took the plunge into the churning waters with laughter which was nearly child-like in its utter freedom and wonderment over what we were experiencing.

I swam freely and with unaccustomed strength, and occasionally I took his shoulders from behind and pressed myself against him. We stayed immersed in total liquid splendor for nearly half an hour, laughing, cavorting, and frolicking like a couple of youngsters spending their possibly first and last day at the beach. And it was wonderful to sneak up on him from behind and dunk his fair, golden-haired head underwater in play. And it was even more wonderful to be pushed closer to him from time to time whenever a sudden rush of water propelled me, powerless, in whatever direction it chose to. And it was heavenly when, crouched behind me in the water, Wayne then sprang forward, grasping me unexpectedly at the waist, and then hurled me forward just as an oncoming wave was about to engulf me in its relentless swirl of powerful majesty.

It wasn't until later, when we were out of the water, that we went for the walk that took me to the realm of physical pleasure that my body, up till this point in my life, had never visited.

There was an expanse of pure and untrammeled earth before us, close to the water's edge. We walked upon this earth in our bare feet and with our hands joined and with the sunlight – God's pure sunlight – illuminating the path before us. The ocean surged on our right, and the seagulls swarmed at a distance on either side of us, and we were alone. Totally alone. The two of us, walking in the golden glow of summer, feeling that we were entwined on an imaginary carpet of supreme pleasure that neither of us had ever imagined existed until now.

"I love you," Wayne said to me, once again as calmly and devoid of all pretense and artificiality as he expressed the words that we both recognized, now, as a constant in our lives. "I love you," he said to me one more time, softer than before, and because he then halted in his steps, I too paused and turned to regard him. "I love you, and I want to show you how much I love you," he said to me, "but only if you feel that this is something you want – and that you want it to be as beautiful as I want it to be, too."

The sun's rays, at that moment, seemed to warm his eyes to an aquamarine and bleached his hair from blond to a hot and sensual white.

"I am sure – " I started to say, and then my heart almost rose up into my throat and caused me to feel a momentary fright, thinking that I was about to expire with pure happiness at that precise moment in time. But I took in a deep breath of salty air, smiled into the radiance of his face, and told him," I am sure that it will be beautiful, Wayne – and even more beautiful than I imagined it could ever be."

It was on that spot of beach that I gave myself to him, slowly and almost methodically at first, until every sensation began to feel so right and so natural, simply because I was being loved by the man I'd already taken completely into my heart. Yes, during that unbelievably unreal stretch of time, I gave him the fruit of my love, the outpouring of my soul, and the essence of my being. I gave. Yes. I gave, and felt rapturous in the giving of all that I had to give him.

The best part of all, as far as both of us are concerned, was when he held me in his arms afterwards so that we were both facing out at the boundless sea in front of us, and he leaned his chin gently upon my right shoulder and let out a sigh that told me quite distinctly that he was as blissfully happy and as totally at one with the universe as I was just then.

Once more, I find that I could write about this momentous occasion, this milestone in my life, for fifty or more pages and still not even scratch the surface of the enormous joy that flooded my being the whole time we spent together on that crystal-clear stretch of sand underneath that benign and voluptuous sky. I only know that there were even more peaks of ecstasy in the hours that followed, moments of sublime tenderness and even stretches of silence while we both reveled in just being close to each other, wherever we happened to be at any particular moment.

This evening, as we sat together in the front seat of that convertible and told each other the story of our respective lives with a calm but gorgeous moonlit sky for our audience, Wayne suddenly drew my head against his shoulder and said softly into my ear,

"This is the real beginning. The real beginning of my life. Just promise me that you won't ever leave me, Betsy. I can't afford to lose you – especially now that I know what it's like to be loved by a truly beautiful woman."

Needless to say, I felt content and fulfilled, just leaning my head against him and listening to the simple truths that spilled forth from his lips. It was not necessary for our passion to mount any further than this, because I – we both were fulfilled.

I now make this vow: that for the rest of my life I will give everything I have to this man. To this man who found me worthy of his love. This man whose soul I know I have seen. This man who found me worthy enough to view it. This man whose hand I was holding when the portals of love unfolded before me.

And I will offer prayers of thanks and words of the highest praise to the good Lord above who gave me this day of such perfect beauty. I pray that He will lend me the assistance to bring about the fruition of all the hopes and joys of the other members of my family as well. May they all be blessed forever and ever, as I have been so wonderfully blessed on this, the most wonderful day of my life.

P.S. No one must know any of this at this point. Not Ellen, not Aunt Lucille, certainly not Mom. Not even Monica. Not until Wayne and I have decided the time is right. We are certain of our own love and devotion, but not quite so certain that the rest of my family will be able to accept the two of us as lovers – not without some sort of resistance and hostility which, sadly enough, I know these people to be perfectly capable of.

CYCLE FIVE

MONICA'S MEMOIRS – April 16, 1986

I have kept my promise, and a cleansing feeling of self-satisfaction has oozed over me to the point where I sense a certain degree of inner peace. It's at least a semblance of the kind of inner peace I thought I could never again experience after blackening my hands and my soul with the crime that sent that despicable, heartless woman into the pit of Hell. I have actually kept my promise – the promise I made to myself – for three days now. In effect, I have not screamed. I have been calm, and it wasn't even that difficult. I didn't even have to pretend to be calm and relaxed when the doctor spoke with me the other day and mentioned the horror of my crime to me. I saw the rather guarded expression on his face when he alluded to that violent night upstairs in Betsy's room, and I answered him unflinchingly and with perfect composure.

Yes. I told him without the slightest desire to scream or to fling my hands to my face in order to tear my eyes out. I told him that I had killed her and that, in doing this, I felt truly justified. At the time it happened, and even now. I told him that I realized I had taken another person's life. Yes, I told him, I realized that the person whose life I took was a person to whom I owed a great deal of love, loyalty, and respect. Yes, I understood that it was unnatural to take the life of one whose ties to me were considered to be of the most sacred kind, ties that any normal person ought to cherish as such; but

I was justified. I told him it didn't matter that we were related, that her blood flowed through my own body, and that she had never hurt me or said anything to me directly which caused me pain. None of that mattered, I told him. It wasn't for my own sake that I had acted as I did. I was justified, I assured him, because I was enacting the revenge of another person who no longer had the power to carry out her own vengeance. A person who, had she been able to do so, would not have acted accordingly, anyway, because it was not in her nature to do violence to another human being. No, it wasn't in her nature to bring harm to another human soul. She couldn't hurt an animal, a fly, a bug that had accidentally found itself under her foot. No, it was not a part of her nature, a part of her psyche, to bring even a fraction of an ounce of pain to another living being. Had she lived, she would have eventually forgiven the person whose life I had seen fit to take. She would have not only forgiven that person, but undoubtedly would have prayed for her soul and begged for a chance to win that person's love.

No. It was not on my own account that I took that gun out of the closet and shot her that night when she opened the door to Betsy's room. It was not my finger that pulled the trigger which released the bullet that propelled itself into her heart. Neither was it Wayne's finger. It was the finger of the dark side of Betsy's soul that did it. The finger that didn't really exist but which I myself chose to create in order to vindicate the horror that that woman had precipitated.

I have been so calm over the last few days, so composed and silent in all my meager activities, that they granted me my request; and this morning her diaries were brought to me. A woman stood nearby as I opened one of the first ones. They were afraid, I guess, that I would open to the very last page, dated September 4, 1985, but I outsmarted them, you see. I was calm, and I moved quite slowly so as not to arouse their undue curiosity, and in doing this, I was able to open to one of the happier pages of her diary. I was able to pretend that nothing as horrible as the events of the summer of 1985 – or the revelation of September 4 – had ever taken place. I opened to the page wherein she described how the three of us came home from school and she excitedly ran upstairs to take out her piggy-bank. I ran upstairs after her, infected by her enthusiasm, and watched her take out all her money, and I saw how radiantly happy she became when she saw that she had enough money to buy the bird. I also remember how she stretched herself out on top of her bed a few minutes later and, smiling sweetly, she gazed up at the ceiling, probably looking right through whatever imaginary spirit it was that always seemed to be hovering near her, and she said,

"I think I know what bird I want. The bird I choose must be very young and very little. I don't care if it's a boy-bird or a girl-bird. It must be small and maybe even have a scared look on its face. A scared look that might turn into an expression of joy if it felt it was being loved. I'll survey all the cages and look carefully at all the little birds. And the one that sings a song of cheer when I draw near it will be the one I choose."

"Oh, but Betsy," I whined at her. "Please don't pick out an ugly one."

"I think I would actually prefer it to be ugly," she said, quite seriously all of a sudden. "Then it will appreciate being loved even more. And then when it knows you love it, it will appear to be the most beautiful bird in the world."

I laughed when she spoke her last words. Typical Betsy, I remember saying to myself. I was only ten years old at the time, but obviously I was old enough to know that birds were incapable of the kinds of feelings she attributed to them. But I kept my mouth closed, not wishing to spoil the serenity of her mood just then.

A little bit later, the two of us ran as hard as we could down the streets. Sidewalks, I should say. Betsy held my hand at the crosswalks, and even though we were hurrying, it seemed as though we would never get to that pet shop we were headed for. At one point in our travels, I whispered to Betsy that the store might be closed when we got there, and Betsy laughed nervously but refused to believe such a dreadful possibility could exist.

And then, just as we finished crossing School Street, we hopped the curb to get up on the sidewalk, and some coins spilled out of Betsy's pocket. It was at that point in time – and I firmly believe this – that the cruel hand of Fate decided to start tightening the noose around our throats, both mine and Betsy's. Our hearts were so geared towards getting to that store and buying that bird that we almost knew, as if by instinct, that something had to go wrong. Something just had to happen to bring a sense of dread upon us, so that our happiness would be ruined, even if ever so slightly. And so, when I saw that money spill onto the sidewalk and noticed that some of the coins began rolling in several different directions, I nearly cried out in a panic. I was sure that all the money would be lost and we'd find ourselves with no other alternative but to start back towards home without the little bird that was to bring such joy and excitement into our pathetic little lives.

But no. I was wrong. Betsy fell to her knees and grabbed up quite a few coins, and I helped, too. And, miracle of all miracles, an elderly woman who had been passing by stopped to help us. She even slipped in a few extra quarters of her own, I'm sure of it, and Betsy and I arrived at the pet store with plenty of time to spare.

We soon found ourselves scanning a whole array of wonderful little canaries, hummingbirds, and parakeets. There was a dull-looking canary in one cage, a bird with feathers of the drabbest colors imaginable. It practically flattened itself up against the walls if its cage when I put my face close to it, and even as Betsy peered inside, with her face next to mine, the bird seemed to be trembling.

"That one's a little sickly," I remember the owner of the pet shop telling us from somewhere behind our backs. "I've got some real beauties down here in this other cage."

Needless to say, we didn't even get to bother to look at those beauties the owner had referred to. Five minutes later, we were at the cash register, purchasing the dreariest-looking little bird imaginable. But that didn't matter, of course. Even if its song were faint and melancholy to everyone's ears, it would still gladden Betsy's heart, and that was what it was all about, wasn't it?

Why am I writing about this trivial event in our lives? How is it possible that she could have found so much happiness in such a small thing? I read the pages of her diary this morning, these very pages in which she described the whole episode; and when I was through, I closed up the book and sat very quietly for a very long time. My attendant stood quietly, too, without even making any movement at all, or so it seemed. Then she was relieved by another phantom-like figure. They exchanged a few words, but I was hardly aware of anything that passed between them. I simply sat there, trying to imagine that we were together once again, enjoying the feelings of peace those memories evoked. I even felt slightly amused when I recalled how Ellen said that she thought the bird was "stupid-looking." Typical Ellen.

Oh, God, I don't want to dwell on it any longer. It's over and done with and cannot be changed. Even though it all lives, awesomely and resplendently, in the pages of her diaries, the events themselves have passed, and nothing can be altered, neither the good nor the bad.

I read a little more later on. "July 8, 1985," to be exact. But I couldn't make it through the entire entry. I had read it back in September, shortly after the funeral, but to sit here this afternoon and read it again was unbearable for me. How could I re-open her diary to those pages and not crumble into dust? How could I allow the

243

blinding light of those pages to strike my eyes and then continue to breathe normally, after being exposed to such luminosity?

Oh, my God! To read those pages again and not gasp for air would be an impossible task for me to accomplish. I thought I could be purified if I were to re-visit those pages describing the blossoming of her love for that man to whom she became totally devoted. I thought that, upon being purified somehow by the experience of re-reading those particular pages, I could actually rest tonight without being convulsed with the internal suffering that is still a part of my daily living.

No. Better to open her diary to the very last page, and once again, feel all the horror that I felt when I first read it. The horror that prompted me to seek vengeance on those people who had been instrumental in destroying her. But worst of all, I couldn't bear to face the horrifying reality which the words on that page reveal.

I am tired of dwelling on this now, because if I dwell upon it any longer, I'll break the promise I made to myself the other day, and the attendants will have to come rushing in here, and their ministrations will ultimately send me into a two-week chloroformed numbness. Yes, as inviting as the prospect of losing two weeks of my God-forsaken life in a state of oblivion may initially sound to me, I must remain calm and as close to being rational as I can possibly get. Because this morning, I did experience a small, yet noticeable quiver of peace enter my body; and if I lose control now, they'll take her diaries away from me and I won't be able to re-enter that fantasy world of long ago. That world that no longer exists and which can never be resurrected, even in another sphere of existence. Not for me, anyway. Because I know, just as I've known ever since they brought me here, that I will never see her again. I will never get to be with her again. Not even for a split second. Ever again.

And in that, I see Hell.

BETSY'S DIARY – July 9, 1985

Dear Diary: This is the second consecutive night that I have come to my room and wondered whether I am really the same girl who has always inhabited this still and quiet chamber, the same girl who used to get up in the morning and move aimlessly about during the daytime before coming to put her head down to rest every night, having accomplished nothing and having meant nothing to anybody during the long, fruitless course of each day's activities. I am still on vacation, not usually one of the most productive periods of the year for me, but today I felt that I had done something worthwhile for a change, and my feeling self-satisfied stems directly from my having found an alter-ego, so to speak, a second individual in this world who seems to be very, very anxious to share my life with me, to even see things with the same eyes that I use, and to feel, along with me, the great and gigantic heartbeat of Nature that governs all of our lives.

I love him. I can now write down this confession with absolute simplicity. I can even face him and tell him those very words with the same degree of simplicity, as if I were stating something as generally accepted as the observation that we all need oxygen to survive. I realize that yesterday I wrote my diary in something of a frenzy. I was like a little schoolgirl, naïve to the bitter end and flushed with excitement almost beyond all reason. Today, however, I have exercised a certain amount of restraint, and I believe that, in doing so, I have put this significant experience into a more realistic perspective.

We both realize that there are distinct disadvantages to presenting ourselves openly to others in this family. Both Mom and Aunt Lucille have already voiced negative feelings towards him. Well, Aunt Lucille has, anyway, but I daresay that if Mom were to learn of our relationship, she would either become hysterical, or treat the idea that Wayne and I are lovers with complete disdain. In either case, I do not believe that I am in the least prepared for what may occur should the truth be made known to her. I would desperately relish the idea of telling Monica what has happened, but I will hold my feelings in check for a little longer, I think, and wait and see what the next few days will bring.

As far as today is concerned, everything went remarkably well. I woke up, feeling the same rather unnatural excitement in my veins that I had felt nearly all day yesterday. I sat before my dresser mirror for the longest time, brushing my hair and looking deeply into my own eyes which seemed to stare back at me in amazement. At times, I felt so completely overjoyed that I felt like bursting into cascades of laughter. At other moments, I regarded my reflection in intense contemplation, wondering if there were really any truth to Wayne's belief in my being beautiful. Then I shook my head quickly, ascribing his admiration of my physical appearance to a certain amount of romanticism on his part. At still other moments, I wondered briefly, although very acutely, whether Wayne was perhaps what people customarily call a "gigolo," and maybe this wild longing that we seemed to have for each other would soon wind down and I would never see him again, after all. Once again, I would shake my head at such upsetting possibilities and continue brushing my hair and wonder when I would see him next and what we would say to each other and what new beauties we would uncover while in each other's company. As usual, I was putting my head in the clouds, but after what had happened yesterday between us, I didn't see any real harm in pampering myself by indulging in such totally uplifting fantasies. The shocking truth of the matter was that they really weren't fantasies any longer. I had found love in the arms of a truly handsome man who professed his love for me in no uncertain terms. It was inspiring to my very soul to have been held in his embrace while the two of us had stood on the rocks at the beach, to be told that I was beautiful and that he never wanted to lose me. Even our child-like gamboling in the waves later on had revitalized my spirit in such a way that, I believe, aided in the transition I made from awe-struck yet still naïve young girl to fully mature young woman, panting with the desire to please the man she loved.

Yes, looking back on what transpired yesterday on that stretch of white, sandy beach, I have no regrets whatsoever, because I know that Wayne and I performed an act of love, pure and simple, and I cannot conceive of how such a natural and spontaneous event could possibly be considered to be anything but good, true, and beautiful.

This morning as I continued to sit in front of my mirror, I heard a sound at my window, much to my sublime pleasure, the sound being that of his ladder being placed against the side of the house. He was out there already, and we would spend the better part of the day together. So many hours of fulfillment, so many hours of a mutual sharing of each other's lives lay before us. I swept across the room and leaned out of my window just as his face lifted itself in the sunlight towards me. He raised his index finger to his lips to caution me to be silent, and I quietly helped him climb over the window ledge to enter my room.

We held each other in a warm and tender embrace that lasted for several minutes without either of us uttering a single word. My heart beat gently against his chest, and I fancied that his own heart was beating a pulse through his body in perfect synchronization with my own. It wasn't until a short time later that he pulled away slightly and held my face in his hands, keeping me at arm's length.

"I can't believe this is happening," he told me. "I mean, I really can't believe this is really, really happening to me. I've never been so happy in my life. You do want me to be with you, don't you, Betsy?"

"I want you," I told him quietly, fighting back tears of the sweetest joy imaginable. "I wish you could simply stay with me forever and ever."

A moment later, he lifted me in his arms and brought me, with him, onto the bedspread where we lay in silent rapture, staring into each other's eyes for a space of time that I seemed to have no way of accurately measuring.

His eyes are beautiful, too. I know it now beyond the shadow of a doubt, and this morning the sadness in them seemed restrained, replaced by a calmness and a peace that I had not seen in them earlier.

The moments passed in stillness while we lay facing each other. Occasionally he would brush a few strands of hair away from my face and gently touch my cheek with his soft fingertips. The corners of his lips would also, occasionally, twitch and force themselves into a smile, almost as if against his will. And I strained myself to keep the spell going, to maintain the trance that being loved by him was putting me into, it was just so sweet and so perfect. Soon the sounds of birds at play outside my window elicited full smiles from the two of us, and feeling a surge of spontaneous vigor enveloping me, I rolled him onto his back and placed myself on top of him.

His body felt enormously solid underneath me, the body of a young and powerful creature that has roamed in the forest all its life without being stained by the corruption of human strife. A fire stirred in his dark blue eyes while I sat straddled on top of him, and I saw the fire in my own eyes reflected in his and the smile on my face complemented by his own wide smile of confident pleasure. I also felt the flame of physical desire begin to flare up in his body, and I slowly drew apart the folds of my own desire so as to enclose his yearning, blossoming urge of love. Waves of bliss soon swept over and through me in surges of the most intoxicating splendor, and while I was experiencing these new and exciting sensations, I ardently sought to discern the undulating flame in his eyes, the flame that seemed to alternately seethe, cool off slightly, and then grow once more in increased intensity. I was only half-conscious of the passage of time once again, feeling as though we were both suspended in a world where unimportant elements like Time and Space held no sway whatsoever. There was no longer any reason to consider that anything else existed besides the two of us, with the cores of our beings bound together in perfect unity.

Later on, we rested together in my bed, and Wayne held me close to him so that I was able to discover the shelter his body made by allowing mine to curl up securely against him. We talked quietly from time to time, and when it seemed we heard a little bit of noise coming from downstairs – possibly Ellen getting herself settled in front of the television set – Wayne stirred, got up, and walked about the room. I, too, got off the bed, and I showed him some of the books I had recently read. He listened quietly while I explained to him that many of these books had brought a great deal of pleasure to me and that I greatly admired the people who could bring imaginary worlds to life so vividly through the power of words and the beauty of the English language. Without wishing to hurt him or offend him, I told him quite simply that the ability to read was a great and precious gift. I told him that, in fact, I had a great deal to be thankful for and that he did, too.

"I do now," he said to me, but his heart didn't really seem to be in his smile just then. As soon as he finished telling me this, he walked over to my dresser and sat down to look at himself in the mirror. Without speaking, and as if I were under a spell which was beginning to dictate my every movement, I walked over and stood behind him, placing my hands gently upon the back of his shoulders while he sat there gazing into my mirror with a seriousness that was beginning to unsettle me.

"If we're going to keep seeing each other," he said into the mirror," I mean – if we're really going to make this last, there are a couple of things I think you should know."

"Wayne, we've been through all that," I said to him, suddenly fearful that he was going to chastise himself for his past sins and errors, and I felt that such severe self-criticism was becoming unnecessary. Hadn't we arrived at a point, already, where neither of us had to justify past actions? Was he still so uncertain of the sincerity of my feelings towards him that he felt further explanations were warranted? What need was there to continue to explore regions that were rife with pain, sadness, and regrets that could never be totally erased, but at least might be repressed?

"No, Betsy," he interrupted me before I could speak another word to stem the tide of the heart-felt speech he apparently was determined to make to me. "These are things I have to get out into the open. I don't want you to find out about them on your own and then blame me for keeping them from you. You're bound to find out sooner or later. You probably even know already."

"Go ahead," I instructed him. "Tell me." And once these figurative serpents were let loose into the air, I added to myself, let them dissipate. Let them become non-existent, just as our very souls were before our conception. Then perhaps, once these diseased words were freed from his system, they would no longer feed the tragedy of his eyes, and he might be able to regard everyone, not just me, with open-eyed candor.

The long and the short of it was that Wayne and Ellen had carried on a physical relationship last spring and he did not wish his failure to disclose this information to me to be used by Ellen as some kind of weapon against the two of us at some point in the future. The news of his and Ellen's past dealing with each other came as little surprise to me, for I had always suspected that her nightly escapades frequently brought her into the "arms" of young men in her age category and older. I was not upset by what I heard, not even considering that Wayne himself had been a party to her nocturnal exploits. I was free to give him my pardon, should he ask for it, since I knew that neither he nor Ellen had any intentions of bringing themselves together again in our house. It was from Mom's own admission that we had all understood that Wayne had been invited to do the painting and the yard work through a casual conversation between the two of them at the auto garage where Wayne worked. I did, however, wonder why Ellen had never mentioned a prior acquaintance with Wayne when he first began coming here to paint the house, but then I quickly recalled that she had, indeed, displayed a rather frenzied desire to leave the premises the first few times their paths had crossed.

Wayne also told me, again without shocking me as much as he probably thought he would by revealing this to me, that Mom had invited him into her bed one day last week. "Yes," I said to him before he even had a chance to proceed much further in relating the incident in question to me," it was on the day it rained. Mom called in sick that day. She had it planned –"

"Right, Betsy. She had it planned from the very first day she sat out on the patio and watched me paint the house. But don't blame her for all of it. I did what she wanted me to do because I knew, all along, that that was the whole reason behind me getting hired to begin with. I know by the way a woman behaves when she's coming on to me, and I've always been quick to react the way I'm expected to. I told you before. I've used people –"

"Yes, you've used people," I broke in hurriedly," but so have they. I'm sure that Ellen used you as much as you think you used her, and I do understand why you felt you had to tell me all of this. I can see now why last night you thought it best to keep our relationship a secret. There's no telling how they would all react if they discovered how much I love you."

"They'll break us apart, Betsy. They'll tell you I'm a rotten bum, and they'll be right, you know."

"No, Wayne!" I shot back at him, and then I realized I was speaking too loudly, and quickly lowered my voice to barely above a whisper, as I continued," None of that matters to me. Anything you may have done in the past is of no importance to me. It's what we are about to do *now* – what we are about to do with the rest of our lives that's important. We're together right now, and there are so many things we can do together in the months and years ahead. I'll help you to forget everything from the past that troubles you right now. I'll prove to you that I can make those memories disappear if only you can learn to free yourself from all guilt. Stay close to me, Wayne, and I'm sure it will be that much easier for you to do."

"How can you possibly forgive me after what I've just told you?" he asked in a soft, almost tremulous voice.

"We are all sinners, Wayne, all of us. Some greater sinners than others, that's true – but we all started out in life basically the same way, didn't we? As you were growing up, Wayne, you were treated a certain way – Certain things happened to you, possibly many of them totally beyond your control, and you formed your own distinct habits, personality, and code of ethics. There's nothing in the past that can't be forgiven, just so long as you refuse to tarnish the future by repeating those same mistakes that are haunting you right now. Hopefully, when the two of us leave this world at some point in the future, we will leave it the same way we entered it. I want you to believe what I'm telling you, Wayne – because if you should die and I should die and the Lord decides that we can't be together anymore, I will find you anyway – wherever you are – and be with you there. Because wherever you may be, darling, it will be Heaven just so long as I can be there with you."

"Don't say these things to me," he said, suddenly timid about looking up at me once again. "I'm too stupid to understand any of it. All I understand is what my body and my feelings tell me to do. I can't think about the same kind of future you're talking about. I'm sorry, Betsy, but my mind can't take it all in."

"You don't understand such things with your mind," I said to him. "You understand them with your heart."

At this point in time, I don't even recall what else we talked about this morning. I do know that, shortly thereafter, Wayne climbed back down the ladder and started painting. I wanted so much to go out there and help him, but the folly of such an action, in plain view of Ellen and possibly the neighbors as well, would have constituted too great a risk.

Wayne did hurry, though. It's true that he had been fired, but between the two of us, we realized that some type of story could be given to Mom, at least, should there be any trouble over it. In fact, when Mom did come home later on at her usual hour, she seemed so delighted over the fact that the house was fully painted that I scarcely had any opportunity at all to tell her that it had been Wayne and not I who had finished the job. Not even Ellen mentioned a word about Wayne having been out there all afternoon, and I attributed her silence to a certain melancholy satisfaction she may have derived from knowing that a man who had once made love to her was so close at hand after the intervening months had passed.

I wanted to talk to her about her feelings, though. I felt that I could perhaps help her to deal with the emotions she might have felt for Wayne and may still, to this day, harbor for him, if she would only open up to me. But I honestly could not determine the exact method I could adopt in broaching the subject with her without opening up a lot of old wounds.

I can't really say that I regard either her or Mom in a different light now that I have been informed of Wayne's former ties with the two of them. That is, Wayne's disclosure has added nothing to the very full picture I already have of them. I love them dearly and wish them every happiness in life, to be sure. But like I told Wayne, all of that was in the past. Even his brief fling with my mother had taken place before he and I had barely exchanged a word, so it is totally absurd for me to view what happened between them that day as a betrayal on the part of either one of them. In fact, if anything, I'm pretty much elated over the fact that Wayne apparently had so much trust and confidence in me that he felt able to reveal these matters to me, confident in the belief that I would not become angry or bitter after having been told about these affairs.

This evening I slipped out of the house again, this time on the pretext of doing some shopping at the mall. As a matter of fact, I did stop there to pick up a shirt and matching bandanna to give to Wayne when we met later on at his place, so it wasn't as though I were lying to Ellen and Aunt Lucille about where I was heading off to.

And I'm glad I bought him the shirt and the bandanna, because I would've been so embarrassed if I'd walked into his apartment, empty-handed. As soon as he opened the door and let me in, my eyes caught sight of the most gorgeous display of white roses in a huge vase sitting in the middle of the kitchen table. Wayne was even holding one of them by the stem, behind his back at first, and he somewhat gallantly pulled it out into the open and drew it in towards my nose so that I could take in its soft and beautiful fragrance. I couldn't help but smile – and even giggle a little – when he did that, and a moment later, he brought me over to the vase itself and showed me the card that went with it which said: "To Betsy, With All My Love, Wayne." Simple, to the point, and lovely enough to briefly take my breath away when I read it.

"I couldn't deliver them to your house, so I thought I'd keep them here," he explained. "I'm sorry if you don't like them, but for some reason, I think of you whenever I think of beautiful things like these. I'm not sure, though, what exactly are the things that you like best."

"This is exactly what I like," was my truthful answer. "And I like other things, too – like being with you, and giving you things, and making you smile – and loving you."

If that's not exactly what I told him at that moment, at least it gives a general idea of how I felt when I responded to him just then. I daresay I'm not getting any conversations recorded here verbatim, but I do know that, in front of Wayne, what I feel and what I say are often two very similar things. I know that he told me he doesn't always understand me, but I don't believe that for a second. I can tell that he knows what I'm saying to him. It's positively uncanny the way the two of us, in such a short time of knowing each other this intimately, have discovered certain common grounds of conversation and behavior. I don't know what directions we'll be going in next, but I'm sure that the journey will be exciting and filled with nothing but loving pleasure. Some day we will stand, hand in hand, before God – either here on earth or in Heaven – and we will be married. I know this to be an inevitable and unalterable truth. And Wayne knows it, too.

I came home rather early. After I had given him his new shirt and bandanna, he brought me into his room and showed me some of the magazines and car posters that made up practically the sole adornments of his sleeping quarters. He also had a weight bench and quite a few sets of barbells lying around. I expressed as much interest in all of these objects as he had this morning when I'd shown him my books, but there was a bit of tension in the air this evening. Wayne mentioned that his father might return unexpectedly from his job, and upon hearing this, I became nervous, recalling the rather threatening image of that rugged, blond-haired man who had raged at his son in the hospital last week. Seeing that I was not completely at my ease, Wayne drew me against him, smiled into my eyes with his own, and said,

"We'll be together again in the morning. Worse comes to worst, I can give you a hand with the gardening; and if it's nice out, we can drive down to the beach later in the afternoon. Whatever you wanna do, we'll do."

Now that it is time for me to go to sleep, I find that I'm wide awake. Not from excitement, or at least it's not the same state of elation I was experiencing all day yesterday. It's just that I simply deplore the idea of sleeping, which necessitates my spending so many hours away from him, of not being able to inhale the same space of air that he's inhaling. I want to do something with these next several hours that lie ahead of me. I want to run downstairs to Ellen's room and embrace her and tell her how much I love her. I want to drive around the city and seek out my mother's whereabouts and, when I find her there with Rick Sellars, throw my arms around her, just for being the woman who initially brought me into this amazing and wonder-filled world of ours.

But most of all, I want to hold Wayne in my arms and thank him for the new life and the new sense of well-being and happiness that his love has created within me. Now, through the miracle of his love, I feel more certain than ever that there is a God, after all, and I now have more reason than anyone else in the world to bow down in gratitude because He has been so good to me. I have never felt so close to Him as I do right now, and I feel blessed. Truly, truly blessed!

Thank God I'm alive!

P.S. When Wayne told me this evening that he'd enlisted in the armed forces earlier this summer and would be sent to boot camp for several weeks, I felt understandably saddened and disappointed – but not alarmed. After all, we have the rest of our lives to spend with each other, haven't we? What harm can possibly come – to either one of us – from a separation of a few, fleeting weeks later this summer?

ELLEN'S MEMOIRS – December 31, 1985

I can't believe it. Twenty minutes to midnight. In twenty minutes it'll be 1986. How many more years till the end of the world? I always thought it was supposed to be in '84. I thought we were supposed to have a nuclear war or some such disaster, years ago, that would plunge us all into Hell. But here it is right now: twenty minutes to twelve, and no sign of nuclear war in the immediate future. Looks like it's going to happen after all. It'll be 1986, and somewhere in this rotten town, that incredible hunk who used to bed me down all the time will be shouting Happy New Year at the top of his lungs – if he's not already stoned to the max at this particular moment in time.

I'm being unfair. I keep imagining that, just because he's not interested in me anymore, he must be living it up with Charlene or one of his other tramps. Don't I know it's impossible for him to ever again shout anything joyful at the top of his lungs?

I don't get it, though. Where *I* was concerned, it was as if he had a goddamned stone for a heart. Even that first night – the night I gave him what no other guy had ever had from me – he simply pulled his pants back up after we were all through, and crawled out of the back of his van without saying so much as a "Gee, thanks," or "Hey, that was great!" to me on his way out. Then, when I finally put my own clothes back on and went outside to join him and the others, it was obvious his pals had been laughing it up just before I popped into sight. Then they all stopped, and I felt real awkward, like they must have been laughing at *me* and they felt kind of embarrassed when they saw me all of a sudden. And I remember, too, how Wayne didn't even come over and put his arms around me or anything. He just leaned against the side of his van, looking down at the dirt under his feet without saying anything at all while his buddies resumed their laughter after a few seconds. Then, when they saw Lisa come out from wherever she'd disappeared to for a few moments, they started goofing on her something fierce, grabbing her butt and throwing her back and forth between them like she was some sort of rag-doll or something. When I told them to cut it out because it looked like Lisa was about to cry, those two jerks simply ignored me and just kept on teasing her some more. Before I knew it, she was crying and even going at them with her fists, and while all that was going on, Wayne calmly got back inside his van, started the engine, and drove off.

And even though he disappeared that night without even saying good-bye or anything, I got it stuck in my head that I'd been the biggest turn-on of his life. The next night, when Lisa and I showed up at Burger King and we saw his van pull up, the two of us practically flung ourselves out the door to rush out there and meet him and his two friends all over again, like two stupid gluttons-for-punishment, would you believe it?

But poor Lisa! It was a crying shame, but her two boyfriends from the night before weren't riding in the van. They'd obviously just been using her. But the love of *my* life had come back to me, and when I climbed in the front seat next to him and he started rolling his van out of the parking space, I just waved Lisa good-bye and snuggled up close to the man of all men.

No, he didn't say anything to me that whole time. Not even hello. He just knew what was going to happen just like I did. We didn't have to exchange a single word, you see. Then as soon as he got his van parked way up on Old Great Road, he turned off the engine, slid out of his seat to move around back and get the rear of his van opened up, and before you knew it, it was like an instant replay of the night before.

At school, though, he was smart enough to pretend he didn't even know me, just in case rumors got started and it leaked out to Monica, and then everything might get back to Mom. That has to be the reason why he so totally ignored me at school, right? Sure, he acted pretty slick those whole two months. I remember how I'd often see him at school, and he wouldn't even look at me. I'd be walking to math class with Lisa or one of my other friends, and all of a sudden I'd see him coming down the corridor from the other end, walking along with his eyes cast to the floor, looking so fit with those tight denim jeans clinging to his buns. And even though he never raised his eyes from the floor, I kept hoping and hoping every single time that maybe – just maybe – he'd glance up in my direction and give me a little smile, or a little wink. In my greatest fantasy of all, however, he'd look up and see me and his face would light up with excitement; and I'd rush over to him, grab him by the shoulders, lean up towards him, and kiss him smack-dab on the lips for everyone to see. If that were to happen, I would then be regarded by one and all as the absolute Queen of the School, and all the other girls would flock over to me and beg me to tell them what it was like to be going out with the most incredible hunk they'd ever laid eyes on.

But no, he never let on at school that we knew each other. And how foolish of me to imagine that he was keeping quiet about us because he wanted to salvage my reputation! Why delude myself into thinking that his silence and his indifference were prompted by any amount of concern for me? I had my fantasies about this great supreme love that he had for me – but that's all they were: Stupid, ridiculous fantasies!

Then I had my accident, and that was really the end of everything. All I had left were memories and fantasies, and they couldn't take the place of the nitty-gritty three-dimensional physical pleasure I'd received from him every time we had sex. Maybe I could have borne this terrible cross of mine a lot better if Mom hadn't bumped into him a month or so after my accident and invited him to do all that work around the house. There never would have been any occasion for our two paths to cross, if only he hadn't re-appeared in my life and stirred up all those old feelings and desires – feelings and desires I'd been fighting like crazy to suppress when the reality of my predicament sank into my brain.

But no. Life was not meant to be easy for me, was it? Wayne Brown came back into my life, strutting his gorgeous stuff all over our back yard, and making me hot all over again. Even after I knocked him off that ladder and Aunt Lucille told him where to go – even after it looked as though he'd be out of my life for good – stupid Betsy goes inviting him over our house for Sunday brunch!

When I ever saw his van pull into our driveway that afternoon, with me, Aunt Lucille, Betsy, Monica, and Carl sitting around on the patio, I thought I was going to faint dead away, or have a serious heart attack, at the very least. And then Betsy calmly rises from her seat when she sees Wayne approaching, and she brings him over to the table to sit with us – like he's one of the family, no less!

Well, I wasn't the only one who was left temporarily speechless, let me tell you. Aunt Lucille looked like she was about to lay an egg as she watched this farce taking place right before her very eyes, and the way Carl shot that look over in Wayne's direction when Wayne parked his butt right next to him, I thought we were going to have World War Three right there in the middle of our patio. Even Monica looked stunned, eyeing Betsy as if she were a creature from another planet all of a sudden.

It wasn't fair for them to do what they did. They must have had it all planned, no doubt. That could be the only possible reason why, out of the whole bunch of us, Betsy and Wayne were the only ones who remained calm and composed. For my own part, I don't know how I kept it all inside. But then again, I didn't stay out there for too long. All I had to do was raise my voice and demand to be taken indoors, and Aunt Lucille was ready and willing to do me the honor. Of course, she was as anxious to get away from that scene as I was, because as soon as she'd wheeled me inside, she leaned over and told me she never thought she'd see the day when Betsy would lose control of herself and actually invite an outright mobster into our very own home, or something like that, and I said to her," Well, what do you expect? She's screwed up in the head, anyways." Or something like that. Then Aunt Lucille swore that she'd sit Betsy down, first chance she got, and straighten her out; and I agreed with her every step of the way: What we had just witnessed was surely scandalous, and we should all make a concerted effort to see that scum like him was never allowed to contaminate our home ever again. Or something like that.

And we would've had our way, too, I'm sure of it. But Mom's timing was way off, because of all days to pick to drop a bomb on us, Mom chose that very same afternoon to let us all in on her stupid little surprise, and Aunt Lucille got so flared up over it that she completely forgot about that incident with Betsy and Wayne, but instead, focused all her anger on Mom's stupidity.

I don't know why I'm reliving all of this right now. It's pretty close to midnight. Also, it's pretty clear that all of what happened last summer can't be undone. There's no sense in thinking about what could have happened or, better yet, what *should* have happened. All I know is I'm tired of thinking about it. It's almost midnight, and I should be dreaming up what my next New Year's resolution should be.

Last year's was a corker. I remember me and Lisa were sitting at Newport Creamery, putting away the greatest hot fudge sundaes on this planet, and Lisa mentioned that, the year before, she'd made a resolution that she'd get high at least three times a week and that, as of that moment, she'd actually kept that resolution and even exceeded it on multiple occasions. Then she came out and told me that her new resolution was to get *laid* at least three times a week and that, with any luck, she'd exceed that one, too.

I was still a virgin at that time, of course, so I just sat there and took this all in. That's when Lisa confessed that she'd gotten laid multiple times by this redheaded stud named Marty (soon to become my Marty, too!) and that it had been supreme and she couldn't wait to get it on with either this same guy or some other guy, perhaps, as soon as possible.

"In fact," she said to me with fudge dripping down her lips (or was it drool?)," I know of this real great party one of Marty's ex-girlfriends is having tonight. Alison McKenna, you know? She told me I could drop by if I wanted to, and that a lot of the guys that'll be there are on the football team, would you believe it? Friends of Marty's, I gather. Can you imagine, Ellen? All those big football hunks, and little old you and me, coming together all in one big house in one big party. Tonight could be the night, if you know what I mean. It's New Year's Eve, kid-do, and anything goes!"

My juices started flowing really hot, you see, when she mentioned that bit about all those football players who'd be there. Plus, I knew Marty by sight, and if his pals were only half as hunky as he was, then this was gonna be the party of the century, let me tell you! I was so excited, I could barely finish the rest of my sundae without making a mess all over myself, and then Lisa started telling me about how she even gave Marty head a few times in between all the other times she'd gone all the way with him, and that was something I hadn't done yet, so I was more anxious than ever to get going. With any luck, Wayne Brown himself might put in an appearance, right?

Well, that didn't happen. I waited till way after midnight and wasn't even getting noticed by most of the guys who were there. In fact, a large majority of those guys were standing around, holding beer bottles in front of them and doing a lot of smoking and talking about the last football game they'd played in, and they didn't even seem to notice me and Lisa and a whole lot of other girls who were trying to get their attention.

It was only a matter of time, though. It certainly didn't take long for me to spot Marty, seeing as he was the only redheaded guy in the bunch, and it didn't take long for him to spot me either. Next thing you know, he's standing opposite me, talking some stupid nonsense about some guy from another school whose ass he just got through kicking earlier in the day, and he's drinking his beer the whole time he's talking to me, too, as I recall. Well, pretty soon, the two of us are smoking it up on the couch in the living room, just the two of us, and before you know it, his hand is sliding in places I'm not used to having guys' hands in, if you know what I mean. Well, I can read the old handwriting on the wall, and after looking around and not even seeing Lisa anywhere in the room, I'm really starting to freak out a little.

Then, out of the clear blue, Marty burps and then says he needs to take a leak, and would I mind showing him to the nearest bathroom? That's all I needed to hear, of course, so I simply took him by the hand and led him upstairs to this little hallway; and instead of us going into the bathroom, we wound up in one of the spare bedrooms. Marty kicked the door shut, and he pushed me onto the bed which, luckily, just happened to be right behind me. A moment later, he's standing there with his pants down to his ankles, and he's telling to get down to business, what the hell did I think we were here for?

Well, I was so spaced-out and even turned-on that I can hardly remember any of the details. I just recall telling myself that this guy had one hell of a body, and he was – let's just say, he was bigger than I expected him to be. Let it be said once and for all, then, that I remained a virgin that night, but I did try out a few things on this guy that I'd never done before. He didn't say much of anything, except a few times he complained that I was doing a lousy job, but he ended up leaving the room with a big grin on his face. And for my part, I thought the whole experience was totally fantastic! What a way to start a new year!

Speaking of which, I've just noticed that it's five minutes past midnight, so we are officially in 1986. Hallelujah! I wonder how many morons are getting their jollies over this, just in this pathetic little town alone. I wonder who's servicing Marty this time around, and if she's as lousy as I supposedly was – according to him, anyway. I suppose, though, that a lot of folks are kissing and hugging and drinking themselves silly over such a miserable non-event as this. Aunt Lucille's asleep, no doubt. Asleep upstairs in her sacred little bed with her virgin-white sheets pulled up over her, and even if she's lying there half-awake, she's probably thanking the Lord and all the saints above for keeping all those vicious snakes out of her bed for one more year of her sickeningly lonely life.

And right now, Monica is lying in her own bed in a dark chamber that is quiet and stinks of chloroform, and she's probably not even aware that this night marks a milestone in history – or in the history of the stupid calendar, at any rate.

And right now, the love of my life is lying in his own chaste bed, with tears streaming down his cheeks, all the way down his chin and even moistening that stupid bandanna he's still probably wearing around his neck. Maybe he's thinking about Charlene, and maybe he's thinking about *her,* and maybe he's thinking about playing with himself. But one thing's for certain: He sure ain't thinking about *me,* and for that, he can go straight to Hell!

And that's my New Year's resolution for 1986: To see Wayne Brown burning alongside of me in Hell before the year is up. And the next time he spits at me, I'll spit back, too!

BETSY'S DIARY – July 14, 1985

Dear Diary: In the space of a mere eighteen hours or so, it seems as though matters have altered their course considerably in my life – to outward appearances, at least. For one thing, the day began with sunny skies, and there was a rather dense humidity in the air that imparted a sultry glow to all of my surroundings. Later on, in the evening, a refreshing downpour dispelled the heat, and now, at eleven-thirty p.m., there is an almost autumnal cast to everything I see, and I feel strangely perturbed by all of it. And for another thing, there is one more person sleeping in this house tonight, in the bedroom right next to me, in fact, and it is perhaps his presence here in our home that has caused me to feel uneasy.

But first things first. I awoke early this morning, nearly at the crack of dawn, and slipped out of the house before Ellen had stirred and even before Mom had returned home from last night's adventures. When I arrived at Burlington Park, Wayne was leaning against the side of his van with the already sparkling sunlight filtering through his blond curls and dazzling my eyes into a state of near-blindness as the sun's rays reflected themselves off his sunglasses. The smile that creased his lips when I got out of my car to greet him was even more blinding; and I slid into his arms and became engulfed in the strength of his solid, yet tender embrace. Over the past couple of days I confess that the need to feel his warm, smooth body against my own has become very potent within me.

It was barely seven o'clock when we joined hands and started our trek through the woods, and almost immediately it felt as though not even the shade of numerous trees which bordered our path could offset the steamy aura of veritable passion that seemed to curl up from the ground beneath our feet and the brush that entangled our ankles. As we walked hand in hand, I was conscious of the fact that this was the last day of total freedom for me, that tomorrow I would be returning to my job at the library, and that I was most desirous of taking advantage of the amount of time and space that I felt I could enjoy this morning with the man I loved.

When the heat started to become almost unbearable for the two of us, we directed our steps to the shore of Lake Palmer and, in total seclusion, swam for over half an hour in its cool waters, made love among the sheltering reeds, and when Wayne carried me into the thick of the woods once again and placed me gently upon the dry earth, I clung fiercely to his neck and arched my body against him while he inclined his face over my left shoulder and told me to rest in his arms for a little while, to stay close to him, and to whisper words in his ears that would delight him to no end.

But we didn't speak, even though he'd asked me to do so as the two of us reclined under that tree, clasped together with our eyes soon closing as we listened dreamily to the music of our thoughts. And a little bit later on, I drifted into a trancelike slumber, my mind quivering in a state that was somewhere between consciousness and oblivion, only to awaken a short time later to find myself strewn with wildflowers and to see Wayne standing over me, in a haze of sunlight, smiling and giggling like a small, young child.

In many ways, even though he is biologically a man, he seems very much like a child. A child that is both scarred and scared. A child who is just now learning to shed his fear and his shame, and to don a cloak of purity so that he can begin to view the world and everything in it with the same kind of awe and delight that I, too, experienced the first time I gave myself to him, body and soul, on the beach earlier this week.

But he is scarcely the only one of us who is learning. I, too, have learned. I now know how to breathe without a sense of shame, how to look upon the years ahead without a fear that they may ultimately lead me nowhere and be utterly devoid of meaning. I have learned to love. To love not only Wayne, but to love my family, my mother, my God, and His gift of life to me, now with complete abandon and with all the youthful power and force within me.

Yes, I am a young woman who is in love with life, who is at that point where she can hurl her passion about her and even find renewed strength in her inner dynamism as she does so. As the years pass and I enter into middle age and, finally, senility, I may never again possess this same capacity to feel and love as intensely as I do now; and I vow that I will not commit the offense of wasting another precious second of my youth by cloistering myself, stemming the tide of my emotions, or in any other way preventing myself from living life to the fullest. It would be a sin to do otherwise, I am sure of it.

Being in love has been such a glorious experience for me that I yearn to see every other human being in love as well. I want to see my mother locked in the arms of a man who is passionately in love with her, to see my aunt's otherwise dreary existence invaded by the incredible torrent of happiness that only true love can bring, to see Ellen's face flooded with joyous sunlight upon hearing words of love directed towards her from the lips of a sincere and trustworthy young man, and to hear Monica's heart singing with ecstasy over the joy that marriage to Carl has brought her. Oh, if only such fantasies could become realities! If only all of us could be happy and be totally consumed by this zest for life and love which I now feel!

And how splendid Wayne is! How gentle, how kind, and how caring! When I hear him laugh, like the way he laughed this morning when he saw my reaction to being adorned with wildflowers upon awakening from a brief slumber, my heart rejoices and seems to be leaping inside of me. When he smiles, I seem to hear the thunder of God's majesty erupting in my soul. And when his eyes fall upon my face, the most divine and tender music throbs throughout my entire being. And to think that this incredible man is mine! He is almost afraid to love me too much, as if he and I both wonder at the effect so much love may have upon our lives after so many years transpired without our being able to feel this way. We need each other so much and draw so much strength from each other – And yet, there is a fear that both of us are aware of. A fear that, after being exposed to so much sheer joy, some sinister disaster may be awaiting us just around the corner and we are too blind in our child-like naivete to be able to perceive its looming presence.

It was there, in the deep shelter of the woods this morning, that we agreed that, whatever may be in store for us, we would encounter it as one; and as a starting point, I suggested that he join me and the other members of my family for brunch later on in the day. It was planned between the two of us that he should step into the back yard and onto the patio with a naturalness that would belie the significance of his presence, and hopefully, the others would accept him without question as a part of our little gathering. This would be the first step in our being able to love each other more openly. We were both fully aware of the risks, but we reminded ourselves that we could pull it off far more successfully if we simply behaved in a nonchalant manner and, even if there were odds that would have to be met even more challenging than we realized, we would remain undaunted throughout the entire episode.

When we separated around eleven o'clock or so, Wayne in his van and me in my own car, the air was unbearably thick with moisture, and I soon found myself pulling into the parking lot of the first church that I passed by, deciding to seek both shelter and peace inside its doors.

It was the first time I had entered a church – the first time since Wayne and I had fallen in love, that is – and I knelt in my pew and thanked God for my continued good health, and prayed for the welfare of my family and friends. Then I raised my eyes timidly towards the church ceiling and said to Him: "I thank Thee for this love that has entered my life, but please don't let it destroy me."

My eyes immediately dropped to the floor in shame and embarrassment, but that final thought had truly been there, perhaps lying in my subconscious, and it seemed to release itself from my mind as if it had a life of its own. For some unfathomable, incomprehensible reason, I couldn't help thinking that I may blindly step off the edge of a cliff one of these days, and the thought of being blind to dangers that might lurk all about me instantly caused me to tremble in momentary fear.

I soon realized that I was being foolish, and after Mass had ended and I was driving back home, I comforted myself with the thought that I would soon be enclosed in Wayne's sheltering arms and as long as his love for me burned as ardently as mine did for him, there was no need for either of us to be afraid.

And so, I was able to remain quite poised during the initial period of our Sunday get-together out on the patio. Monica and Carl helped me get everything fixed up while Aunt Lucille and Ellen sat out back and complained about the heat. I had no idea where Mom was, but Monica, Carl, and I conversed so pleasantly for a while that I scarcely bothered to let Mom's mysterious whereabouts trouble me.

It was at about two o'clock that Wayne's van pulled into the driveway. Monica was leaning across the picnic table, telling me about some shopping she was planning on doing in a few days, and Aunt Lucille was talking about the heat wave of '75 during which the temperature had soared to an all-time high of 104 degrees Fahrenheit. I heard his van pulling closer to where we were all sitting, and I wondered if anyone else had even heard it because they were all carrying on as if nothing out of the ordinary had taken place. Then I reminded myself that that was exactly it: I was to assume an air of nonchalance and behave exactly as though nothing out of the ordinary was taking place.

I saw him first, and my heart immediately jumped into my throat. He looked so handsome with his hair bleached almost white by the sun, and his head-band clung tightly to his temples, so tightly in fact that it looked as though a pair of veins were protruding slightly through the skin of his tanned forehead. He was also wearing one of the bandannas I'd given him, and it hung loosely at his throat the same way his shirt hung loosely over his body. He tried to smile. In fact, he did manage to grin a little, very briefly, as our two sets of eyes momentarily met, and then he immediately dropped his glance to the ground underneath him; and all of my family members became perfectly still and quiet within a matter of seconds.

"Wayne," I said briefly, the sound hardly coming across as anywhere near as pleasant or carefree as I'd intended it to, and I swept up from my seat and went over to escort him closer to where we were sitting. "Wayne," I said a little more brightly than before. "You remember my Aunt Lucille, and Monica and her husband Carl – and Ellen, of course."

Wayne kept his eyes to the ground, and I inwardly cursed at myself for not having suggested to him that perhaps the ordeal might have been a little easier for all of us if he'd been wearing dark glasses; but since nobody in my entire family even bothered to say a word to him, except for one feeble hello from Monica, it didn't even actually strike anyone as being rude that he was unable to lift his eyes from the ground.

In a few moments, I had him seated at the picnic table on the bench right next to me, between me and Carl, and while Wayne calmly took out a cigarette from the pack that was in his shirt pocket, Carl directed such a seething look at him that I thought it to be downright hostile. Not to mention the sour look Aunt Lucille was wearing on her face, only her expression of pure disgust was directed mainly at me, not at Wayne, and I immediately offered them all another sandwich and then turned back to Monica in an awkward attempt to revive the conversation we'd been having earlier.

Fortunately, Monica got her burst of energy back and proceeded to ramble on about a big sale they were having at the mall during the upcoming week, and she even went so far as to include Wayne in her smiling glances from time to time. For my own part, I remained as warm and charming in manner as I possibly could, and luckily we were able to keep the conversation going for quite some time on neutral territory. Both Wayne and Carl, however, preserved a rather icy indifference towards each other, and in a way, I preferred it to any outright mutual abuse erupting between them. The two of them just sat there in silence, as if making their distance between them remain both physically and emotionally as great as possible.

Finally, during a lull in the conversation, Monica turned towards Wayne and quite sweetly, I thought, complimented him on the excellent job he'd done painting the house, and at that very moment Ellen remarked to all of us in general that it was really quite hot sitting out there on the patio and that she would like to be taken indoors.

"Yes," Aunt Lucille piped up in a strident tone of voice. "I fully agree with you, dear. In fact, I find the atmosphere out here to be quite stifling."

There was a distinctly sharp edge to both her words and the tone of voice she used in expressing them, but I was actually relieved when she and Ellen went inside. It wasn't until I was satisfied they were both shut up indoors that I felt a great sigh escape my body and I immediately put my arm around Wayne's waist where he sat next to me and pulled myself in a little closer to him.

Monica noticed the movement, and her lips creased themselves into a smug little grin, and then she said, taking Carl into her regard as she said it,

"You know, I really feel we should be spending more time together. Carl and I would love to have you drop by for a little visit. Any day of the week, in fact, would be fine. Wouldn't that be nice?"

"Oh, Monica," I said to her," I'm so glad you said that. I've just felt kind of funny about doing that, though. After all, you two are still newlyweds and –"

"Nonsense," she said with a little laugh. "We'd love to have you. Both you and Wayne, of course."

What happened next was very odd, but not really unexpected, I suppose. No sooner had Monica issued her invitation to me and Wayne, than Carl climbed to his feet, stepped away from the table, and began striding back and forth behind where Monica was sitting, and I will never forget the fierce look he was wearing while he kept pacing and then said to her in tones that I've never heard him use before,

"You know, Monica? You never know when to stop, do you? You never know when you've gone too far."

"Really?" my sister said to him, and she turned her head to watch him pace a little; and while she did that and her husband continued to brood, I clutched Wayne a little more tightly and felt his own arm slide about my waist and bring me in against him more forcefully than ever.

"Just do me a favor, will you?" Carl said to her, and he paused in midstride to give her a stern, whining type of look. "Don't go opening your big yap and saying stupid shit before thinking first, O.K.?"

"But darling –" Monica started to say, and I was taken by surprise when I heard the jeering tone of voice when she used when she said the word "darling."

"Look, you're really pissing me off," he said to her, and then he actually stepped in towards her in a somewhat threatening manner, and that's when my sister rose to her feet and glared at him. At the same moment, I found my arm becoming disengaged from about Wayne's waist as he, too, got to his feet and stood quietly with his arms hanging loosely at his sides while he watched my sister and her husband shooting figurative daggers at each other with their eyes.

There was a tense silence, even more tense and agonizing for me because it gave me time to absorb the horrifying significance of the scene I was then witnessing. Plus, my inability to deal with what was happening – to deal with it in any constructive manner, that is – held me motionless in my seat as I watched the three of them standing there in their own strained immobility.

At length, Monica emitted a forced sort of laugh and turned slightly in her stance so that she was able to take in all three of us.

"Come on," she said in a fruitless attempt to sound cheerful. "Let's not stage a scene in front of Betsy and Wayne."

"Right," Carl sneered, moving between where Monica was standing and where Wayne himself had assumed a silent standing position of his own. "We mustn't stage a scene in front of Betsy – and Wayne."

As soon as he was through spitting out Wayne's name, he turned his back on us and strode off to the rear of the yard where he found a spot against a tree, folded his arms across his chest, and leaned his back against it to stare down at his shoes.

I felt sorry for him even though I couldn't understand the reasons for his unbelievably strange reaction to Monica's invitation to me and Wayne. The sight of his brooding form, hunched up against that tree at a distance from the patio, stirred an eerie sort of compassion inside of me, and as soon as Monica mentioned going indoors to get some watermelon, I excused myself from Wayne's side and walked over rather timidly to where Carl was standing.

"Don't be upset," I said to him, reaching out my hand and rather lamely touching one of his wrists while he remained slouched against the tree with his arms folded in front of him, still looking sulkily down at his feet. "It's a beautiful day," I continued, having failed to get any kind of a reaction out of him when I touched him lightly on the wrist. "We're all here together to have a nice, relaxing afternoon. What is it that could possibly be upsetting you like this?"

He shifted his weight from one foot to the other and only slightly altered his position against the tree, but his arms remained enclosed about his body. And so did his eyes remain riveted to the ground under his feet, and I honestly couldn't decipher the precise cause of all this suffering on his part. It all seemed so unnecessary.

"Please come back and sit down with us," I said to him, leaning in towards him a little bit and pulling ever so slightly on his wrist. "I won't be happy until you've sat down with the rest of us and had some watermelon."

I thought I was speaking to him in my sweetest voice possible, but he suddenly yanked himself out of the already insecure grip I had on his wrist, and he lifted his eyes from the ground to look at me.

I was totally shocked to see real, honest-to-goodness tears coming down from them. This wasn't just an act to garner sympathy. These were genuine tears being shed by a man who was racked with some indefinable pain, and I stepped back in instant alarm upon seeing the state he was in. I was speechless, and I honestly didn't know whether I should move back in towards him and seek to comfort him in his distress, or to run into the house and seek some form of assistance from Monica in how to deal with her husband's strange behavior. So, I simply stood still in my indecision, and oddly enough, the strangest feeling suddenly came over me that maybe I personally was responsible for his tears.

His lips trembled slightly, and he moved them apart a few times as if he were going to say something to me; but then a look of complete fright came over his face, and he dropped his eyes back down and kind of shrank even farther against the tree, and it was then that I realized that Wayne had sidled up next to me.

He pulled me in towards him by the waist, leaned his face down towards my ear to ask me if everything was O.K., and when I shook my head rather uncertainly, he released me completely and walked right up to Carl who was, needless to say, still slouched against the tree, but on his guard now that Wayne was standing before him.

"Why don't you come on back and sit down?" Wayne said to him, not quite as sweetly, to be sure, as I had spoken to him only a moment earlier, but still in a remarkably low-keyed manner. And when Carl didn't stir a muscle, Wayne stepped in towards him a little closer, laughed rather uncomfortably, and then said," It's because of me, right? You want me to leave, huh?"

"Wayne," I started to say, rushing forward to take his forearm in both hands, but Wayne simply shook his head a few times, looked down at the ground momentarily, and then back up in Carl's direction.

"Just give me five minutes," he said to him," and I'll get the hell out of here, O.K.? Then you can go on back and sit down. Five minutes, O.K.?"

Then, much to my alarm and perplexity, he turned on his heel and went striding back out onto the patio and, even more unexpectedly, towards the driveway where his van was parked. I tore myself away from where Carl was still standing, and rushed to follow Wayne. I called his name a couple of times, reminding myself that I ought to be as nonchalant and casual about everything as I possibly could, but found that I just couldn't manage that.

Finally, when I saw Wayne pull the door to his van open and get inside to sit behind the wheel, I stopped just outside the window where he was sitting, wanting to fling myself upon him and pin him down bodily so that he wouldn't leave me, but feeling restricted by a sense of self-dignity and, at the same time, numbed by the shock of watching his abrupt departure from the premises – a departure which bore too striking a resemblance to the one he had taken from our house on the morning when Aunt Lucille had terminated his painting services and I thought I'd never see him again.

"Wayne," I said to him when I saw the fierceness with which he got the engine started and shifted into reverse.

I'm sure my voice must have come out sounding meek and helpless and tortured with fear, but it was apparently loud enough to get his attention; and before allowing his foot to let out the clutch and start the van rolling backwards out of the driveway, he grasped the steering wheel in front of him with both hands and then furiously drove his forehead straight against it with such sudden force that I expected to see blood spurting from his temples as soon as he lifted his head into view once again.

Instead, when he did raise his forehead away from the steering wheel and turned to face me, there wasn't any blood at all streaming down his face. There was, however, that unmistakable look of supreme sorrow smoldering in his dark blue eyes, and that was far more devastating for me to look at than if he had actually been bleeding from his forehead – because now I could see, quite clearly, that he was bleeding from his soul instead.

"Don't cry, Betsy," he said to me in a voice that itself sounded so saturated with tears that my own feelings just then seemed negligible in comparison. "I've failed. I know it. And that's why I've got to get out of here right now."

In the next moment, his hand came out briefly through the open window of his van, and then he took my face and gently caressed it with his soft fingertips. That was all that was needed for my distress to be instantly dispelled, and a few moments later when I returned to the patio, I was relatively composed.

Carl was just making his way back towards the picnic table when I got back out there, and then both Monica and Aunt Lucille emerged from the house, my sister carrying a plate with slices of watermelon on it and my aunt bearing a pitcher of pink lemonade. The tears were no longer on my brother-in-law's face, but he did seem rather pale and tense, even after we'd all gotten seated and were eating watermelon. No one mentioned the fact that Wayne had suddenly disappeared, and I was glad that I was, thus, spared the necessity of explaining what I still didn't know how to describe. They, no doubt, spoke about Wayne and his sudden disappearance later on because it wasn't more than half an hour later that the phone in the kitchen rang, and luckily, I was just going inside with some empty plates when it started ringing, so I was the first to reach it.

It was Wayne. He was calling from a telephone booth at the mall, and I jumped at the opportunity of being able to see him again, so that with only a minimum amount of explaining, I managed to get out of the house all over again and drive out to the mall. Once inside, I directed my steps to the Newport Creamery and found him sitting way in the back, all alone, with a practically untouched hamburger in front of him and a nearly full glass of soda a little off to the side. His eyes were cast down to the floor, and he sat with his back half-against the wall and half-against the back of his seat. Without saying a word, I slipped into the booth so that I sat directly across from him, and my movement caught his attention to the extent that he drew his back away from the wall, but his eyes remained lowered.

"I'm sorry," he said before I had a chance to speak, and his voice sounded very low. Not tragic. Not even sad, really. Just kind of drained and defeated.

"Wayne," I said to him once again, and I tried putting my hand out to him across the table, but he took his own hand and put it up to half-cover the lower portion of his face, then shifted his position uncomfortably in his seat. I could see the sweat starting down from underneath his head-band, and his shirt, which had seemed to hang loosely over his body earlier in the day, was now sticking to his muscular arms and shoulders.

"I fucked up, right?" he said to me, still without raising his eyes from the floor. "I gave it my best shot. I really tried to – What's the use, though? I fucked up, right?"

"You didn't," I told him quietly but firmly. "You didn't do anything wrong."

"I'm bringing you down with me, right?" he suddenly said to me, straightening up a little and setting his shoulders back a little more firmly. "There's gonna be trouble in your family now because of me, right?"

I couldn't believe I was hearing this. Not now! Not after everything we had been through. Not after we had vowed that we would surmount all obstacles anyone in the world intended to throw in our way. We had been so happy this morning, so deliriously happy. The sound of his child-like laughter in the woods early this morning came back to haunt me like a wistful melody that one associates with a wonderful dream-like and bygone era. How could this transformation have taken place so rapidly?

"I'm sorry about everything," he said to me. "Sorry I ever embarrassed you in front of your family –"

"Wayne, no!" I said shrilly, but it seemed pointless for me to try to interject a single word of protest in the face of his sudden desire to unleash his bitterness in my presence.

"What can we do about it, Betsy? Can you tell me that? What can we do about it? You gonna send me to college, teach me how to read maybe, show me how I can get to be good enough so your brother-in-law'll be able to accept me into his apartment?"

"No, Wayne," I said to him, and this time I raised my voice loudly enough and with enough conviction behind it so that he wouldn't try to go any further before I had a chance to speak my piece. "I honestly hope that you didn't call me on out here to listen to this speech of yours that really amounts to nothing more than a desperate plea for sympathy. If you want to sit there like a mope and feel sorry for yourself, that's one thing, but I would prefer not to be a spectator to such idiotic wallowing in self-pity."

"Betsy." It was his turn to attempt to interject some sort of remark, and he actually managed to lift his eyes from the floor for a second when he did so, but I wasn't having any of it. I had started the flow, and I was determined to allow it to pour forth, uninhibited, until I was satisfied that I had driven my point home.

"I love you for the man you are, the person you are, the individual that you happen to be," I told him. "I couldn't care less whether Carl considers you worthy enough to step foot inside his apartment. If that's the case, fine. It only serves to detract from *his* character, not yours. The man I fell in love with is a strong and kind-hearted individual who can take pride in himself as a unique member of the human race. He's a loving and tender creature with the strength of a lion and the soul of a child. He is the man that I have chosen to cling to for the rest of my life, and then some. Now, if you don't want to lose me, then I suggest that you start acting like that man again, instead of sitting there sulking like a spoiled brat. It's really beneath you, and I sincerely hope that you never ask me to witness a scene like this again. And that's all I have to say."

The dear man blushed in humiliation during my entire lecture, and even after I was done talking and had leaned back in my seat rather out of breath and shocked at my own behavior, the redness stayed in his cheeks, and when he lifted his eyes, finally, to my own, there was a gleeful sparkle dancing within them.

"You're right about everything – as usual," he said to me, and then before another second had passed, his whole face lit up and he said," So, what are we wasting time sitting here for?"

Within the hour, we were clasped in each other's arms on the mattress of his bed in his poorly ventilated bedroom, and I don't believe I ever perspired so profusely without even paying attention to it, I felt so fully and completely wrapped up in layer upon layer of loving tenderness. And later on in the evening, after the rains had come and the humidity in the air outside had dispersed, there was still a great deal of heat in the apartment while we changed back into the clothes we'd been wearing before.

Watching him for a moment as he pulled his shirt back on, over his head, and then smiled across at me with such open and unrestrained happiness when he had it mostly all buttoned up again, I couldn't help pausing for a moment and telling myself that this wonderful young man was like a god to me. There is no other way of defining it. He is the one I adore – totally, rapturously, and with my entire being.

And when I returned home later in the evening, I felt as though I were leaving behind me a vital and thriving counterpart to my own persona. I long for the day when it will no longer be necessary for the two of us to part company for any length of time whatever. True, there is the fact of his being inducted into the marines in the very near future, but we are both confident that, after he completes his stint in the armed forces, there will be absolutely no impediments to our being wedded for all eternity. Of that, we are both absolutely positive.

And now I come to the part of the day which seems to have lent a rather peculiar cast to all of my surroundings. Perhaps I'm making too much of this in my own mind. Maybe it's just a trifle, something that is only temporary, and we'll all be laughing about it at some not-so-distant point in the future.

When I returned home, feeling flushed and exhilarated, I was taken aback to find Mom and Rick Sellars sitting in front of the television set. The fact that they were sitting there together was not, in and of itself, at all noteworthy. Rather, it was the fact that both of them were dressed in barely acceptable attire and, more so, the fact that Mom instantly rose from the couch and approached me with arms extended and brimming over with smiles – this fact alone was enough to unnerve me, at least momentarily.

"Betsy! Darling!" she enthused, wrapping her arms about me before leading me over towards the couch where Rick Sellars was sitting, clad only in a pair of quite skimpy-looking shorts. "You remember Rick, don't you? You've met him before, haven't you, dear?"

I told her that I believed we'd met at least once and waited for the man to rise from the couch to acknowledge my entrance into the room in some manner, although he hardly seemed inclined to do so. Instead, he reached over to the coffee-table in front of him, picked up a can of beer, took a swallow, and then put it down so that he could settle back in his seat and belch contentedly.

And then Mom took me aside, told me how pretty I was looking, asked me what I thought of Rick, and then before I had a chance to reply, she fondled the collar of my blouse a little bit, dropped her eyes coyly to the floor, and told me that she really hoped that I liked him because, from now on, he was going to be living with us.

Under other circumstances, I probably would have fled from her sight in a panic of some sort, regarding such a change in our living conditions as nothing less than a betrayal, not only of me and Ellen and the privacy we had grown accustomed to enjoying over the years, but also as a betrayal of our father's memory, even though his death had occurred over fifteen years ago. I mean, I have usually found it difficult enough to accept the fact that Mom has, over the years, led a rather promiscuous social life, but it had never dawned on me that she would go so far as to invite one of her boyfriends into the house to live with us.

As I said before, under other circumstances I might've reacted differently to what she was telling me, but flushed as I was with the excitement of my own happiness, I barely moved a muscle while she

284

delivered this news to me; and my silence evidently was some kind of justification in her eyes for her sudden change from playful flirtatiousness to sour indignation.

"Of course," she stated, moving away from me and pretending to interest herself in a floral arrangement that was in the center of the kitchen table," if you don't find this arrangement agreeable to your high-and-mighty sense of decorum, Betsy, you can always feel free to move out and get an apartment, you know – some little cozy place of your own, where Rick and I being totally in love won't bother you so much."

"Please, Mom," I said to her, raising a hand to my forehead," I'm not in the proper frame of mind right now to discuss –" and then she cut me off by saying that she wasn't in the proper frame of mind, either, to deal with any of my childish tantrums and that maybe it would be best if I would just go to bed and get out of everyone's hair.

It was amazing, I told myself, how she had managed to regulate her emotions so skillfully in the short space of time that we spoke to one another. The long and short of it was that, even though it had certainly been only a short space of time, she had succeeded in upsetting me, and I lost no time in coming on upstairs here to my room and jotting all of this down here in my book.

It has been a long day, and tomorrow will be a strange one insofar as I must go back to work. It will seem so odd to fall back into the routine of my daily living, yet to be aware, at the same time, of all the changes that have taken place in my life since the last time I stepped foot in that library. It has really been, for me, a tremendously prosperous and pivotal two-week period, and I can honestly say that there isn't a single action that I performed during this whole time that I feel I should ever regret having done.

With that said, let me now retire for the night. I'll try not to dwell upon the deft manner Mom possesses whenever she intends to throw me off-balance, and I'll try to put out of my mind the passionate love-making that may be going on right now, at this very moment, in the bed that my mother once shared with my father. No! I will not allow my mind to veer off in that direction. Over fifteen years have passed. She has a right to anything and to anyone that she believes will make her happy; and if inviting Rick Sellars to move in here with us will succeed in doing that, then I wish her the best. I wish them both my best, in fact.

P.S. I wonder what Aunt Lucille will say when she finds out about Mom and Rick Sellars.

AUNT LUCILLE'S DIARY – December 31, 1985

I really blew it this time. This afternoon after work, Kathy and Melanie invited me to join them at a nightclub this evening to celebrate the coming of the New Year, and I actually said Yes. Then, as soon as I got home, it hit me that I didn't have anything in my entire wardrobe that would be suitable for the kind of evening I'm sure the girls had in mind. Not that Kathy and Melanie are wild party-goers, far from it, but they are certainly more liberal in their outlook than I am, but for some cock-eyed, immature reason, I wanted to impress them with the idea that, if I put my mind to it, I could dress as stylishly and party as uninhibitedly as the best of them.

How foolish! And really, when you come right down to it, how utterly childish and stupid! Who am I really trying to impress? At my age, all I can ever hope to accomplish by going to a nightclub on New Year's Eve is to surround myself with an artificial, bland commotion of sights and sounds that would ultimately prove to be more dizzying and sickening than an actual boost to my dwindling spirits. And this realization was driven home to me quite effectively when the three of us arrived at that horrid place down by the beach, and one look told me that I'd committed probably the all-time error of gross stupidity of my entire life.

For one thing, the crowd largely consisted of men and women in their twenties and early thirties, and although Kathy fancies herself as looking a good deal younger than her biological age, nobody can convince me that even a thirty-eight or thirty-nine-year-old man – even a desperate one, at that – would give her more than a passing glance. Not that I myself am what you'd call a raving beauty either.

Well, that one man did ask me to dance. First, he'd offered to buy me a drink, and I went and specified that I would like a Diet Pepsi, so from that, I guess you could say we more or less started out on the wrong foot. The man was semi-attractive, I'll say that much for him. A little gray at the temples, but he had enough hair on his head to cover the bald spots, and he smelled of cheap cologne, which is a darned sight better than what a couple of the men who talked to Melanie smelled like. So, I thought I'd give it a try and sit for a while and talk to this man even though I was frankly quite nervous and uncomfortable, especially when I caught Melanie's eye and noticed the way she was winking at me as if to say," Go for it." Well, I purposely kept the conversation very low-key and impersonal. I spoke about where I worked and that I had a very lovely niece who happened to be crippled but that one of my other nieces was in an institution for the criminally insane and that a third niece of mine had recently committed suicide. I didn't go into any of the details, mind you, but the man seemed to be only half-listening to what I was saying anyway, and with the music blasting so loudly the whole time, it's highly unlikely that he really heard a small fraction of it. Well, no sooner had I started telling him about how my sister had been shot to death than he suddenly interrupted me by saying, "That's nice," and then he asked me to dance.

I noticed that a very slow, romantic song was being played – something by one of those black singers, I think – and before I realized what was going on, he had me by the hand and was pulling me up from my chair.

I must confess that the dance started out quite well. He kept his distance from me like a perfect gentleman, and I was careful not to lean in too close because I felt it my duty at this point to make it clear to him that I was not a loose sort of woman or anything remotely resembling such a thing. But for all the strength of my convictions, wouldn't you know that, before the dance was over, that man actually had the audacity to squeeze my buttocks? The song wasn't even over yet, and I pulled myself out of his arms and went back to the table where Melanie and Kathy were sitting. I was quite flustered – understandably so, I would think! – and I'm certain my face was flushed with embarrassment and shock, but I earnestly tried to remain calm and self-composed; and everything would have been all right, too, but then that horrible, lecherous sex-fiend displayed the out-and-out audacity to come back to where I was sitting and, right before my very eyes, he asked Kathy for the next dance!

That was it. I took up my purse, barely said good night to Melanie, and took a cab home. I just couldn't stay there in that pit with all those voracious animals and watch those subhuman creatures carry on their disgusting mating rituals like that. Such antics, I daresay, are really just a feeble attempt on the part of mankind to disguise the mating process, pure and simple. I am sure that at least three or four of those women that were at that club tonight ended up having sex with the men who met them there. At least three or four, I'm sure! Not that I honestly believe that my two friends would have sunk to such a base level. I'm sure that they possess enough self-control – enough self-dignity to avoid falling into the clutches of the type of playboy who managed to put his hands on me tonight. But it was just so obvious that the men who stood around watching us all night were playing some type of game whereby, if the game were played with enough skill and finesse, they would wind up taking one of us to bed with them tonight. It was all so brazenly obvious that it makes me sick to my stomach to think that I actually allowed myself to be taken in – that I actually danced with that monster and ended up being fondled by him, right there in the middle of the dance floor! For several minutes there, I actually became his toy, his little plaything – his sex object!

Well, I'm home now, and in a little while, hopefully, I'll go to bed and fall asleep. It's about a quarter to twelve, and Lord knows, I don't want to be aware of what's going on when it finally hits midnight. Nosiree. I can still remember that time, many years ago, when Arnie took me with him to that New Year's Eve party, and he started making passes at that tramp Fran Woodstone. It was right around midnight, too, when I caught him in the hallway bending down and kissing that slut on that disgusting swan-like neck of hers; and a few minutes later, when everyone was ringing in the New Year, he embraced me, displaying the utter gall to kiss me on the lips, and I wanted to run outside immediately and vomit all over the sidewalk. I should have learned my lesson right then and there that men are animals, pure and simple. All they care about is the gratification of their own physical desires, and they think all of us women are fair game, too. Well, this happens to be one woman who is determined not to become any man's toy. I've been fondled and mistreated far enough for one evening, thank you, and I know I should just consider myself lucky that that oversexed beast didn't rape me tonight, right there on the dance floor in front of everybody, my two best friends included.

What time is it now? Ten of twelve? God! It's actually coming. It's actually going to be here before you know it. 1986. What a huge number! I can remember when Jean and I were little girls. I think if somebody back then had told me I'd still be alive in the year 1986, I would've considered the person a total freak or something. And if I'd been resourceful enough to stand there and count out the years to determine that I'd be only forty years old when 1986 got here, I probably would have said," Well, bless the Lord, I certainly do hope I'm still alive and kicking when 1986 gets here."

Well, here I am, and here it is. And I'm still alive, though not exactly kicking. And the sad part about it is I honestly wish it weren't so. I honestly wish it had been me, and not those other two, that they would have had to bury last September. Wouldn't life for everyone else have continued a lot more smoothly and happily if it had been me instead of them? Why, my death would have devastated the family, I'm sure. For a reasonable period of time, at any rate. But Monica would certainly not be where she is today, and so would Jean, for that matter. And as I do recall considering a few days ago, even though Jean had recently been abandoned by a man whom she felt she had fallen in love with, she had enough inner strength and perseverance to weather the storm of loneliness that would have resulted; and in no time, she would have picked up where she left off with Rick by going into some other man's bed.

Yes. Jean would have been able to endure just about anything. Look at the way she managed to preserve such utter calmness and poise during her very own daughter's funeral. In fact, she conducted herself with such coolness and such detachment that it infuriated me, and I'll never forget how I verbally attacked her when we got home after the funeral. My attack was intended, on my part, to be complete and relentless, but then when Monica lost control, I had to run over to her instead and was compelled to relinquish the attack I had been prepared to make against my sister.

Oh, God, what a day it had been! We were all sitting in the living room when the hearse arrived to drive us to the church, and I remember how tense I was because Jean was still upstairs getting dressed and I actually said to myself: "Maybe she's not coming after all. Maybe she intends to remain upstairs in her room and not even bother to attend her own daughter's funeral." And then I quickly shoved those horrible thoughts out of my mind, and I told myself: "Of course, she'll be down directly. She loved her, just like she loves her other two daughters. We all loved her." Then, quite suddenly, we saw her come down the stairs, dressed to the hilt; and I breathed a little more easily and forced myself to keep quiet about how worried I'd been that she wasn't going to be ready in time.

The church service was very brief, as I recall, although I was pretty much in a daze during the whole thing. Carl, I remember, looked as though he were ready to faint as soon as we all set eyes on the casket, and I instinctively reached out and took his hand, even though I really had never felt all that close to him.

Well, we all made it through the church service fairly well, I think, but the service at the cemetery itself was excruciating. For one thing, Carl was sobbing out loud a few times, and I honestly thought, at one point, that Father Andrew was going to pause in mid-sentence and ask him if he were all right. But what struck me as quite bizarre was the way Monica seemed content to simply stand there alongside her husband without trying to hold him in her arms or take his hand in hers as even I had done when we'd entered the church.

And, omigod, I just remembered how embarrassing it was when the wind suddenly kicked up for some inexplicable reason and Jean's dress started blowing up towards her face, and of all times for her to lose her sense of dignity, she actually started giggling and said, "Don't look, anybody," and that remark even produced a little snicker from Ellen. At least, in her case, all I had to do was shoot a stern look over in her direction, and that was enough to silence her; but my sister was a totally hopeless case, so I simply stood there and prayed that the wind would die down and stop blowing her skirt up so that we could all be spared another tasteless remark. And all of this, right in the middle of the cemetery, no less!

Well, it was horrible, no matter how you looked at it, and then – just to top everything off! – as we were departing in the funeral-car, we all saw that van speeding past us, and I knew that it was headed for her grave, and I was so shocked. Even puzzled. I'd been given to understand that he was in basic training for the marines or something like that, and I was going to ask Monica how it was possible that he could have been right here in Maplewoods. But it all seemed so irrelevant, really, so I simply tried to push the whole incident out of my mind just as quickly as it had taken place.

And just two days later, I lost my sister Jean, and it was such a scandal for all of us – for the entire family, in fact – that I can't even go into it. I was sure that that madman from the marines had been responsible for Jean's death, and when I was told that the man had actually confessed to the murder, I told the police detective," Of course! I could have told you that myself. I knew it from the beginning." I didn't tell the detective, naturally, that I had known, from the moment I'd seen him outside in Jean's back yard painting the house, that he was trouble and that anyone who associated with him would end up either being murdered, raped, robbed, bludgeoned, or abused in some way, either physically or emotionally or both. That he was actually capable of taking a gun and shooting my own sister was something I honestly didn't want to believe to be within the realm of possibility for that young man; but when I heard that he'd confessed, I was sure that I'd been right about everything. He was a bad one, despite what Betsy tried to tell me. For one thing, he was a man, so he had one strike against him from the start. For another thing, he was attractive to women. My own sister, God rest her soul, even commented on the curvature of his buttocks, as painful as it is for me to remind myself of that incident. And furthermore, he never looked a person in the eye, and that, in itself, was a dead give-away that the man meant nothing but trouble for anybody and everybody. Add to that, those silly kerchiefs and the like that he always wore. I was surprised he wasn't covered from head to toe with tattoos. Definitely a suspicious character, though, no matter how you looked at it.

Then, lo and behold, it turns out it was Monica, not that hoodlum, that was responsible for Jean's death, and I was devastated. First, it occurred to me that some mistake had to have been made and that some ludicrous type of joke was being played on me by God Himself for all my past sins. Then I became seized with disbelief. I mean, how could it be possible for a child to take her own mother's life? Such things are unheard of, at least in this day and age. I remember when the detective informed me that it was a case of "matricide," I peered at him for some time in total perplexity, shook my head, and said to him," No, it wasn't. It was murder, remember?" Then, when he explained the meaning of the word and said that Monica was the culprit, I just couldn't comprehend it. I just couldn't absorb this information and take it into my brain as part of its storehouse of knowledge. In fact, I believe that one reason why it took so long to accept it was that I was not prepared to deal with the horror of it all.

I remember my last intelligible conversation with my niece. She was being held in custody for the murder of her own mother, and they wouldn't even let me speak to her in total privacy, the monsters! I had to sit there and face my niece with that horrid prison attendant standing guard, and I looked that poor, pale child in the eye and said to her,

"Tell me it isn't true, honey. They're telling me that it was you who killed her. You, my little baby Monica. Tell me it isn't true. It's not possible for a little girl to kill her own mother. Oh, God, Monica! Don't put me through this! I'm finding it difficult enough to cope – after what happened to your sister – and then Jean – Tell me it isn't true, baby. It's not possible. Such things don't really happen. Not in real life."

Then my niece, my very intelligent niece who graduated at the top of her class only a few months before any of this had happened – my niece then took it upon herself to look me in the eye and tell me,

"This is real life, Aunt Lucille. As brutal as this is going to sound to you, I'm going to tell it to you, anyway: I killed her in cold blood. And I'm glad I did it, too."

Then she turned away so coldly that a fever shot through my system, and I lashed out at her with all the force I had inside of me: "I hate you! Monster! I'll never forgive you for this!"

I could barely make out what was happening at that point because I was being led away by a pair of powerful arms of what felt like superhuman strength, but I do recall catching a glimpse of my poor little niece as her whole body seemed to crumble, and those are the last words she probably remembers my having said to her – because the next time we came face to face, she didn't even recognize me. Didn't even look up at me, in fact. And after that, it was pointless my even bothering to drive up there to see her.

I vowed, just a few short days ago, that I would go visit her and find out, once and for all, why she did what she did. Nobody kills his or her own mother, then states that the crime was warranted or brought pleasure to the perpetrator of that crime. Nobody in his right mind, that is, would do such a thing. But I know Monica had to have been in her right mind when she pulled the trigger. It's true that, in a sense, you could say that she was still mourning the death of her sister, but to my way of thinking, grief doesn't usually manifest itself in outright acts of violence against one's own relatives. What awful dark power motivated her to take the life of her own mother – my sister?

I drove out there two days ago, and this time, they did let me see her. Finally. I was so scared because I remember that the last time I went to see her, I was told that she'd been so heavily sedated that it was impossible for me to even take a peek at her. Well, at least this time we were able to come face to face, but what good did it do? I mean, I wanted to interrogate her. I wanted to ask her, very meekly and very sweetly, why she had done what she had done.

But when I saw them bring her out, my heart inside of me burst open. She was so ugly, so drawn, like the picture of a walking death, and I held her in my arms and wept bitterly for nearly fifteen minutes straight. I couldn't talk to her. I couldn't ask her anything. I couldn't utter a single word, a single syllable, although I desperately, with all my might, wanted to tell her that I loved her and that I would never leave her side, never desert her, never for a single moment nurture any ill feelings against her because she was like my baby girl, my little baby Monica who used to rush over to the front door, along with Betsy, when she saw me coming up the walk. My little girls used to get so excited when I came for a visit. They were my little girls, my little babies, and I loved them, and I love them still, and I want to die, just knowing that they can never be happy again, never be re-united, never know what it's like anymore to be able to run through open fields, splash one another in the water, sing Christmas carols together on a cold but cozy Christmas Eve. No, they'll never be able to do those things ever again. None of them will.

And neither will I.

It's all over now. It's after twelve o'clock. Another year has begun. Ellen is probably lying in bed right now wondering, as I do, how much worse this new year could possibly be than the last one we both lived through, both she and I. She and I, the survivors! Yes, she and I have both survived, and in that respect, we are victorious. But why does this victory taste so sour? This is not a victory. No. It's a punishment. We are being penalized by having to live through the rest of Time without peace. Without our loved ones. Without hope. And without the comforting assurance that at least our past existence was fruitful and worthwhile. I've often said, in the midst of a depression, that it would have been better if I had never been born, but the same would hold true for so many others. There should be a better way, a more efficient system of running this universe. At a certain point in a person's life, all of that person's options should be examined, as well as that person's innate ability to cope with the difficulties that may lie ahead. Should the person be judged ill-suited to meet the challenge, a painless death should be arranged for him or her so that all the horrible elements of daily living can be avoided for that poor soul. If such a system could have been arranged, Betsy and Monica would have been spared the ordeals that Fate saw fit to put them through, and maybe I wouldn't be here right now to even think about this the way I'm doing. God, am I smart! I have all the solutions, don't I? It's such a shame that I haven't the means or the power to see them to fruition, isn't it?

1986, are you going to be kinder to me than 1985 was? Well, let me go to bed now and sleep on it for a few hours. Even if the powers-that-be cannot guarantee a full year of happiness for me and Ellen, maybe we can be given at least one full day of it. Perhaps. And maybe, God willing, it'll be tomorrow.

That's it for today.

Correction: That's it for 1985. Amen!

BETSY'S DIARY – July 15, 1985

Dear Diary: I am thoroughly exhausted, both emotionally and physically, and yet, I can't go to bed and rest for the night until I've recorded the events of the day. The events of a day which involved my having to come to grips with a few too many issues in my life than I actually had the strength for. There are times when I look upon this all-consuming passion that has entered my life and can view it only as a divine blessing that causes my mind to reel with the sheer intoxication of knowing that all this happiness is actually being directed towards me, and not somebody else or some character in a novel. And then there are other times, perhaps not quite so frequent, when I long for the kind of peacefulness that used to characterize my life before I became involved with Wayne. Of course, I have not, for one single moment, regretted having given my love to him, but I do see that, by entwining my life with his, I have increased the flow of activity in my life, and I daresay I am not altogether sure that I can handle everything with the degree of polish that I would hope to possess so that I can come to grips with everything that's happening lately without ending up hurting or disappointing any of the people I have loved all my life.

My day basically consisted of four rather upsetting confrontations. I have never been a skillful conversationalist, especially under tense circumstances, and have often contented myself by remaining silent, even when I felt I had something important to say, rather than antagonizing another person, intentionally or not. I know it may sound overly romantic of me to say this, but I feel that my love for Wayne aided me, to some extent, in that I was able to withstand the pressure accompanying these four confrontations without falling apart emotionally, as I may have done without the strength that Wayne's love for me seems to have given me as of late.

I should have known, when I got up this morning and started down the corridor towards the bathroom to take my shower, that the day would progress in a manner that would be considered far from normal because, as soon as I approached the bathroom, the door opened, and Rick Sellars emerged. It hadn't actually dawned on me that he might be showering at the same time that I might want to do so, so I was a bit taken aback, especially when I noticed that all he had on, when he stepped into the corridor, was a towel wrapped around his waist. The presence of a nearly naked man in our home at such an early hour of the morning after so many years have gone by since Pop passed away – this masculine presence unsettled me for a moment, and when he passed by me without even saying Good Morning but with a rather crooked smile on his face, I hurried on into the bathroom and closed the door behind me, locking it with a sort of angry determination.

It's silly and immature of me, I suppose, to have reacted in such a manner. I guess I just wasn't ready to encounter a man stepping out of our bathroom – especially a rather burly, hairy-chested man like Rick Sellars – and for him to be wearing only a towel around his waist when he passed by so close to me. All I could think of while I took my shower was that this incident was just one indication of the fact that, with Rick living here from now on, certain adjustments would have to be made in the way I conducted my daily affairs if I expected to stay out of his way and vice versa.

I would have been able to start off for work in a better frame of mind, even after my initial shock of running into Rick in the corridor, had Mom not decided to pay me a visit in my bedroom while I was sitting at my dresser, brushing and blow-drying my hair. First of all, Mom rarely enters my room. In fact, one of the things she said during her little visit this morning was that she never realized I had so many books, even going so far as to suggest that I hold a yard sale some day and get rid of them, so then my room wouldn't look so cluttered. Of course, I thought the whole idea of getting rid of my books was utterly preposterous, but I didn't let it upset me, so I simply withheld voicing my thoughts on the matter, and kept brushing my hair in silence, all the while wondering when she would get around to addressing the main point of her whole unexpected visit.

Well, it didn't take very long for that to happen, although she did it in a rather roundabout fashion. When she saw that I was being reticent about everything she was saying, she paused and then asked me to turn around and look at her, which I did.

She was dressed in a very chic outfit, the kind of clothes that enhanced her shapely dimensions, and before she even had a chance to ask me for my opinion of the way she looked, I told her quite sincerely that I thought she looked absolutely stunning. I also noticed that she was wearing the shoes I'd bought her a couple of weeks ago, which she never even thanked me for, but I never brought the matter up while in her presence.

"Oh, I'm so glad you said that," she told me in a very bright manner, alluding to my compliment regarding her appearance. "I feel quite wonderful this morning. Now that Rick and I are living here together as if we were husband and wife, I feel happier than I've ever felt in my entire life."

I tried not to flinch when she referred to their living conditions as being similar to that of husband and wife, but Mom's too sharp to let anything get past her, so she immediately stepped towards me and said,

"Betsy, please be patient with me for once, won't you? I realize you have very little knowledge of such matters, so I'll forgive you for not understanding me. I just love Rick so much, I can't help but think of him as if he was really my husband. You don't know what it's like to love a man as much as I do. I know that all you can think about right now is that, somehow, I've betrayed your father in inviting this other man to live here with us, and that's why I came in here this morning to see you. I know how you are, Betsy, and I don't want you to feel that way about me and Rick at all. I want you to accept Rick as if he were your own father."

At that moment, I recall that I turned back towards my dresser and resumed brushing my hair. I felt very uneasy during her entire speech, and even more so when she expressed a desire for me to regard Rick Sellars as a second father. I've always wanted to please her, yes. I've wanted that perhaps more strongly than I've wanted anything else in my whole life – but if, to please her, I would have to embrace her newest boyfriend as a daughter would embrace her own father, I heartily feared that such a task would be totally beyond me. I had nothing against the man, I wanted to tell her, but I didn't see how, at this stage of affairs, I could be expected to blindly accept him into my affectionate regard as quickly and as easily as she apparently expected. Naturally, I didn't verbalize any of my feelings to her just then, but she evidently sensed the crux of my thoughts.

Before I knew what was happening, she clapped her hands sharply together and commanded me to face her while I was being spoken to, at which point I swallowed my bitterness, put down my comb and brush, and turned to face her.

"This is exactly what I don't want, Betsy," she started in by saying to me. "I don't want Rick to see the two of us fighting. This man is a saint, I tell you, and if he were to see any sort of – friction, shall we say, between any of us, I don't think he could tolerate it. He already left three other women this year alone, because their children wouldn't get along with him, and if the same thing were to happen – I couldn't take it if he were to leave me, Betsy. I just wouldn't be able to survive the breakup without slipping into the deepest depression of my life."

There were actually tears, I believe, straining to come out from under her eyelids, and I really felt sorry for her upon witnessing a vulnerability that I never knew existed within her. Instinctively, I rose from my seat and took her hands in my own. I tried very hard, in my own insignificant and awkward manner, to assure her that he would never leave her if he truly loved her, and that I would do my best to keep the harmony and peace in the house so that his stay here in our home would be as free of tension and anxiety for him as possible. I said all this with complete sincerity because I could see how important it seemed to be to Mom that this man should remain in her life; and since I, too, valued the constancy and fidelity of a lover, I fully sympathized with her in her distress. For those few moments while I held her hands in mine and spoke softly as I looked into her somewhat vexed countenance, I experienced a sudden closeness to her that I'd never thought possible.

In any case, Mom then stated that she really hoped I would co-operate, and repeated her belief that life without Rick Sellars would be unbearably difficult for her. Then she released my hands and walked over to my dresser and contemplated her own reflection in my mirror, frowning at herself as she did so.

"I'm not as young as I used to be, I'm afraid," she said to me while she continued to gaze critically upon her own reflection. "But I can still get what I want from a man. Even after all these years and after bearing three children, I've got the kind of figure, the kind of body that can really turn a man into a wild animal. Oh, I know," she added with a little, girlish laugh," this is all Greek to you, darling. It's like trying to explain what filet mignon tastes like to a person who's never even eaten a hamburger. But I can tell you this: That man is ten times the man your father ever was – in bed, which is where it really counts the most, you see."

Hearing this, I involuntarily brought my hand to my mouth and let out a little cry. I thought, at the time, that I was being unusually calm and that I was doing a terrific job of restraining all the words I might otherwise have spoken to her – But upon hearing her assertion that Rick was superior, or more sexually fulfilling for her, than my own father, I could not help but react, and Mom quickly responded, turning around to face me in a patronizing way, and informed me that it was hardly suitable for a girl my age to entertain notions that her deceased father was a saint.

"I know," she continued," that because he's dead, you feel that we should all continue to mourn his passing away and pretend that no other man exists who could possibly fill his shoes – or his bed either, for that matter."

"Mom, please –" I said, and then I broke off quite voluntarily because I heard that there was a sob in my voice. A sob that I didn't want her to hear. A sob that would simply re-enforce her opinion of me as being naïve and immature. A sob that would elicit scorn and hostility from her rather than the compassion and understanding I craved at that crucial moment.

"This adoration you have for your father is very touching, Betsy," she explained to me, placing her hands on her hips in a truculent attitude," but it is precisely this kind of thing that I just finished warning you about. Rick will certainly sense this resentment you feel towards him, and that will make him feel uncomfortable and unwanted. I swear, Betsy, if I should lose him because of something you've said or something you've done to drive him out of this house —"

I turned away from her completely and faced the window. I didn't actually cry – not audibly – but inside, a part of me was screaming. Screaming for justice. Screaming for relief. Screaming for an end to come to her harshness, her severity, and worst of all, her threats. How could I get in a word edgewise even if I'd wanted to speak? I'm weak. I know it. And I'm always the loser when it comes to confrontations of this nature, but I was so afraid (and I'm still afraid at this very moment) that if I were to say one word that could possibly be construed as argumentative or contradictory, a possibly violent and hysterical scene between the two of us would be the end result, and a chasm would be created that would exist between the two of us forever.

So, I turned my back on her and kept quiet, and after a time, she ceased her threats and stood in back of me, breathing heavily but without uttering a word until just before she reached the door and I heard her footsteps stop as she paused to tell me that I had gotten her very upset and that perhaps I should think over what she had told me and to give it a lot of serious thought, too.

"By the way," she mentioned just before leaving my room," I've written out a list of a few things I'd like you to pick up at the store on your way home from work today. I'll leave it on the kitchen table."

And thus ended my first confrontation of the day. As disturbing as it had been for me, I did manage to get dressed for work in a fairly rational frame of mind. The thought occurred to me that perhaps I should consider moving into my own apartment. Such a change in living conditions would certainly make life easier for both Wayne and me and, on the surface of things, for Mom and Rick as well; but on second thought, I realized that Ellen needed me to a certain extent, not the mention the fact that my absence from the house would put a strain on Mom as it would necessitate her doing the cooking and washing and other chores that she hasn't been responsible for in many years.

As it turned out, I was able to leave the house without having to encounter her of Rick Sellars, and for that, I was relieved. It was actually something of a pleasure to get back into the swing of things at the library this morning, and when one of the girls asked me if I'd had a good vacation, I was able to face her with confidence and state that it had been the best two weeks of my entire life. She didn't pry any further into the matter because we all had a lot of work to do, but I was hoping, just a little bit, I confess, that she would bring it up later on, so that I would have an excuse to gloat as I visualized describing how I had met Wayne and how we had fallen in love with each other. In fact, the sheer act of fantasizing over the pleasure of letting the other girl in on my little secret was so stimulating for me that the morning hours seemed to slip right by, and that encounter I had had with my mother was out of my mind completely, and for that, too, I was relieved.

At around a quarter to twelve, Mrs. Evans walked over to me and told me that there was a young man at the front desk who had specifically asked to speak with me, and I practically dropped the whole pile of books I was holding when she told me this because I knew that Wayne had mentioned he would stop by to see me some time during the day if he was able to get away from the garage for a little while, and I was so anxious to see him as I was beginning to view him as my very rock of stability.

Unfortunately, my delight in expecting to see Wayne at the front desk was cut short, and little did I realize it at the time, but I was about to have my second confrontation of the day.

Standing at the front desk with a bouquet of red roses in front of him was Carl Peters, looking for all the world like a bright-eyed little schoolboy who is excited about pleasing his teacher with an unexpected gift.

"I didn't know how to apologize for the stupid way I acted yesterday in your back yard," he said to me, holding out the bouquet," so I was hoping you'd accept these as a token of my remorse."

Needless to say, I was very gratified by the gesture, and I told him quite warmly that the flowers were really quite beautiful but that, as far as I was concerned, the incident would have been forgotten even had he neglected to atone for his actions in this way.

"It's O.K.," he said, smiling a little self-consciously while I sniffed the flowers' aroma in my obvious pleasure. "I've often wanted to give you things – like flowers, for example. I just never had an excuse or a pretext to do so, that's all." And then he just stared at me, but without smiling, and so, it was my turn to smile self-consciously.

"Well, you needn't have," I said to him," but thanks just the same."

There was a period of silence. I certainly felt the strain of it, even if it's possible that he didn't, but after a time elapsed during which neither of us spoke, he shuffled his feet a little bit, looked down at the floor briefly, and then told me that that wasn't really why he had come here and would it be possible for us to sit down and have a little private talk.

Immediately the possibility that Monica was ill or suffering from some problem or misfortune sprang into my mind, and I quickly sought permission from Mrs. Evans for a five-minute break and then found myself sitting in the lounge area in a chair opposite Carl's.

"Is everything O.K.? Is Monica all right?" were the first words I came out with, as soon as we were alone.

"Betsy," he started to say, then lowered his eyes in discomfort or distress or embarrassment – I really wasn't able to figure out exactly what he was feeling at first – and then he continued, looking back up at me rather disapprovingly," I've noticed that you've decided to – associate yourself with – with Wayne Brown these days –And I just thought you ought to know – just in case nobody's told you this yet – I think you're making a very bad mistake."

This was hardly what I'd been expecting to hear, but I was willing to sit quietly and hear him out. After all, he is my brother-in-law, and being a member of the family as he is right now, I was willing to give him some "air time" since I felt that, as a brother-in-law, he couldn't help but take something of an interest in my personal affairs.

So, I didn't say anything in response to what he'd just said. I simply lowered my eyes and told myself to be patient and to sit still. If I refrained from jumping to any sorts of conclusions as to his motives for coming here to tell me this or his interest in my affairs, I could then assume an objective stance in the matter and not say anything impulsive or upsetting to him.

"You see," he finally resumed when he saw that I wasn't about to make any verbal comeback to his initial statement," Wayne Brown is – I don't want to shock you by saying this, but – He's a – Well, I guess the common term for it is 'bum.' Now, I know you're going to disagree with me on this and tell me that you know him a lot better than I do – But you don't know him as well as you think, Betsy. I – I went to school with this guy. He and I were in the same grade and everything. I saw him on a day-to-day basis, and I know – I was able to see first-hand the kind of – the kind of shit he –"

"Oh, Carl," I quickly cut in. "I don't want to sit here and listen to you enumerate all his bad qualities." Not wishing to sound disagreeable, I had intended to say more, but he quickly cut me short, leaning forward in his seat and gazing at me so intently that I was practically hypnotized by the force of his stare during the entire time he spoke to me.

"I know you don't want to hear this, but I think you have a right to know exactly the kind of person you're allowing yourself to get involved with. I know the way you are, Betsy. You're trusting. You're always ready to see the good in other people and always eager to overlook the bad. I admire you for that. In fact, I love you for it. But when it comes to a situation like this – where you're obviously wading through territory you know nothing about – I feel the line has to be drawn somewhere. Wayne Brown is a bum, Betsy. A bum, pure and simple. Worse than that, he's a stupid loser."

"No, Carl, I don't –" I started to say, rising to my feet with the desire to escape this entire scene just as quickly as possible. I mean, of course, Carl had no idea that I already knew all about Wayne's past. Wayne himself has already confessed every detail of it to me. I heard Wayne tell me these things himself, and it wasn't that hearing them again would upset me. It wasn't that that compelled me to rush away from this scene. It was the awkwardness of having to sit there and hear all of this from my own brother-in-law that was most disturbing for me. It had been obvious from the way Carl behaved yesterday out on our patio that he had no desire to even be civil towards Wayne, and now his coming here and telling me all of this was beginning to impress me as a premeditated attempt on his part to discredit Wayne, and *not* a well-intentioned effort to spare me some sort of unnecessary grief which is what he expected me to believe to be the case.

As I said, I just had such a need to escape from his presence and to wish that I could simply vanish and no longer act as a participant in this conversation. But as soon as I was on my feet, Carl shot to his feet as well. He apparently anticipated my movements because, in the very next instant, his hand was clamped upon my wrist, and I was unable to squirm out of his grasp.

"I'm not going to let him do this to you," he persisted, speaking in a tight whisper straight into my face as he held me in his grip. "I'm not going to stand by and watch him drag you down to his level. You! You are too good, too beautiful, too pure to allow yourself to become contaminated by the likes of such a filthy --!"

"Carl, don't!" I pleaded with him. My pleas partly stemmed from my wish to have my wrist released, he was holding me so tightly; but for the most part, I suppose it would be fair to say that I listened to everything he said in a state of shock, and the pain of being held so tightly by the wrist was only a part of the feeling that accompanied the complete amazement and disbelief that I was then experiencing.

Maybe he saw my physical pain suddenly becoming manifested in the expression on my face, because he then let go of me, his face turned perfectly white, and he looked upon me in almost incredible pain himself, as he said,

"Betsy, I'm sorry. I would never hurt you. Never! Please forgive me. I just think about all the danger you're in, and it drives me crazy. Betsy, please. Please give it some thought – everything I've told you – Give it plenty of thought because – because it's important to me. It's very important to me that you don't let him get to you. Do you understand?"

To that question I was unable to offer any response. As far as I could tell, this whole scene had been so bizarre, so unexpected, so completely beyond anything I had ever experienced in his presence that I was hard put to answer him with a positive reply when he asked me if I understood what he'd said. I had certainly come to understand that his feelings for me and his concern were, strictly speaking, beginning to exceed the normal limits of concern and affection I would expect from a brother-in-law. I might have found his concern for my well-being to be somewhat endearing, if only he hadn't been so forceful, so physical in his persuasiveness. But, even though it pains me to say it, I've begun to be a little afraid of him. I just don't know what his next move might be, should we ever find ourselves alone together once again, and I still didn't want to plumb the depths of whatever strange and mysterious passion it was that had actually brought him here in the first place.

"Oh, Betsy," he wound up by saying, and he put his hand to his forehead and laughed a little, rather self-consciously once again. "You probably think I'm some kind of nut-case right now. I just get carried away sometimes, that's all. The thought of seeing you getting hurt –"

He had been shuffling his feet around and stammering in his speech for the last couple of seconds, so that his sudden pause would have seemed to indicate that he was simply unsure about what he wanted to say next; however, a look of incredible alarm suddenly came into his eyes, and without saying another word, he quickly walked away from me.

As I turned to watch his retreating figure, I saw what was probably the reason for his hasty departure: Wayne was standing in the doorway wearing dark glasses and with his arms hanging loosely at his sides.

When Carl started to walk past him, I noticed that Wayne deliberately stayed planted in the spot he was standing in, even though a slight movement to the left would have afforded Carl additional room by which he could make his exit more smoothly. As soon as he was gone, though, Wayne took off his dark glasses, smiled brightly upon me with both his lips and his eyes, and my second confrontation of the day was brought to an immediate close as my rock of stability came towards me with the light of heavenly joy dancing in those beautiful dark blue eyes of his. When we met in the center of the room and he held me in his arms in a long embrace, I quickly forgot that, only moments ago, I had stood in pretty much that very same spot and experienced so much physical and emotional discomfort.

When we finally drew apart, Wayne raised his chin slightly and asked me in a rather teasing manner,

"Aren't you going to tell me what Pretty Boy was doing here a few minutes ago?"

The question was put to me in so laughing and light-hearted a manner that it was impossible for me to feel the least bit threatened by it, although I must confess that I wasn't one hundred per cent truthful when I answered him. I simply told him that Carl had dropped by with a bouquet of roses to apologize for his actions yesterday and then had concluded by warning me about the dangers of associating with the likes of Wayne Brown Junior.

"Oh, he did, did he?" Wayne retorted, feigning a mixture of astonishment and good humor, and he raised his chin once again and looked upon me in an oblique manner. "Did you tell him it was impossible for you to give me up? Or did you say,' Oh, sure, whatever you say, Pretty Boy?'"

The long and short of it was that Wayne and I barely had five minutes to ourselves. I had obviously used up a good deal of my free time in Carl's company so that, by the time Wayne came along, there was really very little time left. As it was about noontime and my lunch break was scheduled for one o'clock, I promised that I would take a run out to the garage, and if he wasn't too, too busy, maybe the two of us could have a bite to eat together. The truth of the matter was that I was already planning on phoning in an order at Glenda's Grinders and intended to surprise Wayne with a huge foot-long sandwich I knew he'd like. As he explained matters to me some time ago, the folks at the garage were usually quite flexible when it came to granting free time to their employees, and even though I only had a half an hour for lunch, I would be certain to spend as much of that time as possible with the man I loved most in this whole wide world.

There was a bit of a sour taste in my mouth, however, after Wayne's little visit to me at the library, and surprisingly enough, Wayne himself was responsible for it. We were standing in the doorway, having just kissed each other good-bye, and I recall that I was very conscious of the way Mrs. Evans was staring at me from where she stood some distance away, when Wayne suddenly took me by the waist and brought me against him rather impulsively. He had his eyes lowered, and his face looked dead-serious when he said,

"He didn't hurt you any, did he? He didn't lay a hand on you?"

I didn't answer him right away. I didn't want to lie, but at the same time, I was afraid of telling the truth. At any rate, my very hesitation was enough for Wayne to guess the truth all by himself, and before I could think of something to say – anything at all! – in order to lessen the tension that seemed to have arisen during those few moments that had just passed, Wayne then said to me,

"If he ever touches you again, Betsy – If any man ever hurts you in any way –"

And then, after a little pause, he simply released me and strode out the front door of the library without looking back at me.

Yes! Although he hadn't finished his sentence, I knew that the unspoken remainder of it contained words that I would tremble at upon hearing them, and I was glad that he hadn't actually said them out loud to me. I was also glad that I hadn't been forced to lie to him by saying that Carl hadn't touched me. Had I successfully uttered that lie, Wayne would have had reason to love me less, because he would have seen that I was allowing myself to become a willing participant in a lie that was tailored to defend another person, and that little white lie would have ended up being a very dark blemish upon the surface of our, as yet, untarnished love. Wayne had been unable to attain high grades in school, but he had certainly been conscious enough of his surroundings early this afternoon, and he had to have seen the tension I was undergoing when he intruded upon me and Carl in the middle of our conversation. For all I know, he may very well have witnessed Carl grabbing me by the wrist because I have no idea how long he'd been standing in that doorway, since Carl spotted him there before I did, and even Carl may not have seen him right away.

But no. If Wayne had seen Carl's hand upon my wrist, I shudder to think of what might have happened. Oh, God! As much as I love him and despite the wonderful gentleness and tenderness he has always shown me, I do fear that there may be a latent streak of violence inside of him, and I fervently pray that I shall never live long enough to see the day that that violence were to suddenly break out – and Heaven forbid if *I* should be the cause of it!

That's why I've got to be very careful where Carl is concerned. There's a definite animosity that exists between him and Wayne. If Carl should ever put his hands on me again, I know that it will be difficult for me not to tell Wayne about it. If I were to even attempt to withhold that information from him, I'm quite certain that he would eventually sense the truth.

But I don't want to think about that anymore. I will just have to be discreet in my actions and in my behavior whenever Carl is around. From now on, I will make sure that the two of us are never left alone together. He is my brother-in-law, the husband of my very precious and dear sister, so it is essential that a scene like the one that took place in the library today shall never again take place in either of our lifetimes.

Thus resolved, I managed to get through the next hour in a reasonably healthy frame of mind. Loretta, in fact, even came up to me at one point and asked me about Wayne as she had noticed the two of us saying good-bye to each other in plain view of both her and Mrs. Evans, and when I informed her that he was someone I'd recently met and of whom I'd obviously grown quite fond, she smiled warmly and told me that she was very happy for me. Even though Loretta and I have never been very close, it touched me so deeply to hear her say this that I'm sure I must have been blushing when I thanked her for her kind expression of friendliness.

Later on, I picked up the sandwiches at Glenda's Grinders and drove to the garage where I instantly found Wayne bending over the open hood of a remarkably stylish-looking vehicle that looked far more luxurious than the car I drive around in. Hearing my approach, he straightened up, told somebody named Larry that he was going on break, and then motioned me around to the back of the building where we soon got comfortable sitting on the ground with our backs leaning against the wall, and dug into our grinders. I would have much preferred a warm hug to the simple smile and hello that Wayne gave me when we were alone, but seeing as his hands and clothing were quite grimy and greasy in appearance, I understood that the physical distance he maintained was probably due to his concern for my own cleanliness. In any event, it felt so wonderful to be spending this short space of time eating our lunches together, that I completely forgot about the morning's strange episodes.

As soon as he was finished gobbling down his sandwich, he got out a cigarette, watched me finish my own sandwich, and then, as I finished eating and he finished smoking, he climbed to his feet and stretched out his limbs in a big yawn.

"Thanks for coming and making my day," he said, looking down at me very tenderly all of a sudden. "I finally have somebody in my life that I can love. I owe all my happiness to you, you know that?"

I laughed rather softly, then rose to my feet as well, and put my hands on each of his shoulders.

Every time I touch him, a renewed sense of wonder comes over me. He is so incredibly strong. His shoulders, his arms – He's so powerfully built that I must say that he is the most muscular specimen of a man I have ever laid eyes on. And yet, each time I find myself enclosed within his embrace, he seems to hold his awesome strength in check, just as one would if one held a tiny, fragile bird in one's big, strong hands and tried to shield it from a sudden gust of wind.

"I love you so much," I soon heard him saying to me, as we stood opposite each other a moment or two later, and I had my two hands resting upon his two shoulders, and our two sets of eyes seemed interlocked in a gaze of pure rapture. "I never imagined I could ever be this happy, or ever feel this strongly about another person. You have saved me, Betsy. You've saved me from having to live a life that was gonna end up being useless and worthless and a complete waste of time. Because of you, I feel now like I'm just too, too happy – like I'm ready to bust wide open, like I wanna scream out at the top of my lungs that I'm a man and that I'm loved by the most beautiful girl in the whole universe."

"If only we had met years ago – when we were mere children," I whispered up at him. "If only we hadn't wasted so much precious time, longing for each other without even knowing that the other existed – And yet, I feel as if you've always been a part of me – as if we were connected by a bond that neither of us knew existed. I spent so many years without you – without anybody I truly loved the way I love you – but I knew that, when I did finally fall in love, it would be wonderful and it would transcend everything I'd ever experienced before in my life. I love you, Wayne, and I'm going to keep on loving you for as long as such a thing as love exists. You do know, of course, that we belong to each other – both now and forever."

He raised his hands towards my face as if to pull it towards his lips for a kiss, but awareness of some of the grease that was still on them caused him to stop, so that he simply held a hand on either side of my face, an inch or two away from the surface of my cheeks. And when those two hands of his suddenly started to tremble with the force of all the emotion that was pulsing through his body, I rapidly drew my hands from his shoulders and seized each of his wrists in them. I then lowered my head and kissed the back of his right hand before bringing it into a closed fist so that I might clasp it firmly against my heart. And when I lifted my eyes to face him once more, having clenched his own right hand fiercely against me with all the power that I could summon forth, I smiled into his eyes and told him once again, quite softly, that I belonged to him forever.

With his face suddenly gone white with emotion, Wayne stared deeply into the blueness of my eyes for several moments, as if straining to peer inside my very soul, and his face seemed to whiten even more when a single, solitary tear slowly began to wend its way down his cheek.

"Who are you, Betsy?" he asked me while I stood, mesmerized, watching the path that that tear of his was making down the entire length of his cheek. "Who gave you the power – the power to reduce me to this? I have never cried in front of another person before. Never. And now, standing here with you and feeling the blood drained from me, that's all I can do. I can't do anything else but cry. Tell me who you are – who the two of us are – why this is happening to me – to the two of us together."

"Isn't it obvious who I am?" I responded, smiling faintly in the face of his lack of composure and, more so, upon his seeming lack of faith. "Don't you know who the two of us are? We are one. You and I, Wayne. We belong together as one. It's something that is simply meant to be, and there's nothing that either one of us can do about it any longer."

"Then it's O.K., I guess, for this to be happening to me. It's O.K. for me to be standing here wanting to die on the spot because I never thought I'd ever be this happy. You know everything there is to know about me, and you still care. You still want me to be with you. Forever and ever, like you said. Even after we're both – dead?"

It was then that I reached out and wiped that tear away from the corner of his lips with my free hand, took in a great breath of air, and increased the warmth of my smile, telling him,

"There's no need for either one of us to be alarmed about that. Now that I've found you, I intend to stick around for a very long time. You're not going to get rid of me that fast, you know."

As I sit here in my room and write all of this down, I wish the day had ended right there with the two of us standing interlocked in spirit and in the common sensation of being destined to remain so, even beyond life on this earth. After all, during those blissful moments, we were no longer conscious of standing in the back of an auto garage, he in grimy shirt and jeans and me in a plain tan-colored blouse and white skirt, and that we were very shortly to become embroiled in what was to be my third confrontation of the day.

In retrospect, I can see that this particular confrontation was perhaps a little less trying than the earlier two, if only because Wayne was present during its entire span of time. However, the element of hostility and the threat of physical harm were both present just as they'd been when Carl accosted me in the library only a short time before this.

It was getting to be that time when Mrs. Evans would be wondering about my whereabouts, and I was just explaining to Wayne that I would try to see him later in the evening, when the two of us suddenly became of aware of the fact that we were being watched. I could see the way Wayne instantly set his jaw when he swung about to face our visitor, and his eyes almost immediately fell to the ground when he did so.

The fact of the matter was that a tall, slender brunette by the name of Charlene was standing at the edge of the building, leaning against the wall with her arms folded against her chest, and she slowly straightened herself up and walked a few paces in our direction as she spoke.

"Well," she began, in a brittle-sounding voice," this is really cute. Big Wayne Brown and – Little Betsy-Wetsy, I believe?"

Neither Wayne nor I said a word, and I caught a glimpse of the way he simply dropped his arms so that they hung loosely at his sides, and he shifted his weight from one leg to the other before hurling a glob of saliva off to the side at a point not too far away from where Charlene had come to a halt.

"Now I can see," she continued," why I haven't heard from you in such a long time, Wayne. After all, how can I compete with this?" And she flung her arm out in my direction as she uttered the final word of her sentence. "Well, Betsy," she suddenly continued, turning her fiery gaze fully upon me and advancing a couple of steps in my direction," did good old Wayne tell you about me and him? Or are you the type that just doesn't give a damn whose boyfriend she decides to mess around with?"

No sooner had the words been spat out from between those vicious lips of hers than Wayne immediately stepped in between the two of us and turned his back on Charlene. In a soft and restrained voice, he told me to leave, and before I had a chance to reply or to respond to his words, Charlene quickly stepped forward, grabbed him by the arm, and whirled him around, bodily, to face her in a horrible burst of fury that actually terrified me for a very brief moment, until I reminded myself that, at least in a physical sense, Wayne was perfectly capable of handling himself in front of this tigress.

"What's the matter, big man?" she railed at him once she had him facing her, although I knew instinctively that he wasn't looking into her face with his ardent blue eyes. "You afraid I'm gonna hurt your precious little Betsy-Wetsy? You think I came here to kick her ass or something? Believe me, if I feel like kicking her ass, I'll do it whether you're here or not."

It was at that point that she became conscious of the way he was glaring down at her hand which still held his arm, and she rapidly removed it, whereupon she drew back from him slightly with an enraged look still in her eyes as she said,

"What's the matter, Wayne? Suddenly you don't like it no more when I touch you? Not too long ago, as I do remember, sweetheart, you really enjoyed being touched by me – especially when we were in bed together –" and she turned to look me in the eye and add, quite unnecessarily," – fucking."

If she expected me to wince at the way she flung that word at me, I suppose I left her grossly disappointed because I was determined that, with Wayne standing there between the two of us, there was no way I was about to allow myself to become intimidated by her or by any obscenities she wished to hurl in my direction either. In fact, there was something almost pathetic in the way she was carrying on, I felt, and while I knew better than to utter a word in sympathy or by way of trying to justify my current association with Wayne, I was becoming increasingly uncomfortable, not only for myself, but also for Wayne whose suffering I could clearly discern in the set of his jaw and the way he kept shifting his weight from side to side as if, at any moment, he would lash out with his powerful fist and drive her, unconscious, straight to the ground.

"Well, I'm glad I came here then," Charlene continued, folding her arms across her chest once again and turning her fierce gaze upon Wayne. "Now I can see what I'm dealing with here. You've picked a real beauty this time, Wayne. I mean, you've always had an eye for the greatest-looking chicks out there, but this time you've really hit the jackpot, haven't you? I just wonder how long it'll take before you get tired of her and decide to dump her, just like you've dumped me. Well, I sure hope she's worth it. And for her sake, I hope she smartens up before it's too late and she finds herself pregnant like me –" And after dropping that bomb on the two of us, she calmly turned around and started walking off, seemingly in mid-sentence, but then stopped when she heard Wayne muttering something under his breath. At that point, she sprang towards us all over again and yelled," That's right, lover-boy! I'm pregnant – as if it matters to either one of you. But don't worry. It's O.K. 'cause I can just get myself a little old abortion, and there'll be no little baby Wayne coming along a few months from now to spoil all your fun. I didn't come here to threaten you guys or to kick little Miss Goody Two Shoes's ass – I just came to see for myself whether it was true or not. Well, that's about all I got to say. How about you, lover-boy? You got anything really deep and meaningful you wanna say to me before I clear out and head for the hills? Nothing? My, my, Big Wayne Brown's got nothing to say. How about that? A man of few words, huh? I come over here and tell him I'm pregnant with his kid, and what's he got to say about it? Nothing. Absolutely nothing. Can you stand it?"

A split second later, she slapped Wayne right across the face, and I grabbed his arm and pulled him in towards me.

"Still got nothing to say, big man?" she continued to taunt him, and although I tried with all my might to interpose my own body between the two of them, Wayne shook himself out from my grasp and faced her all over again, shielding her countenance from my sight with his wide shoulders and heavily muscled frame.

"I'm not through with you yet, you bastard," I heard her tell him. "You're gonna pay for this! – Big-time!"

After that, I didn't hear her voice anymore, and seeing Wayne's shoulders relax a bit, I stole a look past him and noticed that Charlene was no longer on the premises. Heaving a weary sigh, I grabbed him by the shoulders and twisted him around so that he could face me completely.

His eyes were cast down to the ground, and when I touched the side of his face where Charlene had struck him, he rapidly tilted his head upwards and stared up into the sky above, breathing heavily and shifting his weight from one foot to the other while he occasionally clenched and unclenched his hands at his sides.

"It's all over, Wayne," I told him, desperately pressing the side of my face against his chest and tugging his body in towards mine. "She's gone. You can relax. It's over now – and she won't come back. I promise you, I won't let her come back here again and hurt you the way she did."

"I deserved it," he said, suddenly breaking away from me and hiding his whole face from me as he turned completely in towards the side of the building and lowered his head. "There's no getting away from it, Betsy. I deserved it."

"Maybe you did, and maybe you didn't," I explained to him, hoping that the rather faint sound of my trembling voice would reach his ears, as well as my words penetrate his comprehension. "But whether you had it coming to you or not, I can't imagine any reason why one adult human being should ever feel justified in striking another."

"You don't know," he replied, shaking his head slowly from side to side while he kept his back to me. "You're smart and all that, Betsy – but there are some things you'll never know – some things you'll never be able to understand about me, and about the things I believe a person should do in order to – get revenge."

Needless to say, I was running so late that I couldn't very well stand there and discuss the issue with him at any great length, and although it pained me to be forced to leave him in such a state of emotions, I said good-bye to him and assured him that I would make it a point to see him later on, no matter what.

When I returned to the library, I also made it a point to apologize to Mrs. Evans for being late and promised it would never happen again. And so, my third confrontation of the day was behind me, but I was very upset all afternoon. The time seemed to simply crawl along, and I felt that I would never find any peace for my troubled spirits, not until I once again found myself in his arms and was assured that he, too, was untroubled by the memory of Charlene's terrible visit.

It was with a sense of extreme irritation that I remembered, after work, that Mom had written out a list of things for me to purchase at the store, and I set about doing what she instructed me to do, all the while wishing that I could just drive home, change into a fresh set of clothes, and then immediately drive out to wherever it was feasible that Wayne and I could meet. But instead, it was necessary for me to spend time picking up odds and ends at the grocery store and even having to make a special stop at a nearby liquor store in order to buy a case of beer which, I knew, was undoubtedly destined to be consumed by Rick Sellars.

I found Ellen sitting in front of the television set when I got home, having to make a couple of trips in and out of the front door in order to carry everything into the house. On my last trip inside, I carried in the bouquet of roses that Carl had brought with him to the library this morning, and the sight of me standing at the mantelpiece, arranging these flowers in a vase, caught Ellen's attention, and she inquired about the identity of the person who'd given them to me. I thought, at the time, that there was nothing out of the ordinary in the way she posed the question to me, but little did I realize it then that I was about to embark upon my fourth confrontation of this already rather harrowing day.

"*Carl* gave them to you?" she asked in a very pointed manner the instant I answered her question.

"Yes, Ellen, I just told you –"

"Don't you think it's kind of weird?" she interrupted, lifting her face towards me in such a way that I could see the devilish sparkle that always comes into her eyes whenever she's beginning to enjoy herself immensely in the pursuit of some strange sort of pleasure that usually comes at someone else's expense. "I mean, why in the world would Monica's husband be giving you flowers, Betsy? Do you think maybe he's got a *thing* for you?"

I laughed a little when she said that and asked her what she meant by that, although I was fully aware of the insinuation that she was making a point of suggesting to me.

"I don't know," she laughed by way of responding to my question. "It just seems to me that lately – within the past week or so – all the guys have been getting their poor hearts broken because of you."

Again I laughed, perhaps only in an effort to disguise my growing discomfort, and I started to leave the room, not liking in the least the direction that I felt this conversation was going in. I would have made it all the way into the kitchen, too, but then Ellen suddenly stopped me by saying,

"It's easy to walk away from a cripple, isn't it? Especially when you've got a lot to hide."

My biggest mistake of the day, I guess, was in letting her get to me with that reference of hers to the ease with which I seemed to be managing my escape from her on the grounds that I was simply taking advantage of her handicapped position. I have always felt a certain amount of guilt, maybe even a little shame, when I happen to reveal a little too much enjoyment out of being able to walk along the beach, for example, or climb the stairs to my room whenever I wish to go there. I know I really have no reason to feel even a speck of guilt since I was in no way instrumental in bringing about her disability. Still, I felt stirred with pity when she referred to herself as a cripple, not to mention the fact that I was curious to find out the hidden meaning behind her assertion that I might have had something to hide. So, I came back into the room and stood in front of her, looking upon her upturned face as squarely and with as much self-possession as I possibly could.

"If I've said or done anything to upset you," I told her, my voice faltering a little," I'm really very sorry."

"No, you haven't done anything to upset me," Ellen assured me, though the words were spoken in a tone of voice that was definitely not very re-assuring. "I just can't help noticing how, for a girl who usually spends all of her free time with her nose buried in a book, you've been leading a pretty active social life lately. Always out of the house on some mysterious errand or another. I'm not blind, Betsy, and neither are the rest of us. We all saw what you did yesterday – bringing Wayne to brunch with you in our back yard as if the two of you were boyfriend and girlfriend." Her eyes narrowed into slits at that point, and she asked me suddenly," What were you trying to prove in bringing him here like that, Betsy?"

"I wasn't trying to prove anything, Ellen –"

"Please!" she cut in sharply. "Just because I'm crippled, it doesn't mean I'm retarded!"

"Ellen, I wish you wouldn't talk like that – and the way you constantly refer to yourself as –"

"Face facts, why don't you?" she once again cut in on me. "I'm crippled. Handicapped. Disabled. Use whatever word you want to describe my condition. It's easy for you to pretend it doesn't exist. You! You've never known a day in your life when you had to look around and see that you had no future – That's the way my life is, Betsy, like it or not. It just isn't worth shit."

"That's not true," I protested, and in an instant, I was on my knees in front of her, and when I reached out to pull a strand of her hair away from the front of her face, she quickly shoved my hand away from her and said,

"I don't need any of your false pity, you know. If you really had any sense of decency, you wouldn't have tried to make a spectacle of yourself in front of me with Wayne—"

This time it was my turn to interrupt her, and with a sense of having been victimized in this conversation without even bearing any guilt that I could see I had reason to feel, I told her quite firmly that I hadn't meant to make a spectacle of myself with Wayne and that, had I known how bitterly she would have been affected by all of this, I never would have exposed her to such a situation.

"If you want," I even went so far as to concede on her behalf," I'll make sure that he never comes here again."

"This is really funny," Ellen next shot back with. "You actually seem to have this crazy idea stuck in your stupid head that you and Wayne have some kind of future together. You really are stupid, Betsy. Mentally retarded, I'd say!"

Upon hearing what I considered highly offensive language being spoken in my presence, I rapidly got to my feet and started walking away from her, and I guess I must've mumbled something to the effect that I had no interest in listening to anything else she had to say – because, in the very next moment, she yelled up at me that I was afraid to hear the truth.

"That's what's bugging you, Betsy," she persisted, wheeling herself towards me in such a way that I was actually being trapped in a corner of the room with no means of escape, short of climbing right on over her wheel-chair in order to flee to a location where her poisonous words wouldn't be able to harm me. "You don't want to face the fact that this thing you think you have going on with Wayne is not going to last. Do you actually think a man like that – a man who's used to being with a real woman – would stay interested for very long in a person like you? I mean, c'mon, Betsy. You don't know the first thing about sex. You couldn't possibly hold onto a man for very long, let alone a man like Wayne who knows what it's like to get bedded down with a woman who really knows what she's doing."

There were tears coming down my cheeks, tears that I wished to God I had not been weak enough to let fall. Tears which seemed to strengthen Ellen's allegation, at least in her own mind, that I was not the kind of woman Wayne would need to satisfy him. And I found it impossible to hold my tears in check as I stood there and listened to her ruthless attack upon my character, not only as a woman, but as a human being who could be capable of giving something of herself to the man she loved.

And all the while she was slicing me to ribbons with her wicked tongue, it slowly began to dawn upon me that she was talking about *herself* when she referred to the kind of woman who could make him happy. She was apparently spurred on by her own hurt and her own rage over having lost him. So now, her bitterness knew no bounds, and she sat there and let it all pour out in one huge display of relentless candor.

"It's all so stupid, Betsy, and you're too stupid to realize it. You're only going to end up hurting yourself by all of this, you know that? I can see it all now: You're going to fall in love with this guy, and because you think it's important for you to hold onto your precious virginity and because you don't know the first thing about what a woman should do in order to hold onto her man – Because you're so incredibly stupid, you're gonna end up losing this guy. Face facts, Betsy. You'd be better off just leaving the man alone. Just go upstairs and read a book and stay the hell out of his life. You'll only end up making yourself look like a damned fool if you keep thinking the two of you could possibly have some kind of future together. Why, I can see it right now: Betsy the Fool finds out her lover's abandoned her, so she goes out and she kills herself over it! What a laugh! You really are a fool, Betsy, you know that? A real fool!"

By the time she'd concluded her splendid butchering of my character and my intelligence, I had already managed to stop crying because, as the words came from her lips with increasing venom and hostility, I could see that I couldn't possibly take her seriously. Her rage and her bitterness were probably fully justified in her own eyes, and maybe she had a valid reason for feeling the way she did. But was that rage really directed at *me?* In a sense, the answer would have to be an obvious Yes. But wouldn't she feel the same way if it happened to be any other girl who was standing there and who she believed was somehow responsible for taking him away from her?

I tried to convince myself that it wasn't really all that personal, but I didn't succeed very well in that regard. I also tried to remind myself that I ought to give her a bit more "wiggle room" because of her handicap – but even then, I couldn't really see that she – or anyone else, for that matter – had any right to speak in such an abusive manner to another human being.

Well, the moments passed slowly, for me at any rate, and Ellen's temper seemed to abate to some extent. I don't know what more she might have wanted to say to me, but it was not meant to be that anything more should be said because, just then, we both heard the sounds of Mom's and Rick's voices as they came up the front path. Ellen quickly wheeled herself out of my way so as to assume a more natural position opposite the television set, and I hastily went for the staircase so that I could escape to my room for a short time. Facing Mom and Rick at that particular point in time seemed to be one of the least appealing prospects I had before me, so I took my time about changing up. When I came back downstairs and entered the kitchen, I saw that Mom and Rick were outside on the patio, sitting at the picnic-table with two cans of beer in front of them. Mom had the straps of her blouse undone from around her shoulders while Rick had taken his shirt off completely and was sitting there, not saying much of anything as he idly scratched his chest.

Dinner went pretty smoothly for the four of us, all things considered. I, naturally, could not erase from my memory the biting words that Ellen had so recently directed at me, but at least nothing was said between the two of us over dinner. Fortunately, Mom was in a wonderfully pleasant mood, watching Rick Sellars stuff himself on ham, potatoes, and carrots, not to mention rolls, butter, and a large quantity of beer. I was pleased, though, to see the look of love that Mom poured upon him all through dinner. I was so moved, in fact, by the sight of her happiness that, just before clearing the dishes from the table, I stopped behind Mom's chair, leaned down, and kissed her on the cheek. I didn't say a word, didn't tell her I loved her, didn't tell her she was looking beautiful this evening either. I just felt like bending down and kissing her, and I felt so good inside after doing that that it didn't really matter to me that Mom just sat there and kept her eyes on Rick, behaving as though she hadn't even noticed the gesture in the least.

Sometime later, after I'd finished with the dishes and Mom and Rick had gone to the movies and Aunt Lucille had arrived to sit with Ellen in the living room, I took Wayne's phone call in the kitchen and heard his request that I come to him in his apartment, and I was there fifteen minutes later.

He took me by the hands and smiled briefly into my face, but there was an awful sadness in his smile.

"Thanks for coming, Betsy," he said to me, squeezing my two hands in his and sending me a kind of unspoken pleading message with his eyes as he did so. "After what happened today with Charlene, I'm almost afraid that you'll stop wanting to be with me – and it's killing me, Betsy. I've never been this afraid before in my whole life."

We briefly discussed the possibility that Charlene may have been lying about being pregnant, then concluded that it would be best to assume, at least for the time being, that she was telling the truth. That being the case, we agreed that the baby's welfare should be a paramount consideration in our future actions, even though Charlene had expressed her intentions of having it aborted. Even so, Wayne insisted that there was no way we were going to let her use her pregnancy against us as a weapon or a tool whereby she might expect to entrap him in a loveless marriage.

In time, we were able to hold each other without the image of that awful scene behind the garage infecting our mood, and when we retired to Wayne's bed, we made love slowly and tenderly at first, as if we were two children just learning how to walk and joyfully taking one step and then another and then another until we reached the point where our actions became sure and confident and full of exuberance. Then, after re-affirming our love in a physical union, we lay quietly, side by side, on his bed and listened, the two of us, to the peace that pervaded the room while our two bodies relaxed next to each other, breathing comfortably – even blissfully – in the tranquility of our surroundings.

"In two weeks I'll be gone," Wayne said to me, breaking the silence at a moment when the peace and serenity I was experiencing were beginning to lull me into a very beautiful slumber.

"I know," I whispered into the stillness of the room.

"I don't want to go," Wayne said to me, and he turned his body on the mattress under us and leaned on his side, holding his hand against the side of his head so that he was propped up slightly over my face. "I know I have to go, but I don't think I'm gonna be able to do it."

"You'll do it. You know you will. You have to."

"Yes," he admitted, and he slowly took one of my hands with his free hand and clasped it gently against his chest. "It'll only be for a few weeks, right? You – you'll write to me, won't you?"

"Every day," I assured him, smiling up at the ceiling and feeling my hand being clasped more tightly than before.

"And when I come back, you – you'll be there for me, won't you?" he said in a child-like voice that was shot through with fear.

"Yes, Wayne."

"We'll be together forever then, won't we?" he said to me, and for the second time that day, a tear started rolling down his cheek.

As I eased my body in towards him and clasped him behind his shoulders, his whole body shook for a moment in my embrace, and he buried his face against the crook of my neck and expelled a long sigh, as if releasing some unbearable anguish from deep inside of him.

Minutes later, we lay facing each other, simply drinking in the beauty of each other's deep blue eyes, and he suddenly began speaking again, his brows creased as he caressed my hands in front of him with his own.

"I always wondered what it would be like," he said," after a person died. I remember my father telling me I was gonna go to hell if I didn't mind him and do what I was told, and I always figured that was one bridge I'd have to cross when I came to it. Never gave it a second thought – until you came along. And now I'm scared to death of dying, Betsy. I mean – I'm scared, not just for my own sake, but – What if it was *you* who died? Like, what if something was to happen to you while I was gone – in boot camp, for instance – What if something was to happen to you *then?* I wouldn't be able to be there with you to say good-bye. I might lose you forever –"

Despite the sincerity with which he was speaking to me and the obvious strain that accompanied this speech of his, I suddenly took it upon myself to break the spell by laughing and telling him to put his mind at rest regarding such matters. We were both young and extremely healthy individuals, and we both had everything to live for, indeed a good deal more to live for than many other people in this world. My assurances did not quite erase the crease that remained in his forehead for a time, I'm afraid, but I did manage to alter his mood to a certain extent by getting him to lie supine while I slowly crept over him and kissed his lips, his neck, and then his chest – actions which resulted in my returning home quite a bit later than I'd originally intended.

Because this diary entry is inordinately long, I'm sure it's high time I got into bed and slept. I began writing here tonight in a state of exhaustion, and right now, if I don't put an end to it, I don't think I'll be able to hold onto this pen without dropping it. So, without further ado and, for once, forgoing my usual postscript, I will record one final request: that the good Lord may bless all of my loved ones – even those who, in some misguided attempt to hurt me, would mean to drive Wayne and me apart.

CARL'S DIARY – January 7, 1986

Dear Diary: This may very well be the last night I'll ever be able to record my thoughts here in my diary. By this time tomorrow night I'll probably be locked up in a prison cell for the murder of Wayne Brown Junior. I don't know whether I'll be given paper or not, so I can do some writing while I'm in prison. I know I'll sure as hell have a lot to write about, once I've seen to it that that prize moron is put to death. He made a big mistake when he decided he was going to beat me to a pulp on the Fourth of every month. Nobody messes with Carl Peters and gets away with it. Nobody. And that's one lesson Wayne Brown Junior needs to be taught, and I'm just the man to teach it to him, too.

Last night I didn't get to write anything here in my diary. I came home sick to my stomach and couldn't even lift my head out of the toilet bowl for nearly two hours, I was so sick. I guess they were right, all those old fuddy-duddies at school, when they used to tell us the kinds of shit that can result when you mix drugs and alcohol. Hey, I learned all that stuff in school, but I'd always managed to live my life with a pretty clear head, and I was always one to mix drugs and alcohol, too. I don't see why the stuff should start affecting me this way all of a sudden. Hell, man, it's like my whole world is beginning to cave in on me, and I sure would like to know what I've done to deserve all this. In the first place, it's not my fault I'm so heavily into drugs. Kenny got me started a long time ago on pot, for example. We were only in the seventh grade, and Kenny was already up to five or six joints a week, not that that sounds like a hell of a lot, but back in those days, we didn't have that much money to go throwing around on that kind of crap. Plus, Kenny was already smoking almost a whole pack of cigarettes a day, so he needed money to buy himself his smokes, especially when there weren't that many kids at school he could bum cigarettes off of.

I remember all the times me and Kenny and some of the other guys would get high, and we'd laugh and joke around and couldn't figure out why our parents and all the teachers and everybody else always seemed to frown upon it, like it was going to make us mental or something. "I mean, what's the big deal, right?" I remember saying to Kenny once, and Kenny just laughed and lit up another joint right after we'd just finished smoking one already. But you see, that's the way Kenny always was. He was always so cool with a capital C, and I wanted to be like him. I looked up to him as some kind of ideal person. He was always better than me at sports. He was always stronger than me and faster than me, and even though I'm pretty tough myself, Kenny and I both knew that he could kick my butt with ease, too. Later on, when he started becoming sexually active, it was the same old thing. Kenny could always get the hottest-looking chicks, and he'd always manage to get laid on a first date. Every single time. And I envied him, man. He was everything I wasn't.

And now I can't stand the prick, and after I take care of Wayne, I'm going after Kenny. No doubt about it. That prick ripped me off of one thousand dollars, and I thought he was my friend. I swear, man, if I get away with knocking off Wayne Brown Junior, Kenny's gonna be next on my list. No doubt about it.

It all started out last night when I began to have my suspicions about the kind of shit Kenny was fixing to pull on me. I'd dropped off the grand at his house early in the afternoon. Kenny promised me he'd give the money to these guys who were going to take care of Wayne for me. I was guaranteed, Kenny told me, that Wayne Brown was dead meat, and that the killing would take place within the week, man. *Definitely,* within the week – give or take, I think he said. Well, you can imagine the state of euphoria I was in, just thinking about seeing Wayne Brown lying dead on a slab in the morgue. As soon as I dropped the money off with Kenny, I drove on out to the cemetery and told my angel about what I had in the works. I assured her that, inside of a week, the two of us would be rid of that prize moron once and for all. Man, if only the dead could rise from the grave and speak, I'm sure my angel would have appeared before me in all her heavenly beauty and imparted her blessing upon me. While she was alive, she may have been unable to give herself to me completely and allow me the chance to prove to her and to myself, even, that I was a real man, you know? But with Wayne in the picture back then, it wasn't meant to be. Hell, I'd already alienated her from Monica, so I'm sure the two of us could have carried out our act of love without raising objections from any other quarter.

I remember the night before I took my angel into my arms and very nearly consummated our love. It was a roasting-hot evening in the beginning of September, and my wife was gazing upon me with those serious dark eyes of hers while I paced in front of her in our cozy little kitchen with those stupid rose-colored curtains on the window. In complete and utter seriousness, she tells me that she thinks we ought to have our marriage annulled.

"You mean, get a divorce, don't you?" I said to her, and I used this real tough voice, you know, so she'd be afraid of saying or doing something that might offend me, or set me off. I mean, by the end of our marriage, I had that woman terrified of me. It's no wonder she ended up falling off her rocker a little while later. You might say she was always afraid of me, especially after I started smacking her around and showing her the kind of man she was dealing with.

"No," she said to me in that dead-serious voice of hers. "Annulled. Seeing as it was never consummated –"

"And whose fault is that?" I shot right back at her, and she actually cringed back as I took a couple of steps in towards her.

But I didn't hit her, like she thought I was gonna do. Not just then, anyway. I'm no sadist, you see. I just wanted to scare her a little, just so I could keep her in line. Then maybe I could even get her to forget about this annulment crap she was suddenly fixated on. Get the marriage annulled! I couldn't believe the idiotic notions that were floating around inside that crazy, psychotic brain of hers. Annulled! And then all I'd need would be for her to start spreading it around that I was impotent or some such garbage. I didn't need that kind of nasty gossip being said about me, no way, man! So, just in case she was planning on initiating some kind of vicious plot against me with all this nonsensical talk about an annulment, I wanted to scare her into submission, so she'd drop the whole idea completely.

And that's when I had my brainstorm, man. If she was going to sit there and toy with the idea of having the marriage annulled, hoping to pin the blame on me for the failure of our marriage to be consummated, I was going to dispel anybody's doubts, even hers, regarding my virility. I'm a man, and I know it, and just because my wife wasn't enough of a woman to arouse me in our bed was no reason for her to threaten to go out and broadcast to the whole town that our marriage had never been consummated.

Like I said, I suddenly got this brainstorm. Seeing that I already had it planned that, in the very near future, I was going to have a very strong and active physical relationship with the most beautiful girl on the planet, I went ahead and told her, straight out, that her sister and I had been having an affair.

"So, you see," I said to her," you can just erase this annulment crap out of your head. I'll give you a divorce, O.K.? And you can have everything. This apartment. The furniture. Those stupid-looking rose-colored curtains, even! All I want is my freedom. The freedom to go out and be united with the woman I really love."

Running true to form, that soft-in-the-head wife of mine rose to her feet and started yelling at me that it wasn't true. She admitted she'd had her suspicions when she overheard me talking to Betsy on the phone a few times over the last couple of weeks, but she refused to believe that Betsy reciprocated my feelings.

"She's in love with Wayne," the bitch screamed at me. "What you're telling me just isn't possible. After all the times she's spoken to me about Wayne and how she's missed him ever since he left for basic training –"

"That's part of the act, Stupid," I remember saying to her, and it was right about then that she started crying, too. I remember noticing how her shoulders hunched themselves up and she bent forward in her chair, and I said to myself: Now she knows the kind of man she's dealing with here.

Out loud, though, I told her that Betsy and I had planned it that way all along. This whole bullshit with Wayne was just a smoke screen, I told her. It was just a way of throwing everybody else off the scent the whole time her sister and I were carrying on the most passionate and torrid affair imaginable.

"Why do you think I'm never in the mood when I'm in bed with *you?"* I yelled down at her. "A man can only take so much, you know – even a man with the kind of awesome sex drive I've got."

"No! No!" she sobbed, carrying on like an actress in a Grade-Z movie from the freakin' Forties. "It's impossible. My sister's not like that. Even if she hadn't fallen in love with Wayne, she wouldn't have entered in an adulterous affair such as the one you're suggesting. Never! You're lying to me, Carl. This is just a sad attempt on your part to cover up for your own inadequacies – as a husband, as a man, and as a human being!"

I could've smacked her right then and there when she said that, but I was actually finding these histrionics of hers wildly entertaining. You see, by this time, I knew I had her. If she so much as threatened to call Betsy and ask her if it was all true, what I'd just told her, I'd simply laugh in her face and ask her if she really expected Betsy to admit the truth. And that's exactly what I said to her, too, when she suddenly went scurrying over to the phone. I laughed in her face, man, because I knew I had her precisely where I wanted her. Betsy would never betray our love, I told her.

"But," I said to her, pulling out my trump card," you can ask your sister Ellen whether it's true or not. She's known about it for months."

And that's when Monica started staring into space for a long, long time. I knew I had her by the gonads just then, and I figured that, by the time she got a hold of Betsy and began probing her for the truth, I would have already managed to win my angel over with my love. We would have already united our two bodies in the most beautiful and supreme union imaginable, and there was no way she'd ever betray me after *that!*

That trump card of mine, I thought, was a real inspiration. I knew that, sooner or later, Monica would be talking about getting a divorce or a freakin' annulment, as she insisted on calling it, so it was only a matter of time before I'd have to justify my disinterest in her as a lover by explaining that I was already involved with another woman. Knowing that this day would eventually arrive, I'd already planted the seeds of suspicion in little sister Ellen's head. I'd call the house in the middle of the day, knowing Ellen would be there to pick up the phone, and I'd ask to speak to Betsy. The little slut would ask me," Who's speaking?" and I'd tell her," I'd rather not say," and hang up, doing very little, mind you, to disguise my voice. Then after a while, the stupid little slut thought she was being really brilliant. She'd answer the phone and I'd ask for Betsy, and she'd say," Carl, I know this is you. C'mon, tell me. Why is it you keep calling here asking for Betsy?"

That day I dropped flowers off for my angel over at the library started the wheels in motion, I guess you could say, because I found out later on that Betsy had brought them home with her from work and had let it slip out that I'd been the one to give them to her. At the end of the week, when we were all gathered out in the back yard for one of those asinine Sunday brunch affairs of theirs, Ellen turns to me and says, right in front of my wife," Those were real pretty flowers you gave Betsy, you know," and when my wife saw me blush, she must've begun to suspect, right then and there, that there was something mighty fishy going on between us. What a shame my angel was the only one who failed to see the glowing love with which I handed her those flowers! She'd accepted them from me graciously enough, that's true, but then she disappointed me by not following my advice when I urged her to drop Wayne like a hot potato. Christ, I might've even gotten through to her just then if that class-A moron hadn't shown up and seen the two of us standing there together. That's when I knew there'd never be any peace for the two of us – not until that sucker was out of our lives for good!

Oh, God, it pains me, even now, to think back on that day shortly before I gave her those flowers. We were all sitting out back on the patio, having a reasonably good time. My angel looked particularly lovely that afternoon. Usually there wasn't that much color in her cheeks, but that day her whole face seemed flushed with joy. Every time I would smile across the table at her, she'd smile back at me; and the joy I felt just sitting there and becoming the object of her love was just so incredible, man. How beautiful she was – especially compared to that insane wife of mine who didn't know the true meaning of love the way Betsy and I did.

Like I said, I was sitting there, just basking in the radiance of her beauty, when that Class-A moron-of-all-morons shows up in his van, and I have to sit there and watch my darling angel go over to him and welcome him into our little circle as if there wasn't anything more natural in the whole world. Right then, I felt like dying. If a real sharp knife had been handy, instead of those cheap plastic utensils we were using that day, I would've plunged the sucker straight into my heart. It would have been better to die, right then and there, than to see her with her arms entwined about that moron's waist. Then, to add insult to injury, my schizoid wife starts issuing invitations to the prick. "Why don't you come on up and see us sometime?" she says to them, thinking she's Mae West or something. The next thing I know, I'm beginning to lose my cool, and then Wayne starts getting ready to interfere, and I'm saying to myself: It's all over. She's in love with him. I'll never get the chance to love her and find out if I'm a man. Never.

I made a fool of myself that day. I realize it now. Me! – who's always got his head together at all times!

When my angel came floating across the yard towards me on those beautiful sandaled feet of hers to see if I was all right, I couldn't help but look at her, and she saw my tears, and this stirred her. I'm sure of it. Right then, I could have died. But I couldn't tell her why I was crying. I couldn't tell her how my seeing her with another man made me want to just sink into the earth and die. Right then and there!

Christ! I went through hell last summer. Pure hell, and there was nobody I could turn to. Nobody. Not even Kenny would talk to me those few times I tried to get in touch with him. I was an old fuddy-duddy of a married man, as far as he was concerned. It wasn't until after they had my wife put away and the scandal died down a little that Kenny started hanging around with me and started borrowing my car something like every other night, just like he used to.

And now what have I got to show for all this? My marriage is beyond salvation, which is all well and good, anyway, because it was nothing but a joke to begin with. My angel has been laid to rest, which is something that is beyond my power to change at this point in time. Wayne Brown is still walking the face of the earth, doing his best to screw up my life even more than it already is. And Kenny, my best buddy in the whole world, goes and rips me off of one thousand dollars!

It kills me just thinking about how easily I allowed myself to be taken in by that sucker. Like I said before, I handed over the grand to him yesterday, went out to the cemetery to visit my angel, and later on in the day when I phoned Kenny to see if the job had been done already and Wayne was dead meat, Kenny's old lady tells me he's out with some of his friends. Partying on my money! She didn't tell me that, of course, but I had a feeling Kenny was pulling a fast one, so I called a few other places, and sure enough, I find out he's over at Patrick's with some of the gang, so I go over there 'round about ten o'clock and there he is, lying on the couch with a babe on each arm. The air was thick with the stench of marijuana, too, and I was getting high just inhaling the fumes in that room, man. As soon as Kenny sees me, he tilts his head up and says Howdy – not Hi or Hello or What's Up, but Howdy! – because he's wearing this idiotic cowboy hat all of a sudden and thinks he's Gene Freakin' Autry or something. I can see right away that good old Kenny is feeling no pain. Plus, he's in a good mood, 'cause he's got those two hot babes all over him while he's got his shirt unbuttoned all the way, and even the top button of his pants undone, too, would you believe it? So, I go over and I casually mention to him that I'd like to speak with him for a few minutes outside, if it's O.K. with him. I was real polite with him, you see, because like I said before, Kenny can kick my butt any time he wants, and he and I both know it. You might say he's had me kissing his ass for as many years as I've known him – not that I haven't had my own ass kissed a number of times myself, I hasten to add – So, anyway, Kenny's feeling absolutely no pain, so he gets up and follows me over to the doorway.

"I'm not going outside into that cold air," he tells me, laughing it up like he's been partying for the past six hours straight. "I got hardly any clothes on. I'll freeze my fucking nuts off, man."

"Yeah, O.K.," I say to him, real agreeable-like because I don't want to piss him off, you see, because he can kick my butt anytime he feels like it. I may have already said that. Oh, well.

So, I decide to broach the subject very carefully with him that I gave him one thousand dollars, and now I find him partying it up like there's no tomorrow.

"What gives, man?" I say to him. "You partying it up on the grand I gave you, or what?"

"Hey," he says to me," chill out, will ya? I took out a little loan, that's all. I can replace the cash tomorrow, no problem. You'll get the job done inside of a month or so, O.K., man?"

"You said it would only take a week," I reminded him, trying my best to stay cool and calm, you know?

"A month, a week, whatever," he says to me, and he sort of turns around because his two chicks are calling out to him.

"Please, Kenny," I then said to him, and I was practically ready to kneel down and kiss his ass, literally this time, right there on the spot just to impress him with the fact that it was of the utmost importance that I see Wayne Brown on a slab in the morgue inside of a week.

"Look, man," Kenny says to me, and he takes a hit on the joint he's been smoking the whole time we've been standing there. "When have I ever let you down before, huh? Just stay cool. Go home and take a shower. Or go home and whack off a few times, whatever turns you on. Me? I'm gonna be banging those two chicks all night long, so I don't really give a fuck what you decide to do with yourself."

I beamed back into his face and told him he was a true pal, even though I didn't much care for his stupid remarks about me and my private sex life, you know? Well, anyway, I started out the door, but before going, I caught his arm as he started to turn away, and I asked him if he could spare a couple of joints, as I was fresh out. Fresh out of cash, too, for that matter, but I didn't tell Kenny that because I didn't want him to think I was so down and out.

"Hey, you think I'm Santa Claus, man?" he said to me, giving me a little push back towards the door. "Go see your old buddy Samuel. He'll fix you up real good."

And that's exactly what I did. Samuel fixed me up so good, in fact, that as I related earlier in my diary, I wound up puking my brains out in the toilet bowl for what seemed like sixteen hours straight.

At any rate, I got up this morning around two o'clock. What I mean is I got up this *afternoon* around two o'clock, and it gradually hit me that maybe I should give good old Kenny a call and find out if

Wayne Brown was on a slab in the morgue yet. His old lady didn't answer the phone this time, nobody did, so I got dressed and hotfooted it on over there, only to find that nobody was home. Then I checked out a few other places like the mall, Burger King, Glenda's Grinders – you know, all the real hot spots in town where a guy looking for some real keen action could go and find it with no trouble at all. Like I said before (I think), my pal Kenny is cool with a capital C, and you can usually find him with all the cool dudes at all the cool places in town, usually having sex with or about to have sex with all the coolest chicks, too.

Come to find out, though, Kenny's over at Vince's place, and I suddenly remembered how I'd gotten Vince to promise he'd take on Wayne with his fists if Plan A should fail, Plan A being that Kenny would use that grand I gave him to pay off these thugs who were going to make sure that Wayne Brown became dead meat real, real soon, like inside of a week, if everything went according to the plan.

So, I headed on over to Vince's place. It was about five o'clock, and it was getting pretty dark out, and the snow was starting to fall, and my head was still aching like crazy from that awful hangover I was experiencing, and I was dying to smoke a joint and maybe even get my hands on some real top-quality coke, and the roads were getting mighty slippery, and before I knew what was happening, I lost control of the car and found myself slap-dab against a damned telephone pole. I went to start the engine up because the whole stupid car had died out on me upon impact, and wouldn't you know it, the goddamned engine wouldn't start!

Christ! I could tell right then and there that this wasn't going to be my day. Not by a long shot. Not unless I could find out for sure, one way or the other, that Wayne Brown would be dead on a slab in the morgue by the end of the week – not the end of the month, or the end of the next millennium, but by the end of the freakin' week, man!

Well, I'm sitting there cursing, using the kind of language I normally refrain from using under ordinary circumstances, and it's snowing heavier than before. Sure enough, not more than fifteen minutes have gone by, and this cop pulls over and starts poking around. As if any of this was any of his goddamned business!

Next, he comes over and asks me if this is my car.

"No," I remember saying to him. "I'm just sitting in it."

I don't know why I said that, but the next thing I know, this pig tells me to step out of the vehicle. Then he throws me up against the side of the car and starts feeling me all over, the faggot! It's a good thing I didn't have a dime-bag on me, or I really would've been in hot water. Well, the long and the short of it was I needed to get the car towed and to file an accident report. I told the guy that I didn't have that kind of money and why did I have to fill out a stupid accident report, but this guy was strictly Grade Z when it came down to your basic average intelligence, and he wasn't hearing any of it. I wanted to tell him that he happened to be dealing with not just any old run-of-the-mill citizen of this town, but with a young man who had been voted Most Popular and Best Personality by the other members of his senior class. I wanted to ask him what his I.Q. was, so we could compare and see for ourselves who it was that should be telling who what to do.

This town is run by a bunch of morons, that's all there is to it. It must have been close to seven o'clock by the time I hitched a cab and got driven over to Vince's place, and I prayed with all my might that both him and Kenny would still be there, so that my running around all afternoon and getting my car racked up against a pole wouldn't have gone for absolutely nothing.

Well, I found more than just the two of them inside Vince's place. There were two chicks there, too, and you could tell I must've interrupted some kind of orgy because it took close to a full five minutes before the door opened for me, and then it was one of the chicks who opened it, too. I walked in and saw the other three lying around in varying stages of being undressed, and when Kenny laid eyes on me, he briefly makes a face and then takes a big hit on the joint one of the chicks had just handed to him.

"Look, can we talk in private?" I said to him, because Vince and the two chicks were there, about to witness everything that was about to go down between me and Kenny, and I do have my pride, you see. I wasn't about to stand around and talk about murdering a guy right in front of the chicks, right?

"No, we can't talk in private," Kenny says to me, so I turned to Vince, figuring that since Kenny was in such a rotten mood, I might fare a whole lot better with Vince. I've only known Vince a few days, but I can tell he's loyal. Loyal with a capital L, and I pride myself on being an extremely good judge of character, too.

But my luck was really reaching an all-time low because, as soon as I was about to ask Vince if he'd consider duking it out with Wayne using bare fists, Kenny got up off the couch, walked right over to me, and gave me a gigantic shove towards the front door, telling me to screw.

I must have been insane. Temporarily insane, at least. But I was desperate, you see, and I couldn't just let Kenny push me out of the house like that – not without first hearing his assurance that the money had been paid over to the thugs who were going to put Wayne in the morgue. So, without thinking, I moved in on Kenny and went to grab the front of his shirt, so I could appeal to his basically kind and generous nature, and before I knew what was happening, he slugged me. Right in the mouth.

I hit the floor, man. Instantly. Kenny can hit hard, and I now realize that I shouldn't have gone to touch him like that. The least little thing can set him off because he's tough. I'd almost go so far as to say tough with a capital T. I remember one time when we were in eighth grade, and Kenny beat the living crap out of three kids at the same time. Of course, those kids were real wimps to begin with, but I remember being so impressed with Kenny's skill as a fighter that I realized the value of having a cool, tough friend like that for a buddy.

Anyway, I ended up sitting on the floor, spitting out blood, and one of the chicks ran over to me, saying to Kenny that he was just a big old bully for punching me in the mouth like that, and then I heard Kenny say to me,

"Just stay away from me from now on, Peters. You're a fucking loser."

Can you imagine that? Christ, when I think of all the times I let him copy my homework, all the times I took him with me cruising in my new car, all the times we smoked together –

He's dead meat! That's all there is to it.

And now I see very clearly what I have to do. Tomorrow I'm going out and getting myself a gun. I've got maybe just enough cash in the bank, too. Screw the car! Sooner or later my old man'll be giving me the money to get the car back, he and the old lady'll be so sick of me being underfoot all the livelong day. Plus, if I happen to be successful tomorrow and end up shooting that sucker in the head, it's altogether possible I'll get caught and wind up spending the rest of my life in prison.

Or better still, they'll lock me up in a ward for the criminally insane. Who knows? Maybe they'll put me in the same cell as that crazy wife of mine. That'd freak me out completely. I just hope, though, that if *that* happens, she doesn't expect me to have sex with her!

347

BETSY'S DIARY – July 30, 1985

Dear Diary: I am tired right now. Extremely tired. But I know that I won't be able to sleep in anything resembling a peaceful slumber until I have written about what happened during the course of the day.

It was a day which started somewhere around three o'clock in the morning. I was sound asleep up here in my room with my window open. A cool, refreshing breeze had been floating inside since around midnight, which was about the time I'd retired for the night, and I lay in bed for a very short while without pulling any sheets over my body and felt lulled into a very peaceful state. I may not have actually fallen asleep, because at around three o'clock I heard Wayne's voice just outside my window calling to me in a soft whisper. Then, when I turned on my bedside lamp and saw the crest of his blond head outside the screen of my window, I could see that he was sweating quite freely. As soon as I helped him over the ledge and on into my room, he explained to me that he'd parked his van a short distance down the road and carried his ladder into our back yard, leaning it up against the side of the house just as he used to do a month or so ago when he was engaged in painting the house. When I had asked what occasioned his visit to my room in the middle of the night like this, he reminded me that within twelve hours he would be boarding a bus for South Carolina and that we wouldn't be seeing each other again, or talking with each other either, for several weeks. He sounded so apologetic in telling me this that I gently placed a finger to his lips to shush him, then smiled and told him that it was all right. As long as we remained very quiet, there was no reason why we couldn't spend the rest of the night together here in my room.

And so we did do just that, remaining quiet even on into the early morning hours. We didn't even make love for fear of accidentally making a sound that might be heard by the other occupants of the house. Instead, we lay next to one another in my bed, and at one point I held his golden-haired scalp against my chest and wrapped my arms around his strong torso while he curled his legs up practically into a fetal position and rested his weary form against me. Occasionally I stroked his hair, occasionally I planted a kiss upon the fair curls that adorned his scalp, occasionally I closed my eyes and imagined that we were resting on a vaporous cloud in another universe and in another time frame – and during every second that passed while I held him in my arms, I could think of nothing, save the absolute rightness and perfection of these moments we were spending with each other.

I don't remember exactly what time it was when it happened, but Wayne suddenly decided to break the silence and began speaking to me, picking the words very carefully out of his mind and staring off into the grayish corners of my room as though he were reliving some awfully distant past.

"My mother died," he said," when I was just a kid. Barely six years old. I remember, because for the longest time after she disappeared, I wouldn't talk to anyone, and they had to keep me back in first grade because I wouldn't do anything in school either, or answer the teachers when they asked me a question. For the longest time, I wouldn't talk to anyone at all – not even my dad. And then one day I heard him tell one of his friends that he was gonna have me put away, so I got real scared. I don't know why, but it just kind of freaked me out, thinking I was nuts, or retarded, or something. So, I started coming out of my shell a little bit. I made a few friends at school and shit. And then my dad tells me we've gotta move. Before I know it, I'm starting all over again in a new school, and even though it was only the next town over from where we used to live, I don't know nobody, and I don't feel like talking to no one either. It wasn't until I was in tenth grade, and my dad decided to move back here, that I started coming out of my shell a little bit, like I did a long time ago. I found things I was good at, and a lot of kids looked up to me for it, and that kind of made me feel like I was somebody special. I got interested in cars – mostly fast cars – and I was good at driving them, too, 'cause I wasn't afraid of getting racked up, I guess. I didn't care how fast I went. So what, if I smashed myself up against a tree! I didn't care. I didn't care about nothing. Nothing except doing the things that made me feel good. Like smoking pot and, once in a while, taking other shit. It made me feel good – and stupid as it sounds, I was good at it, too. Nobody ever gave me credit for anything, but as I grew older, they began saying I could outfight and out-smoke just about anybody. And it made me feel good to have some kid come up to me and ask me to kick some other kid's ass for him. A lot of guys looked up to me, and I made a name for myself in that school, and it made me feel good. I'd walk down the halls, man, and those kids feared me. I never even *looked* at any of them, either. It made me feel good to think that all those people who were really so much better than me – were actually afraid of me.

"And then I met you, Betsy, and it all seemed so stupid. All that respect, all that fear, all those girls who wanted to go out with me. I had nothing. Nothing real and good and meaningful to be proud of in my life. Not until I met you. And you loved me from the start, I think. You didn't know the first thing about me, but you fell in love with me. God, I was so embarrassed – so ashamed of myself when you found me in pain in back of your house. I felt like crying, I was in so much pain, but I was afraid you'd think I was weak. I was ashamed to cry in front of you. But you took me anyway. You didn't know the first thing about me, but you took me to the hospital and stayed with me and acted like you really cared about me, and I hadn't even done anything to make you like me or respect me like all those kids in school did. And when I woke up after my operation, you were there, looking down at me, and I said to myself: 'This is unreal, man. This can't be happening. Nobody ever cared about me as much as this. Nobody.' I felt like crying just then when I saw your face staring down at me, so I closed my eyes and held your hand – and while I had my eyes shut, I cried so hard inside that I thought I was gonna explode. I couldn't believe there was really somebody out there who cared. Somebody who didn't even know me for the stupid ass-hole that I was, but was ready to love me on the spot.

"That's why, after the first day we spent together at the beach, I was afraid I'd lose you. There was no way a girl as beautiful and as smart and as wonderful as you could stay interested in a bum like me. I thought you'd tell somebody you'd been with me, and then you'd find out about some of the rotten things I've done – but it was unbelievable. You didn't care. You were ready to forgive – to accept me on faith. I told you I loved you, and that was good enough for you. I didn't have to be able to read or talk like a scholar or anything – All I had to do was be me, and you were ready to love me. This whole month I've spent with you has been unreal. I go to sleep at night and I say to myself: 'It's a dream, and it's gonna come to an end. It can't last. She loves me, and I love her, and the whole thing is just too good to be real.'

"That's why I'm so afraid to leave. I am more afraid of this than I've ever been afraid of anything else in my entire life. I don't want to leave, because that would be like breaking the spell. I don't want to break the spell. I want to keep living in this beautiful dream-world of ours – 'cause if the spell is broken and I wake up, you might – you might not be there anymore. I—I can't risk losing you. If I leave, Betsy, and while I'm gone, something bad should happen to you, it'll be all over for me. If anything happens to you, Betsy, I'll just have to kill myself. That's all there is to it."

His voice was starting to rise ever so slightly just then, so I clutched his head even more tightly against my heart and rocked him in my arms for several minutes. His body gradually became less taut, and he didn't speak another word, and before I even realized it myself, he was sound asleep in my arms.

For my own part, I stayed awake. A thousand different thoughts raced through my mind, making it impossible for my body to find complete rest; and at this moment in time, I cannot specifically recall exactly what those thoughts were which kept me awake. I know that I thought back upon our first encounters with each other and how I wasn't even consciously aware of the fact that I was falling in love with him. I thought, also, of how lonely I'd been, previous to our meeting – but most of all, I suppose, I thought of how lonely I was *going to be* within the next twelve hours, as I was soon to embark upon a period of my life wherein an inner strength would be essential if I were to successfully hold onto my conviction that Wayne and I would surely be together again just as soon as his basic training period was completed.

Wayne didn't leave my room till about six-thirty. I was beginning to worry about Mom or Rick possibly suspecting that there was someone in my room, even though we were being very quiet. At any rate, it was with a certain amount of difficulty that I was able to send Wayne off, reminding him that I would be at the bus station to see him board his bus later on in the day and that there was no reason to fear anything at all in speculating upon the sorrows of our imminent separation.

I was then able to shower and get dressed for work without running into either Mom or Rick, and when I got downstairs, I peeked into Ellen's room, saw that she was sound asleep, and then went out to my car and drove to the library.

Although I shook my head in mild disapproval, I was hardly surprised when I pulled into the library parking lot and saw Wayne's van parked there. He was standing outside, leaning against it, with the early morning breeze swirling through his blond hair, and he smiled sadly upon me when I approached him. He didn't say a word, but he took me in his arms and held onto me for a very long time. Then he slowly drew away from me, took me by the hand, and escorted me to the front door of the library. Once inside, I explained to him that I would be very busy this morning, in part to compensate for the time off this afternoon that Mrs. Evans had been generous enough to grant me when I'd informed her that a very good friend of mine was leaving town for several weeks and that I would like to see him off. Wayne nodded his head, walked over to the magazine rack, found something that caught his interest, and sat down while I hastened to apply myself to the business of the morning.

The hours passed slowly and laboriously. Once in a while – quite frequently, in fact – I peeked into the lounge to see what Wayne was doing, and every time I looked, I'd see him sitting in the same spot. The same magazine lay open to the same page on his lap, but he wasn't looking down at it at all. He simply sat there, very silent and very still.

When it came time for me to take my morning break, I entered the lounge and sat opposite him. He looked at me sadly for a moment and then dropped his eyes.

"Maybe you should go home and get packed," I said to him, trying to sound nonchalant.

At the sound of my voice, his eyes immediately went to my face, but after he absorbed the contents of what I'd just said, he dropped his eyes to his lap once again and shook his head almost imperceptibly.

"Wayne, look at me," I said to him, quite softly, and I fought back the urge to rush over to him and take him in my arms when I saw that he was unable to raise his eyes to face me, even thirty seconds after I'd asked him to do so.

"What would you like me to give you when you get back?" I put to him, trying to sound bright and cheerful all of a sudden. "I'll save up my money over the next few weeks, and I'll get you whatever you like. Just name it, darling, and you'll find it waiting for you when you get back."

A moment passed – a very brief one – during which he didn't stir at all. Then he suddenly rose to his feet, nearly dropping the magazine to the floor, and started walking away. For one second of dizzying panic, I thought he was about to walk out on me completely, but he simply made his way over to the huge, wall-length window opposite him and stared outside for the longest time with his back turned towards me.

I sat quietly, absorbing his pain and wishing that, in so doing, I could just make it all go away so that, somehow, things could go back to the way they usually were between us. But time was against us, because Mrs. Evans had her head poked in and she reminded me that it was time to get back to work. I nodded my head, waited for her to go, and then walked over to Wayne.

With my hands gently touching the back of his shoulders, I told him that it wouldn't be too long now before I would be released from my duties here at the library. Then I would go with him and help him pack and we would be together for a short time.

Unfortunately, my words failed to elicit much of a response from him. I could see his reflection in the window directly opposite him, and it was apparent to me that his eyes were still cast downwards. Also, for one brief second, his hands at his sides started to clench themselves into fists, but soon relaxed into their former position as he barely nodded his head in agreement, and I walked away from him for the last time that morning.

Around twelve-thirty I followed him in my car to his apartment building. Neither of us spoke while we mounted the stairs and entered the apartment. Once inside, I alluded to the fact that I had expected his father to be there, at which point Wayne actually opened his mouth to speak to me, saying that his dad would probably meet us at the bus station later on.

The two of us packed his suitcases, quietly and without saying anything important to each other. Occasionally, Wayne would inquire as to the time, and after I'd tell it to him, he'd say," We don't want to be late," and then continue what he was doing. As soon as we were finished packing, we brought the suitcases downstairs and loaded them into the trunk of my car, and then I drove the two of us in my car over to the bus station.

We found a bench inside, close to the big windows that afforded us a view of the various buses that were pulling into the terminal, and Wayne sat forward, his shoulders hunched, and didn't say a word. I asked him if he wanted a coke or anything, and he merely shook his head and kept his position, sitting forward and with hunched shoulders.

' At one point, I mentioned that his dad ought to be showing up at any minute, and Wayne nodded his head and said," Yeah, any minute," but he didn't turn his head to see if his father was approaching.

At length, we saw his bus sitting outside, and an announcement was made over the loudspeaker that passengers and luggage were being boarded at that very moment, and both Wayne and I stood up at the same time and started outside with his suitcases. There were other young men about his age who were boarding the bus as well, and many of these people were talking loudly and excitedly, filling the air with their high-spirited conversations.

And the breeze swept through Wayne's hair as he stood before me, having just handed his luggage over to an attendant, and he stared right through me and calmly informed me that he wasn't going.

"Wayne," I said to him, trying to smile in an understanding fashion, but whatever it was I meant to say to him at that moment simply refused to come out of my mouth. The truth of the matter is that I, naturally, had been dreading this moment all along as well, and had actually feared that my knees would have buckled under me long before this. However, in the face of Wayne's stony obstinacy, I strove with all my might to reach down inside – deeper than I had ever reached before – for those reserves of inner strength I felt each one of us possesses, those reserves that, in some cases, keep many of us just this side of insanity at moments like these.

"I'm not going," Wayne repeated while I stood opposite him, unable to speak the words that would effectively stifle all of his fears and all of his doubts. "I don't want to. I can't."

"But you must," I told him, getting the words out with far more ease than I thought would be possible for me to do so.

"I can't Betsy, I can't," he told me, and hearing a sob entering into his voice, I reached out my hand, grabbed his shirt-front, and brought him in against me.

"I'll be writing to you every day," I whispered up into his face which was lifted to the sky above us. "Three or four times a day, if necessary. And I'll be praying for you and thinking of you always. Now, be strong for me, Wayne. Please, darling, show me how strong you are and walk onto that bus for me. Do that for me, please, darling. I love you. You know that. There's nothing to be afraid of. And when you come back, I'll be standing right here, darling. Trust me. Believe me. I love you, Wayne. I'm yours forever, darling. Remember that. Forever."

And then I rested the side of my face against his chest, but I struggled to hold back the tears I wanted to shed, even when I felt his arms enclosing me against him, powerfully at first and then more gently, and when I looked up at him again, his face was still turned upwards towards the heavens above us, and his complexion appeared to be pure-white – possibly even lacking in color, it was hard to tell in the sunlight that poured down upon his upturned face. But I was shocked – even a bit terrified – by the way his whole body seemed to stiffen up just then, as if he was being gripped by something more powerful than either one of us had ever known.

Once again, it was with extreme difficulty that we were able to disengage ourselves from each other, but once we were separated, Wayne turned his back on me and walked inside the bus just before the doors closed in behind him. I rushed to the side of the vehicle and saw him, just in time, sitting by a window towards the rear. I instantly caught his attention as the bus started pulling away, jumped up and down in something of a girlish frenzy, and waved to him.

Wayne smiled down upon me through the window. He raised his hand very slowly and waved back. Very timidly. And he gazed upon me with incredible sadness dripping out from those deep blue eyes of his. Then the bus took a sharp turn, and he was out of my sight completely.

As I walked back towards where my car was parked, I prided myself on the amount of self-possession I'd been able to summon forth during our last few moments together, and I was actually a bit relieved upon realizing that the experience was now behind me. Behind both of us, in fact, and now I could devote my life, for the next several weeks, towards a conscious awareness of the need to remain strong, the need to stay firm in my resolve to keep the faith, and the need to look ahead to our reunion in a mature and level-headed fashion, a reunion that would be so joyous for the two of us that this separation which was now upon us would fade away into pure inconsequence as soon as we were, once again, in each other's arms.

I say that I was proud of myself for being so strong; and yet, when I got inside my car and started pulling out of the parking lot, I found myself driving rather aimlessly for nearly half an hour. Finally, I pulled into the mall parking lot, hoping to keep my mind occupied by roaming from one store to the next, my eyes falling upon this shirt or that hat or this bandanna or that head-band which might suit Wayne's fancy when he returned and I would present them to him as just a few of the countless gifts I wished to be able to shower him with upon his return.

Then I laughed at myself for entertaining such far-fetched thoughts. He'd been gone for scarcely an hour, and I was already envisioning how wonderful a greeting I would have ready for him when he came back to me.

Nonetheless, I did buy him several shirts. One dress shirt because I had never seen him all dressed up, and perhaps we could go to a fancy restaurant when he got back. I was sure that, dressed in a suit and tie, he would shine in such handsome attire. I also bought him two T-shirts to replace the many T-shirts he already owns which are either torn in certain places or spotted with paint and grease. And I also bought him two pullover shirts, instead of the kind that hang loosely which he normally wears. In a pullover shirt, he would look absolutely splendid, being so well-built. It's a bit of a shame that he seems to be disguising his muscular physique by wearing all those loose-fitting shirts all the time. Yes, he would look simply wonderful in all the different clothes I was buying him.

Then, like a supreme idiot, I walked into the pet store at the mall, and I stayed there for the longest time, just looking at the fish swimming lazily and aimlessly in their tanks, and gazing upon all the colorful and lively birds that were flitting about in their cages, and watching with intense delight as a group of golden retriever puppies played with one another in their own little cages. When Wayne returns, I said to myself just then, we'll come here and pick out a puppy, and we'll find a place of our own where we can keep a pet. We'll be like a mini-family – me, Wayne, and the puppy – and nobody will bother us. We will, all three of us, play together and grow strong together and smile together and laugh together for many years to come.

It wasn't until I arrived home and brought Wayne's shirts up to my room that it really started to dawn on me that I wouldn't see him again until sometime in September.

September! It seems so far away. It's one of my least favorite months, too, because it signals an end to the flourishing blooms of spring and summer and a diminishing of the strength of the beautiful sun's rays upon the earth. I always feel a strange sadness when September arrives; but this September I will have something to really look forward to.

I took the shirts out of the shopping bags and put them away in one of my dresser drawers. Then I slowly changed into a fresh clean blouse and a pair of shorts. Pulling the blouse over my head had mussed up my hair, so I walked over to my dresser, sat down, and brushed my hair a few strokes. For a moment, my own eyes seized upon their reflection in the mirror opposite me, and I gave a sudden start.

I know that it sounds incredibly bizarre as I relate this experience, but for one extremely eerie second, I thought that these were Wayne's eyes staring back at me from the mirror. They were the same dark blue, and yes, they were of the same profound and mysterious sadness that very often characterizes his eyes as well.

I slowly put down the brush, got up, and walked over to my bed. First, I sat at the edge of it and stared down at the floor, biting my lower lip momentarily with my upper teeth. I don't know what I was thinking at the time, but I do know that, when I finally stretched myself out on top of the bed and stared up at the ceiling, I felt tremendously alone – as if I were detached from every other human being in existence. I closed my eyes in sudden fear, only to open them again a moment later, and remind myself that I wasn't alone, after all. I would never be alone, ever again, for the rest of my life. I had found another person, another entity, with whom I could bind my whole being. And we were perfect for each other. In a few short weeks, we would be together again, just as we had been for this one glorious and joyful month, and just as we always should have been from the moment of our births.

Later on, while I was getting dinner prepared, I looked outside the kitchen window, and with a smile, I remembered how close he had always been to me, how he had spent many hours right outside this very window painting our house, and how silly it had been for me to feel a little nervous about his being there. I hadn't known at the time that underneath that strong and rugged exterior of his there beat the heart and soul of one of God's most blessed children. Again, with another smile, I recalled how dear Aunt Lucille had been quick to judge him as a dangerous punk who had come to our house in order to rob and steal from us. Dear Aunt Lucille, motivated, no doubt, by a desire to shield her three little girls from all the hostile elements of the universe. I am so lucky to have her in my life, even though she rarely understands why I do some of the things that I do. I love her so much, and I want her to be as happy as I have been this past month. I must tell her how much I appreciate having her in my life, and I must thank her for all the love she has given me over the years.

After dinner was over – a dinner which I ate in relative silence while Mom and Ellen chattered about some scandal that had taken place on one of the soap operas, and Rick basically consumed as much food as was humanly possible in the space of time he allotted himself to actually sit at the table with us – I soon found myself driving on over to Monica and Carl's apartment. It's been a week since we've had any kind of contact with one another, and I was stimulated by a desire to confide in my sister the sense of loss which I could not help but feel at the present time.

When the door to their apartment opened up, it was Carl whose face immediately came into view. He didn't seem to be entirely in possession of his faculties, regarding me through eyes that were mere slits when his face first appeared to me in the doorway. Upon entering the apartment, I smelled a strong odor of marijuana in the room, and I realized that this probably explained why he seemed to be a bit out-of-it. I may not be the most liberated woman around these days – far from it, I'd say – but I've learned to at least understand that people, often members of the same family, sometimes lead different lifestyles from others, and it's certainly not my place to pass negative judgments, as long as no one is being harmed or being forced to do something against their will.

But I couldn't help being rather annoyed at Carl's inability to talk to me or respond to any of my initial questions in a normal, rational manner. For example, I had a hard time ascertaining Monica's whereabouts. In a very roundabout manner, I learned that she'd gone to the mall to do some shopping but would be back within the hour. Once that information was received, I was tempted to simply excuse myself and come back another time, but Carl insisted that I stay, even going so far as to pull my by the hand into the living room and bring me over to a seat.

"Monica will be back within the hour," he told me once again, and as soon as he got himself seated, he picked up a very small fragment of one of those marijuana cigarettes, lit it with a lighter, and began inhaling smoke, making a good deal of irritating noises in the process. I'm sure he was able to read my discomfort in my face because, after one more inhalation, he looked at me and said," I take it you don't approve of what I'm doing. Well, I'm sorry, Betsy, but we can't all be as perfect as Wayne Brown Junior who, by the way, used to smoke with the best of them. In the good old days. Before he became – purified by your love."

I admit that, even though I'd braced myself for the worst as soon as I realized he was going to keep smoking despite my discomfort, I wasn't quite prepared to listen to the bitter remarks he suddenly came out with. I was on the point of rising to my feet then, when he hastily put out the cigarette in an ashtray and took my wrist in one of his hands – not very hard, I must confess.

"That was very unkind of me, I know," he said to me in a changed tone of voice from before," and God knows I wouldn't want to say or do anything that would offend you. It's just that – I start smoking this stuff, and I kind of lose it, you know? I don't have a very strong hold on my emotions to begin with, and life has been rough on me the last few weeks. Extremely rough. Your sister's always on my case about all the days I take off from work. She comes home and

362

starts in on me as soon as she steps in the door. Life is rough. So I smoke, and I drink a little – here and there, you know? Luckily, I've been able to keep everything pretty much under control, but some days – Look!" He suddenly brightened up, and even straightened up a bit in his seat. "Why don't we stop talking about me? Tell me what you've been up to lately, Betsy. Christ, you never come by to see us anymore. You're always driving off into the sunset with your big hero Wayne Brown Junior." Then, before I had time to react, he pushed on by saying," Hey, I heard he's going to boot camp. He get bussed down there yet, or what?"

By the time he'd finished his last sentence, he had risen from his seat and started pacing back and forth in front of me, although he didn't actually stop and turn to look at me, not even when I spoke up, saying,

"As a matter of fact, Wayne left this afternoon. He'll be gone for six weeks, minimum."

"Six weeks, huh?" Cal responded, even more brightly than ever. "Six weeks! I'd no idea basic training was that long. Christ! That means Wayne Brown Junior will be out of the picture – I mean, he won't be around for quite some time then, will he?"

"I'm afraid not," I answered him, and I lowered my eyes a bit, put off by the way he was suddenly looking upon me with bright enthusiasm. "But I'll be writing to him every day, keeping him up-to-date on everything that goes on here at home."

"Six weeks," Carl said all over again as though he were actually treasuring the very thought of it, and I began to feel increasingly uneasy as he resumed his pacing, nervously clutching and then unclutching his hands in front of him. Finally, after mulling over the same information we'd already shared together, he paused directly in front of me and said," I suppose you're going to miss him a great deal. That is, I imagine you'll be feeling very lonely in the weeks to come." And when I agreed that that would undoubtedly be the case, he leaned over towards me and placed his right hand affectionately upon my shoulder. "Well, I want you to know," he said, lowering his voice a little," that anytime you're feeling lonely or depressed, you can feel free to call me – or Monica. That's what we're here for, do you understand?"

For the next fifteen minutes or so, we engaged in nothing but small talk, which was perfectly fine by me. Carl would occasionally remark that Monica would be home shortly, and I'd smile and nod my head, without knowing what to say.

Then, without warning, he picked up the marijuana cigarette he'd put out a few minutes ago, took out his lighter, and went to re-light it, only to put everything away, almost in a manner indicating either disgust or impatience, and then he turned to me one more time and said to me,

"So, I'm hoping you've given some serious thought to what I said to you the day I visited you at the library and gave you those roses – you know, the advice I gave you about not pursuing any kind of relationship, serious or otherwise, with good old Wayne Brown Junior." I started to say something, but he quickly jumped in and continued," I'm also hoping that in these next six weeks, you'll come to realize that it wouldn't be a good idea for you to throw your life away on the type of person Wayne Brown Junior happens to be. Both Monica and I agree that you'd be much better off without him."

"I don't believe that Monica –" I began, feeling that since I was in the midst of this uncomfortable conversation, I'd might as well be permitted to participate in it. But again, I got interrupted.

"Don't let your sister fool you," Carl persisted in earnest tones that still failed to convince me that what he was saying was true, when I knew that the exact opposite was true, instead. "To your face, Monica will tell you that she's happy for you and that she fully

364

agrees with you that he's a changed person. But in front of me, she says that she's very concerned – in fact, she's alarmed at the idea of you degrading yourself by associating with the likes of him. I mean, the guy is a bum, Betsy. Can't you see that?"

I reminded myself of the resolution I'd made two weeks ago when Carl had used these same stale arguments at the library – my resolution that I would avoid being alone in his company for any length of time. I remembered how tightly he'd held onto my wrist, and I was not in any frame of mind, not on this evening of Wayne's temporary absence from my life, to undergo a scene even remotely resembling the one that had taken place back then. And so, I quickly found the energy to get up from my seat and start for the door.

"Betsy, for the love of Christ!" he called out to me, not chasing after me or reaching out to grab my arm to detain me as I thought he might do, but remaining in the center of the living room, his voice ringing out in such desperation that I stopped and whirled around to face him once again. Then I said to him with complete openness and a sincere desire to get a direct answer,

"Would you please tell me what it is you expect from me, Carl?"

"Oh, Betsy!" he sighed, and he lowered his voice as he continued by saying," I wish you could understand that the only reason I'm so concerned about this unnatural attachment you seem to have for Wayne is that I regard you as one of the most wonderful people on this whole planet. I'm just so afraid of seeing you get hurt." There was a pause, and he knitted his brows as he looked across the room at me and sounded quite sincere when he said," My intentions, as far as your well-being is concerned, are strictly honorable. You do believe me when I say this to you, don't you?"

"Oh, Carl, I want to believe you," I told him, dropping my gaze in an attempt to disguise the regret I was beginning to feel for having attributed sinister motives behind this whole discourse he insisted upon having with me. Then I continued," I want to trust you, too, because I really do need a friend right now – since Wayne is gone. Somebody I can talk to and explain my feelings to. That's why I came over here, I guess. I thought maybe I could explain to Monica how I was feeling. She and I have been very close over the years, and it would be so wonderful if I could open up to her – to the two of you, in fact – But I admit that I strongly resent the way you constantly refer to Wayne in such a negative fashion. It's really quite offensive to me. You can surely see that, can't you?"

"O.K., O.K.," he said, stepping closer to where I stood, and putting his hands out in front of him, palms facing out, as if to placate me. "May God strike me dead on this very spot if I should ever speak or think any evil against Wayne Brown Junior from now on. How's that sound?"

Then he laughed, and even though he'd just made a rather absurd vow, his laughter was somewhat infectious, and I found myself laughing a little bit, too.

"So? We're still friends?" he said to me, and with a big smile, he held his arms open and tilted his head back in a rather playful manner, so that I felt far more relaxed just then and actually walked into the friendly embrace he was offering to give me.

As it turned out, we were just pulling away from each other when the front door opened, and Monica came into the apartment. At that exact same instant, Carl suddenly pulled me back in towards him and kissed me lightly on the neck, then pushed me away a bit roughly and said,

"Oh! Monica! I didn't hear you come in!"

Then he laughed again, rather self-consciously, I thought, and we both watched silently as Monica put the few bags she was holding down upon the kitchen table, looked at him with absolutely no expression on her face, and then turned to go into another room without speaking to either one of us.

"Monica!" Carl called out to her in a sing-songy tone of voice. "Didn't you see who's here? Aren't you even gonna say hello to your favorite sister?"

Since Monica seemed totally oblivious to the sound of his voice and had kept on going into the other room, I ignored Carl completely and went, myself, into the bedroom where my sister seemed bent on secluding herself.

I found her there, lying on top of their big double-bed, and for a moment, I thought, upon looking down at her weary and motionless form, that she appeared to have aged since the last time I'd been with her.

"Monica," I whispered over to her, tiptoeing into the room and not daring to step any further into its interior than I deemed permissible on my part as a guest in their home. "Monica, honey," I whispered down to her silent form. "Are you all right?"

Then the big shocker of my whole day occurred: I'd no sooner approached the bed and peered down compassionately upon her when, as if possessed by some sort of alien, demonic power, she shot to a sitting position and commanded me to get the hell away from her.

As I have said so many times in the past, one of my most glaring deficiencies lies in my inability to handle myself during a crisis or in the middle of a tense confrontation, and on this disastrous occasion, I am afraid that I ran true to form. The instant that I found myself face to face with the rage that was stamped all over her countenance and I heard the venom in her voice when she screamed at me, I hastily did what she asked, bolting out of the room and failing to heed Carl's attempts to detain me when, as I shot past him, he tried to take my arm, asking me what was wrong.

I drove all the way back home in a state of disbelief. Earlier in the day, I'd prided myself on having mustered the necessary strength and courage to face the separation from Wayne that loomed in front of my immediate future. And now, hearing the almost insane rage that was in my sister's voice when she basically told me where to go, I felt numbed to the point where I wasn't even conscious of what streets I was driving down as I went back home – or at least, that's the way it seemed at the time.

What is wrong with her? What in the world could have possibly taken possession of her that she could have lashed out at me in that manner? Could it be possible that she's been under such tremendous stress lately that she's no longer able to handle daily living as a rational human being? Could this account for her otherwise unexplainable behavior towards me?

Even physically, she seemed so worn, even haggard. What is happening to her? Oh, God, maybe it's just as well that this new crisis in my life has arisen at this time, as if to fill the empty space that Wayne's absence has brought with it. Maybe now I can devote all of my energies, more fully than ever, towards finding out what it is I can do to bring peace of mind, at least, to my dear sister to whom I've always felt so very, very close. This is so bizarre, so unreal, that I'm beginning to be frightened by it. But I can't let fear take over. Only by being strong and facing head-on whatever opposing and threatening forces I may have to deal with in the weeks to come – only in this way will I be able to overcome them and put an end to these irrational and disturbing episodes that seem to keep taking place in my life.

And so, I pray to God for this strength, and I pray that He may ease the torment of Monica's soul, and Carl's as well. And I pray for

Mom and Rick, that their mutual love with continue, unabated, for many long years. And for Aunt Lucille who deserves to be far happier than she is right now. And also for my little sister Ellen whose bitterness needs to be replaced by a fresh outlook on life, if this is at all possible for her at this stage of affairs.

And I pray that, at this very moment, You may wipe the brow of that splendid young man who's brought such happiness into my very soul. I pray that You may love him and place him in such a deep sleep, at this hour, so that the hours of our being separated may seem to pass more quickly for him.

P.S. He loves cars. Fast ones, especially. Maybe when he comes back, I'll have been able to save up enough money for a down payment on one of those sports cars he was showing me pictures of in that magazine a few days ago. I have no idea how expensive they are, but I'll see if I can find out tomorrow. Oh, God! How wonderful it would be to see his smiling face once again! The face of the man to whom I have pledged my undying love.

CYCLE SIX

MONICA'S MEMOIRS – May 25, 1986

At last, I have something to live for, something to look forward to, something to devote all of my energies towards seeing come to pass. I have been calm and good and co-operative for so long in this rotten hell-hole that the doctors have agreed to granting me this one request. The doctors have even gone so far to express their belief that my very sanity hinges upon my being able to go there tomorrow and experience the peace that, they hope, may restore me to my former self, the peace that for so many months I have despaired of ever being able to recapture.

Tomorrow is Memorial Day. That one solitary visitor who comes here each month – on the Fourth of each month – will break his regular tradition and come here tomorrow. He will be dressed in a three-piece suit – one of the ones that was purchased for him on a radiant day sometime last August. He will come here to me in his three-piece suit with his golden blond curls plastered down closely against his scalp, and the two of us will enter a car, along with the doctor and an attendant, and we will be driven to the very spot where

370

she was laid to rest. Tomorrow is Memorial Day, and we two will join hands and approach her final resting place together, and her spirit of light and purity will enclose us both in its warmth and glowing splendor.

I yearn for this event to take place. I positively can't rest until I see it happen. Then, and only then, will I know for sure whether I can ever get on with the rest of my life.

Yes. Tomorrow my solitary visitor will arrive here in his three-piece suit. When our eyes fall upon each other, I will once again, just as I do every Fourth of every month, perceive the piercing sadness that haunts his entire being. We will stand opposite each other for a few moments, as we do once a month, until his footsteps gradually bring him into my arms where I will hold him securely and press his golden head against my chest, and together, we will listen for the slightest sound, the slightest stirring in the air around us, the slightest indication that she is with us and that, wherever her radiant soul resides, we two are being blessed by her and experiencing the only soothing comfort either of us will ever again know here on this earth.

Oh, dear God, let it happen. Give me the strength to make it through the night and into the morning so that this wonderful and therapeutic event may take place in my life. Let me remain strong throughout this entire period, although I know I shall fear a disintegration of my mental stability, just as I always do as of late. But I must have faith. I must keep reminding myself to be calm and to be patient.

What rare commodities calmness and patience were for me last summer! How senselessly I allowed myself to be driven by reckless, disloyal thoughts – the thoughts which tore us apart during those last few days of her life. Even after the news had been delivered to me that she had taken her own life, I was unable to shed a single tear of remorse, my mind being so infested with serpents of doubt and with a sense that I had been horribly betrayed. I, who never even gave her a chance to defend herself against those vicious lies, had felt betrayed, so betrayed and wronged and hurt by something that didn't even exist that I closed my heart up completely and refused to mourn, absolutely refused to join in the general sense of bereavement that we were all supposed to feel.

Yet, even in my cold-heartedness, I sent that telegram off to Wayne and prayed that it would reach him in time so that he could, at the very least, attend her funeral. At the same time, I had prepared a test for myself. If he were to arrive and express genuine grief over her passing away, then I would know that she must have sincerely reciprocated his love, and if that were the case, I would then know that what my mind had been dwelling on for so long was a mere string of outright lies.

When the funeral car started to leave the cemetery and we all sat inside of it and watched his van screech past us, I clutched onto the folds of my dress and said to myself: Wrong! I've been wrong about her these past weeks! Totally wrong! – And I felt so relieved in finding the power within myself to forgive her that I actually felt a sense of contentment spread throughout my entire body. She was innocent. She was guiltless, and that meant that my faith in her innate goodness had been restored, and I could feel the weight of my bitterness floating off my body and into the air around me, never to return; and so, I experienced a strange, almost unearthly contentment all the way back to the house.

Once inside the house, amid the ranting and raving of my aunt and my mother, I then lay upon the couch and said to myself: She's gone forever.

And then the darkness closed in on me, and I wailed and lost touch with reality for several minutes of the most intense and most relentless agony I had ever felt in my entire life. The next thing I

372

knew, Aunt Lucille's face was peering down at me, and I heard her voice entreating me to compose myself, and my husband's voice was begging me to get ready to leave the premises.

I still don't know how I made it off the couch, across the room, outside, and into the car that brought us back to our apartment. Once there, I sat at the kitchen table and stared down at my hands which rested on the table-top in front of me. I was exhausted beyond description. I felt as though I'd aged twenty years in the space of only a few hours. My desire to get on with the rest of my life had already deserted me, and I was essentially the same shell of emptiness that I have often considered myself to be during my stay here in this hell-hole.

Only half-consciously did I hear my husband demand to know whether it was I who had informed Wayne of what had happened. His voice was harsh, powerful, and grating, but I couldn't have answered him, even if I'd wanted to. My strength to continue living had already vanished by then. And when he struck me in the face, I could barely feel it. There was just no point to it. No point to any of it.

I was a zombie for the next two days. My employer had graciously allowed me the time off from work that was normally granted to those who had experienced a death in the family. Carl didn't go to work either, but he was generally out of the house. I didn't know where he was, although I would imagine, in retrospect, that he was either out doing drugs with his old chums – or at the cemetery.

And all that time, the doubts began gnawing at me again, the uneasiness of not knowing the whole truth, the nagging suspicion that there may, after all, have been even the smallest iota of a reason for my having felt so justified in my wrath against her. Then, like a bolt out of the sky, I remembered those diaries. What better proof, what more final an end to all my doubts and suspicions could I ever hope to find if I were to ignore the information that I was certain would be contained in those diaries?

Ellen was already asleep in her room when I let myself in the front door with the old key that I would always use before my marriage to Carl. I mounted the stairs as quietly as possible so as not to disturb her from her sleep. It was only two days after the funeral, but my mother was already gone for the evening in her never-ending search for another man to share her bed. I had the house virtually to myself. I was alone, sat alone for nearly two hours in the silence of her room with those diaries on my lap, and everything that had happened to her all summer long came to life all over again as I sat there, perfectly quiet in the stillness of her room, and read page after page, my eyes refusing to give in to weariness even after I'd been reading for two hours straight – because the truth kept assailing me. Page after page after page revealed to me that I had been wrong about her. She had loved me. She had loved Wayne.

She had loved all of us.

When I came to the pages where she described her loneliness upon being separated from him due to his compliance with the rules and conditions of basic training in the armed forces, I put the book down and went downstairs to call him. It was well after midnight, but he answered the phone on the first ring.

No, he hadn't been sleeping, he told me. He hadn't slept in two days, and yes, he was going to come right over.

I went into the living room and waited there, so that I could open the door for him as soon as he arrived. The downstairs room was still and dark, just as her bedroom was, just as the whole house was, and just as, as far as I was concerned, the whole universe had now become now that she had chosen to divorce herself from it completely.

Scarcely ten minutes passed before I heard his van pulling into the driveway, and I walked stiffly to the front door and opened it wide. The last time I had seen him, he had appeared tall and rugged and sturdy. But the man who walked into the house on that horrifying evening was stooped and utterly shattered by the pain that had already begun to take hold of him. I took him by the hand, gently, as if he were a very small child about to face human error for the very first time, and brought him with me up the stairs to her room.

He stood in the doorway for several moments and looked around. I had turned on the bedside lamp and gone over to sit at the edge of her bed. I motioned for him to sit down next to me, but he wouldn't move. Not an inch. Not at first, that is. So, I sat there by myself, holding her diary on my lap, and I read aloud to him for forty-five minutes. An expression of glorious peace passed over his face as she gradually came alive for the two of us, and slowly he made his way over to where I was sitting and placed himself beside me in a very careful manner. Another stretch of time passed, and he clenched me by the hand and let out a blissful sigh.

As time passed, we came to the concluding pages of her diary, and his hand separated itself from mine; and when I read aloud to him the words that were contained in that last entry of hers dated September Fourth, the two of us became still. Very still.

I looked at his hands, and he looked at them, too. And then those hands of his started to shake as he lifted them to his face. And then he covered his face with those trembling hands – those trembling white hands of his that he didn't want to believe were his any longer.

Then his body suddenly lurched forward onto the floor, and his scream sounded like it came from Hell itself.

I sank to the floor with him and fought to get his body under control as it lay under me, convulsed. But he was too strong for me, and I rushed downstairs with the intention of calling an ambulance.

As I rushed into the living room, the headlights of an approaching vehicle shone through the picture window as it began pulling into the driveway, and I stopped suddenly in the middle of the room.

Who was it that was pulling into the driveway at this ungodly hour? Was it Carl, driving over here to find me after noticing that I was absent from our chaste bed so late in the middle of the night? Or was it Mom, now returning home after spending hours in the definitely un-chaste bed of a man who had obligingly satisfied her animal hunger so that she could make it through the next day without attacking anyone in her unbridled quest for sexual gratification? Either way – whether it was Carl or Mom – I knew what I had to do.

I walked over to the closet where Pop used to keep his hunting rifles. I found what I wanted and scooped up a handful of ammunition in the process. Then it struck me that I had no idea how to use the rifle or what to do with the cartridges I was holding in my hand.

In a state of panic, I took the gun and ammunition with me and ran back up the stairs to her room where I found Wayne still lying on the floor, his body wracked with sobs of the utmost pain. I don't know how, but somehow I managed to get close enough to him to explain to him that I needed his help just then. In effect, I started begging him to load the gun for me.

"We're going to kill them, Wayne!" I hollered down at him. "We're going to have our revenge – *Her* revenge! Just help me load this gun!"

I heard the front door slam shut and then Mom's voice calling out to me, and still, Wayne hadn't heard what I was saying to him. He had no clue as to what I was begging him to do for me – for the two of us – and for *her* as well! In my intense hatred of that woman downstairs and in my overwhelming desire to punish her for all eternity for what she had done to us, I could think of nothing, except the need to get Wayne to load the ammunition into that rifle so that, when she walked up here and stood in the doorway to Betsy's room, I could send her straight to Hell in one mighty burst of horrible violence.

Finally, hearing Mom mounting the stairs and still calling my name, I crouched on the floor next to Wayne and tried to start loading the gun myself; and while I was doing that, a crazed look came into his face, and he grabbed the rifle out of my hand and loaded it himself with such unbelievable speed that I was amazed at his dexterity in handling the weapon under such trying conditions; but I didn't realize at first why he'd been so anxious to load it – not until he turned the muzzle in towards his own chest.

The gun was about to go off, sending its deadly cargo in the wrong direction, and I screamed, "Wayne!" and in a split second, I grabbed it and wrenched it out of his grasp, yanking it away from him with all the strength of Satan governing my movements, and when my mother stepped upon the threshold and gazed at me with those dark angry eyes of hers, I squeezed the trigger and nailed her.

I watched her sexually seductive body fly back against the opposite wall without even realizing that Wayne had grabbed the gun away from me in the meantime and was standing beside me, shivering in a cold sweat. And seeing her body slide to the floor a few moments later, I said to myself: Good. Now Justice has been done. Finally I have found the courage to do something that needed to be done.

I stood there, gloating in my victory, for several minutes straight, not even aware just then that Wayne had gone downstairs and called the police and was prepared to admit to the murder himself, hoping to be found guilty so that he could rot in prison for the rest of his miserably lonely existence.

Instead, I'm the one who chose to step forward and assume the burden, rightfully so, of paying for this crime that needed to be committed. It was the only way I could pay her back for her cruelty and heartlessness against a woman who didn't even know the meaning of such qualities.

There! I have written it. I have said it to the doctors as well. I have finally gotten it out of my system, and the horror is gone. I killed my mother, and the stark horror of this unnatural act has ceased to stun or amaze me or render me insane.

If I ever get out of here, I will stand trial. I will plead insanity or whatever my attorney wishes me to do. It doesn't matter. I have no life worth living. Neither has Wayne. We couldn't care less what happens next in this world. All that matters is that that great reunion should take place. That great reunion which shall make us whole again. To be sane when that great reunion takes place is all that I desire.

BETSY'S DIARY – September 1, 1985

Dear Diary: Here it is, ten o'clock in the evening, and it is finally quiet in this house. The uproar has abated, and I feel confident that, when I retire to my bed shortly, I will be able to sleep without being aroused by some new scene of hysteria. And yet, the day started out so calmly and routinely. I woke up, slightly grateful for the fact that it was Sunday and I wouldn't have to go in to work, and then I realized that being in the library and applying myself to the sundry duties that my job entails usually manages to take my mind off the plodding passage of time that I am normally all too aware of when my mind is challenged by nothing at all.

I have been doing a lot of reading lately, consuming one book after another with amazing quickness, digesting very little of what I have read, and feeling strangely unfulfilled after I have finished each one of them. The last book I completed was truly preposterous. The heroine's name was Zambia, of all things, and her most grievous trial lay in her inability to acquire enough wealth and social prestige to attract the attention of the illustrious and powerful entrepreneur Deacon Forsythe who just happened to own a yacht and his very own tropical island in the South Pacific. Lo and behold, at the end of the novel, Zambia learns that her true ancestors were descended from an Inca tribe, and as soon as she comes into her wonderfully abundant inheritance, she and Deacon realize they're in love with each other, and the two of them go sailing off into the warm blue horizon.

Why do I keep reading these fluffy bits of nonsense? I used to read them all the time, even with a sense of awe, and I used to believe in my heart that such things really happened in real life and that one day some sort of miracle would take place in my own life whereby I would stumble upon an incredible treasure chest and fall rapturously into the arms of a powerful business magnate by the name of Deacon Forsythe or Bartholomew Meriwether, or one of their kind, at any rate. I used to feel enormously satisfied, merely in the act of fantasizing over such splendid events possibly occurring in my own life. I did it constantly, and then I used to wonder why everyone considered me hopelessly naïve.

Oh, well. I went to church this morning by myself, and afterwards, I walked through the park, holding my latest paperback acquisition in my hand, looking for an appropriately secluded spot where I could settle myself down upon the grass and immerse myself in my book. Instead of doing so, however, I sat beneath a tall maple tree, my book unopened on the grass in front of me, and delighted in the sounds of the birds all around me and the activity of the numerous other creatures of the woods stirring freely about me. And the sun felt warm and comforting upon my shoulders, and it struck me once again that I was so lucky to be alive and to be able to partake of this wondrous beauty.

I dozed off at the foot of that tree for about half an hour. When I awoke, I discovered that the air had become more humid and that my clothes were sticking to my skin, so I picked myself up and drove home.

Nobody was about. Our weekly Sunday brunches have ceased to be important enough for any of us to bother having them anymore. The family is no longer as closely knit as it once was. Lately, even Aunt Lucille and Ellen have formed a kind of bond of bitterness, and they always seem to be off together, commiserating with each other in their common view of the world as a ghastly and depressive sphere of existence, populated mostly by male predators who ought to be avoided at all cost. Mom and Rick are never around the house anymore either, and when they do happen to come home, the bedroom is the site of their activity, and that's about it. Not even Monica has seen fit to call me or try to establish any sort of contact with me as she continues to avoid me and fails to appear when I set up appointments to meet her for lunch, for example. When I show up at her apartment, she retreats into her room, and I am left alone with Carl who does little to satisfactorily explain to me why my sister has become so distant over the past month or so – and we've never even resolved the issue between us concerning that horrible outburst of hers, yelling at me to get the hell away from her.

I see what is happening to my family, to these people whom I love with all my heart, and it is all I can do to resist giving in to a mood of terrible despair. Then I remind myself of my vow from several weeks ago, and I make a supreme effort to stay strong, no matter how upsetting everything around me seems to be.

Tomorrow is Mom's birthday, and in an attempt to get all of us back together again at least to assume a semblance of conviviality, I have arranged that all of us meet for dinner tomorrow evening at the Embassy Club Restaurant. The dinner will, naturally, be on me, since the dinner was my idea to begin with. I do hope this affair will successfully re-affirm the bond of love that I know really still exists between all of us. I'm sure that, as soon as we are all together again, it will seem as though nothing has changed over this past summer – Or am I being naïve once again?

Well, I can hope, can't I? It's just possible that when Mom opens up the gift I've bought her and tries on the pearl necklace, she'll be all smiles, and maybe she'll even direct one of those smiles at me and then thank me in such a way that I will be freed of all my doubts of her ever having regretted bringing me into the world twenty-one years ago.

So, entering the house this afternoon and finding no one on the premises, I immediately made my way upstairs here to my room and, knowing that I would be torturing myself by doing so, I took from my dresser drawer the stack of letters Wayne has sent me over the past several weeks. Even though they are all very brief and re-reading every single one of them would not have taken up too much of the afternoon, I purposely selected just a few, spread them out on my bed, and reveled in the simple avowals of love that were contained in each of them. Why, after all, should the obvious always be expressed in extravagant language? Each of his letters is, to me, as priceless and unique as each beautiful stone that lies on the ocean's floor. Hopeless romantic that I am, I even fancy that, in their simplicity, they rival the most intricately constructed novels I have ever read in terms of sheer emotional truth and sincerity. And as I re-read a few of his letters this afternoon, I reminded myself that, within a few weeks, I would once again be able to look into those dark blue pools that are his eyes, once again hold onto those granite-like pillars of solidity that are his arms, and once more listen to that vibrant and love-filled throbbing which is his heart.

Once more, I extracted those three pictures he sent me last week and spread those upon my bedspread as well. They are almost comical, one of them being terribly out of focus, another one off-center, and the third much too dark to clearly make out any details at all.

The first picture shows him sitting down with his back propped up against the trunk of a tree. He's wearing khaki slacks and a sleeveless T-shirt, and although he's looking at the camera, the picture is so blurred that it's impossible to tell whether his eyes are fully open or not. I would like to think that they are, but upon closer scrutiny, it looks as though he's staring down at the ground.

In the second picture, he's standing with a group of his friends. They're all smiling and kind of goofing around, making faces at the camera and flexing their muscles in exaggerated poses. However, the picture is so off-center that nearly half of Wayne's body is cut off, and it doesn't look as though he's emoting for the camera-man.

He's all by himself in the third photograph, wearing his full uniform. His hair is clipped so short, of course, that none of his curls are visible protruding from the base of his cap, but he's standing very erect, as though a superior officer had suddenly commanded him to stand at attention, and his jaw is set in an extremely serious manner. In fact, there's no humor at all in the way he's looking at the camera. The picture came out very, very dark. All the same, it's probably the best of the three, and I'm considering having it blown up and then framed so that he can hang it on the wall in his bedroom or wherever else he would like to put it.

After putting the letters and pictures away, I idly fanned my hand through all the clothes that were hanging in my closet. I've bought so many of them that the idea of buying him the sports car is now a very impractical one, at least for the time being. There are two three-piece suits hanging in my closet along with all of my own clothes. I've only approximated the size that he actually takes, but even if they don't fit him when he gets back, we can have them altered, I suppose. And one evening, just for the fun of it, he can put on one of these suits, and I can put on one of the party dresses I bought a long time ago and never wore – and the two of us can go out dancing. While he holds me in his arms and sweeps me lightly across the dance floor, I can imagine that my name is Zambia and that his is Deacon and that we are two very wealthy and sophisticated people who do this sort of thing whenever we get bored playing billiards, backgammon, and cricket.

I say these ridiculous things to myself if only because I want to hold onto my equilibrium. The truth of the matter, of course, is that I'm beginning to find his absence almost unbearable. "To the max," as Ellen would say, I guess. While Wayne was here and I gradually attempted to bring him into the inner circle of my family, one of my greatest desires was to convince all of them that he was a changed person and that he was far from being the stereotypical punk they were all so anxious to categorize him as. Well, I think that I've changed a bit myself. At least there are certain times when I feel that I'm handling things remarkably well, considering my prior inability to cope with some of the normal pressures of daily living. I am aware of an increased amount of inner strength that I never thought I could possibly achieve – not until this summer of '85 took place and changed my life completely.

I had closed my closet door and was just heading downstairs to get some sort of dinner prepared when the explosion occurred, although in calling it an explosion, I am not accurately characterizing what actually did happen in this house today, but now that it is all over, it certainly feels as though an explosion did indeed take place.

I heard Mom's and Rick's voices raised in anger as they entered the house through the front door. They had apparently been attending some function this afternoon where one of Mom's young female associates had flirted with Rick and, according to Mom, received encouragement from him as well. Rick told Mom to forget the whole incident, saying that she was exaggerating in stating that he had encouraged the woman, but Mom wasn't hearing any of it. Finally, Rick said that he was going upstairs to take a shower, and Mom came into the kitchen where I was preparing dinner.

"What!" she cried sharply, gazing ostensibly upon the, as yet, bare kitchen tabletop. "Dinner's not ready? Don't tell me there's nothing to eat, Betsy. If Rick doesn't have his quota of the five basic food groups, I'm really going to hear about it."

I calmly told her that dinner would be ready shortly, and she settled down at the table and started reading a section of today's newspaper. In fact, dinner was just about ready when Rick came downstairs in shorts and sandals, opened the refrigerator, and started fishing around for a beer.

"What!" he cried out suddenly, turning to Mom with an ornery look on his face. "Don't tell me we're all out of Sam Adams." At that point I hastened to explain to him that there was plenty of a different brand, I forgot which, way in the back, but both his and Mom's nerves were stretched to the limit. "Jean," he said, whining over at Mom," you know how much I enjoy my Sam Adams when I get out of the shower. What's today?"

"Sunday," Mom told him, without looking up from the newspaper.

"Jeez!" exploded from his lips. "Liquor stores are all closed, I suppose. And tomorrow's Labor Day. Jesus Christ, Jean! Don't you know how to run a fucking household?"

Despite my conviction that I'd grown emotionally stronger over the past several weeks, I was unable to stay in that room with them and listen to such inane bickering so I hurried outside onto the patio and walked all the way over towards the tree at the far end of the yard. It wasn't enough, however, because I could still hear Rick's whining voice as he complained about the mismanagement of our household and even, at one point, yelled at Mom to look up at him when he was talking to her. I put my hands over my ears and leaned back against the tree trunk, and I could still hear him. No matter how hard I tried, it was impossible for me to shut the scene out of my awareness.

Then suddenly, just as I expected would be the case sooner or later, Mom raised her voice in retaliation, and a prolonged and furious shouting match ensued. I stood at the tree, dropped my hands by my sides realizing that it was useless trying to shut out the sounds of their hostility, and I said to myself: Tomorrow is her birthday, and it's going to be ruined. It will take a long time before the effects of this argument blow over and she can feel free to celebrate her birthday with the rest of the family.

At long last, the shouting died down, and a few seconds later, I heard sounds of some sort of activity taking place from beyond their bedroom window upstairs, though there were no voices being raised in continued rancor. With a sigh of relief, I re-entered the house and found Mom pacing the kitchen floor.

"Mom," I said to her very softly, and when I caught her attention, I foolishly came out with the question I should've known would irritate her even more than she already was: "Is everything all right?"

"Stupid!" she shot back at me. "You heard us yelling at each other, didn't you?"

Just then, Aunt Lucille wheeled Ellen into the kitchen, and I was fortunate enough to be spared any additional attacks from my mother. She instantly turned to Aunt Lucille and told her that Rick had just threatened to leave the house for good. There was a little sob in Mom's voice when she told her this, and I wanted to go over to her and put my arms around her; but the fear that my actions would be misunderstood held me back. So, I watched helplessly as Aunt Lucille stood there and told Mom not to shed any tears over it.

"It's for the best, don't you think?" she said to her. "I, for one, knew that this arrangement between the two of you wasn't going to last for very long. Look at what happened to *me* when my Arnie abandoned me for that tramp twelve years ago."

"That's right, Lucille," Mom stood there and practically spat right into her sister's face. "It happened twelve years ago, so let's not stand here and talk about it as though any of us really cares."

And then, just to add a further note to the ridiculous dispute the two of them had embarked upon, Ellen clapped her hands in senseless delight and applauded Mom for successfully putting Aunt Lucille in her place.

Aunt Lucille then accused Mom of being heartless, and I was really grateful to Ellen for then taking it upon herself to suggest that we all just sit down and have dinner. Aunt Lucille wheeled Ellen over to her usual place at the table, I put a few more dishes out that had been sitting on the counter, and we all got settled in our chairs, even Mom, when suddenly we heard Rick lumbering down the staircase in the living room, accompanied by the dragging of a pair of suitcases. This, of course, was enough to induce Mom to bolt right out of her chair and go running into the living room to stop him, and before they'd even begun shouting at each other, Aunt Lucille followed suit, and then Ellen wheeled herself frantically into the other room as well, so as not to miss out on any of the action that was beginning to take place. For my own part, I remained riveted in my seat and nervously clutched my napkin between my fingers as I heard Mom yelling at Rick that if he were to leave the house, she'd never take him back. Rick answered by saying that that was fine with him, and I heard the front door open, followed by a brief struggle, a stifled cry from Mom, and then the sound of the door being closed as, it seemed, Mom had successfully prevented his departure – for the time being, that is.

"You want to leave so you can go to that bitch, admit it," I heard Mom scream at him, and once again, Rick responded that she was right about that, that he had been "banging" her every day during his lunch hour for the past two weeks, and that she was younger and prettier and "a much better lay" than my mother ever hoped to be.

There was a lot more to what they flung at each other in the most vicious, high-pitched tones of voices imaginable. I was amazed that Ellen and Aunt Lucille chose to remain in such close quarters to such a hateful scene. And I wanted it to end and for Mom to come to me in her grief, and I'd enfold her in my arms and try to make her forget that this whole awful experience had ever taken place. When all was said and done, the scene between those two lasted no more than five or six minutes, but it seemed an eternity. When the door finally did shut and I realized that Rick Sellars had walked out on her, I rose from my chair and resolved to go into the room and see if there was anything I could do on Mom's behalf.

But the nightmare continued. As soon as the door closed behind him, Mom tore into Aunt Lucille, telling her that it was because of her, Ellen, and me that Rick had found it unbearable living in our house. Aunt Lucille began by defending herself and the rest of us in a fairly calm and sympathetic manner, but as Mom's hysteria heightened, Aunt Lucille's reserve vanished, and then she, too, began screaming back at Mom. Their argument raged from the living room, on into the kitchen where I remained seated, and then on back into the living room over a period of at least fifteen minutes.

Finally, Aunt Lucille disappeared out the front door, slamming it behind her, and Mom sharply commanded Ellen to go to her room and to stay out of her sight for good.

"Hey!" I heard Ellen yell back at her. "Don't go taking it out on me!"

It was only then that the tension started to lessen, and I heard Mom admit, in a tearful voice, that Ellen was right and that she had no right to take this out on her little baby.

Hearing that, I rose from my seat and cleared off the table. If anyone cared to eat anything, it certainly wasn't me. While I was getting rid of our untouched dinner, I heard Mom go upstairs and, shortly after that, her bedroom door slammed shut. I felt relieved that, at least, she was able to find some means of escape from her grief by sheltering herself in her room. There, I hoped, she might manage to calm herself to the point where I could rest assured that there would be no further shouting in the house for the remainder of the evening.

After tidying up the kitchen, I found my way into the living room and sat on the couch to watch T.V. with Ellen. Neither one of us spoke, and although our eyes were on the television screen, I doubt that we were actually paying the slightest bit of attention to what was taking place in front of us.

At about nine or nine-thirty, the telephone rang in the kitchen, and when I got up to answer it, I heard Carl's voice on the other end, inquiring as to whether everything had been suitably arranged for our little dinner-party for Mom at the Embassy Club Restaurant for tomorrow night. I assured him that everything was all set, but in my desire to dwell as little as possible on the rift that had just taken place between Mom and Rick, I neglected to mention to him that Rick probably would not be among us.

As soon as I got off the phone and reseated myself in front of the T.V. with Ellen, she turned to me and asked who had just called, and when I informed her of my conversation with Carl, she regarded me with a very peculiar expression on her face and asked,

"Are you sure that's all you two talked about?"

I was about to answer her when we both noticed that Mom was coming downstairs. At the foot of the staircase, she looked at me and asked me who it was that had just called. I could tell by the anxious look on her tear-stained face that she was hoping I'd be able to tell her that it had been Rick who had just phoned, but in telling her the truth, I was forced to watch her leave to go back upstairs, looking utterly defeated and forlorn.

On my way here to my room a little while ago, I paused very briefly outside the door to Mom's room. A part of me urged me to knock so as to inquire if I could come in and talk with her; and yet, I could find no power whatsoever to bring myself to do that.

Now that I am here in my room, ready to go to bed, I feel that tomorrow morning I really should make the effort to talk with her. I won't mention the incident that just occurred here tonight, either. Not unless she happens to bring it up herself first. I know that, if I were in her position right now, I'd certainly want to see a friendly face or feel an affectionate arm go about my shoulders.

Oh, God! Will I finally get the chance to demonstrate, once and for all, how much I love her? Even though many hostile and hurtful words were exchanged in this house tonight, might it yet be possible that the tender words I wish to say to her should at least partially erase the memories of this horribly depressing evening?

Tomorrow is her birthday, too. Poor Mom! She has so much to live for, and she doesn't even realize it. That, in itself, constitutes her greatest failing.

P.S. Tomorrow is Labor Day, so there'll be no mail delivery. And since today was Sunday, that means on Tuesday I should receive two days' worth of his correspondence. Two more precious jewels to add to my already priceless collection.

ELLEN'S MEMOIRS – January 1, 1986

This New Year didn't exactly get off to a roaring start, but it may be more promising than I expected. Last night when I went to bed, I was feeling pretty down. I remember all the years when I was growing up, Aunt Lucille used to complain about New Year's Eve, calling it the most depressing time of the whole year, and I used to tell myself what a nut-case she was for thinking that. Wasn't New Year's Eve the time to party? And what could be less depressing than partying? Then when I lost the use of my legs and wound up in this wheel-chair, I said to myself: Aunt Lucille's right, after all. When you've got nothing to look forward to except more bullshit, New Year's Eve only re-enforces it, making you sit up and take a look around you so that you begin to see Life for what it really is: Bullshit.

Well, last night I was feeling pretty down. Throwing myself off a bridge seemed like a pretty good way of spending New Year's Eve, but today things got a little better. I woke up this morning and said to myself: What the hell, it's 1986, and I'm still here, and there's still plenty of dick out there, even though none of it seems to be pointing my way. So, when Aunt Lucille told me we'd be going to the mall this afternoon, I got pretty excited. First of all, I figured I could watch a few tight buns strolling by. Second of all, I might see my redheaded stud-man Marty hanging around with some of his cool-ass pals, and like I've said so many times before, Marty was always up for it, any old time of the day or night. Third of all, I've got Aunt Lucille wrapped around my pinkie, so all I have to do is pout a little and she buys me something to cheer me up. And fourth of all, going to the mall sure beats sticking around this dump and watching the old bag mope – which is what she does when she's got the day off and nobody except me to complain to.

So, we got to the mall, and I saw these pretty earrings. I asked Aunt Lucille what she thought of them. "Oh, they're much too pretty for me to wear," she said to me, and I told her," It wasn't you I was thinking of," as if she couldn't figure that out for herself. Next thing you know, she's buying them for me, and I guess the experience of digging way down deep in that crusty old wallet of hers and having to spend a little money got her all dizzy, because on the way out of the jeweler's, she ran my wheel-chair right smack into this other oncoming wheel-chair that had this guy in it. Come to find out, the guy who was wheeling this other guy around was an old chum of Aunt Lucille's from way back around the turn of the century when they used to go to high school together. I don't know how this guy ever recognized her, she's deteriorated so much over the last few years, but anyway, Aunt Lucille recognized him, too. Like a stupid jerk, she said to him," Didn't everybody used to call you Chubs?" Truth of the matter is the guy is positively gross. A real blimp, you know? But compared to what Aunt Lucille's used to, I'd say he was about a 9 on a scale of 1 to 10. Even after she talked about him being called Chubs and even went so far as to tell him she thought he'd put on a lot more weight since high school, the guy just stood there smiling and making pleasant conversation with her, probably figuring that, compared to what *he's* used to, Aunt Lucille was a 12!

While those two were standing around getting hot for each other, the guy in the wheel-chair started talking to me, telling me about his accident and how he used to play football at Glendale High before that. I took one look at his upper body and said to myself: I don't doubt it for a second. What a hunk this guy is!

As it turned out, the fat guy who was wheeling him around was his Uncle Bradley, and he was a bachelor, never was married, and he spent a lot of his time taking care of him because he didn't have any kids of his own. Hearing this, I immediately told this hunk that the old prune who was wheeling me around was my Aunt Lucille and that, as he could see by the looks of her, she'd never been married either and she sure as hell had a lot of time on her hands, too, so I kind of filled a void in her life by letting her take care of me.

A few minutes later, the gorgeous hunk turned to his Uncle Bradley and told him that the two of us would like to roam around on our own for a little while. When I heard him say that, I almost rose from my chair and started dancing through the mall, I was so ecstatic! Then Aunt Lucille, like a real crab, said that that would be too dangerous, and then the fat dude said," Why not? This way the two of us can have lunch together and talk over old times."

"That sounds like a wonderful idea, Auntie," I said to her in the kind of sweet way that only a living doll like me is capable of.

So, the next thing you know, this handsome hunk and I were wheeling ourselves along the mall, looking around, talking about this-and-that, and having a hell of a time. The best part came, though, when we wheeled ourselves outside and over along the side of the building, and the hunk reached into his shirt pocket and pulled out a couple of joints.

"You look like a real party animal," he said to me. "Whaddya say we spark 'em up?"

I mean, what could I say? I was so totally in love with this guy that I would have done anything in the world for him, assuming he could enjoy himself the same way good old Marty always did whenever I'd "entertain" *him.* Anyway, we smoked those joints, and it's been so long since I've smoked, I really was starting to feel totally zonked. It was like the greatest feeling in the world! – On second thought, the greatest feeling in the world being with Wayne - - But that's beside the point now!

Before very long, this guy started talking about us getting together again, and I was like so turned on, I couldn't believe this was happening.

"Only problem is," he said to me," we'd need a chaperone. That means we'd probably have to double with Uncle Bradley and your Aunt Lucille."

Me? Go on a double-date with Aunt Lucille? Even if I hadn't been stoned, I would've keeled over in my chair with laughter. I don't think I've laughed so hard in ages, and this guy was just so cool, the way he kind of laughed along with me, you know? So, I told him that the idea of doubling with the two old folks sounded super!

So, then this cool dude wrote down his name and phone number on a piece of paper and gave it to me, and I did the same for him. His name is Duane – rhymes with Wayne, get it? – and he lives with his parents way the hell out in Glendale. But that should be no problem. He told me he's got his uncle wrapped around his pinkie, so all he has to do is ask him to drive him over to Maplewoods or to the mall or someplace, and it's party-time for sure!

When I got back to the car with Aunt Lucille and she started driving us back home, I turned to her with my most charming smile and asked her,

"Well, how did things go between you and Bradley?"

She looked down at me briefly in some distaste before saying,

"I guess he's not bad – considering he's a man."

BETSY'S DIARY – September 2, 1985

Dear Diary: I thought I was calm, that the horror that took hold of me two hours ago would have blown over by now – but my hand is still shaking as I write this, and my resolve to remain strong has deserted me completely.

Oh, God, I need to talk to him! I need to tell him that I love him and to hear from him that his feelings for me are as strong as they have always been. How else am I going to get through this? How else will I ever be able to put this nightmare behind me and get on with the rest of my life?

But they wouldn't let me talk to him. I placed a long-distance call to South Carolina and was informed that the rules could not be broken except in extraordinary circumstances. I stood by the phone and heard this, and I forced myself to accept it, to get a grip on myself, and then I realized that, even if they let me get through to him, I couldn't possibly relate to him what happened. If I were to tell him, he would fly here immediately and earn a dishonorable discharge in doing so, and once he got here, he would literally kill my brother-in-law, adding one more horrible act of violence to the already brutal and demonic thing that has just taken place this evening.

How could I have been so stupid? I had vowed that I would never let myself be alone in Carl's company, ever since that awful morning in the library when he seized me by the wrist and sought to impose his will upon me. I was so stupid, telling myself that, over these past few weeks, he had actually become my friend. Even my confidant, to a certain extent, since Monica no longer wished to have anything to do with me. I took this man into my confidence and lowered my guard and –

No. Let me start from the beginning, and in relating the events that led up to this terrifying experience, perhaps my hand will stop shaking and my fear that additional anguish may be heading my way in the days ahead will slowly vanish.

The day started out reasonably well. I stepped into Mom's room this morning at about ten-thirty. I was concerned that, being an early riser and not having risen yet at such a relatively late hour of the morning, Mom might have been subject to some sort of illness or trauma. So, I went into her room, walked up to where she lay in bed with her eyes closed, and sat gently upon the edge of her sheets. I sat there quietly for quite some time and closed my own eyes, fondly relishing the peace that I felt we were both enjoying at that time. When she finally began to stir, I opened my eyes, saw her own eyes begin to flicker open, and then I smiled down upon her and wished her a Happy Birthday.

She didn't respond to me at first, but after yawning and stretching a little and then rising to a sitting position in her bed, it suddenly dawned upon her that today was, in fact, her birthday, one of the rare occasions when both her birthday and the Labor Day holiday coincided, so that she had the entire day to herself in which to celebrate it. At the same time, I felt so sorry for her because Rick Sellars had chosen the day before this to hurt her so cruelly, and I instinctively leaned over her and kissed her on the cheek when I saw that she was wide awake.

"It's a beautiful day, Mom," I said to her. "Is there anything I can get you?"

Mom shook her head No and started to squirm her way out of bed. As she did so, she noticed that I was holding her birthday gift in my hand, and I smiled and told her that I would give it to her now, instead of waiting till we were all assembled at the Embassy Club Restaurant later on this evening, if that was O.K. with her; and she smiled a little at me and admitted that she was really looking forward to finding something that might cheer her up, so she took the little box out of my hand and began unwrapping it while she was still sitting there in bed.

When she opened the box and extracted the pearl necklace I had bought for her, her face lit up in joy, and I laughed a little and told her that it really wasn't anything special, just a strand of costume jewelry that I'd picked up for her at the mall.

"Well, I really didn't think they were genuine pearls," Mom said. "I didn't expect *that* much from you, Betsy."

I let the matter drop and moved off her bed to approach the door, content with the thought, at least, that opening the box and laying eyes on the pearls had produced a smile on my mother's face and that I had been partially responsible for bringing that small bit of happiness into her life this morning. The next thing I knew, she called out my name just as I was about to leave the room. I stopped, half-expecting to hear a remark that might jar me out of my state of contentment, and when I turned to look in her direction, I saw that she was smiling at me with a sweetness that I don't remember ever having seen in her face before this.

"Thank you, Betsy," she said to me. "Thank you so much."

I immediately got a bit choked up. I even wanted to throw all reserve aside and rush over to her and hold her in my arms. I wanted to absorb into my own being every hurt and every pain she may have been experiencing since her separation from Rick. I wanted her to be able to feel like a whole woman again and to see that she had everything to look forward to in her life that so many other less fortunate people couldn't dream of ever finding in their own lives.

Instead, I smiled back at her rather timidly and left the room. I certainly did not want to do or say anything that would make her retract her thanks for the gift. The moment was perfect in its beauty just the way it was, and I had no wish to tamper with its glowing perfection.

Later on in the day, my brother-in-law phoned to make sure that everything was still on for tonight. I remember this conversation, now, as being so natural and unaffected that I shudder once again at the thought that that man was able to hypnotize me into a state that rendered me so helpless and unsuspecting. Little did I know at the time that, when he phoned me this afternoon to re-confirm tonight's plans, he did so, so as to solidify in his own mind his intentions of making this evening the one in which he would turn my whole life into a horror show.

I see by the trembling of my whole body as I am writing this that it will take a lot longer than the expiration of a mere twenty-four hours before I am totally free of these anxieties – these fears that, even now, he may be standing outside this house, contemplating the means of entering it without Mom's or Ellen's knowledge, coming up here to my room, and finishing what he started two hours ago.

But no! Such things couldn't take place in real life, could they? He is a sick and disturbed person, it's true, but I keep telling myself that he couldn't possibly go any further than he's already gone. I successfully averted the ultimate disaster that he's had in mind for me. He knows that the force of Wayne's loving protection is behind me, and he won't go any further with this. He's too scared, too frightened that Wayne will find out about this. Even though I don't have the heart to tell Wayne everything, I must at least lead Carl to believe that I would tell him the whole story, if only to guarantee that there won't be any further attacks upon my physical being.

Getting back to the events of earlier in the day, I recall that I was in my room getting into some fresh clothing for the evening when I thought I heard the front door open and then slam shut. Then when I got downstairs, Ellen and Aunt Lucille were seated together in the living room, and Aunt Lucille told me that she didn't think we should have the dinner-party at the Embassy Club Restaurant.

"Your mother just walked out of here," she informed me, "telling us that she was going to Mackenzie's for a few drinks and that she'd meet us at the restaurant later on. Knowing her, 'later on' could mean ten or eleven o'clock."

"But Mom knows that dinner reservations are for seven-thirty," I explained to her in a feeble attempt to assure her that everything would take place just as we'd originally planned, but Aunt Lucille is too wise and she knows Mom's idiosyncrasies far too well. And later on, while we all sat at the Embassy Club Restaurant, delaying our dinner orders so as to give Mom the benefit of the doubt, Aunt Lucille turned to me and said,

"I told you we should have canceled this whole affair. Knowing Jean the way I do, she's probably feeling no pain right now."

"And knowing Jean the way *I* do," Ellen piped up," she's probably getting –" But she didn't finish her sentence, thank God, although all of us sitting at the table knew that she had purposely made the remark, only to allow all of our own suspicions to come to the surface, as distasteful as the experience of doing so was for all of us.

At about nine o'clock, we were all done with the cheese and crackers that were on the table and everybody was quite distraught over our long and unproductive wait for Mom to show up. Finally, Monica, who had not spoken to me all evening long, stood up and announced that she was extremely tired and was going to drive herself back to the apartment. She made a point of turning to her husband and suggesting that he hitch a ride home with me, of all people, and I now know why she allowed her lips to curl back slightly from her teeth when she said that. I'd phoned Mackenzie's a while back and was told that Mom had left and, as far as the bartender knew, was heading off to Parts Unknown, so nobody thought Monica's desire to leave was the least bit uncalled-for.

In fact, within fifteen minutes, everyone was standing up and getting ready to leave – except me, that is, and I can now see how foolishly I was behaving. In my ill-conceived desire to keep the faith and believe against all evidence to the contrary that Mom would appear sooner or later, I was silly enough to accept Carl's advice when he expressed his opinion that it might be a good idea for the two of us to wait for her together. So, once again, I was left alone with him despite my former resolution to avoid such a situation at all costs.

Well, things were kept fairly low-key at first. He agreed with me that there was still a chance that Mom would show up after all, and at least he and I would be there to greet her when she finally did arrive. In the meantime, he was drinking one cocktail after another, and as time went on and very few people were left in the restaurant, he leaned in towards me and said,

"I don't want you to take offense by what I'm about to say to you right now, Betsy – but you look really gorgeous this evening."

In my naivete, I smiled and told him that he was exaggerating, but that I was flattered nonetheless and couldn't possibly be offended by such an extravagant compliment. Of course, I see now how utterly brainless and simple-minded I was in allowing myself to remain there in his company like that, especially when he put his arm around my shoulders and I told myself that he was my brother-in-law and, as such, was entitled to occasional demonstrations of warm affection of this sort.

Oh, God! How utterly stupid and naïve I have been all this time! I never would have thought he could be capable of such actions. I never imagined he could be so unfeeling towards Monica either. I should have known. I should have seen it coming. He'd always impressed me, in the early days of his marriage to my sister, as an ardent young man with a fiery gaze. I should have suspected that, lurking within him, there would be this cauldron of fierce and violent passions.

And now it's too late. It's already happened, and I can't undo it, no matter how hard I try or how hard I pray.

I know that when he leaned over and kissed me behind the ear, I felt distinctly uncomfortable, knowing that an imaginary line had definitely just been crossed, and then – Then! When I felt his hand slide under my skirt, I scrambled to my feet and started towards the door.

He yanked me by the arm and pulled me in towards him, and I almost slammed into his chest by the force of the pull he exerted on my arm. One whiff of his hot breath against the side of my cheek, and I cried out and tore myself away from him once again.

There were no patrons remaining in the dining area of the restaurant at that time, but I thought, for sure, that one of their employees might be in the vicinity and would intervene on my behalf – And in looking back on it now, I probably did more harm than good by rushing away from him, because I ended up in the restaurant's foyer, which was totally deserted. And yet, I remember telling myself just then that *somebody* must have seen what was happening, and with any luck, that person would stop Carl from following me out here.

Just as I finished telling myself that that was the way it just had to be, I found that he had burst through the door to the foyer and was coming towards me.

"Betsy, listen to me," I heard him say, but I ran out of the foyer and out into the cool evening air. I was in a total panic, but even so, I quickly remembered where I'd parked my car, and I headed straight towards it. I ran fast, too, and without stumbling over anything or losing my balance or anything of the sort, and when I reached the outside of my car, I said to myself: God is on my side. He let me get this far, and I'm all right, and I'm going to get through this!

I dipped my hand into my purse to extract my keys from it, and as I stood there trembling and looking down into my purse, the nightmare began all over again, only worse.

I don't think I can describe exactly what took place. All that mattered to me was that surely some bystander would intervene and put a stop to all this; and at the same time, the horrifying realization that there was no one standing about in the parking lot – no one at all! – began to creep up on me, and I panicked. I found myself pinned against the side of my car, breathing in fits and starts, while he held me and kept repeating over and over again that he loved me and that he wanted me and that he was going to make love to me.

And I screamed once, very softly, it seemed to me, and his hand came over my mouth to silence me. Then he pressed his groin against me so that I squirmed out of his grasp and, freeing myself, swung my arm out in a wild, haphazard motion. I don't think I hurt him at all, or even struck him, for that matter, but the unexpected movement of my arm seemed to have fended him off long enough for me to get my keys out of my purse and unlock and open the car door.

I started to get inside, and he fell upon me. I was pinned once again, only this time I was being held motionless against something inside my car, I don't know what, and that's when he tore my blouse down the front, and I threw back my head and cried out that I was being raped. I was actually resigning myself to it, too, when he pulled my bra off, and his hands went to my breasts at the same instant that my mind slipped into a pit of darkness for several moments during which I knew nothing and cared about nothing, I felt so close to death.

But nothing else happened. My mind leaped back into consciousness as I realized that I wasn't actually going to be raped after all, that his physical drive had apparently diminished, and he backed away from me almost as suddenly and as violently as he had come on top of me. I had my eyes closed, but when I heard his sobs coming from outside my still opened car door, I opened them and saw that he was leaning against the car parked next to mine, with his hands covering his face.

I lay there panting, not knowing what to do, and then the idea came upon me that he might stop sobbing and then renew his attempts to assault me, so I quickly leaned over and pulled the door shut. Then I placed the key into the ignition with trembling fingers, got the car started, and tore out of that parking lot with a recklessness that I never would have thought I could have carried off under ordinary circumstances, not without bringing both myself and the car to considerable harm.

It wasn't until I was on the road, heading back home, that I realized that the front of my blouse was torn open and that my bra, too, was completely disengaged, so I pulled over to the side of the road. I stupidly sat there and tried putting everything back to the way it should have been, my hands trembling the whole time. For some insane reason, the need to cover up everything that had been exposed seemed to be the most important thing in the world to me. It wasn't until several minutes had passed that I actually remembered what had just happened to me, and I burst into tears. But I fought them back almost as soon as I began realizing that I was losing control of myself.

I got back on the highway and continued the rest of the way home in something of a daze. At one point, I thought I caught a glimpse of Carl's automobile in my rear-view mirror, but when the car turned a second or two after I noticed it, I felt a huge sense of relief, but was still feeling far more paranoid than usual, and with good reason, too.

As soon as I stepped into the house, I closed the front door and locked it. Like a complete lunatic, I stumbled about the house and locked every window of the ground floor as well and, after my brief but fruitless attempt to contact Wayne on the phone, I came upstairs and locked myself here in my room. I threw myself onto the bed and lay quietly for over an hour, thinking about nothing in an attempt to prevent myself from thinking about the attack that had just been made against me —something that I always thought only happened to other people, and now I was one of those other people.

But I had escaped. Nothing had happened – in a technical sense, at least. I kept telling myself this, hoping to be comforted by it, but to no avail. On two separate occasions, I took my pen in hand and sat at my desk to record the day's events, but found that I couldn't get anything legible onto the paper, and this, in itself, caused my hand to shake even more.

I am calmer now, a lot less frantic than I was even fifteen minutes ago, because as minute after minute goes by, the likelihood of his coming here to this house and trying to get at me all over again seems to diminish.

And yet, the threat still exists. He is my brother-in-law. There will be times in the future when our family will be together, and the others will consider it totally natural that we should be in each other's company. But it is impossible for me to continue this way. It is impossible that any kind of wholesome family life can continue, involving both me and Carl, without my having to relive in my mind the horrible events that took place in that parking lot tonight.

It's over. The delusion that he ever truly loved my sister. The delusion that we could ever be a happy family. All of it is over. I will stay here in my room. Oh, God! I wish to stay here for the next two weeks until Wayne comes, that's how dreadful the prospect of my going out and facing each one of them appears to me right now.

If only he were here. If only he hadn't left me in the first place. If only I had someone, right now, who could put his arms around me so that I could totally blot out the memory of what happened tonight.

Oh, Wayne, my dearest, my treasure, my love. It grieves me to say that I need you now more than I've ever needed you before. How incredibly sad it is for me to find that I cannot cope, that I cannot live from one day to the next without your loving support.

No. He must never learn of this. He must never be told that Carl actually tore my blouse from my body. I shudder to think what would happen if he should ever learn the truth of what happened to me tonight. Carl is sick. He needs help. How could a second act of violence erase the sin of the first?

No, Wayne, you will never hear from these lips that that disturbed young man attempted to use me as the object of his carnal desires. This incident will cease to have any significance for either of us, Wayne, because when you return, when you re-enter the fold of my love, I will see to it that there will be no stain or blemish that shall mar the perfection of our reunion. And only God can give me the strength to see that this may be so.

P.S. Tomorrow is another day that must be endured. If it weren't for the fact that Wayne will be returning in a few weeks, I don't believe that I would have the strength to continue. And that alone is what scares me the most. It positively terrifies me, and I cannot allow myself to give it another moment's thought.

AUNT LUCILLE'S DIARY – January 1, 1986

When I woke up this morning, all I could think of was how foolishly I had allowed myself to be talked into going to that nightclub last night with Kathy and Melanie. I hated myself for exhibiting such weakness, especially at my age, as to entertain the notion that there could possibly be anybody out there for me, anybody who could even come close to meeting my standards, anybody who might turn out to be the noble, upstanding, and loyal individual I had once considered my Arnie to be – until that dreadful day nearly twelve years ago when he abandoned me for that tramp, leaving me high and dry in the prime of my womanhood. How stupid I'd been to allow myself to be taken in by his wiles. I should have known that, as soon as I permitted him the intense pleasure of sharing my bed with me, there would be nothing more I could entice him with. You see, I am convinced that, once you have given a man the pride and glory of your womanly treasures, you've automatically lost his fidelity and respect because you've already given him the very thing (the only thing?) he wanted in the first place.

Like I said, I woke up this morning, feeling like an absolute fool, and I said to myself that today was the start of a new year, and I'd be damned if I was going to let myself be taken in by anything or anybody, man, woman, or child. I'm forty years old, at the twilight of my life (or so I've been told – by Ellen, anyway). The least I can do is act in a solidly mature manner and not allow myself to be persuaded into doing anything that I know will only bring me emotional pain and disillusionment.

Being thus resolved, I made up my mind that I'd take Ellen to the mall with me and spend a little money on myself. Usually when I get in moods like the one I was in early this morning, I can manage to pull myself out of them by buying myself some small trinket at the store, some little bauble that will take my mind off the fact that I can't stand the thought of being alone all the time.

I did end up doing one thing I'd already decided I wouldn't. In one of the stores, Ellen spotted an extremely over-priced pair of earrings, and the next thing I knew, I was buying them for her. It's a shame that she'll probably never get a chance to wear them at a party, for example; but even if she can put them on and look at herself in a mirror and get some pleasure out of doing that, I figured it would be worth it. And besides that, the earrings might look pretty good on me, too, if Ellen ever decides to let me try them on someday.

Well, wouldn't you know, Ellen and I had been at the mall barely half an hour when I literally ran into one of my old high school friends. I say "literally" because I wasn't looking exactly where I was going, and I accidentally ran Ellen's wheel-chair straight into the wheel-chair of this young man that Chubs was wheeling in front of him. I remember Chubs as being a rather heavy-set individual from way back when the two of us were in high school together, but I don't recall his being so absolutely obese! I mean, the man is positively obscene-looking with all those rolls of fat hanging over his belt. But he really is such a harmless and sweet person, so when he offered to buy me lunch at the mall (and I've never been one to turn down a free meal), I hesitated only a second or two before accepting such a gallant invitation. As it happens, Ellen seemed to be getting along very well with the boy in the wheel-chair, so everything seemed to work out to everyone's satisfaction in the end.

When Ellen and I got home, we turned on the T.V. and watched a couple of soap operas, the way we usually do when I get a day off, and Ellen was in a remarkably good mood. In fact, during the entire evening that followed, she remained in high spirits, even while we were playing cards at the kitchen table, and she didn't even complain when she caught me cheating, just a little bit, a few times. I even beat her at gin rummy, which is a game she usually excels at, and when she realized she'd lost, she didn't even fling the cards across the room, which is what she always does whenever she loses a card game. I suppose I really shouldn't have cheated those few times that I did, but I think the psychological significance of that aspect of my nature stems from what happened twelve years ago when my Arnie deserted me for that tramp. Ever since then, the thought of another woman getting the best of me, even if it's only my niece and it's only a card game, has a very unsettling effect upon me. I guess I just can't help being the way I am.

Nevertheless, Ellen and I did have a jolly old time, all things considered. We even ate some ice cream at the table and talked a little bit. That's when I found out that Ellen and that boy in the wheel-chair must have really hit it off, because she mentioned to me that he said he would call her sometime this week, and I laughed out loud and told her,

"Don't be surprised if Chubs ends up calling me, too, before the week is over."

By the time the two of us retired for the night, I felt that we'd actually come a long way, in the space of a mere twelve hours or so, towards an awareness that 1986 might have some potential for the two of us, after all.

P.S. I forgot to mention earlier that Chubs is what people nowadays often refer to as "gay" – So, even if he does ask me to go to the movies with him or something, at least I won't have to go to bed with him afterwards.

BETSY'S DIARY – September 3, 1985

Dear Diary: As truly incredible as it seems after this long and harrowing day, I can actually state that I will retire to my bed this evening feeling that there is a certain amount of hope that Mom and I will, very soon, experience a closeness that has always been absent from my life; and I pray that the miracle will take place tomorrow – the miracle that will bring about a permanent change in the regard that she has always held for me.

I woke up this morning after an extremely fitful sleep. I'd had a lot of trouble falling asleep, to start with, and I remember waking up several times in the middle of the night, the remembrance of Carl's attack upon me pressing in on me from all sides so relentlessly that I even got up and took a couple of pills, hoping that they'd provide me with the sleep my body so desperately craved, but the pills were largely ineffective. It wasn't until nearly four-thirty that I was able to get any prolonged period of sleep worth mentioning, and when my alarm clock went off at six-thirty, I felt that I was unable to face the day ahead. And so, I did something that I've never done before since working full-time at the library: I went downstairs and called in sick, as soon as I saw that it was the usual time for Mrs. Evans to open up the library for the day. If she should ask me to work Saturday, I'll agree to that, so as to make up for today's missed hours. For the time being, at least, I felt that I had the time off coming to me. There was no way I'd be able to function if I were to go in to work this morning. Plus, I had an idea that, if I had the whole day free, I could make an attempt to visit Monica at the office and get her to face me and listen to me, once and for all, so that somehow or other we could return to being on good terms with each other once again.

As it turns out, I never should have gone there.

I waited outside her office from eleven in the morning until noontime, just in case she should take her lunch break at a different hour than usual and I would miss her when she stepped out of the office. Sure enough, no sooner had my wrist-watch told me that it was twelve o'clock than some of the girls she works with poured out of the office, and finally, the last to emerge, Monica walked out into the corridor where I was waiting. It startled me to see how pale and drawn she appeared to me just then, bearing only a very faint resemblance to the buoyant, energetic young girl I had always known her to be.

She didn't see me at first, walking stiffly and all by herself and with her shoulders sagging a little, so I stepped forward and touched her briefly at the elbow. She turned towards me with a hollow look on her face and asked me what I was doing there in her office building. I told her that I needed to talk to her and suggested that we have lunch together.

"I'm not having lunch," she told me in that strange, cold voice I have come to know only too well over the course of the past month or so. "I'm just going to go driving around for an hour."

"I'll come with you then," I offered. "We can take my car. We can drive around, or stop and grab a bite to eat somewhere, or just sit and talk. Whatever you'd like."

"Why?" my sister asked me with a pained expression coming into her languid dark eyes. "What could we possibly have to say to each other?"

At that moment of almost insurmountable coldness, I suddenly had a desire to blurt out the events of last night, to tell her how brutally her husband had attacked me and torn my blouse open, but I held my emotions in check. I stood quietly during that awful moment and bit my lower lip with my teeth so hard that I thought I was going to draw forth a bit of blood from it. Finally, I reached out a hand towards her and said,

"Monica, whatever you're thinking – whatever you've been told about me – whatever he's said – it just isn't true."

At that point, she started walking away from me, and I simply stood motionless for a few brief instants, foolishly indecisive as to whether I should rush after her or stand quietly and accept defeat. At length, however, I ended up pursuing her, and was able to catch up with her just as she opened the door and began to walk out into the blinding sunlight.

"This is crazy, Monica," I said to her, following behind her as she accelerated the pace of her footsteps which were conducting her across the parking lot and over to the spot where her own car was parked. "Why won't you even give me a chance to speak? Please listen to me, Monica," I said to her, and I was all too well aware of the fact that I had begun to cry.

"Don't!" my sister suddenly cried out, and she whirled around to face me so abruptly that I immediately drew myself to a stand-still and faced her myself, trembling in my inability to believe that all of

413

this was happening between the two of us. "Don't come on to me with that pathetic act of yours," she said to me in tones of bitterness, the likes of which I'd never heard coming from out of her throat before. "I've known for over a month that you and my husband have been lovers."

At the sound of that accusation, I took a step backwards, and she took a step forward so that the same distance between us was maintained as she continued,

"Last night the same thing happened, didn't it? Carl didn't come home until after midnight, and when he did, he told me the same thing he's been telling me for weeks: that you're a better woman than I am and that you've been satisfying him in a way that I never could."

I shook my head and stopped crying.

"No," I said to her, astounded, but keeping my voice firm and steady. "It's not true. It's impossible. How could you believe such – such trash?"

"Trash, right. I'm glad you said it, not me."

"Monica!" I cried out, but my voice sounded almost stifled, as if I were about to somehow suffocate myself.

"That's what the two of you have been having. A trashy affair. Don't deny it. Even Ellen knows –"

"Ellen!" My voice was weak when I spoke that name, and I recall that I was about ready, just then, to throw my hands into my face in sheer hysteria.

"And to think," my sister continued, and now she was sobbing in her own version of hysteria," that I listened to you and believed you when I saw you and Wayne together. What a façade! I actually thought, at first, that you were too good for Wayne, and now – Now I know what you *really* are!"

"No, Monica. No. Don't say it –"

"You're nothing but a –"

"No, don't," I said, and she stopped without my even having raised my voice just then. I lowered my eyes to the ground and remained as calm as was humanly possible, as I said to her, "Don't say any more. I'll leave. I'll leave you alone from now on. You – you won't ever have to see me again if you don't want to."

I put my fingers to my throbbing forehead – briefly – and turned around and went to my car. And I didn't look back when I heard her enter her own car, start the engine, and drive away. I had told her that I would leave, and so I did. I had told her that she wouldn't have to see me ever again, and I must remain firm in this, too.

I have lost my sister forever, and I must resign myself to that. Even if – even if a day should come when the truth is known to her, I will remain apart from her and I will refuse to face her ever again, knowing that I have inadvertently brought so much shame and grief into her life.

Her life, her marriage – everything is a disaster now for her because of me. What she believes in her heart and in her mind to be true will ultimately corrode her very soul, and there's nothing I can do. There's nothing she would even *let* me do. Nothing. I am as worthless and ineffective in bringing about human happiness as I ever was. All I am successful at doing is bringing about disastrous heart-ache and unhappiness, even to the ones I love.

God help me!

Later this afternoon, I drove to the beach. I had no inclination to return home and find Ellen sitting in front of the television. I must avoid her, too, because she is in this with the rest of them. When she looks at me, she must believe, just like the others do, that I really am that shameful unspeakable *thing* that Monica takes me for.

I went to the beach and sat on the rocks, and I looked out over the blue horizon of the ocean in front of me and I trembled to think that there was possibly no place I could go where I could forget about the horrible gulf that now existed between me and my sister – Not even beyond that beautiful horizon where the earth seemed to fall off into nothingness.

Where was I to go? When Wayne returned, where was I to meet him? How could I ever look him in those beautiful deep blue eyes of his, knowing that my family has branded me a traitor and an adulteress? Monica will tell him. In her spite and in her rage, she will tell him that, while he was gone, I entered into a sordid affair with her husband, and Carl and Ellen will both lend support to that lie.

Wayne is strong, and he still loves me. I firmly believe that. But what, dear God, will he think of me when these people tell him that I have been guilty of such filth? How could I defend myself – And if I were to bring up the attack against me in the parking lot last night, Carl will simply deny it, and everyone will accuse me of covering up for our affair by inventing fantastic lies. Not to mention that I would be exposing Carl to a possible violent attack from Wayne if I were to breathe a word to anyone about the attempted rape.

I always wanted Wayne and I to be happy, to lead a pure and uncorrupted life together that would be so noble and even radiantly spiritual that God Himself would be anxious to bless us in our love. But that is impossible now. It would only be possible if I were to drive down to South Carolina myself and confront him as soon as his freedom is given to him, and we could flee to a distant place where he would never have to find out about any of this – but in doing so, we would only be living a lie.

Will it eventually blow over? Is that possible, dear Lord? By the time Wayne returns, will all the lies be sorted out from the truths so that everyone will know that I am innocent of any wrongdoing whatsoever? And when Wayne comes back, will I be able to love him freely and spontaneously without the nagging suspicion that he might believe there to be some truth behind rumors he might have heard about my being unfaithful?

I sat on the rocks for the remainder of the afternoon and on into the evening hours, in fact. I forgot about my duties at home. I was even afraid that, upon returning home, Carl or Monica or both of them together would be waiting to ambush me and drive me insane with threats and accusations. Would it reach such a point as that?

So, I forgot about my responsibilities. About dinner, the laundry that needed to be done, the telephone, the television, the crippled girl who was sitting in front of it – I forgot about everything except the day when Wayne and I had stood on this very spot and declared our love for each other.

I should have died on that day – when I was at the peak of my happiness.

Then I scolded myself for entertaining such wicked thoughts. Not only would it be sinful to contemplate death in such a fashion, but I should also remind myself that there was not just one single peak of happiness during the days Wayne and I were able to share our lives together. There were literally hundreds and thousands of moments of such indescribable bliss, that it would be even more sinful if I were to seem ungrateful for so much happiness and good fortune.

It was already dark outside when I got home. Nobody was home, in fact, and I assumed that Aunt Lucille had dropped by to take Ellen out shopping or to a movie, and that Mom was out socializing somewhere for the better part of the evening. It was with this realization that I vowed that I would wait up for her and attempt to share a little of my concerns of the day with her, and I slowly gathered together the mail that had arrived while I'd been out during most of the day, and took two new letters from Wayne up to my room – letters that he'd been having a friend actually write for him, though the words themselves were totally his own.

"Dear Betsy," the first one said. "It's so hot down here today, you could fry an egg on the sidewalk. Pretty funny, huh? I miss you, and I wish we could be together again. Keep writing. I miss you. Love, Wayne."

In the second letter, he says: "Dear Betsy, I miss you and wish we could be together again. It's real hot down here, so hot the hens are laying hard-boiled eggs. One guy passed out, too. Sometimes I feel like I'm going to pass out, too. It gets so hot, and I'm so lonely. I think about you all the time. Sometimes when I'm jogging, or setting up camp, I look up at the sun, and I pretend that it's your light that's shining down on me. Sounds stupid, I know. Betsy, do you think we can get married as soon as I get back? I don't want anything else except to marry you and live with you forever and ever. And I don't want to stay in Maplewoods. I want us to go somewhere far. A place where the sun is always out and the birds are always singing. You'd like that, wouldn't you? And I could get a job and make lots of money, so I could buy you furs and rings and diamonds and things, and everybody would look at you and think you were a queen. Think about it, O.K.? Because I miss you, and I love you, and I'm going nuts here without you. Please? Please be there for me when I get back? Love, Wayne."

I put the two letters away as soon as I finished reading them, stretched myself out on the top of my bed, face-down, and slept.

When I awoke, it was a little after midnight, and I heard Mom's footsteps entering her room right next door to mine, and then the door shut behind her. Rousing myself from where I lay on top of my bed, I walked over to her room and knocked gently on her door.

"Mom?" I said. "Can I come in for a second?"

"Yes," I heard her say somewhat irritably. "But only for a second."

The door swung open, and I saw her standing there, wearing an alluring outfit that fully accentuated the lush contours of her body. But her eyes looked tired and were without humor, so I hastily lowered my gaze and said to her,

"Never mind, Mom. I just wanted to know if – if we could talk a little bit tomorrow. I have so much I want to tell you."

Mom laughed, a little huskily, and said,

"You're just like your father, always got something important on your mind, huh? Well, all right – but tomorrow, O.K.? Not right now. I promise." And she shut the door upon me before I had a chance to say Thank You or Good Night.

That was the very last thing that happened before I came back in here and sat down to write this latest entry in my diary.

I feel confident right now that tomorrow will be a better day. When Mom and I have our talk, I will try to let her have a glimpse, for the very first time, of what really is the essence of the little girl she gave birth to, quite sadly, twenty-one years ago.

P.S. It's very odd that she should have referred to my being a lot like Pop. She never talks that way, and yet, I've always felt that he and I were very much alike. In fact, several years ago Aunt Lucille bitterly commented that Mom had had so many boyfriends before her marriage that she was totally taken by surprise when Mom announced that she and Pop were actually going to get married!

CARL'S DIARY – January 8, 1986

Dear Diary: Today my parents finally did it! They kicked my butt out of the house. In fact, right now I'm writing this, curled up on a park bench with the wind howling all about me. I'm running out of paper, so this will probably be my last diary entry. Plus, I'm running out of ink, too, and I don't even have enough money to go out and buy another pen!

I went out this morning to buy a gun, hoping to get one on some kind of credit or something, so I could shoot that moron and put him on a slab in the morgue; but the wise guy behind the counter told me I needed a license in order to purchase a gun, so I had to figure out another way to kill that sucker. I figured I could knife him in the back, but Wayne is tough and quick and I'd probably end up receiving the worst end of it myself. Then I thought about putting poison in his food, but that would be too tricky and he'd probably get suspicious if he caught me tampering with his lunch-box or something. Then I thought, the next time I saw him crossing the street, I could run him down with my car – then I realized I don't even have a freakin' car anymore!

I've got no place to go right now. A little while ago, I trudged all the way over to Samuel's pad and knocked on the door, and when he answered, I asked him if I could stay there for a few days, just until I got my head back together again. But Samuel looked at me and said No, he didn't take in any welfare cases. When I started telling him that I could hardly be considered a welfare case, having been voted Most Popular and Best Personality by the entire graduating class of 1985 at Maplewoods High School, he quickly slammed the door in my face.

If I don't get some money fast, I'm a goner. I need a joint, man. Real bad. Actually I need something a hell of a lot stronger, and real soon, too. But without money, it's practically impossible – Unless I take my chances on ripping off a supermarket or something and pray that I don't get caught, because if I do, they'll throw me into the slammer with a whole bunch of homos and, with my superlative good looks, I'll end up being voted Most Popular, all right – but for all the wrong reasons! But hey, at least then, I wouldn't be a virgin anymore.

So, where do I go from here? Wayne Brown is still walking the face of the earth, and I can't touch him. My angel has been removed from this planet, and I can't touch her either. I'm fast running out of time, paper, and ink, and there's no place to go.

Tomorrow I'll go begging on the streets for money, and when I get enough accumulated, I'll go out and get zonked on acid. In the meantime, I guess you could say I'm fucked. Truly fucked. With a capital F!

BETSY'S DIARY – September 4, 1985

Dear Diary: It's all over now – or it will be very shortly. I have nothing left. Nothing and nobody – not even Wayne whom I must push out of my sight forever.

It happened a few minutes ago. I saw my mother and held her in my arms, and I told her about Wayne and the love that we shared for one another.

She thrust me away from her in disgust and told me who my father was.

"You've been having sex with your own brother," she said to me. "Wayne Brown is your real father, Betsy. Wayne Brown Senior. Get away from me. You're nothing but a freak."

My first impulse upon learning this was to run screaming through the streets.

But I will do better than that. I will end it all silently in the bathroom with a couple of sharp razor blades.

I have lost everyone and everything I ever lived for. The one pure and basic truth I ever treasured has been transformed into the most unspeakable horror. Oh, God Almighty! –

No. I have offended God Himself, so I must not pray.

We had the same eyes. I should have known. And I'll never see him again. And it's better this way.

Mom was right. I am a freak.

E P I L O G U E

MONICA'S MEMOIRS – May 26, 1986 ("MEMORIAL DAY")

I woke up this morning in the gloom of my chamber and, for the first time in months, took air into my lungs without wishing that it were no longer possible for me to do so. I was alive for one more day, and I was glad that God had carried me through the interminable night so that my eyes would open this morning, even though the sun failed to shine through my window and the birds refused to spring into song for any of us either.

I felt anxious and restless when I realized that I was awake and that a new day was beginning to unfold itself and that it was Memorial Day and the doctors had agreed that I could go to that peaceful sanctuary where her soul was laid to rest many months ago. I was tense and nervous, but as soon as one of the attendants stepped inside my own gloomy sanctuary, I forced the muscles of my body to make the effort to convey calmness and tranquility lest my inner anxiety show itself and possibly convince the doctors that they should revoke their earlier agreement.

Slowly and very carefully, I stood up beside my cot and let the attendant disrobe me so that my sanitary black dress could be put over my incredibly white and pallid body. Slowly, I sat back down upon the edge of my cot while she stood behind me and combed my musty, almost limp hair away from my forehead and on down the edge of my shoulders. When she asked me if I wanted a mirror, I smiled faintly and shook my head. Then she got up and left the room, and my heart started racing as I wondered if he had already come here and if we would be leaving in a matter of minutes.

But no one came for nearly two hours, and I sat quietly at the edge of my cot with my hands folded on my lap. At the end of the two hours, one of the nurses came in and took my pulse and my blood pressure and encouraged me to have a bit of breakfast brought in. I shook my head silently, and the woman left me alone without making a fuss, and so, I continued to sit there quietly at the edge of my cot for another two hours.

While I waited, the sun refused to reveal itself from behind the clouds, and a cold dampness seemed to filter into my chamber by way of the cracks in the walls and through the floorboards beneath my feet. I forced myself to sit calmly with my hands folded on my lap, and I waited patiently for the muffled sounds beyond the door of my chamber that would announce his arrival.

I kept the faith and remained calm and patient for what seemed like another two hours. I kept the faith, of course, because I knew that he would come.

When he arrived, the sun seemed to be clothed in darkness even though it was still day time. But I stopped noticing that in a matter of seconds, as my mind started aching all over again when he stepped before me and stood in his three-piece suit with his curly blond hair combed closely against his white and drained forehead. And he gazed upon me, as always, in his pain, tried to smile but failed, and then walked forward and let himself be cradled in my arms.

While I held him there with his face buried against my chest, I listened – We both listened to the heartbeat that keeps the universe alive and functioning. We both listened, our ears straining to hear anything at all that would indicate to the two of us that she was near and that she cared and that she still loved us.

When the doctor and the attendant came upon the threshold of my chamber, we disengaged ourselves and rose to our feet to embark upon the splendid journey that would take us ever so closely towards the serenity that we desired to experience.

The drive to the cemetery was long, so incredibly long, and we sat side by side without looking at each other or out the window or at anything in particular. Neither did we speak.

I thought of the time, many years ago, when I was barely eight years old and had just finished second grade. It was the first day of summer vacation, and I was still in bed, even though it was after ten in the morning.

Betsy ran into the room and jumped onto my bed, laughing and giggling her silly head off as she playfully threw my bed sheets over my face and then pulled them away from me just as quickly as she had covered my face with them. And she kept laughing as she said, "It's summer! It's summer, Monica! We can play all day long now! All day long we can play!" And the tears came down her cheeks, she was so happy.

I even thought about the night she was to attend her high school junior prom and how she'd been kept waiting downstairs in the parlor for so long because the boy who was taking her to the prom had had a flat tire, only we didn't know what the delay was all about because he couldn't get to a phone to call us.

"He'll come, Betsy," I said to her, coming down upon the cushions of the sofa and putting an arm around her shoulders because the look of sadness on her face stirred me in a way that nothing else on this earth had been able to do. And while I held her, she told me how good it felt to be held close to somebody, especially somebody like me whom she loved with all her heart. I remember now how wonderful it felt to be told this, and I promised myself that I would never desert her or turn my back on her for as long as I lived.

That was several years ago, but the memory of that evening and of that promise I'd made to myself came into my mind, burning in the intensity of the pain it brought me. But we were nearing our destination, so I was beginning to feel oddly stirred, and that cold, pale figure sitting next to me remained detached from me, unaware of the remembrances that had begun to haunt me as I sat next to him, just as silent as he was.

When the gates to the cemetery appeared before us, I felt his hand groping for my own, and our two hands became entwined as the car we were in passed through the gates, and in a matter of minutes, we came to a stop only a few yards from where she lay.

The attendant and the doctor disembarked before either one of us had been able to find the strength or the courage to move a muscle. It seemed so dark out, but it couldn't have been too much later than one or two o'clock in the afternoon. But we got out of the car before anything was said by either the doctor or the attendant, and Wayne walked on ahead of me.

At her tombstone, he knelt down and extracted a single white rose from the inside of his jacket, placing it gently upon the soil at the foot of her grave. As I say, the rose was white, perfectly white in its purity – but his face, in comparison, looked even whiter, and after placing the flower upon the earth, he then inclined his head and appeared to have sunk into meditation.

I approached the place where he was kneeling, put my arms around his strong shoulders, and knelt there beside him, while the doctor and the attendant stood off to the side, maintaining a silence that was almost unearthly.

Nothing happened. Nothing changed while the two of us knelt there in our sterile calmness. The sun would not pour forth its rays upon us, neither did the birds allow us to hear their song. Instead, all was quiet, without movement, perfectly still.

Then, without warning, his body began to shake beside me, and he began to fall face-first to the ground.

I took in all of my strength so as to prevent that from happening, and seized him from behind, clasping onto his shoulders in my intense desperation to stop him from hitting the earth with his naked, white face.

"Don't," I said to him, while I clutched his shoulders tightly against me. "This isn't what's supposed to happen. We're supposed to find peace here, not sorrow. We're supposed to pick ourselves up from the ground now and walk back to the car and get on with the rest of our lives. Life continues, Wayne. It continues, and it's got to be faced. She wouldn't have wanted it this way. It would pain her to see your suffering, so you mustn't do this. For her sake, you've got to find the strength to go on living. You've got to do this – for her!"

With his hands thrust in front of his face, he seemed to bend over even more, wilting, and began to sob.

"Don't you want to make her happy?" I whispered into his ear. "Don't you want her to see that you can continue with the rest of your life and face it like a man? Wayne, please – Please don't do this to yourself."

He took in a deep breath – a breath which seemed to conquer his indomitable grief, if only for a moment, and he then struggled to his feet while I sank to the earth and wrapped my arms around his legs.

"She was your lover, Wayne," I cried, gazing down while I spoke, down upon the earth which covered her forever and ever. "She was your lover, your best friend, your sister – and she should have been your bride. And she will be, Wayne. She will be. Didn't she say it once – more than once? Didn't she say that she belonged to you forever?"

The sun was starting to break through the clouds, and I lifted my face up towards where he was towering over me, and I saw him with his own face uplifted towards the heavens, straining to quench the flood of tears which continued to stream down his cheeks.

"Feel the air," I said to him. "Smell the trees. Taste the glory of living, Wayne, and show me that you can smile again. Isn't it wonderful, Wayne? Isn't it wonderful to be alive and to be able to say that you've been loved?"

His body stiffened momentarily as I felt him take in another great lungful of air, and when he let the air out of his body, he sobbed one last time and then closed his eyes which were lifted to the sky, and he tightened himself up from head to toe in one great spasm of agonizing grief.

"Oh, God!" I cried, clutching his legs against my face. "Speak to me, Wayne! Say something to me! Anything! Just tell me that you believe what I'm saying and that you'll try to overcome this – Please, Wayne? Will you tell me that? Will you say – just one word to me?"

In so saying, I brought my face away from his legs for the moment and threw my stare up towards his face – his own face which was pure-white and drenched with tears and lifted towards Heaven in his immense suffering.

But he would not answer me. He would not speak. He never speaks to anyone anymore, and he never will. Ever again.

Not, that is, until God's grace allows him to be with her again so that he can love her just as freely as before.

THE END

Made in the USA
Middletown, DE
20 July 2016